GIRLS DON'T CRY

PETER KESTERTON

BLOODHOUND
— BOOKS —

www.bloodhoundbooks.com

Print ISBN: 978-1-5040-8329-4

To my wife, Adriane

ONE

Boggart Hill, Bristol

D arren stopped to gaze at the lone tree at the top of the grassy slope. Hanging among its slender yellowing leaves were mementos of a once happy life.

Toy Dinosaurs.

He'd placed them up there ten years ago. Time had weathered and washed the plastic so they were now pastel echoes of the original primary reds, greens and blues, but he was pleased to find that they were still there.

Boggart Hill was a lonely spot and his sense of isolation all the more acute because this patch of land was only a mile or so from the city centre. A forgotten corner caught between the railway and the grimy inner-city streets. Back down the hill was the metal chain-link fence he'd pushed through a few moments ago. Beyond the fence, a row of squat Victorian terraced houses, but from up here he could see over the roofs to the high-rise buildings near the city centre. A siren echoed off the office blocks that loomed like tombstones in the haze.

He felt for the letter in his jacket pocket. It had arrived that morning after Kerry went to work. His plan was to keep it unopened until this evening so that good or bad, he and Kerry could face whatever it said together. But filled with an irrational fear that it might get lost, he tucked it inside his jacket pocket and headed off to work.

He was working on a new accommodation block in Chippenham, installing the cabling. It was a half hour drive from Swindon where he and Kerry had lived since severing ties with Bristol. But on the journey he felt the weight of that letter. Dying to know what it said, yet dreading it as well. Told himself, he didn't care if they released the bitch or not. But his stomach lurched just the same.

He didn't take the turn-off to Chippenham. Didn't want to have to be nice to people today, particularly the project manager, who was a jerk. So drove on until he reached Bristol and Boggart Hill.

He pulled the letter out and stared at the logo.

National Probation Service.

As long as Grady was in prison, his murderous thoughts about her remained locked away as well. The move to Swindon was a new start. And he tried to live like a normal human being: Go to work. Eat three meals a day. Sleep eight hours. Get teeth checked every six months. He and Kerry had even managed a couple of holidays. Camping in Wales. A boat on the Norfolk Broads. But without his daughter, what was the point of a holiday? What was the point of anything?

A gust of wind caught the dinosaurs making them jump and twirl, as if the spirit of his Riley was here, playing with them.

One day, shortly before the horror, he padded into her bedroom and watched her in her secret child's world. She was talking to the dinos, telling them off, like they were naughty kids.

2

'I'm not talking to you, Daddy, I'm talking to Tall Boy and Big Tail,' she said without looking around.

Ten years ago, there were flowers at the base of the tree – hundreds of them. Kerry appreciated the outpouring of respect and emotion from the community. But he wanted something more, something that wouldn't wither and die. That would stay the passage of his grief. So he lugged the big aluminium step ladders up here and placed Riley's dinosaurs high up in the tree, securing them with cable ties and wire.

Her body was buried in a woodland cemetery north of Bristol and he and Kerry visited twice a year. But this was where Riley had died. Where her spirit was. Except she didn't just die. She was killed by a monster. An older child: Caitlin Grady.

Traumatic brain injury and asphyxiation.

He hadn't wanted to look at the photos displayed as evidence at the trial. But made himself face them. Riley's small, ruined body, propped up against this tree. Like a discarded broken plaything.

When the lawyer for the prosecution called Grady a monster against nature, she grinned. Actually grinned. Not once did she show any remorse. No emotion at all about what she'd done. In harsher times they'd have drowned her as a child of the devil.

They didn't drown her. They simply locked her up. Not in an actual prison. No, she was in some cushy children's home, allowed to watch TV and play video games and goodness knows what else. Oh, he knew it was all about therapy and rehabilitation. He could dimly see they meant well. But evil is evil. You can't sit down and have a cup of tea with it. And what about Riley? She couldn't be rehabilitated, could she? No video games or TV for her.

He took a deep breath, as though he was about to dive into deep cold water, then ripped the envelope open.

Dear Mr and Mrs Burgess…

The words swam before his eyes, he blinked and shook his head.

For your information we enclose a summary of the parole hearing for Caitlin Grady: Having considered the evidence presented regarding her participation in interventions to address her offending behaviour…

This kind of blathering preamble gave him a bad feeling. They were trying to sweeten the pill.

The decision.

He felt his chest tighten as he read on.

The panel is satisfied that Ms Grady is suitable for release. The release is subject to several licence conditions…

The bastards! He scrunched up the letter and threw it at the tree. Suddenly short of breath, he gasped to get some air. Could hear the blood pumping in his ears.

How could they do this to him? Bloody weak-minded do-gooders.

His chest felt constricted. Heart pounded. Began to feel dizzy.

He staggered towards the top of the steep embankment where the main line to London cut its way through Boggart Hill.

Told himself he wasn't having a heart attack.

Deep breaths, Darren. Take deep slow breaths.

The first time this happened he thought his heart really was failing. That his grief had killed him.

The panic attacks started when Riley disappeared. Got worse when they found her body. The doctor gave him beta blockers, but he avoided taking them. What was the point in treating the symptoms when there was no pill for his disease? Besides, he didn't want to cover up his feelings for Riley with drugs. He wanted the pain. Might even have preferred an actual heart attack.

He watched a long-distance train rumble past on the tracks below. Imagined the passengers settling into their seats with laptops and lattes. Why the hell should they be allowed to go about their business when his world had just collapsed for the second time? Fuck them and their cotton-wool lives.

'Looking for business, mister?'

He swung around to see a young woman, hardly more than a teenager. Bare legs, short skirt, nose piercing. Thin. Far too thin to be healthy. Dark eyes flicking around nervously.

For a horrid second, he thought it was Grady, come back to visit the scene.

'Only twenty for a blowy.'

'What? No! I don't want any bloody business,' he snapped, disgusted. Of all the places to suggest such a thing.

'All right, keep your hair on. I'm only asking.'

'Look, I came here to be on my own, all right?' Of course this girl wasn't Grady. Ten years might have passed but he'd recognise that nonchalant look and vacant blue eyes anywhere. Besides there was bound to be a delay between the parole hearing and the actual release. It wasn't her, but he carried on gazing at the girl. Part of him couldn't help but wonder if being let out of prison was his chance to finally get his hands on her.

'If you don't want business, what are you looking at?'

'Nothing.' He turned away and wandered back to the tree. The scrunched-up letter was still there on the ground. It was like part of Grady herself was here. He couldn't leave the letter to desecrate this place and so picked it up. He'd burn it – later. But for now stuffed it in his pocket. Kerry would be as outraged as he was by the release. They could both watch it burn.

The girl called over, 'Saw you park your van. Had that look about you, like you was after something.'

Did he really look like the type of loser looking to pay for sex? Truth is, sex had all but dried up since Riley died. For a long time, it had just felt wrong somehow. And now, things with Kerry… He sighed inwardly. He still loved her but the marriage needed rewiring. Only he didn't have a clue how to even begin.

'I recognised you that's why. So there's no need to be shy,' she said in a sing-song voice that made him squirm.

'You don't know me! We've never met.' How could he have met her? She'd have been a child the last time he set foot in Bristol.

'You quite sure our paths have never crossed, my love?'

'I don't live in Bristol.'

'You're not on the telly are you?' she said, coming closer.

'No! I'm not on the telly and our lives have never crossed.' Getting irritated with her persistence, he retrieved his wallet from his jeans pocket and got out a tenner.

'What d'you think you're gonna get for that?'

'It's for you to take your *business* somewhere else.'

'All right then. If that's what you really want.'

He glared at her. She tilted her head, gave a weak smile, turned and sloped off down the hill to the fence.

Darren was lying about the telly. He'd been on the telly plenty. But that girl was too young to have remembered him from the TV. Unless she had a special reason not to forget.

His phone vibrated. A text from Ben, the project manager. He should get to work. Being a contractor meant his hours were his own business, but there'd be questions if he didn't show up at all. He headed down the hill taking the path past a row of small back gardens that backed onto Boggart Hill. Each tiny parcel of land was a snapshot of a private life. Neat flower beds in one, scruffy uncut grass in another. Several had evidence of children: abandoned toys and bikes, a swing, a plastic Little Tykes activity gym, like the one they'd got for Riley on her last ever birthday.

Happy families hurt.

Passing through a dank underpass running beneath the railway line, he quickened his pace and emerged into Pennywell industrial estate where his van was parked. It was a miserable area of drab breeze-block and corrugated-steel units, their unseeing mean windows obscured by closed blinds; white vans, like his own, on the forecourts. He still wondered why no one had stopped Grady as she dragged Riley along these streets, having snatched her from Pennywell City Farm half a mile away. He felt drawn to retrace their path and go back to the place he'd lost Riley. But he needed to get to the job in Chippenham. Besides what good would it do to churn things up even more?

The phone rang. Thinking it was Ben on his case, he was tempted to ignore it. But it wasn't Ben; it was Kerry.

'Is everything all right, love?' she asked, sounding concerned.

'Yeah course.'

'Well, where are you?' There was an accusation in her voice he didn't like. Besides he better not say where he was.

'Where do you think I am – Butlins?'

'You're not at work.'

'Aren't I?' he mumbled, feeling foolish.

'So where are you?'

'Checking up on me?'

'No, Darren, I am not checking up on you. I was worried about you,' she said evenly, like he was being a dimwit. 'Got back home after my shift and there's a tonne of messages on the landline. "Are you coming in today? First fix had better be done by Friday."'

'Bloody Ben. Cut a guy some slack for fuck's sake.'

'So, where are you?'

He sighed heavily not knowing what to say. After Riley's death, he got a bit obsessed with going up Boggart Hill and staring at the tree for hours. He'd been almost suicidal then and had to promise to stop going up there for the sake of his mental health.

'Took the morning off that's all. I'm with Mum and Dad.' It was the only thing he could think of.

'Why did you go there?'

He mumbled some vague reason to do with not having seen them for ages. Kerry didn't sound convinced. She knew how he avoided any encounter with his dad or brother if possible. His half-baked explanations were drowned by a train roaring over the underpass only a few metres away.

'Is that a train?'

'No.'

'Sounds like a train.'

'Look.'

'What the fuck is going on?'

'I'm in Pennywell if you must know.'

'Oh, Darren. You been up Boggart Hill?' she said in a voice saturated with disappointment.

'Maybe. Maybe I have. So what!'

'There's no need to lie about it is there?' Kerry hated lies, and he should apologise, but why shouldn't he go to Riley's tree if he wanted to. It's not like suicide was on his mind anymore. If anything, it was the opposite. Murder was closer to his heart.

'I'm leaving now anyway,' he said as though the duration of his visit would lessen the lie.

'Fine. Whatever you say.' Her voice was ice cold and she hung up, leaving him with a sour gut.

TWO

Studio flat, Westcliffe

She lay on the bed staring at a brown stain on the swirling Artex ceiling. Was something unpleasant oozing through from the flat above? Blood? Standing on the mattress she could reach the ceiling easily and traced the outline of the stain with her finger. It was dry to the touch. Probably from a leaking pipe ages ago. All the same, she didn't like the idea of living with that ugly blemish above her head.

When George told her that her accommodation was to be a studio flat, she pictured a cool loft apartment where celebrity DJs and beautiful people hung out. All high ceilings and exposed brickwork. A film star life in New York or Paris.

Well, she was a celebrity of sorts. The sort you didn't celebrate. Her so-called studio was a room barely large enough for the double bed and the grotty kitchenette in a small alcove. Through a door there was a toilet and shower – that was a plus at least – first time she'd had private facilities in her life.

She'd been desperate to get parole, but now she was out, she wasn't sure she was ready.

Been locked up in one way or another since she was eleven years old. Institutionalised, they called it, didn't they? All right, so she may have been incarcerated, but there was constant noise and activity. Thornhill Open Prison was a primitive place: full of gossip, arguments, and fights sometimes. But she could handle that.

There was friendship, affection and love there too. An older woman, Donna, had taken her under her wing and they'd got close. It became physical after a while, but then they moved Donna to another wing, so that was that.

Happened all the time. Friendships formed and broken. Ships in the night, but at least there were ships.

Now she was out, she was alone. The flat was deathly quiet. It's bare magnolia walls mocked her somehow, reminding her of the void that lay ahead. Inside prison she'd felt many challenging emotions: anger, fear, resentment and despair. But never loneliness.

The door to the studio flat wasn't locked. She could come and go as she pleased. But go where?

THREE

Appletree Avenue, Swindon

D arren had stayed on at the building site after hours to appease the project manager, so it was starting to get dark when he finally pulled into Appletree Avenue and swung the van into his own short drive.

Appletree Avenue didn't have any apple trees, merely disappointing bushes placed at intervals on the manicured verge. Set back from the verge were neat houses of buff-coloured brick with white uPVC doors and window frames. Scaled down versions of an Edwardian style, so they looked like doll's houses to Darren. Some had four bedrooms and double garages, others were red brick or pebble dashed, which might provide the illusion of variety to some people but to Darren, they were soulless places that all looked the same.

It is true that the estate was a 'good area'. Safe for families, hardly any break-ins and you could walk around the quiet streets at night with no fear. But there was no scruffy green-tiled local where he was in the darts team. No decent football team either – he hadn't seen his team play since before Riley died. This doll's house street had never felt, and would never feel, like his home. He was existing here, not living.

He sat for a moment unable to get out of the van, ambushed by a pang of nostalgia and an overwhelming desire to put the clock back. Going to the footie, sitting on the red seats and shouting at the referee. Drinking with his mates in the pub afterwards. How many mates did he have in those days? Hundreds. What a laugh his life was. When did he last have a real laugh? Laughing so much you spit out your beer, or can't get your breath.

He banged his fist on his forehead to try and make his brain stop thinking and forced himself to get out of the van to walk the few paces to the front door.

Even before he put the key in the lock, he could hear the to-and-fro of the vacuum cleaner. That was a bad sign. He shouldn't have lied about visiting his parents. But sometimes he didn't know what to say and white lies came out of his mouth before he could stop them.

He found Kerry in the front room grappling with the hoover as if it was something needed taming. 'Bit late for housework, isn't it?' he shouted above the din.

She stared at him for a moment. 'Funny guy.' She shook her head and then turned back to her task.

'Come on, Kerry...'

She kicked off the hoover with her foot and turned to face him. Gave him a look while the high-pitched motor wound down. 'Had a good day, doing whatever it was you needed to lie about?'

'No.' He pulled out the screwed-up letter and thrust it at her.

'What's this?'

'Reason I went to Boggart Hill.' He withdrew, as though the letter might explode and went through to the kitchen-diner. Opened the fridge vaguely looking for something to eat, but didn't find anything much, so simply took a beer and sat, hoping that the letter might at least do something to get them both on the same page.

'Came this morning,' he said as Kerry entered. She sat down at the table and placed the letter between them, carefully smoothing its creases. Did she think that would make its contents somehow more palatable?

'Why didn't you tell me when I phoned?'

'Dunno. Too upset, I suppose.' He took a sip of beer. Kerry watched him, waiting for more. 'And didn't want to say I'd been up Boggart Hill.'

A shiver seemed to pass through her. 'How was it? Going back up there?' She bit her lip.

'They're still there, in the tree. Her dinosaurs. No one took them down; that's something,' he said, giving a sad smile. 'And don't worry. I'm all right.'

She nodded. 'Good.'

'Seemed the right place to open the letter that's all.'

'We should have opened it together.'

'I'm sorry. I just couldn't bear not knowing.'

'Okay. All right.' She reached over and squeezed his hand. 'Well, we knew we'd have to face this one day.'

'Ten years,' he muttered, shaking his head. 'Not enough.'

'There *is* no enough, is there?'

'Should be a life for a life.'

'You don't mean that.'

'Don't I?' he said, giving her a hard stare. If he'd known Grady was the killer before the police picked her up, he'd have squeezed the life out of her himself.

'Come on, love, even if they still hanged people for murder, they would hardly hang an eleven-year-old child. It wouldn't be right.'

He wasn't sure what he expected Kerry to say, but she was being a bit bloody reasonable. He let go of her hand and took a sip of beer to stop himself from saying anything.

'At least it's out of the way,' Kerry went on. 'They were

never going to keep her in prison for ever were they? So that's it. It's done now. End of the story.'

'Doesn't it bother you?' Why was she trying to close the book on something he felt as keenly as being knifed in the stomach?

'Course it bothers me. But there's nothing to be done about it. We need to—'

'How can you be so fucking calm about this?' he said, with growing resentment.

'I have to be calm. Detached in a way. Otherwise I'll go insane. We have to try and put it behind us.'

'Try and forget. Is that what you're saying? Forget Riley?'

She shook her head. 'I think about Riley every day. Of course I do. And I think about what that girl did to my baby.' She swallowed hard, her eyes glistening with held-back tears. 'And every single day it hurts. That hurt will never go away. Not ever. But nothing I can say or do will bring Riley back to us. Nothing. So I put a wall around it. Not forget. But tell myself, there it is, there's the pain. Then hide behind that wall. Protect myself from being destroyed by it.'

He nodded. They hadn't talked like this for a long time, but at least now he understood her. And maybe that was one way to deal with it. It just wasn't his way.

She gave him a weak smile. 'How about we get a takeaway?'

'A takeaway?'

'For dinner. A pizza.'

'Is that supposed to make everything all right, is it? A takeaway bloody pizza.' He shook his head.

'Darren, please, don't be like this.'

'It's an insult to Riley.'

'What?'

'Treat ourselves to a takeaway dinner on the day her killer is set free.'

She opened her mouth, but no words came. Her eyes flicked between his. When she spoke it was with an uncharacteristically small voice. 'We still have our lives ahead of us. Lives to live.'

He wasn't sure if he did have a life to live. Wasn't sure he deserved it.

The phone rang, the landline. No one ever called the landline. 'Don't answer it,' he said, 'probably a scammer'. But Kerry got up and headed to the sitting room to take the call. Perhaps she was expecting someone to phone, but more likely she wanted to get away from him.

He heard her pick up and found himself wondering if it might be his mum as she was one of the few people who phoned the landline. He hadn't seen her for ages and now wished he'd actually gone there today. She'd listen to him. Share his anger about Grady's release.

He couldn't make out what Kerry was saying but her muffled voice had a distinctly agitated ring to it. Not his mum then. When she returned to the kitchen she had a thin-lipped look about her.

'Fucking Harvey Pringle,' she muttered.

'Still working for *The Daily Herald*?'

'How the hell did he get the number, that's what I want to know,' Kerry said. It was a good question, they were ex-directory.

'He *is* a journalist. It's their job to find things out.'

'Poke their nose into other people's business, and then splash it all over the papers.'

That was a dig at Darren. He'd been quite open with Pringle about the suffering he went through at the trial. 'What did he want?'

'What do you think?' Kerry said in a disgusted voice. 'Had we heard that Grady is to be released? What do we think about it? Has justice been done? I shut him down, told him not to harass us.'

Kerry had been pissed off about some of Darren's choicest comments about Grady, printed by *The Herald* after the verdict. Felt it reflected badly on Riley's memory. In retrospect he had got a bit carried away. Understandable though surely?

Part of the reason for the move to Swindon was to put their fame, if that's what it was, behind them. Kerry had made new friends at the depot amongst her fellow bus drivers. None of them knew about what happened to their daughter and Kerry was determined to keep it that way.

'Promise you won't talk to him, Darren. He's a leech.'

'No fear. Learned my lesson about talking to the papers.'

'We should get him blocked as a nuisance caller.'

He grunted his agreement. But later found himself wondering what Harvey Pringle might know about Grady. Perhaps he'd know where to find her when they let her out. In which case he, Darren might be able to get to her. Confront her at last.

FOUR

The pier, Westcliffe

The view from the end of the pier made her feet tingle. The steely ocean stretched away forever and waves rolled in from faraway places she could only imagine. Above her, a vaulting glassy sky with milky clouds.

Two weeks of freedom and she still wasn't used to the bigness of outside. But she refused to be intimidated; it was her world too. One day she'd travel over the ocean to those faraway places.

She'd have preferred to meet George in the pokey room at the probation office, even if the coffee-stained carpet did smell of stale cigarette smoke, despite the no smoking signs. But George insisted they meet on the pier, claiming the sea air would be refreshing. 'Refreshing' was the sort of thing they said in toothpaste adverts. She didn't feel refreshed, she felt naked. Over exposed. Out here, you never knew who might be scoping you with a telephoto lens.

Still, she was grateful to escape from CoffeeTime, the café where George had managed to get her a job. The work itself was okay. Boring, but okay. A *start* as they say. And to be honest what else was she going to do? Stare at the ceiling in her flat 24/7?

The reason she wanted to escape the coffee shop had nothing to do with the job; it was one of the customers – a middle-aged man in a tired grey suit. He sat near the counter hunched over a bruised laptop and kept looking up at her.

She didn't like him. He had the look of something second-hand, like he'd been raised in a charity shop. Been there for hours in his grubby suit and crumpled grey face, pretending to be typing something important.

When he came up to the counter for another skinny latte and a lemon drizzle muffin, she winced at the white flakes of dandruff on his shoulders. But it wasn't simple revulsion of dandruff or his coffee breath. Something else curdled her insides. Something she recognised as dangerous. He could hurt her, but she couldn't put her finger on exactly how.

The tingling seemed to be spreading from her feet and up her spine. Got behind her shoulder blades, making her restless and jumpy. She was too unsettled to hang about here and headed back down the pier towards the crowded entrance. George could meet her in the throng milling around the chip shop and amusements. He'd find her easily enough; the probation service tagging app on her phone was militarily accurate.

Walking down the pier she passed a couple of amusement stalls. She stopped for a moment by the glittering Ten Penny Falls, ambushed by a sudden memory of a rare childhood holiday. Her mum had been flush and rented a caravan in Wales or somewhere. She was allowed to bring her best friend, Tracey.

It was about a year before the bad days started. She and Tracey were ten years old and they spent hours entranced by the Ten Penny Falls, watching the unstable piles of silver coins. The money stubbornly clung to the precarious edge, despite the magic she and her friend willed on the coins to make them drop into the chute. But occasionally, their magic worked and some coins would finally tumble down into their gleeful hands. They'd go to the sweet shop with their booty. Free sweets!

Her mum might know how Tracey was doing. She'd ask next time she saw her. But when would that be? She wasn't talking to her mum and refused to see her last time she visited HMP Thornhill. She shrugged off the unwanted desire to see the old bitch again and carried on walking along the wooden boards, through which she could get glimpses of green water.

A sharp crack of a rifle made her flinch. Bloody hell, she was jumpy as a scared kitten. It was only the shooting gallery. She stared at the row of rabbit cut-outs – holed and pockmarked from gun pellets. She would have liked to have a go, but if George found her taking aim at small animals, he'd probably mark her as a *potential risk to the public*. That is, a fucking psycho. Her probation officer was too warm and fuzzy to use a word like psycho, but that didn't mean she wasn't one.

The truth is, she'd never understood exactly how she'd come to kill Riley. The thought made her wince. A kid holding an ice cream topped in luminous red sauce was staring at her. *That wasn't me!* she wanted to scream at the kid. *Not the real me.* But it was her, and the kid looked like he knew it. She forced a smile to try and break the spell, and to her surprise the kid grinned back.

She breathed easy. And began to feel comforted somehow by the crowds surrounding her. Watched a girl taking a photo of her friend under a sign that read *Golden Nugget*. Smiled at an old lady sitting on a bench sipping a can of Guinness.

But then she spotted the grey-suited man slinking off into the throng. Had he been following her? What if he was a journalist? Her chest tightened. If her identity was exposed, her life wouldn't be worth living.

She mustn't be paranoid. It probably wasn't him; she'd only

seen the back of the guy for a second. All the same, she moved away from the pier to wait for George on the promenade.

Leaning on the white railings, she watched a few misguided people defying the blustery chill in an attempt to sunbathe on the pebble beach. Salt was eating at the railings; the white paint bubbled and was stained with rust. You couldn't see the salt in the air, but it must be there.

A seagull landed nearby and gave her a sideways look with its insolent yellow and black eye. She pulled a face and it flew off, circling high above a couple on the beach. They looked like tourists: taking pics of each other eating fish and chips. The gull squealed and dived at them. She laughed as they panicked, waving their hands about and wailing in a language she couldn't understand. Another bird joined the attack. The couple dumped their chips and ran for cover in a cumbersome dash across the pebbles.

No way she'd be terrorised by seagulls. She'd catch one and break its feathery neck before she'd give up her chips. More shrieking brought a whole mob of gulls flocking down on the discarded lunch in a feeding frenzy.

It was gross.

She grimaced, but was compelled by a grudging respect for the birds to watch them ripping the fish and chips to pieces. They knew how to get what they wanted.

'Vermin, aren't they?' George said, joining her on the promenade.

'Thought you'd be more sympathetic.' Pale sunlight glinted off his bald head and caught the grey stubble on his chin. 'If they were a gang of teenagers nicking chips because they were hungry, you'd be all sympathy and understanding, wouldn't you?'

'Ah, but it's my job to understand difficult teenagers.'

'Like me?' she said.

'You're not a teenager anymore.'

'But I am difficult.'

'Now, I did not say that.'

'So, I'm easy then? Easy Anna.' She laughed.

'I hope not,' he said with a hint of sharpness.

'What's the matter, George, don't you like easy girls?' She fixed him in the eye.

He took a breath. 'I'm not playing this game, Anna.'

'I bet you've met a few. In the line of duty,' she added, enjoying his discomfort.

'Easy or difficult, makes no difference to me. It's just my job.'

The way he said it made her feel dismissed and diminished. That's all she was to him. A job.

'So, if you get fired, I'll never see you again,' she mumbled before she could stop herself.

'I'm not about to *get fired*.'

'What about when you retire?'

'Jesus! How old do you think I am?'

She grinned. 'Ancient.'

'Westcliffe isn't exactly a metropolis, so I don't suppose I'd manage to completely avoid you.' He turned to look over the beach, stroked the back of his neck and let his hand rest there for a moment. The seagulls finished off the dregs of their fish and chip dinner and soared into the air, patrolling like belligerent drunks looking for someone to pick on. He turned back to face her. 'You are my job, but I will always do the best I can to help you, Anna.'

'Do you have to call me Anna?'

'We talked about this—'

'But you know the real me. You know Caitlin.'

George nodded. 'Think about it like this, Caitlin grew up, and she grew into Anna.'

'The ugly duckling turned into a beautiful swan,' she said in a mocking voice.

'I think the jury's out on that one.'

'Oh no, George. The jury already gave its verdict.'

He opened his mouth to speak, but said nothing.

'Can we get chips?' she said to break the sudden awkwardness.

George claimed to be on a diet and passed on the chips, but he bought her a bag. They took refuge from the birdlife in a wrought-iron Victorian shelter. Sat together on a green wooden bench while she worked her way through the chips. Maybe it gave him a secret pleasure watching someone enjoy the thing he denied himself.

'Want one?'

'Better not.'

She held the chip bag under his nose. 'Smell good, don't they?'

'Things that seem good are sometimes bad for you.'

She shook the bag. 'Don't be such a misery.' He looked at her for a moment and then snatched a chip and popped it into his mouth.

'They are good,' he said, savouring the taste, before taking several more in quick succession. The chips made his lips glisten with grease.

It didn't bother her the way George got grease on his lips and then wiped them clean. Whereas the other day, when the grey-suited man came into the coffeeshop and ordered his toasted teacake, his chewing and the way the crumbs stuck to his buttery lips made her want to puke.

'Are you watching me eat?' George said, frowning.

'No. Sorry, miles away.' She told him about Grey Suit and the way he spent hours in the coffeeshop, and seemed to be keeping an eye on her. 'Do you think he could be a journalist?'

'What makes you say that?'

'Kept looking at me.'

'Well...'

'Well what?' she snapped, cross that George wasn't taking her seriously. Again.

'You know…' He cleared his throat and swallowed. 'Sometimes, men look at young women.'

'You trying to tell me he was perving on me?'

George shrugged. 'Maybe.'

'That's supposed to be okay is it?'

'I'm not making excuses for him. I'm just saying. All right?'

'What are you *just saying*?'

'He can't know who you are. No one knows what you look like or where you're living.'

'Says you.' She got to her feet and wandered over to the steps leading down to the beach.

'Watch out for the seagulls,' George shouted after her.

She gave a dismissive wave over her shoulder and descended the worn granite treads to the pebbles. Waved the chip bag around in the air, baiting the gulls. One came flapping down and she ran off spinning around, as if she was a whirling dervish. The gull spiralled around her head – her unknowing dance partner. Then it swooped down towards the chips. She used her free hand to try and punch the bird. She missed. The gull wheeled away, only to return for another go. She jumped up shouting, hit the bird on its wing. It squawked and flapped off. She laughed, finished her chips and crumpled the empty bag into her hoodie pocket.

George clinked over the pebbles to join her. 'You know they're a protected species.'

'Vermin you said.'

'I don't make the rules.'

'Gonna report me then? A danger to gulls.'

'Rules are rules.'

Surely he was joking. Wasn't he? Suddenly she didn't know.

He laughed. 'I hate seagulls.'

'Bastard.'

'Language!' But he was still smiling. She grinned back and caught his eye, but then felt embarrassed and looked over at the promenade where a couple were leaning on the railings – a middle-aged man in a red football shirt that was too small for his belly and a young woman in an orange onesie. The woman was staring right at her.

'Can't I do anything without being watched?'

'Just because someone looks at you doesn't mean they know who you are.'

She wanted to feel reassured, but deep down she knew she was different to other people. Ugly duckling. The ugliness inside must be visible to the world.

There goes Caitlin Grady. Child killer.

George picked up a pebble, considered it a moment and then said, 'This one's no good, too dull and grey.' Dropping it, he went on, 'Let's find one that's special, different from the others, easily recognisable.'

'Why?'

'Bare with me.'

She pulled a face, but found herself searching the beach, picking up pebbles that caught her eye. The stones were mostly boring blue-grey, some had sandy-coloured or white streaks. Nothing striking about any of them. Then she found it. Burnt orange with dark blue and ruby markings.

She showed it to George. 'Cool isn't it?'

He nodded. 'Examine it carefully. Remember all its details.' He gave her a look. 'Its secrets.'

She scrutinised it, turning it over and over, until its markings were seared into her brain.

'Give it to me.'

Suddenly possessive she said, 'Finders keepers, George.' But he held his hand out and after a moment, like an obedient child, she placed it in his palm. He clasped his hand around the stone, felt its weight and then threw it into the air. It landed with a faint clatter, a little way down the beach.

'What the fuck! Why did you do that?' It was a dick move. Get her to hand over a stone and then throw it away. Did he want to throw her away, was that what he was trying to say? He seemed to sense her anger and adopted his professional look.

'The point is, can we find it again?'

She snorted and marched off to where the stone had landed. It was only a stone, but it was her stone and he shouldn't have thrown it away, just to make some bullshit point. Anyway, she'd find it to prove him wrong.

Looking for it was one thing, finding it another. To be fair George did his best to help, but despite searching and searching, neither of them could find her cool orange stone. She could be here for days and not find her own stone in the mass of pebbles on the beach, no matter how distinctive and special it was. Giving up on the search she wandered down to the shoreline where waves were washing the pebbles, rummaging them around and mixing them up. The water made them shine and shimmer in the sunlight.

George might have a point. But she wasn't a pebble on the beach. She was a person and there was such a thing as facial recognition software.

She picked up a stone, wondered if she could skim it across the water. She threw it, but it didn't skim, it just plopped into the water and was gone.

FIVE

Appletree Avenue

K erry would normally get up with him. Even if she was
on lates and could afford a lie in, she'd still get up to
keep him company. Not this morning.

'Too tired.'

He didn't know why she was tired, she'd slept like a well-fed
lioness. He was the tired one. His back ached and his brain was
buzzing like there was a wasp in his skull.

He filled the kettle. It had once been bright stainless steel,
but was now discoloured with limescale that neither he nor
Kerry could be bothered to clean off. Then he spooned an
extra-large measure of instant coffee granules into his old
Oasis mug – a survivor from when they'd first moved in
together. A time when she'd make him sandwiches in the
morning. No chance of that now.

In bed last night, he tried to snuggle up to Kerry, but she
complained she was too hot and moved away. Too hot? She'd
never said that before. Despite actual sex being almost non-
existent, there'd always been affection between them. But this
moving away from him in bed? What next, separate beds?
Separate rooms? No wonder he couldn't sleep. Instead he spent

the night listening to Kerry's slow rhythmic breathing and his own pounding heart, his mind haunted by Caitlin Grady.

Don't think about her; don't give her that power; move on, he told himself uselessly as he tried to lie still despite his churning insides. He'd tried to bring up the Grady situation a few times, but Kerry refused to be drawn and if he persisted she'd walk off and leave him to it. Leave him going over and over the same shit: Grady being allowed a normal life while his family had been blown apart. Was still being blown apart.

Last night Kerry had even taken her tea into the lounge and sat on the sofa to eat it in front of the telly. Watched a lot of telly these days. Soaps. He resented the way Kerry took the goings on in Albert Square so bloody seriously when it was all made up anyway.

He stared out of the kitchen window at the patch of overgrown grass in the back garden; the clothesline they hardly used, faded yellow pegs perched on it like strange plastic birds. They'd never made this place their own. They hadn't really moved in – they were just squatting. Temporary accommodation, like the rented properties he did jobs on sometimes. Houses that were reasonably well maintained, but weren't loved.

Heading off to work, he hesitated at the front door. Should he shout a 'goodbye, love' up the stairs? Or even go up and plant a kiss on her sleepy cheek?

Better leave it. He slipped outside, stepping into the street where he felt like an alien. If only he could feel he belonged. Somewhere. Imagined going back to Bristol and living his old easy life. Impossible; he wouldn't fit in there either. The people he knew, his old mates, were no good to him now.

After Riley's murder it became clear he was no longer in their tribe. Oh, they were sympathetic and that, but he could see they didn't know what to say. Treated him and Kerry like they had an affliction that was catching and kept their cool distance. Maybe thinking if they got too close their own kids would be abducted and murdered.

He swallowed back the resentment and went to his van to check the rolls of grey electrical cable in the back. Tried not to think about coiling that cable around Grady's neck.

A car door slammed and he turned to see a man shambling towards him. It was Harvey Pringle, the journalist, jacket flapping open to reveal a tight shirt struggling to contain a generous belly. Tie worn loose.

'Word in your ear, Mr Burgess.' He seemed short of breath as he approached. 'Shall we step into your office?' He tapped the side of the van.

He'd promised Kerry not to talk to the man, so mumbled something about being late for work and headed to the driver's side. Pringle went to the passenger door and got in anyway.

'You're a hard man to get hold of,' Pringle said as Darren slumped in, tutting to himself at the man's gall. The years hadn't been kind to Pringle. Nose mottled with burst blood vessels. Eyelids hooded. Insincere smile on his purple lips.

'What's this about, Mr Pringle?'

'Unplugged your landline, have you? Because I can't seem to get through.'

Had Kerry really gone ahead and had Pringle's number blocked? 'There's a fault on the line,' he said in a tone that wouldn't convince a child.

'Just wanted a catch-up. See how life was treating you.' Pringle tilted his head and gave a look. 'You know.'

'Mr Pringle, if this is about Grady, I don't want to open that can of worms.' Who was he kidding? The can of worms wasn't just open, it had spewed its contents all over him.

'Doesn't it bother you she's out?'

'I didn't say that, did I? Now if you don't mind…' Darren puffed and stabbed the key in the ignition.

'Let her go three weeks ago. Even before the official announcement.'

'What!?' Grady was already free by the time they got off their arses to tell him. Like he was the last person who should know. Felt like a stab in the back.

And Pringle wasn't finished with the news. 'The word is, she'll be going to university in September.'

'University! They're gonna send her to uni?' No one in his family had ever been to university.

'You know she got top A-levels while she was inside?'

He wanted to spit. Bloody students with their party-party lifestyles. Sex and drugs and never having to do any real work.

'Meanwhile, she's free as a bird. New identity, secret location.'

He couldn't look at Pringle, stared straight ahead. His annoyed gasping breaths were misting up the windscreen in the early morning cold. He wiped the glass with his hand. Out there, behind closed doors people were waking up, having breakfasts and getting ready for work, unconcerned about Grady.

'It isn't right,' he muttered. 'It isn't right she can live it up like that and no one is even allowed to know where she is.'

'Human rights, isn't it?'

'What about my human rights?' Darren spluttered.

'I'm afraid your human rights don't seem to count for sod all, mate.'

Darren realised he was digging his fingernails into the back of his neck, so stopped before he drew blood.

'Look, Mr Burgess,' Pringle was saying, 'I'd like to help. Really.' He sounded almost genuine. But not quite.

'Help? Then tell me where the bitch is. What university? Tell me that for starters.' He spat the words out, not enjoying whatever game Pringle was playing.

'Sadly, I don't know.'

'Is this a wind-up?' He didn't want to listen to Pringle for another damn second. Wanted him out of the van.

'Take it easy, mate. The informant doesn't know which uni she's applied to.'

'You trying to piss me off?'

'But here's the thing. If we work together, we might just be able to winkle her out of her hiding place. Make her face the light of day.'

Pringle didn't actually know anything! Waste of breath talking to the fucker.

'Someone somewhere knows where she is, so we need to keep up the heat. That's where you come in.'

'Oh yeah? How's that then?'

'Give us a peg to hang a story on. An in-depth piece about Caitlin Grady's release.'

'A peg? What do you mean?'

'Listen.' Pringle leaned in. 'I know how hard it's been for you, mate. Everybody talks about Grady. No one listens to you, right?'

Darren nodded. Could feel himself softening.

'So what I'm saying is, put the record straight,' Pringle continued. 'We can tell your side of the story. How it feels having Grady out there, living amongst us, in secret.'

Darren knew how he felt. He wanted to strangle the life out of her. But he couldn't let the paper print that. Kerry would murder him for a start. He might even get a visit from the police. He shook his head. 'No comment, Mr Pringle. No. Comment.'

'So that's it. Nothing to say?'

He wanted to say more, spill his heart and guts to the newspaper. Have them shout it out loud and clear. But the truth was, Pringle was using him. Trying to get him to say stuff that would make people click on *The Herald's* grubby website, and meanwhile he'd end up in a whole heap of shit. He clenched his jaw. He needed to close this down before he said too much. Especially if he valued what was left of his marriage. 'Now if you don't mind…'

Pringle sighed. 'Pity. A quote from the victim's family really helps.'

'Helps what?' he snarled. 'Helps you sell papers!' He turned the ignition, the engine roared into life as he throttled the gas.

Pringle raised his hands as if Darren had a gun and got out, but then leaned in. 'The right quote from yourself would help loosen tongues.' He placed a business card carefully on the passenger seat and shut the door.

Darren floored the gas and accelerated down Appletree Avenue, ignoring the irritating twenty-mile-an-hour sign painted in the road. Drove as fast as he could, like some boy racer in his first car, or like he wanted to get stopped by the police. Perhaps he did. Perhaps he'd give them a run for their money. He didn't know whether he was angry with Pringle for trying to use him or himself for not saying what he felt about Grady. Or, simply angry with the whole damn world.

He jumped some red lights at the roadworks on Paternoster Way. An oncoming car, some large Audi, appeared out of nowhere and was forced to stop. The Audi flashed his headlights and honked his horn. He leaned on his own horn, causing a long continuous blast before going on the pavement to get round the bastard. Fuck him in his fancy SUV.

On the building site, at the half-finished residential block, he kept pacing around or staring out of the window. The development was near some railway sidings and the tracks glinted in the sun like thin curved knives. He thought about Grady. Bringing her here at night. See how she liked being snatched, taken to an isolated place and fearing for her life.

'Working to rule?'

'What?' He swung around to see Ben, the project manager, smirking at him.

'Or thinking of jumping?' The man gripped him by the shoulders, and pushed him against the glassless window frame.

'Hey!' Darren forced Ben off.

'If you are thinking of topping yourself, do let me know. So I can get someone else in.'

'Very funny.'

He'd known Ben since school. It was Ben who'd got him the job in Chippenham so he should be grateful. But to Darren, the guy was still a snivelling lad two years below him. Baby Ben they'd called him. It was hard to get his head around the fact that the kid was now his boss.

'You've had a face as long as an undertaker's coat all morning.'

'I'm fine.'

'Trouble and strife, is it?'

'I said I'm fine.'

Ben puffed himself up, trying to look more like an actual boss. 'Listen, you've done sweet FA this morning and the plasterers are due in Friday. You know what I'm saying?'

Had he really done nothing? Maybe he should tell Baby Ben what was on his mind. But couldn't bring himself to make excuses, especially to the likes of Ben. So he simply looked at the guy, goading him to say more.

'Are you deaf? I said–'

'Yeah yeah, whatever.' Being project manager had gone to Ben's head.

'Get a fucking move on, buddy.'

'I'm not your buddy. Don't call me your buddy, you little fuck.'

Ben's mouth hung open, looked like he was back in school, scared of being hit. His voice went up an octave. 'I can get someone else in, you know.'

He stared at Ben. His arm twitched. Fist clenched, he felt like punching that stupid face. Hard. Instead he shoved his manager out of the way and headed towards the concrete staircase.

'Oi, where do you think you're going?'

'None of your fucking business. Prick.'

'Then don't bother coming back!'

———

He was carrying a bunch of flowers as he walked up the path by the railway cutting. Lasianthus and chrysanthemum – blues and purples. Riley always liked blue. It was his favourite colour too – when he was a kid anyway. Electric blue.

When he got to the brow of the hill his heart sank. The girl, the prostitute, was standing at the edge of the embankment, smoking and looking over the railway. The acrid smell of burning tobacco drifted over, spoiling the atmosphere. She'd better not be waiting for a client. But perhaps this is where she brought them. He felt sick. He'd have to say something if she started to do *business* up here. It wasn't on. But for now he simply ignored her, hoping she'd finish her fag and sod off.

He stooped to place the flowers at the base of the tree, reading the message he'd scribbled on the attached card.

To my Riley. Love, Daddy.

He'd thought about putting something more poetic like 'you'll always be in my heart'. But decided greeting card expressions weren't him.

Whatever words he wrote though, it could never be enough. Every cell in his body was screaming to get to Grady. People, most people anyway, would say justice had been done and that he needed to move on.

Move on.

The words made him want to retch. He shook his head and looked around, as if in search of someone to witness his fury.

He couldn't move on. He knew that now. Not until he found Grady and made her pay.

The girl finished her cigarette, flicked it away and wandered over, stopping a few paces from him. 'Them flowers are lush.'

He kept quiet.

'Where d'you get 'em? Asda?'

He nodded.

'Worked out where I've seen you before.'

Turning to face her, he noticed her trainers. Bright neon pink, brand new by the looks of it.

'You *were* on the telly, weren't you?'

He gave a reluctant smile. Still didn't say anything.

'And you was all over the papers.'

He closed his eyes. Breathed. Mumbled, 'Long time ago.'

'I'm sorry. What happened was…' she trailed off, shook her head. 'Seared into my brain. Never forget something like that.'

'How old were you when…' He swallowed. 'You know?'

'Last year of primary.' She let out a single ironic laugh. 'Well, anyway. Just wanted to say…' She looked over at the tree and then shrugged. 'Best be off.' She turned to go.

'Which school?'

She stopped but didn't turn to face him. Raising his voice, he repeated the question. 'Which primary school did you go to?'

She swung around. 'We all went to Vernon Road from round here, didn't we?'

Same school as Grady. Same school Riley would have gone to if she'd lived. Been due to start reception class in the September. Of course she remembered the crime. All the families with kids at that school would have been riveted in horror. Before Grady was arrested, the police went there to talk to the kids and warn them about wandering off alone.

'Last year of primary?'

She nodded. Her face looked strange, almost broken.

'Caitlin Grady must have been in your year,' he said, his voice croaking.

'It was a shithole. Spent most of year six bunking off.'

'Did you know her? Did you know Grady?'

She shook her head quickly, like electricity was passing through her. 'Got to go.' She turned away and hurried off.

'Wait! Hang on. Please?'

But the girl didn't wait, she increased her pace, jogging through the dry grass down the slope to the fence. That girl knew something. Maybe she was still in touch with Grady. Maybe she knew where the bitch was hiding.

He followed her down the hill.

SIX

Tesco Express, Westcliffe High Street

W as it pervy to stare at the boy like this? Probably, but
she couldn't help herself. She was hanging around a
display of discounted car windscreen wash from where she
could eye him up discreetly as he stood behind the checkout.
She found it actually painful to take her eyes off him. It was
weird and disconcerting. She'd never felt this way about anyone
– this need to stare. What was it about him? The highlighted
blond hair that flopped down over his forehead? His pale blue-
grey eyes? The tanned face, or the hint of muscle under his
shirt?

Looking at the boy made her want him. It was almost as
painful as not looking at him. Ridiculous that she was having
her first teenage crush at the age of twenty. But then, she'd
spent her teenage years in a secure children's home. Hands-on
experience with boys was forbidden and pretty much as soon as
she turned eighteen, she was shipped off to a women's prison.
A convent girl would have more experience of males than
she had.

He looked over and smiled. Embarrassed at being spotted,

37

she pretended not to notice him and quickly looked away before heading to the rear of the store.

It wasn't the first time this week that Brig, her boss at the café, had sent her to Tesco to get a four-litre carton of milk. Today, she was particularly glad to get away from the café because Grey Suit was there again, creeping her out.

'You like your milk don't you?' the boy said in his soft cream-tea accent as she heaved the carton onto the counter. Was he being a smart arse?

'Hate the stuff!' she snapped.

He looked bewildered and scanned the carton.

Feeling suddenly awkward, she stammered, 'It's for the café. CoffeeTime. Work there, don't I? Boss never gets the milk order right.'

He nodded. 'I know the place.' He held her gaze. She stared back determined not to look away. It reminded her of staring contests she had at primary school. But her cheeks began to flush, so she gave in and looked down at the milk.

'Will that be cash or card?' The way he said it, you'd think he was asking her on a date. Was he taking the piss? She pulled a fiver from her black pinstriped uniform trousers and tossed it on the counter.

He gave her the change, grinned again – God was that all he ever did – and said, 'Have a nice day.' Then he winked. What the fuck?

'You taking the piss?'

'No I–'

'Fuck off.'

'Hey!'

She grabbed the milk and got the hell out of there. Arsehole.

Outside, she took a deep breath and tried to calm down. The air was sea-fresh and salty, albeit with a hint of chip shop. There were fish and chip places every few metres down

Westcliffe High Street, along with bucket and spade places, the Las Vegas amusement arcade and weird souvenir shops like Kute Kollectables, with its china figurines and model sailing boats. Shop windows were still a novelty and she liked to take in the different displays.

In the fishmonger's window, a row of slack mouthed silvery sea bass lay in a bed of fake parsley, expressions frozen into wide-eyed looks of horror, as if still shocked by their own deaths. She stared, fascinated by their strange beauty. But there was something unsettling in their unblinking eyes. Like they knew bad things about her.

She shivered and scurried back to CoffeeTime where she was dismayed to find the grey-suited man was still there. She slammed the carton of milk onto the counter.

'Careful! You'll burst it!' Brig said.

'Sorry.'

'Who rattled your cage?'

'No one, I'm fine!' She forced a bright smile.

Brig gave her a crooked smile back. Her manager had a tendency to only smile with half her mouth, so you were never really sure if she meant it. Her cropped ice-blonde hair and glossy scarlet lipstick added to the sternness of her look.

Grey Suit was looking over now and she swore silently at herself for attracting his attention. Grabbing the carton, she took it to the kitchen out the back, put the milk in the fridge and lingered there to avoid having to clap eyes on him again.

It had taken a while to get used to Brig. At first, she was convinced the woman secretly hated her, as she didn't chat much. Didn't talk about herself or ask about 'Anna's' life either. But Brig had given her a job despite knowing she'd been in prison. In the end she was grateful that Brig never asked what she'd done to be put away. Meant she didn't have to lie to the woman. Anyway, Brig trusted her with balancing the till at the end of the shift and so she was beginning to relax around her.

Even took comfort from being in her company, like they were a couple of feral cats that got used to each other.

A skinny latte and lemon drizzle muffin later and Grey Suit still hadn't gone. He kept looking at her. Well, pretended to look around in thought, but she caught him scrutinising her a few times. She told herself he was simply a sad man in a used suit. Nothing to be worried about.

Some computer nerd had taken the official photo from when she was arrested and electronically aged her, so it was supposed to show how she looked now. The original police photo of her staring into the camera was all over the internet. Her unflinching wide eyes were familiar to everyone. Even she had nightmares in which that eleven-year-old came back to torment her.

The new photo was posted up on HuntAKilla – a website based in Israel that liked to expose 'dangerous criminals'. She'd stared at that picture for hours trying to decide if there was a resemblance. In the end she simply didn't know. She wondered if Grey Suit had seen it.

She complained to Brig about him.

'Keeps giving me the eye.'

'What sort of eye?'

'You know. Staring.'

'That's men for you,' Brig said. 'And the thing is, you are quite striking, you know.'

She pulled a face.

'It's true. Anyway, something you'll have to get used to I'm afraid is the male gaze. Don't worry though, sometime after your fortieth birthday, you become invisible.'

Never mind the male gaze; she knew all about the female gaze. When she'd been transferred to Thornhill women's prison, inmates and screws alike were keen to get eyes on her notorious self. She didn't want to be striking. She wanted to be invisible.

Perhaps she should do something about her eyes then. People always commented on her piercing blue eyes.

'Stop looking at me with them witchy eyes,' her mum used to say. Her mother had brown eyes, as did her aunts and uncles. So the blue probably reminded the woman of her father, whoever he was. Her mum had never told her and refused to talk about it. But she couldn't help wondering about him. Maybe knowing her dad would help her understand herself.

That night, faced with the bare walls of her studio flat, she worried she'd over-reacted, telling the boy to fuck off. Pushing him away for no reason. But the way he winked at her was a piss-take, right? Even if it wasn't, and was an attempt to flirt with her, how was she supposed to know? She tutted to herself at the way this thing with the boy was bothering her.

Maybe it would be easier to deal with boys via a dating app, then she wouldn't have to figure out how to behave in real life. So she downloaded an app called Butterfly. First problem was setting up her profile with a mandatory pic. The last thing she wanted was for her real image to be out there in cyberspace.

SEVEN

Pennywell City Farm, Bristol

A *place where people grow.*

The sign was written in cheerful coloured letters across the whitewashed building and was accompanied by murals of ducks and sheep. You'd think nothing bad could ever happen here.

He hesitated on the threshold wondering if he had the guts to set foot on the city farm again. However, maybe the prostitute had come here. He'd followed her down the hill at a discreet distance, afraid of spooking her, but lost her somewhere in Pennywell industrial estate. He'd carried on walking and his legs had taken him here.

He stepped into the tiled reception area feeling like a visitor from another world. Yet the café, farm shop and community noticeboard were as familiar as an old family photograph. The place smelt the same as he remembered: stale milk blended with garlic soupiness from the café, with an acidic whiff of disinfectant. For a moment he bathed in the warmth of nostalgia, until it was tainted by something darker.

Kerry's strained voice. 'Where's Riley?'

He flinched at the memory. The woman at the reception

desk caught his expression and fixed him with a sour look. Didn't she know he was once a regular here? A proper dad who loved looking after his kid. They even knew his name in the café, for God's sake. But now childless, he felt the object of suspicion. He hurried past her into the farmyard.

A couple of women were sipping tea at a trestle table and one of them, a black woman with a nose jewel flashed Darren a bright smile as he walked by. He felt the tension drain from his shoulders. It was okay to be here.

The farmyard hadn't changed. There was the barn, the whitewashed sheep pens, and the duck pond – around which two kids were chasing each other. He breathed in damp hay and animals. Earthy and wholesome.

He went to the duck pond and stooped to dip his hand in the green-black water. The kids, boys, about four years old, careered around him regardless. The water was cold. He held his hand there till it went numb.

It was suddenly quiet. The boys were gone. The tea-drinking mothers were distracted by a woman in dungarees, one strap of which was undone, bib carelessly flopped down. He wanted to go over and tell them to watch out for their kids. That he was a parent once and he'd got distracted.

But he didn't, instead just thought back to that terrible day.

'Where's Riley?'

'Over by the duck pond.'

Only she wasn't by the duck pond. The place was heaving and he couldn't see her anywhere. Panic rising, he searched the crowds. Then he spotted her on the other side of the yard heading towards the allotments. She was holding hands with a tall, thin woman. He raced towards her, but the way was blocked. Pushchairs, mothers, babies, children, bikes and push along trikes. Someone in a mobility buggy across his path. What were they all doing here? Get out of the way!

He shouted, 'Riley. RILEY!'

Fought his way through. Barged, elbowed shoved and jostled. Didn't care.

But it wasn't Riley.

A wave of nausea went through him. The mother looked at him like he was a child snatcher.

'Please! I've lost my child. Have you seen my child?'

The memory was so vivid it hurt his chest. His heart pounded. Wanting to stave off one of his panic attacks he headed out of the yard towards the allotments and gardens. Those boys were probably there somewhere and it might make him feel a bit better to check they were okay.

There was more cheerful signage in the gardens, with names like *Healing Herb Corner* and *Community Garden*. Signs that were decorated with drawings of sunshine, flowers and cute frogs. It was so wholesome it stung him.

They were such regular visitors here that Riley knew her way around. Sometimes he pretended to be lost.

'Silly Daddy,' Riley would say, leading him by the hand and shaking her head in mock disapproval.

Kerry would laugh. 'Yes, Daddy is very silly.' Then she'd give him a playful thump.

He was still Daddy when she died. Not old enough to call him Dad.

He stopped by the herb garden, soothed for a moment by the aroma of lavender. He could feel a faint echo of Riley here. Imagined her giggling as she hid amongst the lavender's purple flowers or the white and yellow feverfew. She could never hide for long – her pleasure was all in being found.

A train roared past in the mid-distance causing a flock of pigeons to take to the air. This was the inner city, not some rural retreat. And there was no Riley hiding in the bushes.

He found the boys looking through a rustic wooden fence into a small paddock where half a dozen sheep were enjoying the languid afternoon sun.

'Does your mum know where you are?' he asked one of them.

The boy stared back with fearful eyes.

His friend jumped in. 'Not meant to talk to strangers.'

'Quite right,' Darren said.

'Oy, Cameron!'

The black woman was striding towards him. The kids ran to her. Darren smiled, expecting a grateful wave, but she returned a fierce stare.

'What did that man say to you?' she asked her child in a purposely loud voice, before leading the boys away.

Pissed off, he turned away and stared at a nearby sheep. That woman ought to be grateful he was keeping an eye out for her kids, not bad mouthing him. Sometimes he wondered if he understood the world at all. The white-faced sheep flicked its ears and munched grass.

EIGHT

Ocean View Residential Hotel

C aitlin was wandering along the sensory path in a sunken garden. Her companion, Moira, a thin, lively woman in her eighties, stopped at various points to pick leaves of rosemary, lavender and lemon balm. Moira squeezed the leaves in her bony fingers and then passed them to Caitlin so she could sniff the aroma.

The gardens were once part of the grounds of some posh person's mansion, but now belonged to Ocean View Residential Hotel. They called it a hotel instead of a care home the way her children's prison had been called a 'secure children's home', to make everyone feel better. That place didn't have a garden, it had grounds where they exercised. Muddy grass, bordered by a scrawny privet hedge that only partially hid the razor-wire fence behind.

This place had an institutional feel: the smell of disinfectant and cabbage, with a hint of urine for a start. Smells which were so familiar Caitlin found them strangely comforting. So even though it was only the second time she had volunteered here, it almost felt like a home from home.

It had been George's idea she should do some volunteering.

He said it showed she was 'putting something back' into the community. It was a box-ticking thing, but what did she have to lose? Volunteering simply meant chatting to the residents and since she had no actual friends, she was happy to come here for something to do. Besides she liked hearing about their lives. Lives that had been lived.

She and Moira reached the end of the sensory path and sat on a bench opposite an opulent display of roses. Moira told her how her husband had loved roses.

'He thought I loved them too,' she said. 'But although one has to admit the blooms have a certain beauty, I've always thought there was an unpleasantness about a rose. Such show-offs, aren't they? Hybrid and unnatural. Something nasty about them I always say.'

'Did you ever tell your husband that you weren't that keen on roses?'

'Oh no. He spent far too much time caring for them, I didn't have the heart to burst his bubble.'

Moira reminded her of her grandmother. She got dumped on her nanna all the time, sometimes for days while her mother was working. She hadn't minded, though, Nanna didn't have a malicious bone in her body and loved her to bits. Always had a pot of stew on the stove. Dessert was biscuits – custard creams. And tea, the woman could drink strong, dark tea for Ireland.

Nanna had an ancient wooden dresser in the front room full of little bottles of holy water. They looked like magic potions to Caitlin. Nanna would tell her where each bottle came from, but she took no notice and instead imagined the magic powers such water might give her. Just as well that the bottles were all sealed, otherwise she'd have drunk one to see what magic she got. She wondered what had happened to those magical bottles after Nanna died.

She'd been given special permission to visit Bristol for the funeral, but when she arrived, the place was surrounded by press. She had to cover her head to prevent the photographers getting an up-to-date photo. Her minder did a crazy U-turn to get away, causing cars to honk in protest, but managed to lose the pack. She knew who'd tipped off the press. Her mum. But that was her mum all over: suck up to the press for a pocket full of cash.

'What's the matter, dear? You look like you've the world's troubles on your shoulders,' Moira said.

'Just thinking about my mum. Haven't seen her for a while. Fell out with her, didn't I?'

Moira frowned. 'Oh dear. That's a shame.'

'Yeah.' It was a shame all right. A shame the only person her mum thought about was herself.

'I know what you mean about roses,' Caitlin said. 'Look pretty from a distance, don't they, but if you get too close, they cut you.'

Later, back at her flat, she rummaged through her knicker drawer and pulled out the old framed photo that was tucked away under her prison-issue underwear. She sat on the bed staring at the attractive but hard-faced woman. Catherine Grady – her mum. The photo was taken over ten years ago, when she'd been sent to Lowood Secure Children's Home. 'I'll be keeping an eye on you,' her mum told her when she gave it to her on the first visit.

With Nanna dead, and aunts and uncles who had never once visited her in the children's unit, let alone Thornhill Prison, her mum was her only family. Whatever else her mum was, she hadn't washed her hands of her. Perhaps it was time to forgive her for the funeral debacle and make contact.

Her mum might be able to shed some light on why Grey Suit provoked such powerful feelings of disgust and fear within her. Somewhere in the back of her mind was a slippery ghost of a memory she couldn't pin down. Had she known a man like him as a child? A family friend or some long-lost uncle?

Even if her mum couldn't help with Grey Suit, she could definitely help with the identity of her father. She was determined to get the truth out of the woman on that score.

Her mum would be horrified to know her pic was stuffed in a drawer with shapeless grey prison knickers. Caitlin smiled at the thought, but decided to promote the woman to her bedside table. Those prison knickers needed binning. She ought to get some self-respect and buy decent lingerie. On the other hand, who'd ever see what she was wearing under her clothes? The boy? No way.

He'd walked past the café earlier that day, stopped and stared in through the window. Looked like he might come inside, so she stared back, eyebrows raised, daring him to do so. When he didn't, she felt annoyingly disappointed.

She consoled herself by checking for *likes* on Butterfly. She'd paid for the upgrade so she could see who liked her before *liking* them back.

To get around the profile pic rule, she uploaded a close-up of her so-called 'witchy eyes'. Luckily it was accepted and she was in business.

She was surprised at how many *likes* she had. Swiped through the pics of her likers until her finger froze solid. OMG. The boy. He'd *liked* her. His name was Bert. She allowed herself a snigger at such an oddly old-fashioned name. Could he tell it was her from the close-up of her eyes? Surely not. He'd probably run a mile if he found out who it really was. But just because she told him to fuck off didn't mean she actually wanted him to run away. So what was it to be? Swipe left or like him back?

NINE

The Pines, outskirts of Bristol

D arren pulled up by the neat hedge, its small lime-green leaves iridescent in the sunshine. The potholed road was narrow with no pavement. Branches squealed against the metal of his van as he parked. Nearby was an old telegraph pole leaning at an odd angle, its wood cracked and stained black with ancient tar.

Hidden behind the hedge was his parents' bungalow. In the quiet of the early morning you could sometimes hear mournful cows in nearby fields. It was only a few miles away from the semi near the centre of town where he grew up, but courtesy of his granddad's will, The Pines was way up the property ladder. He still hadn't got his head around them living in a place so posh it had a name instead of a number.

He headed around the side of the bungalow, to the garden with its large lawn and herbaceous borders. The lawn needed cutting. Dandelions were pushing through the grass which was surprising, because his dad was religious about keeping it neatly shaved.

His mother was over by a border of ruby coloured peonies

and a mass of pale blue forget-me-nots, on her knees, hands in the earth.

He watched her for a moment as she pulled out a clump of groundsel. Wondered whether she knew about Grady's release. Both his parents would be angry. Angrier than Riley's own mother probably. He kicked a seeding dandelion, disintegrating its head. The seeds drifted away in the gentle breeze.

'Mum?'

She stood up, an earthy hand on her back, her movements slow and deliberate. She looked stiff. 'Well!' she said, a warm smile filling her face, eyes shining. But she looked old in the harsh afternoon light. He went to hug her, but she held up her earth covered hands to stop him.

'Sorry it's been so long,' he said.

'I know how busy you are.'

He smiled. She would never want him to feel guilty. 'Dad home?' he asked, trying to sound casual.

She nodded. 'He's put his back out. Had to take time off.' She looked away and wiped her hand on her heavy gardening apron. Pointing out a robin perched nearby, she added, 'That one is as tame as anything. Cheeky little thing will come right up to you.'

'My favourite bird,' he said.

'Dad's too.'

His dad was in the lounge. The TV was on, some news item about the government.

'Hi, Dad.'

'Shush. I'm watching.'

Darren had only been in the house two seconds and already he felt his stomach tensing up.

'I'll make some tea,' his mum mouthed and left the room. The TV blathered on, but the silence between himself and his dad was the loudest thing in the room.

He had to say something. 'I suppose you heard about Grady.'

His dad nodded and turned the TV down but didn't face him. 'What does Kerry think?'

'Reckons there's nothing to be done about it.'

'Nothing to be done about it?' his dad repeated, shaking his head, while still looking at the TV. 'That what you think as well?'

'No I—'

'Being as how she does the thinking for the both of you.' His dad had blamed Kerry when they left Bristol. Felt it was a betrayal, or perhaps weakness on Darren's part. The fact that his mum and dad had also moved out of Bristol, albeit to a nearby village, didn't seem to enter the equation.

Darren shrugged off the dig at Kerry and tried again, 'I don't like it, but what can we do?'

His dad turned to face him. 'Something. Anything is better than nothing.'

'What do you think I should do, Dad?'

It was the first time he'd asked his father for advice since he was a kid. 'That's down to you isn't it?' the man said, giving Darren a hard look. Took a breath and then added, 'If Troy were here, he'd know what to do.'

Troy, his brother. The favourite. 'Well he's not here is he?'

Darren had always known his father didn't like him. The man did his duty, like taking him to see Bristol City play, but even then, he seemed uncomfortable in Darren's company. His sister Sarah, the baby of the family, was originally the one doted on. Until she came out as lesbian and moved in with a refugee from Syria. Lived in Brighton and he hardly saw her. So now it was always about Troy.

'He's in Africa as we speak,' his father said, as though being *in Africa* was some great achievement in itself.

'Apparently there's a lot of mosquitos. Poor lad's got

terrible bites,' his mum chipped in as she arrived with a tray of tea and plate of biscuits.

'A few mosquitos aren't gonna bother him,' his dad insisted. 'Training their lot in anti-insurgent warfare,' he added, tapping his nose. 'Teaching them a thing or two.'

'I bet he is,' Darren said, unable to cover his sarcasm about his brother's wonderful army life.

'They've given him his own fireteam,' his dad announced, taking a chocolate biscuit and dropping crumbs on the table as he broke it in two.

What the hell was a fireteam? Something dangerous no doubt. He turned to his mum. 'Shall I cut the lawn for you?'

He pushed the old bottle-green mower up and down the lawn. The rotating blades threw grass into the front bucket, shaving the lawn in regular stripes. Like a football pitch.

Troy would know what to do.

Bloody Troy. So what would he do then? Get his 'fireteam' and gun Grady down?

He mowed into a patch of dandelions. The blades sent yellow flecks of broken petals into the grass box.

Troy had been an aggressive little thug when they were boys. Getting into fights, breaking windows and doing other acts of vandalism. As a teenager he was a known troublemaker and the police came to the house more than once. He was surprised when the army took him on. Must have thought they could tame him.

But if Darren was honest with himself, his dad did have a point. Troy might well know what to do. And Troy had his army mates. People like that wouldn't fuck about would they? Darren was family and they'd help find the bitch wherever she was.

He breathed in the sweet aroma of freshly cut grass. Relaxed. It reminded him of a summer long ago. In another lifetime, before he trained as an electrician, he had a job with the parks department. It was a legend of a summer, fragrant with promise. Blue sky days mowing, cutting and strimming. Eternal sunset evenings drinking at riverside pubs. The summer he met Kerry.

He'd spotted her on a barge, moored by the Jolly Sailor. He caught her looking at him. He knew he looked good, tanned and muscled from his job, and he raised a glass to her. She invited him aboard. Kerry was the opposite to him; pale, thin and dressed in a Metallica T-shirt. Jewelled nose stud. Spikey black hair. They argued about Metallica. Her mum joined in: she was a bit of an old rocker and it turned out the barge belonged to her. She and her mum were going to the Fleece later in the week to see an up-and-coming band called Coldplay. They had a spare ticket, and would he like to come?

A legend of a summer.

By the time he finished helping his mum in the garden, it was getting late, and the sun was going down. He made his excuses. Kerry was expecting him back, he said and he had to go. But he didn't drive straight back home. He went to Pennywell instead.

It was dark when he got to the industrial estate. Quiet. The forecourts of the drab units empty. No lights inside. He drove slowly around the empty streets, through pools of sodium orange from intermittent street lights.

A girl stepped out of the shadows. He slowed down, scrutinising her face as he cruised past. She wasn't the one. There were a handful of other girls around. The light made their features difficult to make out. Boots, pale legs, short skirts. Sallow faces. None of them had neon-pink trainers.

He parked up. Perhaps if he waited, she'd show her face. But then in his rear-view mirror he saw another vehicle approaching. Police car? Sudden panic. Last thing he needed was a ticking off by the cops for kerb crawling. He floored the accelerator, heart banging at his ribcage. The police car didn't follow him. He breathed. What the hell was he thinking, lurking around a red-light area?

When he got back home, Kerry was in the sitting room watching TV. He popped his head in to say hello. She gave a brief, 'Hi,' and turned back to her programme – a hospital show where someone seemed to be in a bad way – struggling for breath. Sort of show he found unbearable, whereas Kerry lapped up that kind of thing.

'I went to see Mum and Dad.'

'Oh,' she said, uninterested. He thought she'd be cross he was late. Tell him he should have texted her or something. But this not giving a shit was worse than an argument. He left her to the TV and went to the kitchen-diner.

He fixed himself some cheese on toast and was pouring a thick layer of ketchup over a bubbling cheddar when Kerry came in to boil the kettle.

'I wanted to tell them about Grady. You know, the release,' he said over the kettle's increasing roar.

She looked at him for a moment, said nothing and then reached to the cupboard for a mug.

'Mum sends her love.'

'What about your dad?'

'Upset about Grady, I think.'

She didn't respond and put a teabag in a cup. 'You know she's been out over three weeks already,' he added, but Kerry still didn't say anything. Simply poured the boiling water into the cup.

'And they are sending her off to university. Can you imagine?'

She turned to face him. 'I don't want to talk about Caitlin Grady.'

'But…'

'Let it go, all right?'

'I thought you'd want to know about the bloody cushy life

they've mapped out for her,' he said, pissed off at being dismissed.

'This anger. It's toxic. I can't deal with it, Darren.'

'I'm not angry, I'm just telling you–'

'Oh no, not angry! Falling out with your boss. Walking off the job. Yeah I know about that. A tonne of messages on the answerphone. Again. Only this time he says not to bother coming back.'

'He's a cunt. You know that!'

'And as for what you wrote on Riley's Facebook page.' She shook her head. 'You are obsessed with Grady. It's not healthy. Not for you and definitely not for me.'

'All right, so what if I am obsessed. I've every right to be obsessed. That bitch killed my child and you don't seem to give a shit.'

Suddenly revolted by the cheese on toast he pushed the plate away, sending it skidding across the table and crashing to the floor. The plate smashed in half. The toast was upside down on the tiles. They both stared at the mess. Ketchup oozed out from under the toast.

'It won't clear itself up, Darren,' Kerry said, walking off and leaving him to it.

He was fucked if he was going to clear it up. So he got to his feet, scraping his chair noisily on the kitchen floor. Headed off out. Slammed the front door on his way.

The Hungry Horse was a 'family pub'. On Sundays it was teeming with parents determined to enjoy a roast dinner while their kids charged around spilling drinks and running into walls. Unbearable. But now it was quiet, apart from a few tables with couples from the estate attempting a date night. There were no other solitary drinkers, and despite hiding in a corner booth, he felt self-conscious. A couple of swift pints sorted that out. The barman looked about twelve, otherwise he might have sat at a bar stool, telling his woes to a sympathetic ear. Did people still do that? Well anyway it wasn't that sort of pub. In fact, it wasn't really a proper pub at all. The day they started doing food in pubs was the end of them as a refuge for the serious drinker.

He stared at his pint. Back in the day, he and his mates called this brand of lager Wifebeater because of its strength. It was a joke back then. It wasn't quite such a joke now.

Lashing out and sending his food onto the floor like that was something he'd never done before.

He needed to stop. Take a breather. It wasn't Kerry's fault they'd released Grady. It wasn't Kerry's fault Riley was dead. It was his fault. He was her father and he'd failed. Hadn't done the only job that really mattered. Let her get killed. He picked up his beer and pressed the heavy glass into his forehead. Held it there until the cold gave him a headache.

Taking his phone, he opened the Facebook page set up in Riley's memory. The post that angered Kerry was about the injustice of Grady's release. It had resulted in a tsunami of angry comments.

Thinking about Pringle, he pulled the business card out of his wallet and considered whether he should give the journalist the quote he wanted.

When he got back home an hour later, the house was in darkness. He stumbled through to the kitchen to find the mess was still on the floor. The ketchup looked like dried blood.

TEN

Westcliffe Pierhead

T he sea was a gently undulating blue-grey sheen. She'd never been much of a swimmer, but leaning over the polished wooden handrail and staring down into the strangely inviting waters, she wondered what it would be like to jump off and plunge in. Cold probably. Exhilarating, for sure. How deep was the water? She tried to see beneath the surface, but her eyes were mesmerised by the dappling light.

'Looking for sunken treasure?' George asked, coming to stand by her.

'D'you think they have sharks and stuff here?'

'Oh yes, man-eaters.'

'Be serious,' she said, nudging him with her elbow.

'Supposed to be basking sharks out there. Somewhere.'

She only half believed him but frowned as a couple of paddleboarders rounded the end of the pier. A tanned guy, bare chested and wearing tight Speedos, followed by a girl in a black wetsuit and orange life jacket.

'They are huge fish, but apparently don't have teeth,' George added.

The guy was pretty fit, so she was glad he wasn't destined

to be shark food. Although the Speedos were a bit much, to be fair, even if he did have a nice tight arse. She wondered if they were an actual couple. No. She was wobbling like she might fall off. He was giving her a lesson.

What was the attraction of paddleboarding? Either do proper surfing or stick to a boat. Maybe the girl just fancied Speedo Boy. She snorted to herself: he wasn't fit enough to do something lame like paddleboarding.

'What's it about?' She cocked her head towards them.

'It's good for inner balance.' George was a bit of an old hippy at heart.

'I think it looks stupid.'

'Don't knock it till you try it.'

She wrinkled her nose.

'Seriously. Might be a way of meeting people.'

'I am meeting people, at Ocean View.'

'The volunteering is good. But I'm concerned that you need to mix with people your own age.'

A small wooden dinghy, blue with a red stripe down the side chugged past heading to the harbour. A fisherman in yellow rubber dungarees at the helm. The bow wave from the boat rocked the paddleboards, sending the girl into the water. She bobbed about in her life jacket, like an orange cork. Speedo Boy looked unbearably smug.

'Have you thought any more about university?' George said, trying to sound casual. But she knew this was his reason for wanting to meet.

'Been thinking more about my mother,' she said, partially to deflect him and partially to sound him out.

'Oh.' He couldn't hide his disappointment. 'I see.'

'I want to arrange a visit, George.'

He cleared his throat. 'Well, it's natural to want to see her. But are we sure it's the best idea?'

He had a point of course. Her mum might let on to the

press about meeting her, like she did at Nanna's funeral. But people deserved a second chance, right? 'She's all I have. You know, family.'

He looked at her and nodded. 'Perhaps we might be able to arrange a supervised meeting. When the time is right.'

'When will that be?'

'Leave it with me for now, okay?'

She didn't reply. Kicked her trainer against the railings realising how much she wanted to reconnect with her mother.

'Now then, if you went to uni—'

'What? If I went to uni, what?' she snapped.

'It's really the best place to make new friends.'

'I don't need friends.'

'Everybody needs friends.'

'They wouldn't be actual proper friends, would they? Not the sort that you tell everything to. Know all about you.'

'Look, I know how tough it is.'

'No! You don't. You just don't.' She glared at him.

He took a deep breath. Nodded. 'Okay. You're right. I don't.' He stared out at the ocean for a long while, massaging the back of his neck. 'I suppose what I'm saying is, university gives you a chance to re-invent yourself. To really become Anna Moreton. And Anna Moreton can have friends.'

'It's living a lie.'

'It's necessary.'

'What? For the greater good?' she snorted.

'For the greater good of Caitlin Grady. And one day, you'll meet someone you can trust. Really trust. Then over time, you can tell them your truth.'

She could not imagine that ever happening. How could she ever tell anyone the truth about what she'd done? It was impossible. Perhaps the best thing was to live the lie then. Pretend she had nothing to do with that psychotic eleven-year-old that haunted her consciousness.

'What would I even do at uni?' She wanted to be a youth worker, but it was on the long list of occupations forbidden by the Ministry of Justice. She was barred from any job where she might be a *bad influence*. 'All the things I wanna be, I can't be. So what's the point?'

'It's still worth going. You'd enjoy it.' A seagull flew overhead letting out a peel of jarring squawks. Mocking bird.

She grunted. 'I don't think so.'

George fell silent and they both watched the girl trying to get back up on the paddleboard. Every time she tried, she wobbled off again and fell back in.

'Lawyer!' George announced like he'd discovered gold. 'You could train as a lawyer.'

'Jokes right? People like me can't be lawyers.'

'Representing young offenders.'

Poor George, he sounded so enthusiastic about his idea, but it was clearly a nonstarter.

'They'd never let me be a lawyer. My past. What happened.'

'It's not on the Ministry list.'

'Anyway, you have to be posh and rich and…'

'Not true. You just have to want–'

'I'm not going to bloody university, okay? Get real!' She marched off down the pier, suddenly pissed off at George's persistence. It was a dumb idea, so why did he have to bend her ear about it? Or did he simply want to get her off his hands?

George was following her down the pier and in the end she sighed to herself and stopped to wait for him. 'It's a stupid idea, all right?' she said as he caught up.

'Some of the best ideas are stupid.'

'That's even more stupid!' But she laughed, despite herself.

They walked on in silence for a while until she broached the subject of boyfriends, asking if he'd be okay with it.

'Have you met someone?'

'No. Not really.'

'Well, if you do meet someone you like, then of course it would be only natural to—'

'So you're okay with it?'

He looked puzzled. 'Why wouldn't I be okay?'

'Just checking it's allowed. That's all.'

'Yes. It's allowed.' He smiled.

She was oddly disappointed there wasn't more of a fight. She'd pushed on a door and it had opened. Why did that not feel good? Perhaps she was so used to locked and bolted doors she didn't like it when they swung open.

They decided to get something to eat. George had been taking her to various big chains like KFC and McDonald's as part of her get-to-know-the-world programme. Places that when she was in prison, had been the objects of her food fantasies.

She'd snuck into McDonald's on her own several times in the last few weeks. Sat down at the wood-effect Formica table and took her sweet time over a cheese burger. And bucket of Coke. She enjoyed the atmosphere. The gaudy illuminated signs – huge burgers overflowing with cheese and salad. She studied the other customers; the whole world seemed to pass through. It made her feel normal just to sit there. One of the millions of people on the planet who go to places like that. No one took the slightest notice of her, which she didn't mind at all.

Today they went to Pret and got sarnies, which they took to a small park. A tranquil place with flower borders, lush with purple and yellow blooms. Manicured grass shimmered in the afternoon sun. In the centre of the lawn there was an ornate wrought-iron bandstand. They sat on a bench and ate.

A couple in their thirties were on a nearby bench making out. Gross! It was awkward sitting with George having to watch a couple engaged in deep French. She tried not to look at them and was relieved when they got up and left. Why did people do that in public? Just showing off, weren't they? Look at how loved up we are! She herself had never kissed a boy. Although she had gone as far as *liking* Bert on the dating app. He responded straight away by saying he thought her eyes were cool.

Sounded Spanish or something, yet his accent was local, so she replied with:

She wasn't quite ready to admit who she was, so typed:

Maybe. 😏

The app showed he was typing, but no reply came. Impatient for a response she added:

Think I'm catfishing you?

Well I don't know what you look like.

Before she could stop herself, she typed:

You do!!!

How?

She hesitated, wondering whether to go for it and reveal herself. Then looking around at her drab empty flat, decided to take the plunge. She sent him a pic of a carton of milk.

No reply. She stared at the app, but there was no indication that he was typing. He'd worked out who she was and was going to ghost her. Awkward. She'd have to avoid Tesco from now on. He could at least have said something. Even if it was 'fuck off yourself'. She would have respected that. Kind of deserved it. Then:

So let's meet?

That was this morning and she hadn't replied yet.

'Bert,' she said out loud, trying the name out.

George gave her a puzzled look. 'What?'

'Stupid name, isn't it?' Although actually she was quite liking it.

'Who is Bert?'

'No one.' She jumped up. 'Can you do handstands?'

'At my age? Are you joking? And definitely not with a belly full of sandwich.'

She took a few steps onto the grass, knelt down, forehead to the cool soft ground, kicked her legs up in the air. The smell of damp grass filled her nostrils.

'That's a headstand, not a handstand,' George shouted.

She dropped her legs back down and leaped to her feet. 'Spoilsport!'

'Just saying.'

She pirouetted like a ballet dancer, held her arms high in the air and threw herself into a series of cartwheels before collapsing onto the grass.

George came over. She stared up at him, but the sun was so bright she couldn't see him properly and had to squint.

'Help me up will you?' she said, holding an arm up for him to grab.

He pulled her to her feet. She stood unsteadily, head spinning. She leaned on him.

'Anna.' He pulled away gently.

'Hey, I'm dizzy!' She pushed into him again and they walked back to the bench shoulder to shoulder.

She flopped down and took a noisy last slurp of the Coke she'd abandoned a minute ago.

'So, would I have to ask permission, before I went on a date or anything?'

'Well, I'd appreciate it if you kept me informed.'

'You wouldn't have to give your approval or anything?'

'I might have a view, if that's what you mean. If this boyfriend or girlfriend was, let's say, unsuitable.'

'So you do care after all.' She couldn't help smiling.

'I care that the person you choose to start a relationship with is—'

'I might not want a relationship. I might just want a quick shag.'

George twisted his face. 'Well, I wouldn't necessarily recommend…'

'A meaningless shag?' She'd got him. He was embarrassed. 'Why not?' He shifted uneasily on the bench, adjusting his position. 'Just cus I'm a woman, I'm not allowed to want a fuck for its own sake?'

'That's not what I...' He stopped. Wiped his brow and looked over at a weathered statue of some sad woman with pigeon shit on her head.

'In my experience, sex is rarely meaningless.'

'Don't be so old-fashioned, Uncle George.'

'And... I'm not your uncle.'

She crushed her Coke can in her hand, got up and went over to a nearby waste bin. Black with a golden diagram of a stick figure tossing trash into a basket. Just in case you were too thick to work it out. She threw her can in. Looked back at George sitting on the bench. She wondered why she couldn't stop herself from winding the poor guy up.

She went back. He turned to face her. 'Just for your information, I am an uncle. Have a niece and nephew. Twelve and fourteen.'

'They could be my cousins.'

He looked at her with sad eyes and shook his head.

'Have you forgotten our cover story?' she said, feeling let down by the way he distanced himself. Reminding her yet again, she was just a job to him. Jesus why couldn't she just get that?

'But that's what it is. A story.'

'I know that, George. But it's a nice story. A nice story of nice uncles and normal cousins.' She let out a hollow laugh. 'You said I had to become Anna. So that's what I'm doing.'

George nodded. 'Okay.'

'Because you know Caitlin? Well she did have uncles. Uncles that bought her things, sweets and chocolates, Harry Potter toys, pound coins.' She swallowed hard, the saliva choking in her throat at a half-formed memory.

'What is it?'

She coughed. 'Mum said we had to be grateful. I had to be grateful. "Give your uncle a kiss".'

George was looking at her intently. Waiting for more. But

she couldn't say more. The words wouldn't come out. Her head was jumbled: Give your uncle a kiss. Coffee breath. White flecks on his jacket collar, falling like snow. Look at the dandruff. Look. At. The disgusting dandruff.

'Are you all right?'

She was shaking. Nauseous. Mouth full of saliva. Salty and thick somehow. She was going to be sick. Made a dash for the bin. Held on to it, looking inside, saw her discarded Coke can. Still hoping she wouldn't actually throw up, she took deep breaths, but the bin smelt of putrid food and dog shit. She vomited half-digested tuna and cucumber onto discarded plastic packaging.

She stood up, breathed. Felt liquid dribbling down her chin. George was already by her, arm on her shoulder. He passed her a crisp white handkerchief. She wiped her face and neck.

'Sorry,' she mumbled.

'You feel okay?'

She nodded. 'Must have been the sandwiches.'

She didn't know what to do with the sick slimed handkerchief. George took it and put it in the bin.

'I'll buy you a new one.'

'No need.'

She hadn't thrown up for years. What was it about her so-called uncles that made her feel so sick? She shook her head to clear her mind. She didn't want to know.

'You look pale. Shall I walk you home?'

She nodded, shivering with cold now, even though the sun was still strong. He took his jacket off and put it round her shoulders. Gave her a hug. She allowed herself to relax into his arms for a minute. Could smell his skin. Soapy. It felt safe. He pulled away and gave a formal little smile. Then they walked back to her studio flat.

She wondered if he might come inside, sit for a bit. But he stood stiffly at the door and asked questions like, did she have any milk in? Perhaps coming in with her would have broken some rule she didn't know about.

Once inside she headed straight for the shower. But found a spider in the shower tray. Spiders freaked her out. Couldn't bear the thought of one in her flat. It might come in the bedroom, and crawl over her skin when she was asleep. Where was George when she needed him? She got a trainer and whacked it. Then, almost shaking with anxiety, picked it up with toilet paper and flushed it down the pan.

The shower was powerful and scorching. Hot as she could bear. She scrubbed and rubbed, made her skin hurt and glow red. Dried herself and lay on the bed staring at the stain on the ceiling trying not to think about the grey-suited uncle. She was sure he wasn't a real uncle, but was one of her mum's 'gentlemen callers'. She needed to question her mum about the guy. She needed his name.

ELEVEN

Bluebell Heights, Chippenham

'Sorry, mate.' The words almost choked Darren as they came out. 'Was under a lot of stress.'

'I'm not your mate,' Ben said, smirking – echoing his own words of the previous day.

He explained the Grady situation. The man listened in stony silence.

'Three warnings and you're out,' was his boss's only response. 'This is your second.'

It was humiliating having to apologise, but he'd promised Kerry as a way of making up for last night. And anyway he couldn't afford to just jack in a lucrative contract, no matter how much he wanted to.

After his shift, he drove to Bristol where he'd arranged to meet Pringle in a pub. The Baltic was another once familiar place that he hadn't been near for years. Just up the hill from Pennywell, it was a tatty dive back in the day, but a friendly place where the landlord, who fancied himself as a DJ, played some banging rock music. He and Kerry had been regulars.

He hesitated before stepping inside. What would he do if he recognised someone? What would he say? Up to now he'd wanted to avoid awkward conversations with people from the past. But things had changed. He may still be the bereaved dad they knew, but now he was on Grady's case. He was going after her. His old mates would approve of that. Something they could get around and pat him on the back for. He allowed himself a smile and slipped inside.

Early evening, the place was quiet with no sign of 'Rockin' Ricky', the DJ landlord. He recognised the landlord's wife behind the bar. She'd put on weight and her jowly features were sagging. Something more than mere gravity was pulling her down. She looked over at him, gave a weak smile, but he didn't think she recognised him.

The pub was quiet at this time of the evening, between the after-work trade and the late evening drinkers. He didn't recognise anyone, nevertheless the place warmed his heart with its beery familiarity, nicotine-stained walls and mismatched furniture. There hadn't been so much as a whiff of fresh paint in the pub since before the smoking ban.

He ordered himself an orange juice and sat down to wait for Pringle.

'Great little boozer this, isn't it?' Pringle said when he arrived. 'Endangered species, places like this.'

He nodded, feeling a curious sense of pride and decided the cynical old hack couldn't be all bad if he properly appreciated a pub like this. Most people wouldn't. People from the new-build estate in Swindon, for instance.

'What can I get you?' Pringle said, looking disapprovingly at Darren's half-finished orange juice.

'I'm all right. Driving, you know,' he mumbled. Drinking orange juice in a pub didn't come naturally.

Pringle got himself a pint and sat down to discuss how the paper was going to handle the interview Darren had tentatively agreed to give.

'You are the victim here, and the victim's opinion counts as far as our viewers are concerned. We need to show how it's affected you. Get people on side. The more personal the better.'

The reporter's face was red and flushed. The spidery blood vessels in his nose looked like a disease spreading across his face. Darren was gripped by the idea it might be catching. If he hung around with Harvey Pringle for long enough, he might end up looking like him. 'I know you want a quote, Mr Pringle, but I'm worried what people will think if I say what I really feel.'

'They'll think you are a bloody hero, mate. That's what they'll think.' Darren wasn't convinced about that, but Pringle hadn't finished. 'You've struggled with your grief and fought to put your life back together. And you succeeded, right? But now, the justice system has let you down, hasn't it?'

'Too bloody right it has.'

'Care more about the perpetrator than the victim don't they?'

'You're not wrong. You can print that for starters.'

Pringle took out a reporter's notebook and scribbled something in it. 'We're on your side, Mr Burgess.'

He stared at the newspaper man wondering whether that was really true. Was Pringle actually on his side? He wanted to believe him. Truth was, he desperately needed someone on side. That's what Kerry should be. His wife should be on his side, but she just wasn't. At least not in the way he needed her to be. All right then, so be it, he'd throw in his lot with Pringle. Speak his mind and be damned.

'This is just the beginning, Mr Burgess. We have a whole

campaign oven ready, as they say. And your involvement is essential to its success.'

'Campaign?'

'Get the law changed so that child killers like Grady can't live amongst us in secret. We want you to be front and centre of the campaign, so here's the deal.'

The deal was that Darren gave *The Daily Herald* exclusive rights to his story and be the face of the campaign to get Grady's identity exposed. It would mean doing interviews, possibly meeting politicians and generally helping to keep the story in the media. Exclusive rights meant money. The thought of coming into some cash cheered him up as he didn't know how long he was going to be able to put up working for Baby Ben.

'If I agree to this. You have to promise to share any tip-offs you get about Grady,' he said before signing.

'There's a gagging order covering what we can publish, but the rumour is she's somewhere in the south of England. Pretty vague I'm afraid, and the lawyers are having kittens about whether we can even say that much. If we get anything more concrete, I can always slip you an "anonymous" tip-off.'

A smile crept across Darren's face. Not a smile of joy. A smile of anticipation, of feeling he was starting out on a path that would inevitably lead to Grady. 'Okay, Mr Pringle. It's a deal.'

'Are you sure you don't want to seal the deal with a proper drink?' Harvey asked.

'I don't mind if I do,' Darren said, ordering a pint of Wifebeater.

TWELVE

Studio flat, Belsize Gardens, Westcliffe

S he was lying on her bed listening to the clicking of high heels in the flat above. The woman upstairs was probably getting ready to go out for the evening. She always wore heels, never sensible trainers. It was the same in the morning: click click click of heels as she got ready for work.

Upstairs, the apartment door slammed. The sound of the key in the lock and levers clicking into place. Heels on the staircase and finally the heavy outside door clunking shut.

She peered out of her own front window, which although ground floor was above street level, there being a basement flat below. The woman was wearing a black lace bolero over a dark maroon velvet knee length dress. Very smart. Perhaps she was going to a business do. In any case, she looked like she was probably a lawyer or something.

She couldn't imagine herself wearing high heels on a daily basis like that woman did. Another reason, if one were needed, she could never be a lawyer.

She had known a lawyer once: Martin Clayton, the poor guy who'd drawn the short straw and defended her in court.

He was okay though. In fact, he was the only thing that was okay about the trial.

She did her best never to think about the court case. The painful, clock-watching days. It was like some interminable maths lesson in a foreign language. She hadn't understood half of what was said. Had to sit still for hours on end and not fidget. Impossible, she was only eleven.

Every morning she woke up thinking it wasn't happening. Sometimes she even dreamt that she'd gone back to Boggart Hill and found Riley alive, then taken the toddler back to her mum and dad. While half-awake she could believe that. Tried to stay in the twilight zone between sleep and wake as long as she could. It was the best bit of the day. Until banging and jangling keys forced her to open her eyes and look at the cream-painted bricks of her cell. The only comfort she had was her old teddy. She'd been allowed to take one cuddly toy when she was arrested and she chose Teddy Tubby. He wasn't very cuddly, but she'd had him for ever.

In court, all they talked about was the dead little girl. She only knew the girl *was* dead because they kept saying it over and over again. But she hadn't killed Riley. Couldn't have been her. Not really. Not made the baba really proper dead. How could she have killed without a gun? Or a magic wand? One time she saw Riley in the courtroom – in the shadows behind the judge. She wanted to shout out: *She isn't dead. She's right there!* But when she looked again, the girl had gone. She squeezed her eyes tight shut and tried to make her come back. But no matter how hard she tried she could not make Riley reappear.

Martin explained she was too young to take the stand. He reminded her of a teacher she liked at school. Mr Smartwell. She always laughed at that name. Because if he was so smart, why was he a teacher at a dump like Vernon Road Primary? However, she liked him and he liked her. Encouraged her, got her into reading Harry Potter while most of the other kids were struggling with Magic Key.

'Your reading age is very advanced,' he said. It was probably the only compliment she got from any teacher – ever. Certainly the only one she could remember. *Your reading age is very advanced*. She still smiled at that.

In the end, he had been too smart for Vernon Road and moved on. Things went down the toilet after that.

Martin Clayton took the time to explain the strange and confusing proceedings and who everybody was, like the judge in his creepy wig and purple robe. The way they were all dressed up made it seem like a weird version of *Alice in Wonderland*. When there was a word she didn't know, he told her what it meant.

'What's a sociopath?'

He was the only one in the courtroom who ever spoke directly to her. Apart from her mum, who spent most of the trial sitting behind her. But her mum didn't so much speak as chastise. Sometimes verbally, hissing in her ear, 'Get your fingers out of your mouth!'

More often it was physical. Surreptitious flicks to the earlobe and pokes in the back when she thought no one was looking.

When the time came for the verdict, the court was completely silent. Her ears were ringing with the quiet. She was terrified of being found not guilty and sent back home. Her mum would beat the living daylights out of her, she knew that much.

So, the guilty verdict was actually a relief. But when the judge pronounced a life sentence, she felt tears welling up. It seemed like her life was over before it had properly begun.

'Don't cry, Caitlin love, you'll show us up,' her mother hissed.

She bit her lip to stop the tears.

Martin tried to say some comforting words like, 'It doesn't mean life,' and gave her an awkward hug. She looked around to see her mum staring at them with dagger-eyes, before the woman turned to face the press gallery.

Catherine Grady was unmoved by the sentence.

THIRTEEN

Pennywell Trading Estate, Bristol

R ed-light district was the wrong name. The overwhelming colour was a toxic sodium yellow. Only the tail lights of the occasional car were red, glowing brighter when the car came to a stop, attracting a hungry girl from the shadows. But there was no sign of the girl he was looking for.

Maybe she'd overdosed on something. Was lying in some filthy den, eyes glazed, needle in her arm. Or a violent pimp put her in hospital with bruises and broken bones. The possibilities were dreadful and endless. He shuddered.

He cruised past The Embassy massage parlour for the third time.

New girls always required.

Maybe she'd answered the ad and moved her trade indoors. Wouldn't blame her, it must be easier than being out on the streets. Safer. Warmer too. He pulled up nearby.

He checked his phone. Opened Riley's Facebook page. He'd posted recently that Grady better watch her back or else. Likes were flooding in. It gave him a salty pleasure reading some of the more graphic comments.

Stitch the bitch.
Drown her.
Shank her.

Would he be able to do anything like that? Was he capable?

He got out of the van and headed towards The Embassy. There was a greasy spoon café opposite. Did the girls pop into the café for a coffee, or snack? It was closed now of course but he imagined going in there for egg and chips. Watching the comings and goings of the girls and punters. Perhaps he'd spot the girl going in to do her shift.

The Embassy's door was wide open.

From here he could glimpse the red and gold embossed wallpaper inside. There was something inviting about the warm lighting and plush carpeted entrance lobby. He was tempted. Not to go with a girl himself, but to get a vicarious thrill from asking inside if they knew the girl with neon-pink trainers. He crossed the road determined to go in, but stopped dead on the threshold, suddenly nervous.

He couldn't go into a place like that. Seriously, what would he say? That he was looking for a particular girl? Which girl? What service did this girl offer? What did she look like, the one you were after? Oh well, so and so offers that. How about her? Or her? No thanks. Why not, what's wrong with our girls? Are you taking the piss? Timewaster.

How would he ever get out of there without feeling like a total loser? He might even end up going with a girl to save face.

What the hell was he doing? He had Kerry at home, even if they were hardly talking at the moment. He tutted to himself and retreated to the safety of his van.

He set off towards Bristol, driving back through the industrial estate and past the city farm. He'd just passed the farm entrance when he saw her. Short skirt, fur jacket, blonde hair, trainers. Even in the orange light, he could see they were pink. He pulled up a few metres down the road. In his rear-view mirror he could see it was definitely the girl. She was looking towards him, but did not come over. After a few seconds she turned away, distracted by the approach of a car. It stopped next to her and she leant on the door to talk to the driver through the passenger window. He could make out a sickly, ghost-like face behind the windscreen. She shook her head and stepped back. Looked about.

Darren got out of the van, slammed the door. Stood and watched. The car accelerated away. He walked over to speak to her. She was chewing gum, nervous and skittish. Shifted from leg to leg. Looked even thinner than he remembered. She needed a decent meal.

As he approached, she turned to face him. 'You wanna be careful wandering around here at night, all on your tod.'

'Just need a word.'

'I'm busy.'

'A quick chat is all.'

'I'm not the chatty type. And I'm busy.'

Another car turned the corner at the end of the road and cruised towards them. She moved away from him, making a point. The car did not stop. She took the gum out of her mouth.

'You're bad for business,' she said, before pressing the gum into a nearby brick wall.

'I want you to tell me about Caitlin Grady.'

'Why?'

He shrugged, wondering how much to say. Being all casual. But inside he was desperate to know everything she knew about Grady. There might be some clue as to where to find the bitch. Maybe, just maybe Grady had even been in touch with this girl. Another car drove past.

'Look. If you don't want business yourself, do me a favour and piss off will you? You're putting off the genuine punters.'

He pulled his wallet out of his back pocket. Offered her a tenner.

'I'm not that cheap, you know.' She looked offended.

'Just tell me about Caitlin Grady.'

She took the note, put it inside her blouse. 'There's not much to tell.'

'But you knew her?'

She scratched the back of her neck; looked up and down the street again. 'Fifty quid for half an hour okay?'

He nodded. She wouldn't talk on the street and insisted they went to his van. They drove to a nearby convenience store which had a small car park at the front. He asked her to tell him her name.

'Crystal.'

He grunted. 'Real name?'

She rolled her eyes. 'Get me a can, will you?'

'Coke?'

'Cider. And a packet of salt and vinegar.'

She looked hungry so he didn't mind buying something to eat. Got out of the car and went to the shop, although he half expected 'Crystal' to have gone when he returned. But she was still there, fiddling with the radio.

'You want to listen to West FM, not that Radio Bristol. It's tragic.'

He passed her the can, which she opened with a percussive hiss. Then glugged down the drink like she'd just walked across the desert. However, the booze seemed to make her less twitchy.

'Want a swig?' she said, wiping her face and stifling a burp.

He shook his head. 'Better not.'

'Suit yourself.' She put the can between her knees and opened the crisps.

He worried that she might spill the cider, making the van stink of booze. Kerry's sense of smell was canine.

She held out the bag. 'Crisp?' He hesitated, unsure for a second, as though she might have infected the packet. But that was stupid. Whatever she was, you couldn't catch it from a crisp, so he took one.

She gobbled down the rest of the packet. She was starving.

'So yeah, I was in the same year as Cait. Not that she showed up much. Hardly saw year six.'

'Why?'

'Why d'you think? Couldn't be arsed. And Miss Chambers had it in for us.'

'Us?'

'Total bitch.'

Miss Chambers was the headmistress. He and Kerry had been on an open day for parents of prospective pupils and she'd shown them around.

Learning together, learning for life, according to the leaflet.

But he remembered her more for her appearance on a TV documentary, saying how Grady was a difficult and disruptive child, known for picking fights. The documentary had shown Chambers dressed in a leotard, leading a dance class to show how trendy she was. How modern. And if she thought Grady was difficult and disruptive, that made it even more true.

'I wasn't there much either, to be fair. Me and Cait, we use to bunk off. Hang out.'

They were friends. Best friends. She was besties with the bitch who murdered Riley. And here he was sitting and chatting about it like they were discussing the weather.

'We'd go into town. Nick dolls and Harry Potter stuff from The Entertainer. Or make-up from Boots. And sweets and chocolates. Caitlin was always after sweets.'

The CCTV shows the victim at the door of the newsagents while another girl, whose face cannot be seen, is filling up a paper bag with sweets from the pick and mix display.

'We never got caught nicking stuff, cus we were fast! Fast

and furious that was us. And if they threw us in prison we were going to use magic to escape. Caitlin said she was a witch.' Crystal laughed. 'Honestly we thought Harry Potter was real. She loved making potions out of fizzy drinks and adding salt and pepper, or ketchup, vinegar, anything we could find. Then we'd dare each other to drink them. Didn't matter how bad it tasted.'

It was dark in the car, but her unfocused eyes looked full of emotion. Made him feel uncomfortable. It didn't seem right that she had fond memories of Caitlin Grady. Not right at all.

'We'd dare each other all the time. Mostly into nicking stuff or being rude to people. But then there was Railway Chicken.'

'Railway Chicken?'

'Yeah, we'd go down the railway lines, stand together on the tracks, holding hands and wait for the train to come. First to jump out of the way was chicken. It was always me. Cait had no fear in her. Bloody stupid. But we thought we were invincible. Cait did anyway. It was exciting to be with her.' She fished in the bag for a last crisp and chewed it thoughtfully. 'Sorry. Not what you want to hear.'

'Which railway line was this?'

'You know, where I met you. You can easily get down to the tracks from there. Boggart Hill was our land. No one ever went there. It's where we'd run and hide if anyone came after us for nicking. Where we took our booty.

'When we were fed up playing with the stuff, we'd put the dolls on the tracks. Let the train mangle them. I suppose that's a bit psycho. Caitlin would be cruel to her dolls. She'd stick things in their mouths. Pens. I just remembered that. Haven't thought about it in years. That's a bit weird, isn't it?'

He wondered if this was linked to what Grady had done to Riley. At the trial, there was no evidence presented of anything being forced into her mouth. Or elsewhere. It was a small comfort.

'The worst thing we did was pile stones up on the tracks. Ballast from the railway. Quite a little mound of rocks. I was scared. I thought the train might come off the tracks. We went up the embankment to watch. But I couldn't bear it. I ran home and hid. Waited to find out if there'd been a train crash on the news. Caitlin thought I was such a wuss.'

They were a couple of little tearaways but really, his brother Troy had done worse. He didn't know what he expected to find out. But it sounded almost innocent. Nicking toys and truanting. There must be more. Something she wasn't telling him.

'Did she ever do anything violent?'

'Only that thing with her dolls.'

'Or try and get you to hurt someone... or...'

She shook her head. 'What are you – a copper now?'

'I just want to know if...' He took a breath, looked out of the window at the dark street. Tried again. 'What she did to... Riley. If she ever hinted about something like that?'

'It's funny. No one ever asked me about Caitlin. At the time, I was scared the police might come to the house and I'd get into trouble.'

'Why?'

'For being her friend.' She gave an ironic laugh. 'But they never did come round. There weren't interested in me, thank God. But afterwards over the years. I did wonder why they weren't more curious.'

'Did you know something?'

'What do you mean?'

'Was there something you wanted to tell the police?'

'They didn't need me to tell them anything. They had all the evidence they wanted.'

There was something here. Something she wasn't saying. Some reason she thought the police might come visit.

'I was shocked as anybody about... what happened.' She

rubbed her hand through her tangled hair. 'I had no idea that Cait could do something like that.'

'But she got into fights. The headteacher said–'

'Already told you Chambers was a bitch.' She scrunched up the crisp packet, looked round for somewhere to put it. Darren sighed and took it from her. Stuffed it in the door pocket.

'Okay so she did get into fights, but not in year six. Chambers was lying about that. Cait was proper hard, so when she did show up at school, no one would touch her. But when she was younger, the years above had it in for her. Baited her. Called her mother a whore. I didn't know what that meant, would you believe it?' She gave a hollow laugh. 'Caitlin knew what it meant though. She'd punch anyone who said it. But then, wouldn't you?'

She was right. He would. But no one would say that about his mum.

He remembered Grady's mother from the trial. She always made an entrance like she was a bloody celebrity. Always late, her heels clacking across the stone floor of the wood-panelled chamber. Often she didn't stay long. She'd tut and sigh loudly at what was being said and eventually stomp out of the courtroom in disgust, flicking her carefully styled auburn hair as she went. Only to come back an hour or so later. The rumour was she went to the pub in the interim.

'Did you know Caitlin's mother?'

'Course. Sometimes she was dead nice. Other times she wouldn't let me in the house and I had to wait outside for Cait. Cait always wanted to get away from her mum anyway. Kept making plans to run off. Maybe find her dad.'

'Her dad?'

'That's what she said. Either that, or we were going to jump a train and find our way to Hogwarts. To us Hogwarts was an actual place. If we could only get there somehow.' She grunted.

'The grown-up world is shit, isn't it.' She emptied the last dregs of her cider into her mouth.

'Once we did actually run away. On a train too. Somehow Cait had got some money. Said she'd had enough of her mum and this time she was running away for good. Got tickets as far as Weston. Spent the day messing around on the pier. Hung out in the amusement arcades. Tried to blag chips off people. Honestly she had no shame. Told people we were homeless orphans.

'Then somehow, Cait found this guy. He bought us chips. Then took us to his house. She trusted him so...' She shrugged. 'I thought she must have known him. I wasn't thinking really. We watched videos. He gave us cider. It's a bit blurred, but I don't think anything happened. You know, like what you're thinking.

'Later, he told us our mums and dads would be worried about us and maybe call the police and then we'd all get into trouble. He drove us back to Bristol.'

What sort of a story was that?

What sort of man would give two kids cider? He didn't want to know.

Crystal looked restless and said it was time she got back. The half hour was pretty much up anyway, so he drove to the industrial estate. But before she got out of the car he asked her if Caitlin had ever got in touch.

'You are joking. She's too important to bother with the likes of me now, isn't she?'

'So you've no idea where she could be?'

She shook her head.

'Well if you hear from her, let me know,' Darren said, giving her one of his cards. 'I'll make it worth your while.'

She read the card. 'Darren Electrics, there's no messing about with you, is there?' She smiled and looked at him with dark sad eyes. 'You're all right.'

'What's your real name?'

'Crystal. I said.'

'I'm not one of your clients.'

'Well, don't get the idea you're my friend.' She opened the car door and got out. But before shutting it, she leaned in. 'It's Tracey.'

She walked back to her stand under the streetlight. She was just a kid. He waited and watched her for a moment. Bit his lip, wishing he could do something. But what? She had a habit to feed, he was sure of that. What did you do with a heroin addict, or crack user, whatever it was?

He felt like bundling her into the back of the van. Take her away from here. Drive her back to Swindon and lock her in the spare room until she came to her senses and gave up the drugs that forced her out on the streets. But he couldn't do that, could he?

He started the engine and accelerated away, not looking at Tracey as he drove past. Forget her. He'd got sucked into something he couldn't deal with. Asking so many questions about Caitlin, too. It was stupid. It didn't do any good. Forget Tracey. She was a dead-end.

FOURTEEN

The Promenade, Westcliffe

The clocktower, all grey stone and ornate turrets, had a gold painted weather vane that squeaked in the sea breeze. Perhaps the clocktower felt ignored by the digital world and wanted to draw attention to itself. Caitlin was sitting on a nearby bench waiting for Bert, having finally agreed to go on a date with him. She watched the clock's hands click towards the appropriate hour with increasing anxiety.

She had a difficult relationship with clocks. When she was a little kid, she thought that clock faces were alive somehow and were spying on her. Trying to annoy her by moving their hands as slowly as possible.

She'd spent her life waiting for clock hands to move: At school. The trial – hours that turned to days. Days that became years at Lowood Secure and HMP Thornhill. Even now she was waiting. Waiting for Bert yes, but more than that. She was still waiting for the moment when her life would properly start.

Bert had wanted to meet in a big seafront pub. A bit full on, particularly as she'd hardly set foot in a pub up to now and wasn't used to them. She didn't want to look like a fish out of water on a first date so she suggested a walk.

He texted back:

I know where we can go

Where?

Surprise.

She wasn't sure she liked surprises. She'd had too many nasty ones in her life. But she didn't think there could be any nastiness in a sleepy place like Westcliffe, so agreed to meet.

She agonised over what to wear, but then convinced herself that it wasn't really a date, just a walk. So went for a baggy sweatshirt and comfy jeans.

She spotted him walking towards her in long loping strides, wearing skinny jeans and a navy body-hugging fleece. She could have made more of an effort with her clothes. Butterfly wings fluttered in her belly.

She stood up and they said awkward hellos. He looked a bit nervous, which made her feel better. But couldn't think what to say. What the hell did people talk about on first dates?

'How's CoffeeTime?' he asked.

'Oh you know. Foaming with caffeinated excitement.'

He grinned. 'Like that, is it?'

'It's a job. How's Tesco?'

'Oh, yeah foaming!'

She laughed. They were both in dead-end jobs.

'Anyway, it won't be for ever. Meant to be going to uni soon.'

'Oh,' she said, feeling a twist of disappointment. What was the point in making an effort if he was just going to piss off to uni in a couple of months or so?

'What about you?' he asked.

'Me?'

'Sticking around Westcliffe, going to college or what?'

'Well, yeah…' she mumbled, feeling a sharp prick of competitiveness. 'Going to uni as well. Doing law.' The words fell out of her mouth before she could stop them. She just couldn't bear to come across as a dumb-arse bitch whose only chance in life was serving up flat whites.

'Law!' He sounded impressed. She liked that. Liked that she'd impressed someone in a good way, even if it was technically a lie.

'I'm supposed to be going to Manchester,' he said as though it was the last thing on Earth he wanted to do. 'Maths.'

'So when do you start?' she asked tentatively.

'To be honest, I'm not sure I'm gonna go. My mum's all for it of course, thinks I'm gonna be an accountant or something. But…'

'What about your dad?'

'I never see my dad, he fucked off back to Brazil a few years ago. So it's just me and my mum.' A shadow of something dark passed across his face before he added brightly, 'Come on. We need to get going. Time and tide, you know.'

She didn't know. 'You expect me just to follow you into the unknown?'

'Trust.' He raised his eyebrows theatrically, so she thumped him on the arm.

'Whaoh!' He rubbed it in mock pain. 'Ever been to Battery Point?'

She hadn't. They set off down the promenade, with him promising it wasn't far. Asked what university she was going to. She didn't know how to answer so just shrugged, then admitted she hadn't even applied yet.

'Was my uncle's idea to do law. He's kinda looking out for me,' she said to keep the conversation going, but then found herself telling him her cover story. How her parents were dead and she'd been raised in a children's home, but her uncle had stepped in and got her a job.

'Sorry to hear about your parents. What happened to them?'

'Car crash.'

He looked awkward. Rubbed his ear.

'So, I'm a product of the system.' She gave a humourless smile. He'd probably never met someone who'd been in care, never mind an actual gaolbird. He lived with his mum. How would they bridge the chasm between their backgrounds? On the other hand, they did have something in common. They were both missing a father in their lives. So maybe there was a glimmer of hope.

Walking on, they left the souvenir shops and fish and chip pubs of the seafront behind. Now there were large solid houses. Bed and breakfast places with names like Sandy Banks and Riviera Hotel. Some had been converted to residential homes for the elderly, like the one she was volunteering in.

The road petered out into a pay and display car park. It had no cars. He led her to a rough sandy path at the far end of the car park which wound its way across a coarse grassy bank towards the sea.

'What the hell is Battery Point?' She began to feel uneasy. The jokey comment about following him into the unknown was beginning to wear thin. Her instincts told her Bert wasn't dodgy, but all the same she found herself dragging her feet.

'What's the matter?'

'Nothing. Just. How much further?'

'Don't worry, nearly there.' He went ahead. Turned back to her. 'Come on!' he shouted. He looked like a bouncy puppy. It was kind of sweet. She relaxed a bit.

The path led to a rocky beach. Just offshore was a kind of low, grassy island with a rock outcrop, on top of which was a squat concrete building. A pillbox according to Bert.

'There used to be an army base out here in the second world war.'

It was low tide, and Bert said he knew the way to the island. Insisting it was safe, despite a sign warning about dangerous tides in big red letters, he led her across a rocky causeway, avoiding the parts that were slippery with seaweed.

'Welcome to Battery Point,' he said as though it was his own private island.

She liked it here. The expanse of sky and sea. The roughness of the rocky outcrop, and wiry grass. The way it felt so remote. The air smelt of ozone and seaweed.

'Come out here to think sometimes,' he said, standing next to her.

She guessed this was Bert's secret place. She hoped nothing bad happened here like it had at her own secret place, Boggart Hill. The thought sent a shiver through her.

Don't go there, Caitlin. Don't think about that.

'Cold?' he said, risking an arm around her shoulder. She allowed his hand to rest there for a moment, deciding whether she liked the feel of it or not.

'It's warmer in the pillbox,' he said.

'I'm not going in there!' It looked like a bad place with its dark slitty windows and pitted concrete walls. God knows what it stank of too. Piss and shit probably.

But he ran off up the slope to the old fort and disappeared inside. Seconds later his face appeared at one of the windows.

'Hi!' he shouted. He really was a big kid.

She gave in and went to join him, peering inside she sniffed at the air like a suspicious cat. It didn't stink bad, just had a damp sandy aroma, so she stepped in. He was right, it was warmer away from the sea breeze and quieter too, the swell of the waves being muffled. She looked out of each of the windows in turn. If anyone was coming, you'd see them miles off. If it was an enemy, you could shoot them well before they got to you.

'Need to keep an eye on the tides,' Bert said.

She turned around to see him watching her. She took a step towards him. Stared into those eyes.

'So? How long have we got?'

FIFTEEN

Appletree Avenue

He didn't like the way Kerry would peer over his shoulder and sigh when he went through the comments on Riley's Facebook page. So he snuck into the bathroom to read them.

Kerry wanted him to turn off the comments. But he insisted that someone might know where Grady was hiding.

'And then what? What are you going to do? Get her and punch her lights out?'

'Maybe. Maybe I'd do that.'

'Oh yeah. Big man.' She shook her head. 'Don't expect me to visit you in prison.'

That was about the longest conversation they'd had since the cheese on toast incident. Most of the time, there was a casual indifference between them, like grumpy relatives putting up. She hadn't even said anything when he got back late the other night after meeting Tracey. Simply gave him one of her looks.

In the bath was a crusty, dull yellow stain on the enamel. A dripping tap had caused it. The tap dripped for months, yet he did nothing about it. The stain was a permanent reminder of his inaction.

In the end, Kerry had fixed the dripping tap. Told him she watched YouTube, got a new washer from B&Q and borrowed a wrench from Jim, a colleague from Express Bus. Made a big thing of how easy it was. But he wondered if the truth was that Jim had been round to fix it, which left a sour taste in his mouth.

Why did he let things slide? It was the same with the back garden. There was something shameful about the forlorn grass and borders overgrown with brambles and weeds. Yet he could not bring himself to do anything about it. Why was it so hard to mow a small lawn? Tidy the flower borders? When he looked at that garden, his body sagged inside, his bones felt heavy, his limbs painful. It blunted his spirit. He missed living in Bristol, but that was no reason to punish the garden as though it was to blame. What was he trying to prove? And to who?

He'd moved to Swindon willingly; no one twisted his arm. He wanted a new start as much as Kerry. But the new start had spluttered to a stop. His whole life had seized up.

The mower was a stupid electric one, sold off cheap. It whirred and complained and strained at the thick grass, bending rather than cutting, missing great clumps so he had to go over and over the same patch again and again.

Kerry was watching from the window with a blank expression. Wondering what the fuck he was up to probably – attacking the grass like someone who howls at the moon. Was it too much to hope she show some pleasure at him cutting the lawn? She was just making a point, wasn't she? Saying, *I don't care what you're up to.*

He smiled at her anyway. Maybe she'd find it in her heart to bring him out a cuppa. When he finished mowing, he saw that Paramjit Patel, from two doors down, had joined Kerry in the kitchen and both women were staring at him through the window. He gave a wave, before making a start on the weeding.

Kerry had told him Paramjit admired the fact she drove a bus for a living which he thought was an odd thing to admire in someone. It was a good enough job, but not like working for the NHS for instance. That's what Param's husband did. An eye specialist, he kept himself to himself and their meetings so far had been formal and stilted. The husband clearly less impressed by Darren's job than his wife was with Kerry's.

He pulled out groundsel and shook off clods of earth. He trowelled out stubborn roots of tough grass. The trowel was old and rusty. His spine started to ache from all the bending and kneeling so he straightened up, rubbed his back and looked round to see the two women were now in the garden. Paramjit's burnt-orange trouser suit looked tight around the midriff; she was putting on weight.

'Paramjit wants to know if you want any samosas?' There was no warmth in Kerry's voice.

'You know I can't resist your samosas!' He gave Paramjit a broad grin. She always brought round especially mild samosas, as she knew he didn't like them spicy. She was generous like that.

'You'll be ravenous after all this exertion,' Paramjit said. The two women exchanged glances. What was that about? 'We had our lawn paved over. We don't have time for it.'

'Especially now,' Kerry said. 'Now you're going to have your hands full.' Another baffling exchange of looks. Paramjit's hand went to her midriff. Jesus, he was so slow sometimes.

'Right,' he mumbled, feeling embarrassed. 'Well, best get on with it.' He nodded towards the tangle of weeds.

The women retreated back inside and he attacked the brambles with some old shears.

Later, as he was washing his hands at the sink, he felt Kerry behind him watching. She was watching him a lot today. Was she working up to something?

There was a time when she'd come up behind him and slide her arms around his waist. And if she was feeling a bit frisky, her hands would move down to his crotch.

He dried his hands. There were scratches from the brambles on his arms and the towel got a smear of blood on it. 'It needs re-laying to be honest,' he said, looking at the lawn. It was uneven and clumpy, like a bad haircut.

'Re-laying?'

'Or re-seeding. But that will take a while and I'm not sure it's the right time of year.'

She moved to the window and stared out at the hacked lawn and half weeded border. 'Are you having an affair?'

He laughed. 'What!'

She turned to him. 'Are you having an affair?' She wasn't joking.

'Who with? Baby Ben?'

'Paramjit wondered if that's what it was.'

'What what was?'

'That.' She nodded towards the garden.

They'd been gossiping about him. Did she really think he was the cheating type?

'It was on *Loose Women*. A sudden, inexplicable interest in DIY can be a sign of guilt.' Kerry fixed him with a stare.

'It's not DIY; it's gardening.'

'Why now, after all this time?'

'I don't know, just…' Couldn't she simply be glad he was doing it? He scratched at the back of his head.

'And you're secretive about phone texts and messages.

Covering the screen, running to the bathroom if you think I'm looking.'

'Yeah, well. That's because you tut at me every time I check the messages on Riley's page.'

'Your obsession with Caitlin. Maybe you should have an affair with her!'

His jaw dropped. 'How could you say that!' Shook his head, wondering how things had got so bad. She bit her lip and looked away. A suffocating blanket of silence descended on them.

After a minute he couldn't stand it any longer. 'I'm not having an affair. I would never.'

She stared hard, probably looking for deceit in his eyes, then went to get the plate of Paramjit's samosas from the worktop. 'We better eat these,' she said, bringing them to the table. 'They're still warm.'

They ate samosas. They tasted good, moist with just a hint of warming spice that wasn't harsh at all. Seemed ages since they sat down like this, silently enjoying food together.

'I was thinking of re-planting the borders.'

'Re-seeding. Re-planting? You want to start again?'

'If you like.'

'I'm thinking it might be too late for that.'

'You can plant sturdy shrubs in the autumn. Roses for instance. You can't beat a good Anne Harkness.'

She grunted. 'And how long after you plant Anne whatsit does she flower?'

'Not sure. Flowers when she's ready.'

'You should put some Dettol on those scratches.'

She rummaged in a cupboard, and produced some Dettol and cotton wool. She dabbed his arms. He asked if Paramjit was pregnant.

'Twins. Due in the spring.' She looked up at him. 'Still,

maybe our roses will flower by then.' She gave a fragile smile, but the hurt still showed.

He swallowed. The conversation he was putting off had crept up and ensnared him. The conversation about whether they were ever going to try and have another baby. The one where he'd say, not yet, I'm not ready, just let me draw a line under Grady first. The one where she'd say, time has run out.

'I still love you,' he blurted. He didn't even know where that came from. Was it just something he said because he couldn't think of anything else?

She took a thoughtful breath. 'Mum wants to move the *Garcia*. She's got a new mooring near King's Lynn.'

'Oh? Where's that? Norfolk?'

She nodded.

'Long way from Padworth. Is it even doable?'

'Via the Thames and Grand Union, but it's quite a trek. Lot of locks involved.'

He nodded. 'Gonna need help.'

'Yeah. That's what I said.'

The first time he'd stayed on the barge, it was strangely exciting. They were left alone on board, her mum having gone to her sister's for a couple of nights. It was their own private den. They chugged up and down the river, stopping in local pubs. It had narrow single beds, and they squeezed into the same one. The fact it was so cramped only added to the frisson.

'We could offer to move the boat,' he said.

'Would you want to do that?'

He nodded. 'If you wanted.'

'As long as you know I'd be the skipper.'

'Aye-aye, captain.' He grinned. 'But what about your mum?'

'She can stay here for a bit.'

'So it would be just the two of us?'

'What about Facebook, Riley's page? There's no wifi on the

Garcia. And I'm not having you rushing ashore trying to find a signal every five minutes.'

'I'll stop. I'll turn off the comments. I'll give it a rest.'

She smiled. 'All right then.'

'We'll see how we go shall we?'

'Yeah. We'll see how we go.'

SIXTEEN

Belsize Gardens, Westcliffe

She'd woken up far too early and lay in bed obsessing over yesterday's date with Bert. In the pillbox she'd been overwhelmed by the need to kiss him. Came from nowhere. Hit her like an express train. He seemed as surprised as she was at the sudden intensity. She gave in to it, losing herself in sensuality. Until he pressed a hand between her legs and felt her softness.

She went rigid. Panicky. Short of breath. 'I don't want that!' she snapped, pulling away.

'Sorry.' He looked ashamed.

The panic passed. He looked so mortified she almost felt sorry for him. Had she over-reacted? All right so he shouldn't have tried it on like that, but she could have just moved his hand away. Why had she felt so panicky and triggered?

'It's the pillbox. Let's get out of here,' she said. So they walked around the sand dunes and rocks at Battery Point. They didn't speak. He looked sad, like he'd lost her. But she still wanted to be around him. Just didn't want – that. And yet, she kind of did too. Sometimes she did not understand herself.

She held his hand for a bit. Found herself softening and ran her hand down his cheek. They kissed again. More tentative, gentle. Affectionate. Better.

The tide started to come in and Bert said they needed to head back along the causeway, otherwise they'd be trapped there for the night.

If they'd had a tent and supplies, it might have been exciting to spend the night on a lonely island away from the world. But a night in the pillbox? No way.

The alarm on her phone finally went off so she got up. In the bathroom mirror she noticed a love bite on her neck. Made her smile. Despite what had happened, she wanted to see him again. He'd got carried away and she'd freaked out that's all. And anyway, he stopped when she said. Meant she could trust him, didn't it?

The love bite would be embarrassing though. She'd have to use concealer to cover it up.

Later, arriving at the café, her first job was to deal with the morning papers. She heaved the bundle onto a table and cut the blue plastic string holding them together. Did string really need to be plastic you can't recycle? The top paper, *The Express*, slid off the pile, and so she placed it on the nearby paper rack. *The Express* was popular in a place like Westcliffe and she picked up the second copy from the pile. Then she froze.

Her eleven-year-old self was staring at her from the paper underneath.

THE KILLER AMONG US

Below the headline, those impossibly wide staring eyes and the small downturned mouth. She hated that picture. She hated that face. Hands shaking, she tried to read the article, but the words jumbled up in her mind. Felt dizzy. Sat down and stared at the text, not taking anything in. Had they found out where she was living? Was Grey Suit a journalist after all? If so, the mob was on its way. She was a dead woman.

'What's the matter?' Brig said, coming over.

She covered up the paper afraid Brig would recognise her. 'Just feeling a bit ill. Sorry.' She made a toilet dash with a hand over her mouth. Locked herself in the cubicle. Although she did feel nauseous, she wasn't going to actually throw up. She sat on the toilet and caught her breath. Relaxed a little.

I was fucked here.

It was scrawled across the cubical door in felt pen. Brig had cleaned it off a week ago, but somehow it got into the door material and was back.

I was fucked here.

Surely no one had actually had sex in these particular toilets. Maybe they just felt fucked. Or fucked over.

She couldn't hide in the toilet for ever. But she was scared to go out. Scared of the mob. Remembered them, shouting and banging at the sides of the van.

First day of the trial, on the way to court and she was in the back of the prison van. Couldn't see them, but heard the shouts and insults clearly. Wild dogs foaming and growling at their prey. They blocked the road and the van had to stop. The hammering of angry fists on metal was deafening, worse was when the van started to rock from side to side. She thought it was going to get pushed over. That she was going to die. If the crowd had got to her, she had no doubt they would have killed her. But then the van lurched forward and left the crowd behind.

When she emerged from the toilets, she half expected to see the same crowd at the café windows, banging on the plate glass, demanding her blood. But it was still early, and no one much was around. The café itself was empty apart from a regular, drinking her morning cappuccino. No sign of Grey Suit. His job done, he'd crawled back to his hole.

'You're as pale as a ghost,' Brig said, concerned. The papers had been laid out on the wooden rack. She could see the face of that eleven-year-old half covered by another paper. There was nothing in Brig's face to say she'd spotted the pic or read *The Daily Herald*'s headline.

'Think I've got a bug.'

Brig sent her home. She tried to resist, wanting to get the chance of removing *The Herald* from the coffeeshop. But Brig insisted, saying that sick staff made customers worry about food poisoning.

Outside she felt vulnerable. She'd started to feel less self-conscious recently, but the jitters were back now, ten times worse. At least at the café she had Brig as some protection. Out on the streets she was alone, like a skittish antelope, on a wide treeless plain.

Told herself to melt into the background. But someone was walking behind her. Too close. She wanted to run, but pushing the fear back inside she stopped suddenly to peer through the window of a souvenir shop. Pretended to take interest in a delicate sailing ship in a glass bottle. The man behind walked past showing no interest in her whatsoever.

She needed to get a grip, there was no need to panic. All the same she took a long and circuitous route home, picking up a copy of *The Daily Herald* on the way. Stopped at the corner of Belsize Gardens wondering if anyone was watching her flat.

The street looked quiet enough, so she walked slowly past the large red brick mansions. Once they must have been posh family houses with their ornate white stone detailing, but now they were all split into flats. She went up the steps to her flat, took a last look around and slipped inside.

Grieving father of murdered toddler Riley Burgess has broken his silence about the controversial release of Caitlin Grady. 'They sneaked her out without any consultation with me or my wife,' he said. 'The justice system has let me down. It cares more about the perpetrator than the victims.'

The evil monster who murdered toddler Riley in a callous and sadistic attack was granted parole more than a month ago. A government spokesman confirmed she has been given a new identity and is living in an undisclosed location, but declined to provide further details. This paper understands, however, that she is being hidden somewhere in the south of England.

Riley was killed after being snatched from Pennywell City Farm in Bristol on a family day out and dragged to derelict railway land nearby. Twisted torturer Grady has never shown the slightest sign of remorse for her unspeakable crime.

'She's still got the same eyes and callous stare as in the picture we've all seen,' according to a former inmate at Thornhill Open Prison, where Grady was being held before her release. 'I'd recognise that look anywhere.'

Mr Burgess worries that now Grady is free she will kill again. 'How many more toddlers will die because the law allows convicted child killers to go free and live in secret amongst us?'

He added in an emotional statement that killers like Grady should never be released. 'They should have thrown away the key when they locked her up,' he said, 'but now that she's out, she'd better watch her back.'

It is estimated that keeping Grady in detention has cost the honest taxpayers of this country in excess of £200,000, which includes the cost of private tutors as well as creating and maintaining Grady's new identity.

The private tuition appears to have paid off as she is

understood to have been educated to A-level grade and is thought to be intent on pursuing a university education.

The Daily Herald asks: Is it right that a child killer should be allowed to live secretly amongst us, where she might have access to children and kill again? She could be living next door to any one of us, preying on our own children and no one would know until it is too late.

Mr Burgess has called for a new law making the whereabouts of child killers public. 'At least that way, Riley's death won't have been in vain,' he said.

She tore the front page of *The Herald* into strips and put them in the bin. Then got them out again, went to the bathroom and flushed them down the pan. It took a couple of goes to get rid. Disinfected the toilet with Harpic, making the water a pleasing blue-green.

She never tortured Riley. That wasn't true. She never did that. She took deep breaths of the disinfectant smell. Made her feel clean.

Her phone rang. George. She didn't pick up. She wasn't ready to talk. A minute later a text:

> Presume you've seen the papers. There is nothing to worry about. But we should meet ASAP to discuss. Can you come into the office?

She didn't reply. Couldn't handle going out again. Not yet. Maybe not anytime. And what did he mean, nothing to worry about? There was plenty to worry about. How had Grey Suit found her? There was a snitch out there. A traitor. Had someone in the probation service blathered to the papers?

She threw herself down on the bed, closed her eyes and tried to relax, but she saw Riley's baby face, eyes bloodshot. Unblinking. Lips swollen.

Wake up, me baba.

She took a shocked gasp of air and her eyes blinked open as though she'd surfaced from a deep cold pool. Concentrated on the pattern made by the swirling Artex on the ceiling. Like it was some weird white ice formation on a distant planet.

Except for the stain. Looked like it was getting bigger. The woman upstairs was pacing around in her heels, again.

'Fuck off to work,' she shouted at the ceiling. 'Leave me alone.'

She couldn't settle. Jumped off the bed and fished Teddy Tubby out of her bottom drawer. She still had him after all these years. His arm had come off ages ago and she hadn't been able to stick it back on. But nor could she throw him away. She sat with him on the bed and watched TV. A show about a couple moving to a new life in Australia. Imagined herself going there and doing some wholesome job like nurse or plumber, or sheep shearer.

The entry phone buzzed. She sat rigid. Not breathing. Listening.

Some bastard journalist had got her address. Brig had recognised the photo and made some quick cash by giving her away. It buzzed again, more insistent. She went to the window and peered out into the street, heart pounding. She couldn't see the front door from this angle, but the street itself was quiet. No pack of newspaper hacks or photographers on stepladders.

Her phone dinged.

Brig told me you went home. Can you let me in?

She sat on the bed clutching a mug of coffee while George sat at the narrow wooden table. He'd made her the coffee, and with him there, she felt the tension draining from her shoulders. It didn't feel awkward being so close to him in what was really nothing more than a bedroom, which was a surprise really.

'I don't think there's anything to worry about,' George said. 'There's nothing to indicate they have any real information.'

'Living in the south of England.'

'Define the south of England? It covers a vast area – practically half the country. Probably just some disgruntled prison officer making a quick quid by convincing *The Herald* they had inside knowledge.'

'Pursuing a university education.'

'You're not though are you?'

'Well maybe you told someone we'd talked about it… and…' She sighed.

'I'm not in the habit of telling tales.'

She gave him a long hard look. She trusted George. She wasn't going to change her mind about that.

'And that stuff about me having the same eyes. Freaked me out a bit to be honest.'

'Well that was just bullshit. Your eyes don't look anything like that old black-and-white picture.'

She grunted and slurped her coffee.

'Your face has changed shape. Not just because you're older. You were a lot thinner then – undernourished probably. Made your eyes look bigger. Believe me, you do look very different to that pic.'

'What about that guy who's been hanging around the café? He might have tipped off the paper.'

'No mention that you work in a café is there? That's something they would put in for sure. It's the sort of personal detail that papers like *The Herald* love.'

She nodded. He did have a point. 'And as for Darren Burgess, did you read what he said?'

'Well, the victim's family. You know how it is.'

'No I don't know *how it is*.' His offhanded manner made her bristle. 'Perhaps you'd enlighten me?'

George stared at her hard before speaking. 'He's angry

about the death of his daughter. You can't blame him for that, Caitlin.'

'Back to Caitlin now, is it?'

George sighed. 'Put yourself in his position. How would you feel?'

It made her sweat to even think like that. It was bad enough what that man said in the papers, but some of his online comments were much more graphic. 'Thanks a lot for your support there, George.'

'Come on…'

'No. You come on. You're supposed to be on my side. Not his.' If this was some bullshit about getting her to 'take responsibility' for what she'd done all those years ago, he could go fuck himself.

'I am on your side.'

She looked away. Felt completely alone now, even with George there. He could just fuck off and leave her by herself so she asked him pointedly if he'd finished his coffee.

He took the hint and drained his cup. His face looked hard and tense. 'I'll have a word with Brig, tell her you have gastric flu. Give you some time to…' he trailed off and put his jacket on. She managed a sarcastic smile as he left.

Freak of Nature. Possessed by the Devil.
Cover up for Killer Caitlin. Born to Murder.
The monster next door

Each headline hurt. But she couldn't stop trawling the internet. A bad news junkie, searching everything, even back to the trial. It may not look as bad as cutting her arm with a blade, but it damaged her just the same.

How could she ever believe herself as anything other than the monster those headlines called her? She was never going to be pure, sweet, innocent Anna Moreton.

Maybe she could have some brutal psychiatric medical treatment. Electrodes, or making cuts in her brain. Erase Caitlin from her memory.

She'd seen a stream of shrinks over the years, trying to straighten her out. The only one she liked was Sandy. Sandy was keen on cushions.

'This is Riley,' she said one day, standing behind a large cushion. 'What do you want to say to her?'

She wanted to say it's stupid trying to talk to a cushion, but she didn't want Sandy to give her one of her patient, yet subtly withering looks.

'I'm sorry,' she mumbled. 'I want to say I'm sorry.'

'I don't think Riley can hear you.'

'Course she can't hear me. She's in heaven.'

'Well you'll have to shout a bit louder then, won't you?'

'I'm sorry, Riley!' she shouted, meaning to be flippant. But she felt something unexpected. 'I'm sorry, Riley,' she repeated. 'I'm sorry, Riley.' Each time she said it, a lump of hurt swelled in her chest. 'I'm sorry, Riley, I didn't mean you to be dead. I never meant it! I never…' Tears came then. Tears she could not stop. She could hear her mother's voice chastising, *Grady girls do not cry*. But the tears still came. She didn't think she had that many tears inside her. Yet still more came, drowning her mother's disapproving voice.

She hadn't meant for Riley to be dead. Not actually proper dead. Never to be alive again, dead.

Wake up, me baba.

Sometimes she thought she'd been possessed. Something evil, disturbed by the railway, came out of the ground and had got inside her. A Tommyknocker. Or a malevolent tree spirit wanted an innocent child, and she, another child, was its instrument.

But the thing was, the really worrying thing was, suppose that evil was still inside her? Waiting for its opportunity.

George called every day to check she was okay and give her updates on the news, assuring her that the papers would soon run out of things to say. She hadn't forgiven him and so was frosty on the phone. Turned out he was right about the papers though: she was soon off the news agenda. More importantly, there were no new details on the internet about her life, or location. Even HuntAKilla had nothing much to say.

But then a tabloid ran a story about her mother. It was classic her mum, going on about how unfair it was that she hadn't been told where her own daughter is living. How a daughter needed her mother. They should have let her come and live in Bristol with her; it was after all the only home she had. She wondered how much they paid her mum for the interview.

Bert texted her. He'd popped into CoffeeTime to be told she was ill. Wanted to know if she was all right. But Bert was all wrong for her. He was too ordinary. Too normal. She'd thought that's what she wanted. But it would never work. She was too much of a freak. Even though he knew nothing of her real past, she still felt silently judged by his sheer ordinariness. She didn't reply to his text.

SEVENTEEN

Appletree Avenue

Spotted the bitch on a train to Guilford.
She's working at McDonald's in Reading.

T he article in *The Herald* had caused an avalanche of postings on Riley's page. He was lying on the bed going through the posts while Kerry was taking a shower.

I saw her in Coventry.

Didn't the idiot know Coventry was the Midlands not 'The south of England'.

Grady couldn't be in twenty places at once, so were any of them actual genuine sightings? He'd end up chasing his tail if he checked them all out.

He deleted the posts. Best if Kerry didn't see them. Nor had she seen the article in *The Herald*, so going off-grid on the barge for a week would be a good thing. It would give him time to explain the deal with the newspaper. If he approached it right, told her about the money involved, he was sure he could get her on board.

111

> **I have a friend in HMP Thornhill. Message me if you want to know where they took the bitch.**

It was a private message from someone who called themselves Jedd. A scammer no doubt. Not something to follow up, despite the mention of Thornhill.

Kerry came into the bedroom wearing a loosely tied white bathrobe, drying her hair. He smiled: she looked sexy with wet hair.

The George and Dragon was a large soulless pub opposite a closed down shopping centre. The place was empty apart from a handful of early doors drinkers perched at the bar. Probably regulars, unlike Darren who had never been to Durbridge before. It was a dismal commuter town you wouldn't bother with, unless you passed through on the way to HMP Thornhill and stopped for petrol and a sausage roll.

Kerry wouldn't like him being here. But if 'Jedd' knew where Grady was hiding, it would be worth the upset. She may not want to talk about Grady, but deep down she wanted justice as much as he did. She'd thank him in the end.

Darren had no idea what Jedd looked like. Could be one of the drinkers at the bar as far as he knew. But Darren's face would be familiar to Jedd. His picture was all over the internet.

Darren Burgess, Riley's heartbroken father.

Sometimes his pic appeared alongside Grady's, which felt wrong. Like someone was trying to say they were similar somehow.

The pub door swung open; a guy in paint-stained overalls came in and Darren looked over at him hopefully. They guy took no notice and went to join the drinkers at the bar.

Jedd was late. Perhaps he wasn't going to show. Maybe he

was a timewaster whose idea of fun was to scam people into driving around the country for laughs. In that case he might well be one of the drinkers. Darren suddenly felt self-conscious sitting alone with his half of pissy lager. A fruit machine let out a couple of bars of a jaunty electronic melody, its brassy flashing lights inviting him to take a chance.

Monkey Business. Mega Prize Payout. £££

He'd give it a whirl for something to do, and if Jedd didn't show up after a couple of goes, he'd cut his losses and get out of there.

He went over and put a pound in the slot and fisted the big red button. It sent wheels picturing jungle animals spinning round to the squawks and howls of a cartoon rainforest.

The wheels stopped one after the other. Lights flashed. Nudge. He banged on the buttons. Couldn't line anything up.

One of the guys at the bar was watching him. Darren gave him a feeble smile and shrugged. Put another pound in the slot. Almost got three bananas. Maybe he'd be lucky next time.

'Darren?'

He looked over to see a security guard. 'Jedd?'

The guy nodded. He was wearing a V-neck black combat sweater with chevron epaulettes and the word security above the breast pocket. His face was round, with smooth pale skin. Short grey hair. It was difficult to judge his age. Relieved that he hadn't been stood up, he offered to buy the man a drink.

'Johnnie Walker. With ice.'

'Double?'

'You're too kind.' Jedd looked like the sort of man he should take seriously. Maybe ex-forces.

Jedd explained that he worked for a contract security company which handled the transportation of prisoners to and from court and so on. Specifically, Jedd was a frequent visitor to Thornhill Open Prison.

'There's a lot of hanging around in the security industry.

People chat.' He tapped a finger on the side of his nose and said he knew a girl in admin who worked in the governor's office. She was disgusted about Grady's release.

His heart jolted. 'Does she know where Grady is?'

'Sort of.'

'Sort of?'

Jedd shifted in his seat and leaned forward. 'When a lifer like Caitlin Grady is released, the relevant police authority has to be informed where she's living. The probation service are responsible for her supervision, but even in a case like Grady's, where there's a new identity, secret location and so on, protocol still has to be followed. My contact knows which police authority had to be informed.'

'Not the actual address?'

'No, but it does narrow the search area, doesn't it?'

He was disappointed. 'How big are these police authorities?'

'It varies. About the size of a county.'

He might be able to focus down on the Facebook sightings with that information. It was something.

A group of men in suits came into the pub, talking too loudly and slapping each other on the back.

'Estate agents,' Jedd said, pulling a face. 'Perhaps they finally unloaded the old shopping centre onto some mug.'

'So which police force is it?' Darren held his breath.

'Well, there's a complication.' Jedd sighed. 'Our informant, Jenny, she's taking quite a risk by talking to us...' The fruit machine came to life again playing its tune and issuing a cacophony of electronic animal calls. 'She could lose her job and even go to prison herself.' Jedd took a swig of his drink before continuing. 'I'm afraid she's going to need some encouragement to tell us what she knows.'

He knew what sort of encouragement. 'How much?' Darren asked, his voice cold and dismissive.

'I'm sorry it comes down to money.' Jedd made a show of looking concerned. 'But you can see her point. It is a risk for her.'

'How much?' he repeated. Not that he was going to hand over a penny. Just wanted to know how big a piss-take this was.

'Hasn't put a figure on it. Grady's location is a state secret. And state secrets don't come cheap.'

He bristled. 'And you, Jedd, do you come cheap?'

'Take it easy, mate.' There was an edge to Jedd's voice. 'I'm just an honest broker, okay?' He paused a moment. 'Whatever you and Jenny decide, that's nothing to do with me.' He sat back in his chair and sipped the whisky.

The estate agents were getting louder now they'd had a drink. The banter was annoying. Like they were laughing at him for coming here to meet 'honest broker Jedd'.

'You can tell this Jenny, if she wants to do the right thing, maybe I'll buy her a drink for her troubles.' He got up to go. 'If I'm feeling generous.'

'I don't blame you for being a bit cynical, mate. I'd be the same. But she may be our only hope.'

'Then tell your girlfriend to do the right thing.' It came out harsher than he intended, but he was pissed off. He turned to leave.

'She told me to give you something.'

'What?' He swung round, irritated. Jedd was holding out a stiff buff envelope. He took it, sat back down and pulled out a large photo of a teenager with cropped black hair. She was sitting on the edge of a bed, in what looked like a prison cell. The girl was looking at the camera. Narrow fox-like face and staring eyes. He'd recognise that look anywhere, the features being so similar to the photo taken when she was arrested. Older of course, but all the same, it looked like her. Still had that defiant expression across her face.

Darren smiled, knowing now that he would recognise her if

he were to come across her in the street. Looking at her was like looking at porn. Fascinating in an unhealthy way that meant he couldn't take his eyes off her.

'It's from the CCTV at Thornhill. Gesture of goodwill. Jenny is not my girlfriend by the way.'

'Okay,' he said slowly. 'So if she isn't your girlfriend, what is your interest here?'

'Same as yours. Sick fucks that kill children should never be allowed to live a normal life. Sooner or later they'll kill again.'

Darren nodded. Couldn't argue with Jedd about that.

'Listen, I know what it's like to lose someone,' Jedd continued. 'My sister, she was killed by a drunk teenager in a stolen car. Hit and run. They got him, but he was out again within five years. Back behind the wheel. That's my interest.'

Darren stared hard at the guy. Jedd's expression was open. Honest. Eyes didn't flicker. He was telling the truth. 'I'm sorry to hear that.'

'Sophie and I were close, you know.' Jedd bit his lip and looked away, clearly trying to avoid showing too much emotion.

'Did you do anything about it?'

'Burned his house down.'

'What?' Darren stared open-mouthed.

'I wish.' He gave a hollow laugh. 'Didn't do anything. The cunt was untouchable. Notorious family, practically ran Pool Farm Estate as their fiefdom. Besides, I didn't have anyone to back me up.'

Darren nodded, thought for a moment. Looked over at the fruit machine. The music had stopped, but it was still flashing its lights.

'Can I meet Jenny?'

Kerry was waiting for him in the kitchen. She was sitting at the table, watery eyes and drooping eyelids. A half-drunk glass of cider in front of her. Two more cans were on the kitchen surface, all partly crushed. It was something she did when she was a bit pissed.

'Did I miss the party?' Darren said as he slung his jacket on the back of a chair. 'Is there any beer in?'

He went to look in the fridge. Perhaps she'd got a raise. Anyway, he had a minor celebration of his own. A photo of Grady and a possible lead. He opened a can of beer and sat down opposite his wife.

There was an envelope on the table. Opened. She pushed it towards him. 'This came.' He picked up the envelope and saw the logo.

`Avon and Somerset Police.`

'Is it Victim Support?'

She let out a sarcastic laugh. 'Oh you're funny you are, aren't you? Right fucking comedian.'

'Kerry?'

She snatched the envelope, pulled out the letter and slammed it on the table. 'Read it.'

`Dear Sir, We would like to bring to your attention, that vehicle registration no…`

He skimmed over the words,

`According to our records the vehicle is registered to Darren Electrics, and has been sighted by officers who need to speak to the driver to confirm no offences have been committed.`

What offences? Speeding?

```
Kerb crawling is defined as the act of
soliciting a person for the purpose of
prostitution from a motor vehicle whilst
on a street or in a public place.
```

His stomach dropped and he felt his face burning. 'It's a mistake. I...'

'Kerb crawling!'

'I never...' he spluttered.

'Show me some fucking respect. Don't try to squirm your way out of it. Kerb crawling!' She knocked back her drink.

'I'm not a kerb crawler.'

'Oh! Really. Gonna tell me someone else was driving the van are you?' She got up and went to look out of the window, even though it was practically dark outside.

'I was driving. You know, around Pennywell and...' How was he ever going to get her to understand about Tracey?

'You can sleep in the spare room tonight,' she told the back garden.

She wasn't even giving him a chance. 'Kerry. Please–'

'And tomorrow I'll go and stay with my mum'

'On the *Garcia*?'

She turned to face him. 'I'll help her move it to King's Lynn.'

'You have to understand–'

'Oh I understand all right. I understand very well.'

'I haven't, you know...' He was struggling to find the words. 'Been with a... paid for...'

'Say it!'

He wouldn't. Couldn't. Something in him was too stubborn. She knew what he meant anyway.

'I thought, I'll be patient. I'll wait. He just needs time. He's never been the most demonstrative person. People said, he's the type of man who works with his hands. Give him a chance, he's a good man in his heart. I thought... I thought finally... Taking the *Garcia* to King's Lynn together...'

'So did I.'

She shook her head. 'Now I wish Paramjit had been right and it was an affair, but it's worse than that. A fucking prossie.'

'I haven't.'

'Do you really hate me that much?'

'Course not.'

'You'd rather get sucked off by some skanky tart in the back of your van than come near me.'

'All right, listen. There was a girl. Tracey.'

'I don't want to know her fucking name!'

'She wasn't in the back of the van. She sat in the front. We talked was all.'

'Is it because you blame me? Is that it? You think it's my fault?'

'What?'

'Riley.'

'No!'

'You look at me and you think. It's my fault. I'm to blame.'

He stared at her, wondering if there wasn't a seed of truth in that. Did he blame her? They were arguing when Riley disappeared. Distracted. Did he secretly blame her for starting the argument? He should reassure her. Tell her he blamed himself more than he blamed her. But somehow it seemed more important to justify himself for having a prostitute in his car.

'I didn't have sex with Tracey.'

'Oh really!' Kerry obviously didn't believe him.

'We just talked. She knew Grady from school.'

'What is wrong with you? You go in search of some tart to

119

have a cosy chat about Grady. I don't understand it. I don't understand you.'

'I won't see her again.'

'Where were you today?'

He couldn't answer that. He daren't tell her about Jedd.

'You just got to trust me,' he mumbled. Not sounding convincing even to his own ears.

'Oh yeah, like I trusted you not to mouth off to the papers and then that's the first thing you did.'

He felt his face flush again. 'It's Pringle. You know he just—'

'Stop. Stop making excuses for who you are. Who you've become.'

They stared at each other for a moment, not speaking. Had he changed, become someone different? Well perhaps he had, but then so had Kerry.

She opened her mouth to speak, and the words, when they came were small and sad. 'This hasn't been much of a marriage for a long time has it? Dead in the water. Truth is, it died with Riley.'

'Don't say that. Don't make it Riley's fault.'

Kerry shook her head and left the room.

'Kerry?' he called after her as she went up the stairs and went into the bathroom. He heard the lock click on the bathroom door. He followed her up the stairs quietly. Heard her sobbing. He tapped on the door. 'Are you all right?'

'Leave me alone. Just leave me alone!'

All right then, he'd leave it for now. Try and talk to her again in the morning.

EIGHTEEN

Ocean View Residential Hotel

She was called into the manager's office, an airless room the woman shared with a dumpy duty nurse. She stood in front of the cheap desk. The manager, a thin woman, with a chiselled triangular face and a chin you could use as a blunt instrument, gave an unfriendly smile. She reminded Caitlin of a particularly sadistic prison officer from Thornhill. The one she got sent to solitary for punching.

'I'm afraid the God of paperwork needs appeasing.' This sort of weak jokey chat was at odds with the woman's po-faced demeanour. Something put on, like a schoolteacher who hated her kids but wanted to appear friendly.

'Paperwork?'

'If you are to be a regular feature here, there's paperwork to be filled out.'

'How can there be paperwork? I'm just a volunteer.'

'Our residents represent a vulnerable section of the population, so I'm afraid there are certain safeguards…' she trailed off, put her reading glasses on and leafed through some papers on her desk.

121

Safeguards. Was the woman trying to say the residents weren't safe with her?

'A quick DBS check, all right?'

It was not all right. 'You think I've got a criminal record?'

'We're just dotting the Is and crossing the Ts.'

'Cus if you don't trust me...'

'It's the regulations. Now, let's start with your full name and home address, including postcode.'

'Regulations!' Caitlin snorted. 'You just don't trust me. Well I'm not doing your fucking DBS check.'

'You can't use that kind of language in here, young lady.'

She couldn't afford to let them run a check. Who knew what it might flag up? That Anna Moreton didn't exist, that Anna Moreton was really Caitlin Grady? No way she could take the risk. 'I'll use whatever language I fucking choose. And you can stick your volunteering job up your tight arse!' She swung around and stomped out of the office, kicking the waste bin over as she went. The manager and the fat nurse stared after her, open mouthed. Not wanting to be held up by punching the exit code for the outer door, she simply went through the fire escape which set off an alarm.

Quite an exit. Caitlin smiled to herself, feeling the rush. It was the sort of performance her mum would be proud of and she thought about calling her and relating the incident. Imagined her mum laughing and agreeing that the manager could go fuck herself.

She still remembered her mum's phone number. School had made them learn it in year five in case of emergencies. She was no good at maths, but she'd learned those numbers off by heart. There was a magic about them now, connecting her across time and space to her childhood home and her mum.

Back at the flat, she punched the familiar numbers on her mobile and smiled at the photo of her mum as the line connected. When she heard the ringtone, her heart gave a double beat. Imagined the old dresser in the kitchen where her mum would put her mobile on charge. Her mum racing to pick up. But she panicked and hung up before anyone answered.

When her phone rang later, for a mad second she thought it was her mum ringing right back, but of course it couldn't be because she'd withheld her number. It was George, checking up on her again. Wanted to know if she was eating proper meals. It would probably be bad press for him if she died while he was meant to be supervising her rehabilitation. Truth is, she was still sore from the way he seemed to have taken Darren Burgess's side when he came round last time. He'd probably take the cowbag of a care home manager's side as well. Go on about how she herself suffered from 'lack of impulse control' which was probably somewhere on her file.

'Must have been a shock getting ambushed with a DBS check,' he said when she sounded him out about the incident.

'I didn't know what to do.'

'Your false name should be clear of any criminal record. But then again, you never know what's on the police computer.'

'You mean the police know who I am? Is that what you're saying?'

'At the highest level. Chief constable. But police being police, you never know. They may have flagged "Anna" up in some way. To be honest, that kind of knowledge is above my pay scale.'

'So, I did the right thing?' she said, feeling a sudden unexpected warmth towards George.

'Well I think the manner of your departure might have been better handled.' Even over the phone, she could hear that he was smiling to himself. 'But I can't see why they needed a DBS check. You were only there on an informal basis. You weren't providing any actual care or services to the residents, so technically there was no need for a DBS.'

'Bitch just didn't like me.' At that moment Caitlin felt like no one in the world liked her. And it must have showed in her voice because George suggested taking her to the pub.

'It's time to get you out and about a bit more,' he said when she resisted the idea. 'Introduce you to the local youth scene.'

It was the last thing she wanted, but agreed anyway having decided to forgive him. The poor sod was trying to do his best for her after all. She had to admit too, that he had a point about Darren Burgess. What *would* she do if she was in his shoes? It was an uncomfortable thought. She hated Burgess for the things he said, for the online campaign to find her, but in the end, she couldn't really blame him. If he'd killed her child, or her mum for that matter, she'd kill him right back.

The King Henry was a large seafront pub modelled on a sixteenth century manor house. High ceilings, oak beams, coats of arms on the walls and portraits of disapproving queens. The carpet was well worn with a faded leaf and flower pattern, but the maroon upholstered seating looked welcoming and comfortable. The pub was known to all and sundry as The Tudor.

The place was rammed on a weekend night, but now, early evening on a Thursday, it was fairly quiet.

She decided she liked the faded grandeur of the Tudor and somehow, being here made her feel she was part of the community. She even got a kick out of flashing her new provisional driver's licence at the barman. It wasn't just about proving her age, it was proving she was a valid person.

The bar itself was a shrine, with its polished wooden surface and beer pumps which had strangely inviting labels like Doombar, or Blacksheep. This bar even had one called Jail Ale, but she'd keep away from that. At the back, the optics and their exotic coloured spirits of gold, blue and green reflected in a mirror behind. It was a place full of delicious temptation. One day she'd work her way through all those spirits, just to say she'd tried them all. Felt the same way in a sweet shop when she was a kid. But sweet shops were tainted now.

She turned to look at George sitting at a table, waiting for her to bring the drinks. He looked kinda lonely sitting on his own in a pub that was clearly where young people came to get drunk and pull. She wondered if he had someone in his life.

'My manager has suggested there is no reason not to set up a meeting with your mother,' George said as she placed the drinks on the table.

She smiled. 'Thanks, George.'

'Don't thank me, because I have to say I argued against it, since she went to the papers at the first opportunity she had. But the opinion is, a meeting may go some way to alleviate her alleged grievances. We can only hope it will shut her up.'

'Don't be such a grump, George. I have to see her eventually.'

He took a swig of his Doombar ale. 'Well,' he said, wiping his mouth, 'I'm pissed off, I suppose.'

'Cus I want to see my mum?'

He shook his head. 'I'm not pissed off with you.' He held her gaze and gave a kind of sad little smile. She wasn't sure what it meant. 'I'm pissed off with your mother.'

'Oh, well. Join the club.'

'Unprofessional of me. Supposed to be dispassionate, but that woman…' He sighed and took another sip of beer.

'Bad old George.' She grinned.

He grunted. 'So I may not be the right person to supervise the meeting.'

'Oh.' She frowned. 'But I want you to be there.' She felt a wobble in her voice.

'It's just… I think maybe I'm losing perspective.'

'What?'

He rubbed the back of his neck, like he always did when he was in a dilemma. She didn't like what he'd said. *Perspective.*

That's something you got when you stepped away from something.

Bert came in the pub. It was a small town, but all the same, bad luck that he should pitch up the one evening she was here. Maybe he was here every night. She would have suggested somewhere else if she'd known. All right, so it was wrong not to answer any of his texts, but she didn't know how to tell him they shouldn't take it any further. Ghosting him was the easiest way to put him off.

She twisted in her seat in an attempt to hide her face. 'Just seen someone I'd rather avoid,' she explained.

'Not so-called "Grey Suit"?'

'God no! I don't suppose he comes here in the evening. Probably goes back to his coffin.'

'Who then?'

'Someone.'

George half frowned and half smiled, then twisted around to try and see who she was talking about.

'Don't look!'

'Tell me who it is then.'

'No.'

'As your probation officer–'

'You're my uncle when we are out and about,' she interrupted, with a wagging finger.

He gave up and downed some more beer. Looked like he'd need another one soon. But she didn't want to be left alone at the table and if she went to the bar Bert would spot her, no question. He was chatting to a couple of his mates now, laughing and joking. He obviously wasn't missing her.

George was going on about university again, but she wasn't really listening. She couldn't stop looking over at Bert. He clocked her and so she reached for her cider, pretended not to see him and took a gulp.

It was no good, he smiled and waved. She raised a half-hearted hand in return. Encouraged, he ambled over.

'Hi.'

'Hi, this is George, my uncle.'

George stood to shake Bert's hand, who introduced himself. She was left sitting down and felt awkward. 'D'you want to join us, Bert?' George said, taking his seat again. 'Take a pew.'

'No, um… my mates.' He nodded toward the lads watching and grinning. 'Just wondered how you were.'

'Sorry yeah. Been ill. Really bad gastric… something. You don't want to know.'

'But you're all right now?' He looked uncomfortable. Was he suddenly getting shy?

She nodded. She'd rather visit a dentist than have this excruciating conversation.

'Okay so. Just checking you're okay.'

'How do you two know each other?' George asked, smiling. Bloody hell why did he have to prolong the pain?

'Oh, we don't really,' she butted in, before Bert could speak. Bert looked crestfallen. 'Anyway, I guess I'll see you around.'

'Yeah.' She picked up her cider and took a swig.

'See you again then, Bert,' George said, trying to be nice.

Bert nodded and went back to his mates.

George looked at his beer as if there was something nasty swimming in it. 'You could have been a bit more charitable to the poor lad.'

Behind George, she could see Bert talking to his mates and glancing over. Bad-mouthing her.

'Don't want to encourage him.'

'Pity, he seems nice.'

'Yeah, a real boy-next-door type.'

'What's wrong with that?'

'For a gal like me? Come on, George.'

'Are you saying you don't deserve a relationship?'

'Excuse me?'

'Perhaps on some level you think you don't deserve a relationship.'

'Perhaps on some level you should stop trying to be a shrink.'

'I'm just saying, he seems to like you. So?'

'Anyway he's going to university soon, so there's no future in it.' She finished her cider. 'Your round.'

While George was getting more drinks, she watched Bert and his mates. A couple of girls had joined the lads. They all seemed very friendly. Laughing and giggling. School mates probably. She felt left out.

One of the girls was pretty hot, to be fair. Dark skin, braided hair, lips to die for. Paying a lot of attention to Bert. She wouldn't blame him if he got off with her.

She felt a twist of jealousy. It took her quite by surprise. Annoyed her. It was just because she felt left out. Nothing to do with Bert, laughing and smiling at the girl. Nothing to do with the fact they were rubbing against each other. She was glad when they all moved off to sit somewhere out of sight.

'But what about you then, anyone in your life?' she asked George as he plonked the drinks on the table.

'Well um… not really.'

'No meaningless sex?'

'As a matter of fact, no. Not that it's any of your business.'

'So, it's okay for you to interfere with my relationships but I can't ask about yours?'

'I wasn't interfering.'

'Still you are a bit over the hill for any kind of hanky-panky, I suppose.'

'Thanks a lot.'

'Seriously, is there no Mrs George? Or mister?'

'I was married. Two kids. They grew up and left home.

Kids were the only thing keeping us together.' He gave a flat smile. 'It happens.'

'You should find someone else.'

'Happy as I am, thanks. A grumpy middle-aged git.'

'Are you?'

'Grumpy?'

'Happy?'

'I'm not unhappy.'

She looked at him. He didn't look old exactly, signs of ageing yes, like the crow's feet round his eyes. But sometimes older things had their charm, didn't they? Like her teddy. He was a threadbare damaged thing. But she still loved him. 'You could probably pull someone half-decent despite your age if you tried. I'll keep an eye out.'

He laughed at that. 'Well, thank you.'

On the way out, they passed by Bert and his group of mates which had grown in number. A regular posse. The girl with the braided hair was all over Bert, taking pouting-lipped selfies with him. She resented that bitch's perfect skin and beautiful deep brown eyes. How could she ever compete with that? She looked straight ahead as she walked, eyes fixed on the door.

Outside, it was still light, and the glare made her flinch. She felt light-headed suddenly. George offered to walk her home, even though it wasn't late. But she wasn't ready to face her empty flat. So sent him on his way and sat on a bench. She watched the darkening sky for a bit, lights coming on along the seafront. Her mind going round in circles. Bert. The braided haired bitch. She wanted to punch her. Pull her hair. Slap that self-satisfied expression off her pouty posing face.

She'd never felt like this. She'd only been on a bloody walk with Bert, what was wrong with her? All right so she'd kissed him. But so what? He was a tart anyway. He only came over to show how little he cared that she hadn't been in touch. He was deliberately flirting with the bitch in order to piss her off. Well fuck him then.

When she got home, she searched through the cutlery drawer for a suitable knife. A short strong shank is what she needed. Pointed and sharp, but strong enough to cut into something tough without bending or breaking. She found a stubby paring knife. That would do.

NINETEEN

HMP Thornhill, Gloucestershire

Thornhill didn't look like a prison. Not that he expected watchtowers and armed guards: he was in Gloucestershire not Texas. But all the same it was disappointing. Where were the high walls? The dog patrols? The formidable fences topped with razor wire?

It didn't have a fence at all; it had railings. Green loop-topped railings, like they had around Clumberfield Park, his childhood hangout.

There was a barrier across the entrance, but no guard post. Simply a pleasant looking reception building. The road behind was verged with colourful flower borders. There were modern brick buildings set back on either side. The place looked like a science park, somewhere where a clever-clogs tech company might be based. Not where you'd lock up criminals, even if they were low risk and about to be released.

Low risk! What a joke. How could someone, who even the judge said committed an act of 'pure evil,' ever be low risk?

He drove into the visitor's car park and checked his phone while he waited for Harvey Pringle and the photographer to show up. Nothing from Kerry. All right, so she was pissed off, but surely she could manage to send one single bloody text to say she was okay. He'd sent her enough. A whole phone full trying to explain about Tracey. No response.

After the kerb-crawling argument, he'd slept in the spare room. She sneaked out next morning before he got up. He didn't even hear the front door or taxi. She barely took more than a toothbrush, she was so desperate to get away. That hurt. But he told himself it meant that she wouldn't be gone long. She'd at least be back for more clothes – a chance for them to make up. But she hadn't been back. It made him anxious. He wanted to know she was safe at least. She was still his wife.

Welcome to HMP Thornhill.

He was posing by the clean blue and white sign while *The Daily Herald* photographer took a series of shots. Harvey made encouraging comments, in between texting on his phone.

Darren wondered what it would be like to peer out of the back of a prison van or police car at the welcome sign. It may not be a proper prison, but he doubted there'd be much of the promised welcome when you arrived. Heavy steel doors reverberating along echo-chamber corridors. Locked into chilly rooms, clothes and possessions taken away. Full body search. He grimaced. The photographer snapped off another shot.

So far, the worst he'd been accused of was kerb crawling. They wouldn't put him away for that, just wag a finger at him. He'd have to do something much worse to get himself banged up. For instance, give a certain person a dose of her own medicine. If he did, how would he handle being inside? He'd been a tough nut at school. But would he be tough enough for prison?

Thornhill village itself was a miserable hamlet of grey pebble-dashed houses, a dilapidated petrol station and a solitary pub. A place thrown up in a hurry to service the prison. He followed Harvey into the pub, which was trying to play the part of a country boozer, with false wooden beams painted jet black and adorned with cheap reproduction horseshoes. There was a large brick fireplace, but instead of a pile of logs or cosy stove, there was a vase of faded plastic yellow flowers. They'd come here to sign some papers regarding his deal with *The Herald*. Things were shifting up a gear now the paper was officially launching the campaign to change the law. They were going to call it 'Riley's Law', which made Darren feel quite proud.

'The mood is changing,' Harvey was saying between gulps of beer. 'Banging on about human rights is political suicide nowadays. We'll get them to make Riley's Law a reality.'

He showed Darren a draft of the front page announcing the launch of the campaign. The picture of Riley taken at her third birthday party. Bright smiling eyes. Striped multicolour T-shirt and her denim dungaree skirt. She was so excited that day, like a little jack-in-the-box, that getting her to stay still and look at the camera was impossible.

His stomach tightened when he looked at the picture. She was wearing that dungaree skirt the day she went missing.

WRITE YOUR NAME FOR RILEY

Below the headline was a form to fill in and an internet address if you wanted to do it online.

'The paper did some private polling. About ninety per cent of our readers are behind us. So, cheers.' Harvey raised his glass and finished off his beer. He was a thirsty man. 'One for the road?' he said, getting up.

Harvey was served by a downtrodden woman in her fifties with untidy grey hair. She looked as tired as the pub. What would Darren be like at her age? What would he be doing? Where would he be living?

When he was growing up he wanted to be a football player, Bristol City of course, and in fact there was a lad in the year above who'd ended up playing for the junior team. But Darren was no football star. He only made it to the Clumberfield School Under-15 Bs.

Then when he was sixteen, they'd shown a video at school about electricity linemen in America. How they fixed powerlines after storms. There were thrilling clips of cables arcing in bad weather, poles and lines coming down in flashes and bangs. He wanted to be one of the cool guys who climbed the poles and got the power back on.

'It's a question of keeping the ball in play by moving the story on,' Harvey said, interrupting his reverie with more beer. 'That's how these things work.'

Was Harvey married? He doubted it. Divorced maybe. What did he do at night alone in his divorcee's flat? Work his way through a bottle of whisky while watching PornTube? So what? For now he needed Harvey and he showed the journalist the photo Jedd had given him.

'D'you think it's her?' Harvey said, looking at it closely.

'Don't you?'

'I'm no expert, but could be.'

He was sure it was her when he first saw it, but now wondered if his eyes were playing a trick. He really wanted it to be Grady, so is that what he saw?

'Is there someone who could tell us. Some kind of expert?'

'Facial recognition's pretty specialised. Most professionals work for the police. Even the freelancers are in bed with the cops, so there might be some reluctance. In any case they don't come cheap.'

'But the paper could publish the picture, if it was genuine. Keep the ball in play?'

Harvey shook his head. 'Nice try, son, but no can do. Fact is, we do get pics from time to time purporting to be Caitlin Grady. But even if they were to be substantiated, we still wouldn't be able to publish. Court order.'

'Even an anonymous picture?'

'Fraid so. But Facebook's a different story. Nothing to stop you posting it on Riley's page. Obviously, you'll cover your arse by creating a false ID to do that.'

That is exactly what he'd do. He hoped she'd see it. It was a way to get to her.

As they were leaving, the sad woman shuffled over to clear their glasses. She had dry smoker's skin and vacant eyes. A woman whose spirit had withered a long time ago.

'Thanks,' Darren said to her. She gave him a surly nod. Perhaps she was on day release from Thornhill. She could be a murderer like Grady. But unlike Grady, she looked like she'd suffered for her crimes, whatever they were.

TWENTY

Westcliffe High Street

Her hand was thrust deep into her hoody pocket, gripping the handle of the stubby knife. She was outside Tesco watching the automatic doors swish open and close as a solitary early morning customer went in.

To avoid the CCTV covering the door, she pulled down her hood and pretended to be fascinated by something on her phone. She stepped inside. She knew where all the cameras were – entrance and exit, the checkouts and the booze, four in total. Scoping out CCTV had been a game she played in Lowood and Thornhill. She liked to know when she was on camera.

Her heart was beating hard. Didn't know why, she used to be so fearless when she was younger. Besides it wasn't like she was going to shank someone.

There was no sign of Bert.

She headed to the back of the shop where the cartons of milk were kept. It was a CCTV dead zone. Nor could you be seen from the tills. There was no one about.

The knife cut into a carton of green topped semi-skimmed easily. She pulled it out but the milk didn't spurt forth like you might expect, it merely seeped from the wound. You'd hardly notice if you just walked past. She stabbed another carton, and then another. Carried on stabbing. The more she stabbed those cartons, the more she felt compelled to carry on, as though under a spell. Not caring if anyone saw her. Not caring about anything. The stabbing and slashing seemed to have its own momentum. Its own meaning, nothing to do with her original reason for coming in here with the knife.

She stopped. Looked around, worried now someone might have spotted her. But the back of the shop was still deserted. She wiped the knife and placed it back in her pocket. Then, resisting the urge to leg it, she sidled over to the vegetables and hung about by the pre-packed salads. One eye on the oozing milk cartons.

A woman took a carton. The cut distorted and gaped, so milk sploshed onto the floor. The startled woman replaced the milk swiftly and picked up another. The same thing happened and she dropped the carton. Milk trickled out across the mottled tiled floor.

TWENTY-ONE

Little Slaughterford, the Cotswolds

L ittle Slaughterford, with its honey-coloured Bath Stone buildings and cream teas, was postcard pretty. A wide shallow stream meandered through the village to a pond where a boy was feeding a downy feathered duckling. The boy was about ten years old, with scruffy brown hair and wore a Man United shirt. He was tossing small pieces of bread, not much bigger than crumbs, into the water, tempting the duck closer to the shore, closer to his hand.

Riley had loved ducks. The ones at the city farm were fluffy and white. Fairy-tale ducks. The last place he'd seen his daughter was by the duck pond. He turned away. The scene was too perfect to stomach and he headed to the small picnic area outside a visitor's centre where he'd arranged to meet Jedd and Jenny. He got a text.

Been a complication. Running late. Be with you soon tho.

Is there a problem?

All sorted. No worries. Meet you there, stay put.

He sniffed the air. There was sour countryside smell on the wind. Probably a farm. Pigs or something. But you got used to a bad smell if you lived with it, didn't you? He got a coffee from the visitor's centre and sat down at the trestle picnic table overlooking the stream. Breathed in the coffee aroma to counter the bad air.

On the opposite bank, there was a village green where a blonde-haired young woman was walking a dog. She was in beige jodhpurs, tucked into brown boots. Green padded waistcoat. The dog was black. He wasn't good with dog breeds, but this one was young and excitable, straining at the leash and barking at a moorhen, which sensibly flapped off.

He'd had trouble with a black dog as a kid. When he was about six or seven, a big black beast would jump up on him in the park. Scare the fuck out of him. The owner never had the thing on a lead. Darren had stood rigid with fear as the dog nuzzled his face.

'He's just being friendly,' the man told him, indifferent to Darren's terror. Then, another time, he must have been older by then, because Troy was with him. The dog jumped up on his younger brother, but far from being terrified, Troy kicked it in a carefully aimed boot to the creature's balls. The thing yelped and whined and limped back to its master. The owner swore and threatened them with the RSPCA. He and Troy had legged it.

Finally, Jedd arrived. He'd swapped his blue security uniform for a green crew-necked jersey with leather epaulettes on the shoulders and buff combat trousers. If his dress-down clothes were anything to go by, he really was ex-military.

'There's been a setback on the Jenny front,' Jedd said, sitting down opposite. His weight made the trestle table rock as though they were on a boat. The guy was heavier than he looked.

'Setback?'

'Cold feet.'

'You telling me she's not going to show?'

'Have they got a toilet in there?' He nodded towards the visitor's centre. 'Busting for a slash.' He got up and headed off without waiting for a reply. Darren stared after him with a bad feeling in his gut.

'Sit!' It was the woman, trying to train her dog. She stood with her hand raised holding a treat. 'Sit!' she repeated in a shrill voice.

It didn't sit. Just barked at the treat.

'Sit!' she said again. The dog barked, again. She gave up and let the dog have the reward anyway.

Jedd returned, clutching a takeaway coffee and chewing a pastry. He wiped his hand across his lips, took a swig of coffee and stared at the woman and her dog. 'What d'you reckon?'

'Eh?'

'Nice arse in them tight pants.'

'Oh. Yeah she's okay.'

'Think she's got a riding crop? Looks the type.' Jedd sat down, rocking the bench again.

'Look, what about Jenny?'

'Pancake arse.'

'Very funny,' he said, not smiling. He noticed a faint scar on Jedd's forehead above his eye. He must have missed it before, but the sunlight brought it out today. He had something similar on his arm from coming off his bike as a kid. A childhood wound that never quite went away. Sometimes it itched.

'The Jenny situation. Basically, she was too scared to show her face and meet you.'

'Like I'm big and scary.' Darren finished his coffee and crushed the takeaway cup.

'Don't underestimate yourself, mate. You look like you could handle yourself in a fight.'

He gave an ironic smile. 'Maybe at school I could. Not now.'

'Anyway. I wasn't going to let it rest there was I? So, I offered some money.'

'I told you I'm not paying her.' Darren felt his hackles rising.

'Chill, mate. Just wanted to see how greedy she was. So I offered a couple of hundred.'

'You didn't give it to her?'

'She said it wasn't enough. Did I think she was that cheap? Anyone would think she was selling her soul, or her arse.'

Darren shifted uncomfortably. He didn't like this undercurrent of sexism. But he wasn't going to say anything. Working on building sites for most of his life had taught him to keep his mouth shut about that kind of thing.

'Uppity bitch,' Jedd added. 'Just cus she works in the governor's office.'

Darren nodded.

'Anyone can work in an office, can't they? But could they wire a house? No way. So who is she to play hardball with the likes of us? See what I'm saying?' Jedd stared at him, like he was working up to delivering some bad news. 'So, I did what you said, I told her that she should do the right thing.'

'And?'

He took a sip of his coffee, and placed the cup carefully back down. 'Then I told her that I knew where she lived and she'd better tell us what we want to know.'

'What?'

'Said if she didn't, we'd be paying her a visit. The two of us.'

'You never did?'

'You better believe it.' He smiled. 'So, what do you think?' There was a childlike innocence to the man's face.

'I don't know... I...' Darren spluttered. Since he'd

registered Jedd's scar, his eyes were increasingly drawn to it. It looked like an imprint of something pointed, like a shard of glass. He frowned wondering what kind of trouble had caused that scar.

'It was your idea, mate. Tell her to do the right thing.'

'Yeah but I never said to threaten her!' What the hell was he getting into with Jedd?

'I wasn't being totally serious. Just applying a bit of pressure.'

It was the sort of thing his brother Troy would have done, and he'd contemplated getting Troy involved in the search for Caitlin, hadn't he? He scratched his head and looked over at the dog trainer. She threw a large stick into the river. The dog splashed into the water, but then seemed to lose track of the stick. Stood in the water barking at the woman, expecting her to find it for him. Turning back to Jedd he asked, 'What if she goes to the police?'

'She won't do that. Because she decided two hundred was enough after all.'

'What?' Darren said, frowning.

'Pocketed the money and gave up what we want.'

'But I thought...' He sighed. 'You shouldn't have...'

'Don't worry about the money, mate. My decision to throw the cash, it's on me.'

Darren stared at Jedd, not quite knowing what to say.

'Really it's okay,' Jedd added.

'Well...' He should feel bad about Jedd paying, but instead felt a surge of adrenaline. 'What did she tell you?'

'Avon and Somerset police were informed Grady was being transferred to their area.'

'You mean she could be in Bristol?' Surely that wasn't possible? What about the court order? She wasn't allowed anywhere near Pennywell. Didn't that count anymore, now she had her secret identity?

'I was a bit doubtful as well, but Jenny had something else. In fact, something much better.' Jedd produced his phone and showed him a picture of a car.

Darren frowned, not understanding. 'A taxi?'

'It's common practice for probation to pick up their charges by taxi. Jenny took this photo of the one they sent to get Grady.'

'So she says.'

'But it makes sense. Yeovil is in Somerset, right? Avon and Somerset Police, yeah? And she's meant to be in the south of England right?'

He had to admit it all added up. 'Right.'

'Jenny wouldn't lie about this. Knows if she does, I'll be round to get my money back. With interest.'

'Would you do that?'

'If she deliberately deceived us like that.' He took a thoughtful sip of coffee before continuing, 'You'd come with me, help me out, wouldn't you?'

Would he? He didn't reply.

'Help me get my money. You'd be my back-up, right?'

Darren took a last sip of his coffee, but it had gone cold and he found it difficult to swallow. Jed was staring at him, waiting for a reply. He looked at the picture again. A yellow people carrier.

Yeovil and surrounds. Long distance and local.

'Sure,' he said, 'I'd be your back-up.'

'Nice one!'

'Now, I reckon you should tell me your real name.'

TWENTY-TWO

CoffeeTime, Westcliffe High Street

'What do you put in a personal statement?' It was her break and she was sitting at one of CoffeeTime's polished wooden tables, staring at an old laptop she'd borrowed from George.

'I was never any good at them.' Brig looked over from the counter, twisting her mouth and frowning. Her lips seemed an especially bright shade of red today.

'It's for my uni application.'

She came over, pulled down the glasses which lived on top of her head and examined the online form. The glasses made her eyes huge.

'Law!' She looked impressed.

'My uncle's idea.'

'There was a time I was deluded enough to imagine I could be a lawyer myself.' She gave a satirical laugh.

'Really?' She could imagine Brig in court. Her short ice-platinum hair and severe appearance made her look like someone you didn't want to get on the wrong side of. Even the scarlet lipstick seemed to add something that said, *don't mess with this bitch*. 'I don't know if I've got what it takes.'

'Give it a shot, girl, because, let's face it, you'll turn into a lardy-lump if you stay in a place like Westcliffe for the rest of your life.'

'You haven't gone lardy-lump.'

'Give me a few more years.' She laughed. 'Actually, I came here to be with someone.' She smiled at the thought. 'Then got stuck. It happens. Anyway, it's no place for a young woman with ambition. Only jobs are care homes, cafés and caravans.'

'Can you really see me being a lawyer, Brig? Honestly?'

Brig stared at her with an intense penetrating look. 'At your age you can be anything you want. You just have to fight for it.'

She'd always been a fighter. Her mum had taught her that. But up to now her fights had been against people. Teachers, screws, other prisoners. She'd never really fought *for* something. Perhaps she didn't have that kind of ambition.

Later, she saw a police car cruise past. Felt a stab of anxiety. Stepped out of the café for a minute, and saw it park up outside Tesco. The fuckers had called the police over some spilt milk. Shit. If they found out it was her, she'd be straight back to Thornhill. Just as she was getting used to life on the outside. Fucking idiot. Why the hell had she been so crazy?

Personal statement: *Crazy Anna Moreton, notorious milk slasher. A danger to milk drinkers everywhere. Your cartons aren't safe while she roams free.*

She donated the hoody to a charity shop and threw the knife off the end of the pier. Days passed. Nothing happened. She avoided Tesco. Bert didn't come into the café either. She started to relax about the milk. Although, perversely, she found herself disappointed that there'd been no consequences to her action.

What did she expect? Bert to come storming into the shop accusing her, so she could lie to his face?

When she finally came across Bert, her jaw hung open in disbelief. It couldn't actually be him surely? Must be his doppelganger. Because this clone of Bert was dressed in brown striped baggy trousers held up by rainbow braces. He was juggling brightly coloured clubs. He even had a small audience of half a dozen people. A woman gave her small boy a coin. The kid ran to an upturned hat, threw the coin in and ran back to hug the woman's leg.

She went to watch. He pretended not to notice her. But then he caught her eye and lost his concentration, dropping a club which spun and rolled towards her. She picked it up and went over to him.

'It was you, wasn't it?' he said, taking the club.

'I can't think what you mean.'

'Spilt milk.'

'Oh that.' She shrugged theatrically.

He gave the audience a small bow and collected his hat which had a pocketful of change in it. The handful of people wandered off.

'You ought to go contactless. No one pays with cash anymore, do they?'

'You do.'

'I'm different.'

'Oh yes. Insane.' Then he laughed, as if insane might be a good thing.

'Have you looked at yourself in the mirror?' She pulled on one of his braces.

'Is it animal rights or something? That's what they think.'

She shook her head. 'Just my way of saying, hi.'

'Well, hi.'

'You joined the circus?'

'I might do that.'

'What happened to maths at Manchester?'

He looked around and lowered his voice. 'They take it very seriously, tampering with food.'

'I didn't tamper. I slashed.'

'Caused a huge fuss. The duty manager called the area manager and when I got to work there were a bunch of suits crawling all over the place wondering what to do.' He grinned. 'Actually, it was quite funny. Panicking bosses.'

'You didn't say anything?'

'I'm not a snitch.' He looked offended that she'd even think that about him.

'Thanks.'

'They looked through the CCTV for evidence. The police are having it analysed, apparently.'

'I know where the cameras are.'

'Two of them don't work properly anyway, luckily for you. But let's hope you don't end up on *Crimewatch*.'

She hadn't thought of that. Tried to remember who had seen her in that hoody. Brig?

'Hey, don't look so worried. The police round here are a dozy bunch.'

She hoped so.

'Can I have a go?' she said, pointing to his clubs.

He passed her one. She gave him a look, so he passed her another.

'See if you can do it with two, first.'

She pulled a face. Patronising bastard. Threw both clubs up in the air, managed to catch one, but not the other, which rolled away down the pavement, she went scrambling after it before it reached the road.

He took back the clubs and demonstrated his skills, throwing them high into the air, behind his back, under his leg. Sparkling colours caught the sun and the clubs' spinning trajectories created shimmering patterns, like something liquid was flowing around him. It was pretty fucking cool.

'Show off!'

'Jealous,' he said in a sing-song voice.

'Can you teach me?'

'Clubs are difficult.'

'Can you though?'

'Takes hours and hours of practice.'

'Well, if you're too busy…'

'It's not that.'

'It wouldn't be a date. So, no need for anyone to get put out.'

Something like regret passed over his face. He looked away for a moment. 'You'll have to start off by juggling soft balls.'

She grinned, wondering whether he'd said that entirely innocently.

———

George insisted they met in the probation offices. The stale cigarette smell had been masked by new paint. The window had bird shit smeared down it.

'Are you fed up with me?' she asked, pissed off at what he'd just told her.

'No, of course not.'

'Then why?'

'My supervisor is of the opinion that I need to share some of my caseload.' He looked sad. Like an old family cat had finally died. 'And the meeting in Weston will be a good opportunity for Tammy to get to know you.'

'You're dumping me.'

'It will be a long day and they think–'

'You can't be trusted in a car with me?'

'Please don't suggest any impropriety.'

'It was a fucking joke!'

'Sorry.' He looked embarrassed. Wiped imaginary sweat

from his brow. Neither of them said anything for a minute until the silence became too much.

'But they don't trust us, do they? They think, if we get to like each other too much, then I'm gonna pull my knickers down and we're gonna cop off together.'

'Oh God, Caitlin.'

'Like that schoolgirl who ran off with her chemistry teacher.'

'Do you have to make this so difficult?' He got up and went to the window. Opened it a notch. That's as far as those windows opened. A notch. Was it so you couldn't jump to your death? Or was it in case you felt like pushing your probation officer out the window? The noise of the traffic wafted into the room. Cars, people. Distant siren.

'Except I'm not a schoolgirl, am I?'

'And I, thank God, am not a chemistry teacher.' They both laughed at that. He was leaning against the radiator. His shirt needed an iron.

'As I say, Tammy and I will be sharing your case from now on.'

'I don't want to be shared. Passed around like some tart at a footballers' party.'

He sighed heavily, but ignored her remark. 'Tammy Woodcock is very experienced and also, everyone thinks you will benefit from some female input.'

'I think I had enough female input in Thornhill thanks.'

'Can I at least introduce you to Tammy?'

'I won't talk to her.' She got her phone out and started playing *Candy Crush*, just to be annoying.

'She's very nice. Honestly, you'll like her.'

'Don't care.'

'I'm sure you two will get on.'

'I thought *we* got on.' She looked up from her game.

He nodded. 'We do. But... Look, it's not unusual for cases to get reallocated.'

'To prevent "inappropriate relationships"?'

He didn't reply. Simply stared at her with an expression she couldn't read. Rubbed the back of his neck thinking. 'Okay. How about if I promise to take you to the meeting with your mum, you promise to meet Tammy.'

She grinned. 'All right then.' She put her phone back in her pocket.

'And be nice!'

'Only cus it's you.'

Tammy was a middle-aged woman with a face that seemed about to break into a laugh even when she was being serious. Untidy auburn hair, greying at the roots.

'You got any pets?' she asked Tammy after their initial hellos.

'Cat.'

'I think I'd have a dog.'

'Lot of responsibility. Have to walk them every day.'

She nodded. 'Has "cat" got a name?'

'Asha. That's the name she came with. Got her from a rescue centre.'

'Rescued from what?'

'I don't know, but she's a bit crazy. Climbs trees and falls out. Never learns. Picks fights with bigger cats and loses.' Tammy gave an ironic smile. 'And she's terrified of pigeons.'

She laughed. 'I think I'd like your cat.'

The get-to-know-you chat finished and George popped out of the room with Tammy. She heard them muttering in the corridor just outside. Tammy was okay though. It wasn't going to be that bad, being shared with her.

'D'you fancy her?' she asked when he came back in.

'What sort of a question is that?'

'She's attractive though, isn't she?'

'She's married.'

'That's a yes then, is it?'

'She's off limits.'

She realised that's what George was. Off limits. It's not that she fancied him. It wasn't anything like that. It was something with more weight. It would be easy to say he was a father figure, but that wasn't right. She didn't see him as a father. It was something else. Something she didn't understand.

Sometimes she thought she was a jigsaw with missing pieces. Perhaps everyone felt like that. Perhaps, that was what life was really all about. Find your missing pieces.

'You have to promise me something. When we go to Weston, promise me you'll not tell that woman anything,' George said.

'*That woman* is my mother. And I do have to actually talk to her.'

'Talk, but don't say anything. Nothing about where you live. Or your new name.'

'She's bound to ask.'

'We'll tell her you're called...' He thought for a moment. 'Beth.'

'Beth! Is that the best you could come up with?'

'And that you're living in... Birmingham.'

'Do I have to lie to her?'

'View it as a test. If she keeps her mouth shut and doesn't blab to the press, then maybe we can think of telling her more next time.'

'A test?'

'A test of her love, if you like.'

Should you test someone's love? That felt wrong. Maybe it's one of those things that if you test, you break.

It was an ordinary garden, belonging to an ordinary house in an ordinary street. Ordinary, made her think of that poem. The one they did for GCSE by Philip Larkin. He'd had a baby or something.

May you be ordinary. She hadn't understood that to begin with. Why would anyone wish their kid to be ordinary?

In fact may you be dull. Even worse! Dull and ordinary. Why would you want that?

'But if that's what it takes to "catch happiness" as the poem implies,' the teacher asked them, 'would you choose ordinary? Do you need to have a certain dullness in order to be truly happy?'

The garden had a swing in it. It was blue, with a red plastic seat. The frame flexed and bent as Bert sat on it. He rocked back and forth, his feet planted on the ground. His feet were enormous, whereas hers were small. Like her mouth.

'Is that thing safe?'

'Probably not. Meant for little kids, innit.'

There were no swings at Lowood Secure Children's Home. Health and safety. She didn't actually know how to swing. She'd tried once in a playground, kicked her legs about, frantic to get some movement. Failed.

'My dad got it for my fifth birthday. He really wanted me to have goalposts, but I insisted on a swing.' He jumped off leaving the thing swinging by itself. 'Want a go?'

It reminded her of a horror film. There's a malevolent presence, and a rusty squeaking sound which turns out to be an empty swing going back and forth, but there's been no child in that house since one was brutally murdered twenty years ago. Now little Tommy wants revenge.

'No thanks.'

She was here for her first juggling lesson. He made her practise throwing a soft coloured ball up into the air and catch it with her opposite hand.

'It's all about the accuracy of the throw.'

Eventually he let her graduate to two balls. Throwing one up, then the other, and catching them in opposite hands. It was impossible. She dropped them all the time. Felt cack-handed and clumsy.

His mum kept looking at them through the window. She had dark charcoal coloured hair, coiffured into a bob and perfect teeth. Didn't she have anything better to do than gawp at them?

Bert's introductions had been mercifully brief. 'Mum, Anna. Anna, my mum.' He gave an accompanying glare telling his mum to back off from the questions that were clearly on her lips. 'We'll be in the garden.'

Eventually she gave up on the balls. Sat down on the haunted swing and watched him impress her with his routine.

'How did you get to be so good, you bastard?'

'Practice. Hours and hours. You have to be a total nerd. It's even more nerdy than getting A-level maths, but juggling hurts your brain less.'

'Makes my brain hurt.'

'That's because you're anxious about dropping the balls.'

'The general idea is to keep them in the air.'

'Lucy says if you focus on the fear of dropping, then drop them you will.'

'Lucy?' Was this the braided haired girl? The girlfriend.

'My juggling teacher.'

'Wow! Someone actually teaches this stuff?'

'Yeah, I went to circus school last summer. Wanted to go this summer too, but Mum didn't have the money.'

'You went to a circus school?' She was astonished that there could even be a school that would teach you such cool stuff. Sounded like her kind of school.

'Had a bit of a shit summer. Mum packed me off to

Fooling Around to keep me out of trouble. Course she regrets it now.'

'Why?'

'For one thing, the noise of me dropping the clubs all the time in my bedroom drives her mad.' He threw a club high into the air, they both looked up at it spinning against the sky. It came down, returning obediently to his waiting hand. Like he'd tamed it. 'But it did keep me out of trouble, so she was glad of that.'

'Trouble? What kind of trouble?' Bert's kind of trouble would be a walk in the park compared to her kind of trouble, she was sure of that.

'Oh you know. Drinking too much. Got into a couple of fights, which isn't me at all...' He looked over at the kitchen window. His mother had gone away. 'I was a bit upset, I suppose.'

She nodded. 'With your mum?'

'Not her. It's just my dad–' He shook his head and wandered over to the corner of the garden to retrieve an old, deflated football. Drop-kicked it between the two sides of the swing's frame. 'I should have had the goalposts that's all.'

'He can't have run out on you and your mum over goalposts!'

'If he'd had a son who was into football, maybe he'd have had more reason to hang around.' Bert swallowed. 'More reason to see me now.' He picked up a club and pulled at a piece of loose plastic round the handle. 'Sometimes I think it would be easier if he'd died.' Then he looked at her and went red. 'Sorry. I didn't mean... Forgot about your parents.'

'Oh. My parents aren't dead.'

He frowned. 'Died in a car crash. You said.'

She fiddled with her ear. Felt suddenly awkward. 'Yeah I know. But they didn't.' Bloody George and his cover story.

'Why would you lie about something like that?' He pulled a disapproving face, not understanding.

'I make stuff up about them sometimes. Cus the truth is not really all that nice.'

'Okay, So, the truth?' He gave her a severe look.

'All right.' She sat on the swing and rocked gently to and fro.

The stern expression melted away. He sat cross-legged on the grass in front of her, looking up at her, eyes full of anticipation as if he actually cared.

'My mum couldn't look after me. She couldn't protect me from…'

'From what?'

There were limits to the truth. 'Stuff. Bad stuff.' She squashed one of the juggling balls in her hand. 'So they put me in care.'

'And your father?'

'No idea who he is. Mum won't tell me.'

'That's not very fair.'

She shrugged. And deciding to leave that thought behind, asked him what else he'd learned at the circus school.

'Acrobatics, high-wire, juggling obviously. Unicycle, I was tragic at that.'

'Can you do handstands?'

Turned out he could, sort of. He needed her to help him balance by holding his ankles. 'Spotting him', as he called it. The only thing she spotted was his firm arse and his thick calf muscles in his skinny jeans. His mother made a badly timed reappearance at the window, embarrassing Caitlin as her face was now inches from that sexy arse.

'She's worried that you're encouraging me.'

'What?'

'To run away to the circus.'

'I'd encourage anyone to do that.' She laughed.

'Thinks I'll give up maths and do circus training with Fooling Around.'

'What a dilemma. Maths? Circus? Tricky.'

Fuck Larkin, his gloomy philosophy was about the most depressing thing she'd ever heard. And as for that teacher, the reason she had no ambition for her pupils was to dull them into submission.

TWENTY-THREE

Dream Inn, Shepherds Bush, London

He was on Boggart Hill. Riley was there too. Somehow, she was alive! His heart leapt, but then he saw she was crying.

'Why did you bury me?'

'They said you were dead.'

'You didn't check, did you? You didn't check properly.'

'I'm sorry, sweet pea, forgive me.'

'You buried me alive, Daddy.'

He woke up. Gasped. Excited and elated that Riley was alive after all. Heart pounding. But guilty too for burying her alive. Then a crippling feeling of loss as he came to his senses. The guilt hung around long after the dream itself faded into the darkness of the hotel room. The guilt always lasted for hours.

The bedside clock showed 5.27 in venomous green numbers. There was no way he'd get back to sleep, so he went to the bathroom to splash water on his face. The soap and body wash in this budget hotel came out of a dispenser, like motorway service toilets. Kerry would have been pissed off about that. She loved collecting the individual bottles of soapy-smelly stuff you got in half-decent hotels when she got the chance, which wasn't often.

'The Dream Inn is where everybody stays when they're on *Wake-Up UK*,' Harvey Pringle told him last night in the 'Brown Bottle Shop', his name for The Duke of York. According to Harvey, the pub filled up with news people after the programme finished at nine in the morning.

'They do a great fry-up. I'll meet you here after the show for debrief.'

Going to the pub at nine in the morning for a beer and a fry-up? Wrong on so many levels.

He had hoped Harvey would go with him to the TV studio and take part in the interview, but that wasn't the plan. Darren was on his own this morning and getting increasingly anxious.

He opened the curtains. The orange glow on the low clouds was giving way to grey morning light. An early Tube train rattled along a viaduct not far away, brightly lit but empty of passengers.

Last time he was on the telly, it was outside the Bristol Courts, facing a battery of cameras. He wasn't nervous then, though. Kerry was at his side and the prosecution lawyer did all the talking.

'Pleased with the verdict and happy with the life tariff.'

He was stupid enough to believe, that at least in Grady's case, life would actually mean life.

His only other appearance on TV was at the police appeal for information about Riley's disappearance. It was the day after she went missing. He wasn't nervous then either; he was frantic. Kerry read out a statement asking for help. Her face was broken with worry, but she managed to read the statement with dignity. He could hardly speak.

'Please find my little girl.' His voice was choked and strange. The detective in charge of the case put a hand on his shoulder. The crowd of journalists and photographers blurred out as his eyes filled with tears. He hung his head, ashamed for not keeping it together.

Be the man, for God's sake.

Afterwards Kerry said she was glad he broke down, proud he wasn't afraid to show his emotions in public. But his father had been ashamed, disappointed that his son had let him down by crying on TV. Didn't say much, but Darren could tell what he thought.

This morning would be his first time in an actual TV studio. Live TV as well, in front of millions. He wished now he hadn't agreed to it.

'The studio isn't that big and you can't see the audience, so you soon forget about them. There's just you and the presenters and a couple of flunkies hanging about in the shadows you won't even notice,' Harvey had reassured him. 'It's just like having a private chat to the presenter.'

'It's for Riley. You're doing it for Riley,' he told his reflection as he shaved.

The receptionist ticked his name off a list and gave him a temporary pass. He slipped the blue ribbon lanyard around his neck and sat down on a sofa overlooked by large posters of *Wake-Up UK*'s presenters. He didn't watch the show. News programmes depressed him.

'Darren Burgess?' A young man in jeans and a pink shirt, top button undone, held out his hand. 'I'm Hugo. We spoke on the phone?'

Hugo had phoned him the other day for a brief discussion about the interview. He led Darren through the security doors and down some steps to the basement, showing him into the green room.

The room wasn't green, it was beige with a wide orange

diagonal stripe down one wall. Hugo explained they'd play a video 'package' to set up the interview, before coming live to the studio.

'Amanda Cheshire will do your interview. Any questions?' Hugo asked.

Darren couldn't think of any. He was trying to remember who Amanda Cheshire was.

'Great, so help yourself to everything,' he said, pointing to the hospitality table which had a generous range of drinks, pastries and buns.

Left alone, Darren took a bottle of spring water. He sat hunched up on an orange chair and tentatively sipped the water in case too much suddenly made him need a piss.

'It's like waiting for the dentist,' he said to a man in a blue suit. The man looked up from his phone, stared at Darren like he'd said something in a foreign language, then looked back at his phone.

Perhaps the man was a dentist.

A few minutes later Hugo returned and took him to the studio, leading him to a curved orange sofa while they were playing the package. He watched a monitor showing a potted history of Riley's disappearance, the subsequent investigation and trial. A technician pinned a mic to him, warning him not to fiddle with it while he was talking. Facing him was a brick wall with a large window, behind which there was a backdrop of central London, as though they were in a swanky studio loft instead of a basement in Shepherd's Bush. He could see the bricks weren't real, but on camera they were quite convincing.

As the preamble was winding up, Amanda left the presenters' desk and headed over. She was a middle-aged woman who you might describe as mumsy. He was reassured that she was a little overweight because it made her seem more friendly. She gave a brief smile and turned to face a camera. A young woman wearing headphones counted down, before giving a hand cue to the presenter.

'Riley's father, Darren Burgess has come in this morning to tell us more about his campaign to get the law changed.' She was reading off autocue, but then turned to face him. 'Good morning, Darren.'

He cleared his throat. 'Good morning.'

'Could you start by telling us what you hope to achieve by calling for Riley's Law?'

'Justice. Justice for Riley.'

'I see. So...' She frowned and glanced at her notes. 'You don't think justice has been served, then?'

'Well, no, I don't really...' His voice sounded nervous, shaky even, so he tried to carry on with more conviction. 'Caitlin Grady should never have been released.'

'Well, some people may not agree with you on that.' Her eyes flicked to the countdown woman in the shadows. 'However, let's move on–'

'Some people haven't had their daughter abducted and strangled...' He paused and took a breath.

'I'm sure everyone feels for your loss, Mr Burgess.' Sounded like an automatic phrase she didn't mean at all. 'Going back to Riley's Law itself. For the benefit of our viewers, could you explain what exactly Riley's Law will do?'

He nodded, took a sip of water, hoped it would calm his racing heart. 'We should be told where child killers live. Riley's Law would give us the right.'

'But if they have served their time in prison...?'

'These killers are out there and people should be able to find out if they are living next door, that's all I'm saying.' He sounded reasonable, didn't he?

'It would be almost impossible for people named under your law to live a normal life though. Don't you agree?'

He and Harvey had rehearsed this question in the pub last

night. The vigilante question as the journalist called it. But his mind clogged up and couldn't find the words he was meant to say.

'Well... they'll have to watch out then, won't they?'

'But if they are no longer considered a threat to society?'

'How can you say that? Course they're a threat. Leopards don't change their spots, do they? Evil is evil.' He took a sip of water, happy he'd made his point.

'I'm not sure use of the word "evil" is helpful,' she said in her know-it-all tone.

'If the judge called Grady evil, then so can I.' He was getting himself riled up. *Keep calm, Darren. Keep Calm.*

Amanda looked past him, distracted for a moment, then nodded slightly. Someone in her ear was pulling the strings round here. 'I don't think that's quite what the judge actually said, but moving on—'

'He bloody did! Called her "pure evil".' Then blurted out without thinking, 'Are you on her side or something?'

'I'm not on anybody's side, Mr Burgess. But Caitlin isn't here to defend herself.'

'Would you want her living next door?'

'Mr Burgess.'

'Answer the question. Would you live next door to a monster like Grady?'

'I'm afraid I'm not here to answer your questions,' she said, giving him a hard stare.

'Grady was only eleven years old when she killed my daughter. What sort of sick freak do you think she's grown into?'

She turned to address the camera. 'I must stress that Mr Burgess's opinions on Caitlin Grady are his own, and in no way endorsed by *Wake-Up UK*.'

'But would you want her living next door? Let's hear it. Tell the nation.'

'Well, as a matter of fact, I would live next door to her. She's served her time and should be given the benefit of the doubt.'

'Well now we know!' He felt sick.

She addressed the camera. 'And Caitlin, if you are watching, and would like to come on the show–'

'You'd invite her into this studio?' He was flabbergasted. 'Unbelievable!'

'In the interests of balance.'

'You are on her side!' Amanda Cheshire's smug expression was making his head boil. He felt like putting his boot through the studio set's false brick wall. 'I'm not putting up with this crap.'

'Mr Burgess, please?'

He pulled off his microphone and stood up. 'It's an insult to Riley.'

Amanda turned to the camera. 'Ladies and gentleman, Darren Burgess, who is calling for Riley's Law.'

Darren deliberately walked between her and the camera as he made his way out of the studio.

He picked up his overnight bag from the hotel and headed back to Paddington, sardined in the rush hour Tube. Nose to nose with commuters. It was hot and the air smelt bad. His armpits were sticky despite deodorant. Should have had a shower at the hotel before he left but just couldn't wait to get out of London.

That bloody presenter was taking the piss. He should not have agreed to go on that show. Someone glanced at him like he needed to be sectioned. He realised he was actually muttering out loud. He pursed his lips and avoided eyes, hoping no one would recognise him from the morning's TV.

He got on the train at Paddington letting out an audible sigh of relief. At least it was cool in here, but the seat felt hard and his skin was clammy. A lad nearby was eating a pasty. The meaty onion smell turned his stomach and he twisted away to look out of the window. He had that pain in the small of his back again, the one he got when he hadn't had enough sleep.

He got a text. He didn't want to hear from anybody. But then wondered if it was *Wake-Up UK* apologising.

> In the brown bottle shop. Waiting to buy you a well-deserved drink.

How could Harvey possibly think he was in the mood for a drink? He felt like breaking something.

> Not in the mood. Thanks.

> You should be. You did well.

> How is being made a fool of on live TV doing well?

He stabbed his phone so hard his finger hurt.

> You did great putting the Cheshire bitch on the spot. She came across as an apologist for Grady. Totally out of touch. It's all great publicity. That walk-off will run and run!!!

He wasn't sure if he liked Harvey's way with words. But as the train left Paddington, he relaxed a bit. Maybe it wasn't such a disaster.

An hour later the train arrived at Swindon. He stared out at a grey steel fence, behind which he could make out the car park where he'd left his van yesterday. It had been raining here, and in a puddle he could see an inverted watery reflection of the name of the town. The thought of his empty house didn't seem to be enough to get him to move his arse and get off the train. He watched the nondescript scene recede as the train set off again. He'd get off at the next stop.

The next stop was Chippenham and as the train entered the town, he saw the half-finished block of flats he'd been working on. Seeing those flats stung him. After Kerry left he couldn't face going to work. Waited at home for her to come back. When she didn't and he finally returned to work, he found he was barred from the site. He tried to explain about Kerry.

'Too bad,' was all Ben said with a nasty smirk, before ordering him off the site.

He didn't get off in Chippenham either, but stayed put until Bristol. Maybe he'd make a day of it and visit Riley on Boggart Hill. But then he saw Yeovil was up there on the departure board in glowing orange letters. A train was leaving in twenty minutes. He felt drawn to catch it, almost as if Grady was calling him somehow. Ridiculous. She wasn't a siren calling him to his doom. And if they did ever meet, it would be her doom not his. He bought a ticket.

The train trundled its way past a slow-flowing river in a pleasant wooded valley, through green fields dotted with contented sheep, and more fields of recently harvested hay bales. The sun had come out; it was a picture of rural harmony. England as it might look in a tourist brochure. Shame that the dirty window only allowed him a grime-coloured view of the world.

He checked into a hotel. There was a posh collection of shower gels and body lotions in the bathroom. He threw a few in his bag for Kerry before taking a shower. Afterwards, while drying his hair on the soft white hotel towel, he got a text from Jedd.

Well done mate. You showed them!

Jedd's real name was Jerry Downing. He lived, he said, in Dursley near Gloucester, but travelled widely with his job with the security company. Jedd had been his nickname at school and people who were closest to him always called him that.

'So, you can still call me Jedd if you like.'

'Okay, Jedd it is then,' Darren had said, feeling slightly awkward. It was a gesture of intimacy he wasn't sure he was ready for. The text cheered him up though. Jedd was on his side.

Then Kerry rang. At last.

'Hi, love,' he said, feeling a rush of warmth. 'Are you okay? How's it going?'

'What the fuck are you playing at?'

'Hey…'

'Dragging Riley's name through the mud on TV.'

'I did no such thing.'

'Showing yourself up. Embarrassing me. My husband ranting about Grady the evil monster. Thanks a lot, Darren.'

'Keep your hair on, will you?'

'Wasn't enough to go mouthing off to the papers. You went one better and got on TV as well. Well fucking done!'

He tried to sound calm. 'I was only trying to explain about Riley's Law that's all.'

'Darren, I… You and me…' Her breath was making the mic crackle. But she didn't say any more.

He clocked the overnight bag open on the bed. 'I got you some hotel smellies, body lotion and shampoo.'

There was a pause before she spoke again, and when she did her voice sounded even and distant. 'This obsession. This vendetta, whatever it is.' She took a breath. 'The way you talk, the anger. I can't have that in my life. I can't handle it.'

'Everything I'm doing. It's all for Riley.'

'No, Darren. No, it isn't,' she said in a voice full of sadness. Then she hung up.

He sat for a long time on the bed. Then replaced the hotel toiletries, putting them on the glass and chrome bathroom shelf.

The centre of Yeovil was neat and smart, with a pedestrianised area, a range of well-kept shops and a church set in manicured lawns. There were paths and benches where you could sit and take in the day.

He imagined Grady was somewhere near, working in an office, maybe popping out for a sandwich and coffee. Or was she in that shoe shop? Or trying on a jacket in the vintage clothes store? But wherever she was, he was walking down the same streets as she was. He felt so close to her now. Any day, any minute, any second, he was going to see her.

He dived into a burger joint to grab a burger and fries. Sat at the red Formica table munching his way through a cheeseburger, wondering if Grady had been in here. Maybe even sitting at this exact table. What would she order? What did murderers eat? Something with a kick to it. The spicy veggie wrap? But then how could a killer not be a meat eater? He shook his head, why did he even care?

He texted Jedd.

Guess where I am?

Still in London?

Yeovil

Nice one. Looking for the bitch?

👍

Want some help?

Jedd was in his uniform when Darren met him on the green in front of the church. His smooth, pale face seemed at odds with the uniform today. Made him look too soft. Not mean enough for a security guard. He needed another couple of scars. But as they walked side by side through the pedestrianised shopping area, he noticed a few people giving Jedd a respectful nod, or acknowledging look. His uniform made an impression. But more than that, it was the way he held himself and moved. Slow deliberate movements which seemed to add to his presence. Made up for the soft looks. Darren found himself unconsciously echoing the way Jedd moved.

Jedd pointed out a young couple. 'Those two are up to no good,' he said. The woman had a large shoulder bag and the guy wore a hoodie in a way that made it difficult to see his face. 'Shoplifters.'

'How do you know?'

'He nicks the stuff and slips it into her bag. Standard. Look like they both done time to me.'

Darren hadn't picked up anything dodgy; they looked ordinary.

'See that store detective.' Jedd pointed to a uniformed guy standing outside Primark, talking into a walkie-talkie on his lapel. 'He's clocked them.'

The couple sensing they'd been spotted melted away into the crowds.

'The thing with your crims, they mark themselves out. Ask any copper. Can spot a hardened criminal a mile off. It's the body language. All that mixing with other criminals, especially if they've done time, rubs off on them. Can't shake off the postures and ticks they've picked up. Prison hangs round them like bad gas.'

Jedd went over to the store detective and showed him the picture of Grady. The guy shook his head, so they resumed their patrol, with Jedd asking other security guys the same question. But all drew a blank.

'You could be a plain clothes detective,' Jedd told him. 'You look the part.'

Darren could never be a detective, but smiled at the compliment.

After a couple of hours of searching, Darren's enthusiasm was waning. His feet ached and he needed to sit down.

'That's the thing about security. On your feet all day. You'll get used to it,' Jedd said, yawning and stretching as they sat at a table in Starbucks.

'Long day?' Darren asked, resisting a yawn himself.

'Up at five.'

'Same,' Darren said, taking a slurp of tea. 'Not sure I'm up for much more searching today.'

Jedd nodded. 'Don't worry, mate, we'll find her one day.'

'Even if we don't, there's Riley's Law.'

'Don't hold your breath on that. You know how the powers-that-be like to drag things out.'

'I suppose so,' he mumbled.

'She can't hide for ever. Someone will give her away sooner or later.'

'You think?'

'I know it.'

Darren nodded. He appreciated the confidence. Unlike some people, Jedd had his back.

'What are you going to do with her when we find her?' Jedd asked, taking a sip of Coke.

Darren twisted his face. 'Not sure.'

'Don't tell me you haven't thought about it, mate.'

'I've thought.' He felt a flash of anger as he remembered Grady at the trial. All she did was fidget. And sometimes she just sat there with her eyes closed. Couldn't even pay attention properly, that's how seriously she took what she'd done. Once or twice she even laughed. When the judge called Riley's death an 'act of pure evil' she giggled. At that moment he wanted to kill her. Do to her what she'd done to Riley. Strangle the life out of her.

'Bullet in the back of the head?' Jedd said.

'I haven't got a gun.'

'I'm sure it could be arranged.'

Darren frowned. 'I don't think—'

'Just messing.' Jedd finished his Coke, looked around, then leaned in towards Darren. 'Then again, if you knew you weren't going to be caught? Would you?' He formed a gun with his fingers and mimed shooting it.

'A bullet to the brain?' Darren said almost whispering, afraid of being overheard.

'Put her down like an animal.'

He shook his head. 'No, doesn't feel right.'

'Why not, too quick?'

'Maybe.' He didn't want to simply end her life. Needed more somehow.

'Want her to beg for her life? That it?' Jedd had a curious smile on his face.

'I want to look into those cold impassive eyes of hers. See. Something.'

'Before you blow her away.'

Is that what he'd do? Take her life in cold blood? He could have done that ten years ago. No problem. But now? Could he still?

'Don't worry, mate,' Jedd said. 'We're just chatting. Right? Just talking.'

He noticed the scar on Jedd's forehead seemed more

prominent just now. But scars are like that. Change with the weather.

'What about the guy who killed your sister. The hit-and-run guy? Would you blow him away if you had the chance?'

'I might.'

He wondered if Jedd was capable of killing. If he'd been in the forces, then he must be. They all were. But when push came to shove. Was he, himself capable of taking a life, even from a creature like Caitlin Grady?

'Would you blame me if I did?' Jedd asked.

'I can see why you would, obviously, I can see that.'

'Would you grass me up?'

He looked at Jedd long and hard. 'Did you burn that guy's house down, Jedd?'

'Suppose I did?'

'Did you?'

'No.'

'Nothing to tell then.'

'But if I had?'

If Jedd burned the house down and the guy died in the fire, would he go to the police? If it was his own sister, Sarah, and some fucker had killed her in a hit-and-run. He might well burn the bastard's house down. 'No. I wouldn't grass on you.'

TWENTY-FOUR

Esso Service Station, Westcliffe Bypass

She was sitting in a dark blue Ford Fiesta, enjoying the new-car smell. It was a hire car the probation service had arranged for the journey to Weston.

'The number plate can't be traced to Westcliffe,' George explained.

They'd stopped to fill up with fuel. George was at the pump and she could hear petrol sloshing around in the back as he filled the tank. There was a frisson about a petrol station on the edge of town. Tanks being filled, tyres checked, snacks and supplies bought. The promise of a road trip. Where could they get to on a full tank?

She imagined driving through the night up to Scotland. Somewhere wild and remote. A castle on a headland overlooking stormy seas. Ever since she was a kid, she'd had dreams of running away. Leaving the past behind. Leaving who she was. In a way she'd done that, hadn't she? She'd left Caitlin behind. Except that today, she was going to revisit her old life.

She hadn't been out of Westcliffe since the day she arrived from Thornhill. So, as they sped along, passing fields and woodlands, she stared through the passenger window with the fascination of a traveller in a foreign country. It had rained earlier, but now the sun was out and the air was crisp and clear. A freshly minted world.

George turned off the dual carriageway, taking what he insisted was a shortcut down a winding lane. It was dairy country, and they had to stop in a hamlet while cows crossed the road. They were big beasts. One came up to her window and stared in with large empty eyes. Strikingly beautiful with long eyelashes. What was going on behind those eyes? Thoughts of grass, clouds, mud, open fields. Electric fences.

Pennywell city farm didn't have cows. It had sheep and goats. She remembered feeding handfuls of grass through the fence to a pointy faced goat on that fucked-up day. Bunked off school with Tracey and went to the city farm for something to do. It was the last time she ever saw Tracey. The last moment of her childhood.

She turned to George. 'Some short cut, mister.'

He grunted and put the radio on. They had a silly argument about what music to listen to. He wanted to find a country station.

'Country and Western is the bee's knees on a road trip.'

She pulled a face and as they set off again, flicked to Radio 1, just to needle him. He insisted the DJs were full of vacuous blather and it was only for kids. They argued the toss for a while, but later, as they joined the motorway, she could see he was smiling to himself.

As they drove through Weston to the meeting, they passed the railway station. Another memory of Tracey. The day they ran away to the seaside. She smiled to herself at their audacity until she remembered the man with the greying beard and curly hair watching them.

'Where's your mum?' he'd said, smiling with his lips, but

not with his eyes. Looked at her bare legs when he spoke. She knew what that meant.

She made him buy chips. Then agreed to go back to his place, because he had *Harry Potter and the Order of the Phoenix* on DVD, which she hadn't seen. He gave them a lift in his big car with smelly leather seats. Drove straight into a double garage that had an automatic door. She was impressed with that.

While they watched the film, he put his hand on her knee. After a bit Tracey fell asleep. He asked about her knickers. Did they have a pattern, or were they plain? She knew to lift up her skirt. Didn't look at him while he unzipped his trousers, but concentrated on Harry Potter and Sirius Black in the Ministry of Magic. He gave her a pound coin.

She wondered why she'd been so matter-of-fact about it at the time. Why she'd gone along with it. How she knew what he wanted. She bit her lip and forced that thought away.

The probation offices in Weston were in a new building with smooth red bricks and small windows. She had to wait in a meeting room while George went to collect her mother from the reception. This room smelt of new carpet. She sat at a table, sipping a bottle of water. Wondered what it would be like to see her mum again after more than two years. She was looking forward to it, excited about telling her about her life and how she was starting to make a success of things.

She heard them coming down the corridor. Her mother was berating George about something. Typical Mum. Making a fuss about this or that. She couldn't help smiling at the familiarity of such a scene. The woman was still complaining when she came into the room.

'The cloak and dagger routine, I ask you. Really! I promised them I wouldn't tell a living soul.'

She was well turned out as usual. Her rich auburn hair looked freshly done and her make-up was immaculate.

'Hello, Mum.' Caitlin stood and gave an awkward hug. Her

mum still smelled the same. Warm and woody. The smell was always comforting, even if the associated affection was unreliable.

Her mum stepped back. 'Let's look at you. Well!' She nodded approvingly. 'You've blossomed, haven't you?'

'Thanks, Mum.' She grinned. Praise from her mum!

'And haven't you got a nice tan? Been on holiday?'

Was she fishing for information already? 'Oh yeah, Mum. Partying in Ibiza!'

'No need to be sarcastic to your mother. I was only asking.'

Caitlin apologised and hugged her again. She needed to give the woman the benefit of the doubt. After all she'd made the effort to come here. Dressed up as well, wearing a smart black dress and expensive-looking earrings, as though she might be going out to dinner rather than meeting her wayward daughter. But then her mum did dress to impress. Her mum had always been beautiful to Caitlin's childhood eyes. Still only in her thirties, she was as attractive as ever. Even if there was a certain hardness to her eyes and mouth.

They sat down at the grey table facing each other.

'Have you seen anyone lately? Auntie Bernadette?' she said, to try and get the ball rolling.

'You know perfectly well, they all fell away after the trial. Besides, Bernadette's full of the airs and graces now. Forgets who she is.' Her mum sniffed and wiped her nose with a handkerchief. 'Got a bit of an allergy.' She looked around the room as if something unpleasant was seeping out of the walls. 'So what have you been up to? Tell me your news and screws.'

Feeling a prick of embarrassment at her mum's turn of phrase she flashed a look at George, who had taken up an arm's-length position at the nearby window. He was pretending to stare at something outside but she could almost see his ears twitching.

175

'Going to university, I hear?' her mum carried on, a hint of disapproval entering her voice.

'Actually I haven't decided yet. But I might apply.'

'Would you rather not get a job, love? Have some cash in your pocket?'

'I've got a job.'

'Well then, why bother with the university?'

She thought her mum might be encouraging. Proud even, that her daughter had an opportunity to go to uni.

'So you don't think I should go?' She found herself glancing towards George again, but he was still staring out of the window.

'What's this job then?' her mum asked.

'Coffee shop.'

'Starbucks, is it?'

George turned to face them, a warning look on his face. But she wasn't stupid, she wouldn't give too much away. Anyway, how many coffee shops are there in the country? Millions.

'I just thought if I went to uni–'

Her mother sneezed and wiped her nose again. 'Maybe it's the carpet?'

'–I might be able to get a better job.'

'Well, if you think you're good enough to go to university, who am I to say otherwise?' She looked over at George. 'What do you think, George? Is Caitlin good enough?'

Why did her mum want to involve George? What game was this? But George wouldn't be drawn and muttered something about only being there to check protocol was observed.

'Don't imagine they'll let me smoke in here, will they?' Her mum got her cigarettes out of her handbag. George suggested they go to the 'smoking garden'. On the way she asked her mum about Tracey.

'Bump into Sandra sometimes, in Asda. She never mentions Tracey and I don't like to ask. The trouble that girl's heaped upon the poor woman's head.' Her mum gave her a look that seemed to suggest all daughters are trouble.

She decided not to pursue the subject, but wondered if there was a way she might be able to catch up with her old friend. Trouble or no trouble.

They went through fire doors to the so-called smoking garden, which was simply a patch of gravel at the back of the building with a couple of potted plants that needed throwing away and a narrow bench. The gravel was littered with cigarette butts.

Her mum offered cigarettes around. George waved the packet away.

'What about you, Caitlin love?'

She shook her head.

'What? No bad habits? Either of you?' Her mum gave a wheezing laugh that morphed into a cough.

She'd smoked a bit at Lowood Secure, but hadn't liked it much. Putting something in her mouth that wasn't food made her feel weird.

Her mother lit a cigarette and drew on it thoughtfully. 'I suppose, if you did go to university, you might come to Bristol.'

'I'm not allowed near Bristol, am I?' Her mother knew this, so what was she playing at?

'But the university is nowhere near Boggart Hill. They could be a bit flexible, don't you think, George?'

'Caitlin's parole conditions are clear. She's not allowed within the City of Bristol. Any variation would have to be approved at the highest level.' George sounded formal and in control.

Her mum grunted and flicked some ash on the gravel. 'I might have gone to university myself, if I'd stayed on at school,' she said, giving an acidic look. Was that why her mum was lukewarm about her going to college? Jealous, because she couldn't go herself?

'Should have given me away to the nuns then, shouldn't you?' Being given away to the nuns was a family threat. A fate far worse than being adopted, or being put into care. There was a mythology about the nuns, being sent away to an unnamed convent, and living under an indescribably harsh regime.

'Oh, Caitlin love, I'd never do that.' Her mum had still been at school when she got pregnant. Younger than she, Caitlin, was now. No way was she herself ready to have kids.

'I know it must have been tough for you,' she said, trying to imagine what it must be like to have baby that young.

'It's the responsibility you're not prepared for.'

'What about my dad?'

Her mum snorted. Took a drag on her cigarette.

'Was he the same age?' She'd always imagined her father as a fantasy figure. Mysterious, rich and famous. But now thinking about it properly, he was much more likely to be a local lad. 'Was he at school with you?'

Her mother looked taken aback. 'Well, Caitlin, there's a time and a place.'

'Was he though?' If her dad had been at school with her mum, she might be able to find out who he was. At long last. Her heart swelled at the thought.

Her mum shook her head. 'No, he wasn't at the school.'

'Then who?'

'I… can't say. I really can't.' She was squirming under the pressure, avoiding her eyes.

'Just tell me his name then? It would be something.'

She shook her head and looked over at George, clearly expecting him to rescue her.

'Mrs Grady, perhaps if you could give Caitlin a reason for not saying, then I'm sure she'd understand.'

'It's Miss,' she said pointedly before finishing her cigarette and dropping it on the gravel. Trod on the butt with her toe and ground it into the stones. 'Any chance of a cup of coffee, George love?'

'Coffee?' He looked nonplussed.

'I've a mouth as dry as a nun's cunt.'

'Mum!'

'What? Don't tell me you didn't hear language in prison.'

'This isn't prison.' She gave George an apologetic look.

'And don't you look to be a man of the world, George?'

'Is there anywhere we could get a coffee?' Caitlin asked George, hoping her mum might say more about her dad if he wasn't there. He grunted and went off to investigate.

'Did he put you up to it, love?'

'What?'

'Asking about things we never want to talk about.'

'Was it one of my uncles?'

'What? You can't say things like that!' She looked genuinely shocked.

'I don't mean my real uncle. I mean one of my so-called uncles, the men that came around to the house. Your...' She sighed. 'Boyfriends.'

'I was on my own, Caitlin. I was entitled to have boyfriends.'

'So was it one of them? One of the ones I met?'

'It wasn't one of my,' she paused, like she was struggling to find the right word, 'gentlemen visitors, just so you know. All right. Let that be an end to it.'

'Name. Tell me his name.'

'We all have secrets, including you. Won't even tell your own mother where you live.'

'In a flat.'

'In the south of England, I hear. Anywhere I might know?'

'I'm not going to tell you were I live, so don't bother trying to wheedle it out of me.'

Her mum sat down on the uncomfortable looking bench. 'You can't blame me for wanting to know about you and your life. You are my daughter.'

She wanted to believe that her mum was sincere. That she could tell her mum about her life and that her mum loved her enough to keep the details to herself. She was supposed to lie, make stuff up. But how could she lie to her mum, when she herself was expecting to get the truth out of the woman. She sat down next to her. Her mum put her arm around her. She rested her head on her mum's shoulder.

'I'm living in a little town on the coast. Nice place. It feels safe. Apart from the mutant seagulls.'

She told her a few details about her life in Westcliffe without going into specifics. Even so it was good to tell her a bit about herself. There'd always been moments like this with her mum. Eye of the storm, in the midst of bad moods and tellings off. A minute or two when they were close. She told her mum that she'd met a boy she liked.

'Thank God for that. I was getting concerned about you and George to tell you the truth.'

'What? Why?'

'I've seen the way you look at him. And the way he looks at you.'

'You're not trying to say that something's going on, are you?'

'He's too old for you of course, but that doesn't stop some of them. I've met men like him aplenty. Sweet on the surface, but a rotten fruit, corrupted and maggoty.'

'Like the guy in the grey suit. There was something rotten about him.'

'Who are you talking about?'

'One of your "gentleman callers". Grey suit and disgusting dandruff.'

'Don't know who you mean.' Her mum shifted away from her slightly.

'Used to be there when I got back from school. Like he was waiting for me.'

'I don't—' She stopped. Seemed to be stuck for words.

'You must know who I'm talking about.'

The woman took a breath and looked towards the fire doors, as if hoping George would come to her rescue. 'He was there to see me, my love. Not you. I don't know where you got the notion that he was waiting for you.' She got her fag packet out and looked at it a moment. 'What would make you think that? Why would you think he wanted to see you?' Her voice seemed to lose conviction the more she spoke.

'What was his name?'

'Well… I don't remember… why?'

'You made me sit on his knee.'

'I did not.' She lit another cigarette, her hand had the merest hint of a shake as she held the match to it. 'Have you been telling tales to the psychiatrists? I told you never to talk to people like that. They'll twist your mind.'

'I remember sitting on his knee. I remember the dandruff, I remember the bad breath, stale fags…' The memory was turning her stomach.

Her mother would not meet her gaze and stood up. The woman was not someone normally troubled by guilt. But she looked guilty now.

'He was kind to us. Gave us money when we needed it, Caitlin. And you… You didn't mind.'

'I did mind. "Give your uncle a kiss." I did mind.'

'He was harmless enough and I never left you alone with him.'

'So, you were there.' She swallowed hard taking in what this meant. 'What did you let him do to me?'

'It was all right… He never made you cry.'

Something pushed down and forgotten was forcing its way to the surface. 'I was sick.' She was shaking. A deep, primitive anger.

Her mother simply stared ahead, with a fixed expression. Jaw clenched.

'I was sick every time. I hated him.'

'You've remembered this all wrong. He didn't do anything…'

'Stop lying.'

'Watch your tongue. How dare you accuse me. Your own mother of…' Her mum shook a finger at her.

George reappeared with the coffee.

'Is everything all right?'

'No!' She snatched a cup and threw it at her mother. It missed, but hit the wall, coffee splattered on shiny red bricks. She ran inside, down a long corridor.

'Hey! Caitlin, wait!' George called after her. But she couldn't stop. She just needed to run. Didn't care where. She had to get away. She remembered running. Running up Boggart Hill. Running to get away from the man after he gave her money for sweets. Being sick.

Then she was outside on the front steps. Tried to spot the hire car, but shaking with rage and tears couldn't focus. George appeared. She couldn't speak. He hugged her and squeezed her tight. She cried into his shoulder, felt the strength of his arms. Felt safe. They stood like that for a bit and slowly she began to feel calmer. Then he gave her the car keys and told her to wait there. She glanced around and saw her mother watching from inside the glass doors of the building. Good. At least her mum would see that someone really did care about her.

Five minutes later George got into the car. Asked if she wanted to talk about what had happened. She shook her head. All she wanted to do was forget. Forget all about her mother. Forget the grey-suited dandruff man.

'I'm sorry. I shouldn't have left you two alone.' He started the engine and gripped the gear stick.

She put her hand on his for a moment, gave it a squeeze and then let go. 'Thanks,' she said.

'What for?'

'Putting up with me.'

'I'm not putting up.'

'Well then, thanks for being you.' She wanted to say more, that he was her rock or something, but that sounded phoney and shit so she leaned over and planted an affectionate kiss on his cheek, then settled back and fastened her seat belt.

When they reversed out of the parking space, she saw her mum on the entrance steps of the building, smoking.

On the journey back, her thoughts darkened to what had gone so wrong with the meeting. Was it her fault for asking too many questions? Delving too deep. Put your hand in the slime and you might not like what you find. She would never forgive her mother. She knew what the dandruff 'uncle' had done. But she wasn't going to think about it. She was going to put that back in a box and seal it up for good.

The light was fading when they pulled up outside her flat in Belsize Gardens. They sat in the car for a while. She didn't want to get out. She didn't want to be alone. So asked George if he wanted to go for a drink.

'I've got to get the car back.'

She nodded. 'Well, we must do it again sometime.'

'Are you a glutton for punishment?'

She couldn't help smiling at that. 'I don't mean my mum. I mean a road trip.'

'Well, I suppose they couldn't object to me taking you to some uni open days.'

She grinned. 'You mean it?'

'I did it for my daughter, when she was about your age.'

'Manchester is top of my list so far. Maybe we could go there.'

'Okay. Deal.'

'I love you!' She got out of the car before he could say anything. Went to her front door, and turned to see the tail lights disappearing down the road.

TWENTY-FIVE

Parkside Hotel, Yeovil

He could hear Jedd pissing in the bathroom. The guy had asked to come up to the bedroom and 'use the facilities', before setting off back to Gloucestershire. He went in the bathroom and left the door wide open. The pissing went on a long time and Darren felt oddly uncomfortable having to listen to it. Eventually it stopped. Toilet flushed. Hands washed. Why was he listening to Jedd's ablutions? Why was it bothering him?

'How long are you gonna stay in Yeovil?' Jedd asked, emerging from the bathroom wiping his hands on the white hotel towel.

'Heading back tomorrow.'

'Pity, I was getting to like it here.' He grinned, forming dimples on his cheeks. He seemed to take up more space in the room than he should. Darren realised he was actually quite a big guy, but somehow had the air of an oversized baby about him. He looked around holding the towel, uncertain where to put it. 'Why don't we give it another shot tomorrow?'

'Aren't you working?'

'I'll come down after my shift.' Jedd threw the towel over the back of a chair. It slid off onto the floor. 'It's no bother.'

'I really should be getting back. Need a change of clothes.' The towel was crumpled in a damp heap on the beige carpet. It annoyed him, but he didn't want to pick it up himself. He wasn't going to skivvy for Jedd.

'Something the matter, mate?' Jedd asked, reading Darren's expression.

Darren's reply was to stare at the towel. Jedd took the cue and picked it up. 'Sorry. I can be a bit of a slut sometimes.' He threw the towel over his shoulder and took it into the bathroom.

Maybe they should spend another day searching for Grady. After all there was nothing waiting for him at home.

'It's a nice hotel this. Far too good for you!' Jedd said with a grin as he emerged from the bathroom. 'Wouldn't mind a couple of nights here myself.' He went to examine the minibar, checking its contents. 'How much is it a night?'

'Well…' He didn't want to say. Felt shy about that sort of thing, saying how much he paid for things. 'Bout a hundred quid.'

Jedd made a show of sucking in air over his teeth. 'You was robbed, mate.'

'You think?' he said, immediately regretting telling Jedd the truth.

'Still, if you can afford it.' He went over to the window. 'And it is quite a view from up here.'

It was a bit extravagant, checking into a hotel. He wouldn't normally do that. He'd have got a late train back. Save money. Apart from package holidays and family weddings, he never stayed in hotels. Even on a job a hundred miles from home, he'd drive back and forth every day. It's what you did. Did booking a hotel mean he was losing touch with who he really was?

'I could bring a uniform,' Jedd said.

'What?'

'If you need a change of clothes.'

'There's no need.'

'Otherwise it's a waste, isn't it? If we don't do another day on patrol since you paid for the hotel and all.'

'It's all right...' he mumbled.

'Got to get back for the wife, is it? Keeps you on a short leash?'

'No.'

'Need a lot of attention though, women. Can't leave them on their own too long.'

'She's not on her own. She's at her mother's.'

'Got a hall pass then!'

'Yeah. Suppose.' He wasn't sure what a hall pass was.

'We have plenty of uniforms at the depot. Let's look at you.' He came over and faced Darren. Placed his arms on his shoulders. Looked him up and down. 'Think I've got the size of you.'

'You really think it's worth another day?'

'Course I do! You need to keep the faith. We'll find her. We'll find Caitlin Grady together. Okay?'

Darren nodded. Perhaps one more day would do it.

'We'll make a security man out of you yet.'

Darren wasn't sure about that. Nor was he too keen on wearing a security guard uniform. It seemed a bit weird. He was beginning to think Jedd was a bit weird. But he couldn't put his finger on what it was about Jedd exactly. Just because he went for a piss and left the door open? Why had that bothered him? He was being stupid. If they'd been on a building site, he wouldn't think twice about a guy taking a leak within eye and earshot. So what was different about a hotel bedroom?

He got a WhatsApp message from Harvey accompanied by a photo.

Is this the same pic?

The photo was the same as the pic of Grady that Jedd had given him from Jenny. Puzzled, he texted back that it was indeed the same.

'Keeping tabs on you is she?' Jedd said, looking over.

'Sorry?'

'The wife?'

'Nah. It's this journalist from *The Daily Herald*.'

> Found it in our picture library. It's a stock image.

'Stock image. What's a stock image?' he mumbled.

Jedd looked at him with a blank expression, as though the words meant nothing.

He texted back:

> But it looks like Grady.

> Coincidence. It's a stock pic from Getty Images.
> Hope you didn't pay for it.

'Fucking hell!' he said to himself through clenched teeth. 'Fucking, fuckin…'

'Hey, buddy, what is it?'

He shook his head and went over to the window. Slammed it with the palm of his hand. Stared out at the view. The shopping centre roof, the church and below him, a woman was waiting to cross the busy road. He'd really believed Grady was out there somewhere in this town. What an idiot.

'You okay?'

Darren felt a hand on his shoulder. He spun round, knocking the hand away and gave Jedd a shove. 'Take me for a mug?' He glared at Jedd, suddenly loathing that smooth soft face.

'What's going on?'

'I think you know.'

'Mate, if you got something to say, spit it out.'

'Look! Look at this.' He held up the phone and showed the pic. 'It's the same pic. Stock fucking photo.'

'No shit?' He didn't seem that bothered.

'Did you know about this? Did you?' He felt the blood pumping in his head.

'Of course I didn't,' Jedd said evenly.

'Lying bastard!' He punched Jedd under the ribs with his left fist. He might as well have punched a rock. Jedd instantly punched back, hitting Darren in the stomach with a powerful blow which winded him. He dropped his phone and doubled up in pain, but driven by adrenaline, lunged at Jedd, knocking him into the bed. He managed to land a fist on his chin, before Jedd grabbed him and somehow got him in a chokehold. He couldn't breathe.

'Calm the fuck down, buddy.'

He tried to say something but couldn't. He was gasping for air.

'Are you calm?'

He nodded. Bloody bastard was strong as fuck.

Jedd released his grip. If he had any doubts that Jedd was ex-military, they were gone now. The guy was a fighting machine. Whereas he, Darren, had gone soft. At school he was good with his fists. Known to be someone you didn't mess with. Well look at him now. He wasn't just useless in a fight; his mind had gone soft too. Being taken for a ride by Jenny and Jedd. What a duo.

He sat down on the bed and looked up at Jedd feeling sorry for his miserable self. But from the expression on Jedd's face, you'd think he was the one that had received a beating, not Darren.

'Make sure of your facts before you hit out at someone next time,' Jedd said, moving towards the door.

'What facts?'

'Does it matter? You've already made your mind up.' He opened the door and stepped out.

'Wait. What facts?' Darren said, standing up, wincing at the pain in his belly.

Jedd turned to face him. 'You're not the only one who feels like a fucking mug. Jenny's made fools of us both. I'm the one who lost money. Okay?'

Jedd's eyes were burning. Angry, but he also seemed upset. Had Jenny really made a fool out of Jedd as well?

'Okay,' Darren replied. Maybe he had been too quick with his fists. The two stared at each other for a moment.

'You look like you need a drink,' Jedd said.

'I guess I do.' He sat down on the bed again.

Jedd went to the minibar and poured a whisky from a miniature bottle. 'Get this down you,' he said, before picking up Darren's phone and placing it on the bedside table.

'Thanks.' Darren wasn't much of a whisky drinker and the fluid burned the back of his throat. But it felt good just the same.

Jedd pulled up a chair and sat down. 'Sorry about the choke hold. It's just instinct. Wasn't a fair fight.'

It wasn't an unfair fight either. He'd struck the first blow after all, not Jedd. He might not like it, but Jedd was a better man in a fight. Then again, it was good to have someone like Jedd on his side. 'Jenny's the one in the wrong here, not you.'

Jedd nodded. 'Mates?' He held out his hand.

Darren took it. 'Mates.' He took another sip of whisky. 'Aren't you having a drink?'

'Driving, but I'll take a Coke if you don't mind.'

'Help yourself.'

They sat and drank in silence for a minute.

'So, what are we going to do about Jenny?' Jedd asked.

'Not sure,' he said, regretting now saying he'd help Jedd get his money back if she'd lied to them.

'We can't let this stand. She needs to be given a talking to.'

All right, so they'd been scammed, but he didn't feel like going round to her house. He doubted that Jedd only had talking in mind.

'How about we do a drive by. Lob a molly through her window. Easy.'

'Molly?' Did he mean a brick?

'Molotov cocktail? You know. Bottle bomb. Petrol, yeah?' he said as though he was talking about throwing a ball to a kid.

'A fire bomb!' Jesus that was a bit extreme. But then Jedd had mentioned burning down a house before.

'You think it's a bit OTT?'

'Just a fucking bit. Yeah I do.'

'Deserves it, though.'

'I don't know.' He shook his head.

'All right. What then?' He sounded disappointed at Darren's lack of enthusiasm.

'Besides it's too risky. If we get caught…?'

'Sometimes you just have to do what's right.'

Jenny might have scammed them, but she didn't deserve to have her house burned down. 'I'm not going to get banged up over Jenny. If I get banged up, it'll be over Grady.'

'Ah, yeah, see what you're saying, mate. So then, first off, I'll help you get to Grady, then when we've finished with her, you help me deal with Jenny.'

'I'm not firebombing her house.'

'Okay. No firebombs. Deal?'

Darren nodded, even though he had no intention of keeping his side of the bargain.

After Jedd left, he went to the bathroom, lifted his shirt and looked in the mirror. He was getting flabby, but there was no bruising so far. If he did come up in a bruise, how would he explain it to Kerry? But then, who knew when he was going to see his wife again?

He noticed the toiletries were missing. The little bottles he'd placed there weren't on the shelf. Jedd must have taken them. Why do that? Why not ask if he wanted some?

He got a beer from the minibar, and lying on the bed opened *The Daily Herald* app on his phone. Riley's Law was the only way to try and get to Grady now, so he checked for updates.

There was a link to this morning's interview and he couldn't help but follow it and watch himself and Amanda. He looked self-conscious and nervous, but when he ripped the mic off and walked out, he felt a surge of adrenaline and satisfaction. A worried expression flashed across Amanda Cheshire's smug face.

There was an update on the petition: A million online signatures, already. That was impressive and over the next few days, more would be coming through the post. It gave him a boost. Surely that guaranteed Riley's Law would come to pass?

TWENTY-SIX

Garland Avenue, Westcliffe

They were practising a thigh stand. His feet were planted apart, knees bent as though about to perform the haka. She stood barefoot on his thighs, her hands gripping his, their arms outstretched.

'You're good at this.' The fine golden hairs on his arms glistened in the afternoon sun.

'You think?' She was only good because his grip was strong enough to keep her from falling. Even so she could feel her calf muscles shaking, she was going to lose her balance any second.

He made her let go of one of his hands, and they both twisted round to face the kitchen window, free arms outstretched in a flourish. Then she felt her balance going and jumped down onto the grass.

'Take a bow,' he said, pointing at his mum who was watching them from the kitchen with an expression she couldn't read. Head tilted, half smiling. Was it approval or disdain? In any case she refused to bow, it was much too dumb. But gave his mum a hopeful wave.

'Is she still against you running away to the circus?'

'Pretty much.'

'And I get the blame for encouraging you?'

'Tell her you're going to be a lawyer. Then she'll think you're a good influence.'

'I might not be a lawyer.'

'I might not run away to the circus.'

The woman disappeared and Bert took the opportunity to give her a full-on kiss. He squeezed her arse as he did so. She moved his hand away.

'Not in front of your mum, please!'

'She's not watching.'

'All the same.'

'We could go to Battery Point later. For a walk.' He grinned suggestively.

'Maybe,' she replied, giving a playful punch. She knew why he wanted to go up there – to get away from his mum's watchful eye. She never left them alone for long, which Bert moaned about since they were both over eighteen and so on. Even his bedroom wasn't private.

She liked hanging in his bedroom. A trip into the world of Bert. There were boys at the secure children's home, but you couldn't go into their bedrooms and anyway this was different.

'You're so nosy,' he said as she went through his pile of video games.

'*Lego Star Wars*!'

'It's fun.'

She snorted.

'Well, it was when I was twelve.'

She liked the fact there was a whole history here. Echoes from his growing up. A formula one car; little plastic Star Wars figures; a big plastic dinosaur.

'Mum can't wait for me to go to uni, then she's going to give all my old stuff to the charity shop.'

'I'll keep it for you if you want.'

'What? Why?'

She shrugged and picked up a guitar, strumming the only chord she knew. 'Can you play?' She passed it to him.

'A bit. Gave up when I did my GCSEs.'

Nevertheless, he played a decent version of 'Perfect', by Ed Sheeran. She didn't know whether he was trying to say something. She was a sucker for a love song, so to avoid catching his eye while he played, she moved over to examine the bookcase. It was stuffed with fantasy must-haves, like *Lord of the Rings* and *His Dark Materials*. Plus, she was glad to see, *Harry Potter*. There were also half a dozen text books. She picked one out, *Further Maths – Modelling with Algorithms*. Every page was full of obscure hieroglyphs.

'Wow, how do you understand this stuff?' It was way beyond any maths she recognised.

'Dunno, I just have a knack for it. But it's not much fun, I don't enjoy it at all.' He twisted his nose.

She felt for him. To have a talent and not to get any pleasure out of it. That was a weird hand to have been dealt.

The real reason he took her to the bedroom was to make out. But they couldn't get carried away, not with his mum bustling around the house, which she was secretly grateful for. Sooner or later there'd be a knock at the door. The woman would wait precisely two seconds before opening it and bothering them with some question or other, like whether they wanted a cheese sandwich or a glass of Fanta.

'Who drinks Fanta?'

'I do.'

'Weird.'

'Something I got off my dad. He drinks it by the gallon.'

A flash of something sad passed across Bert's face and she felt her heart go out to him. Maybe they should go back to her place. Get close under the sheets. She did want that. To feel his body next to hers. Touch his perfect skin and feel his touch on her. She really did want that. But something was holding her back.

Later they were in the kitchen sitting at the breakfast bar, as his mum called it, having a snack and a lurid orange Fanta. Bert was demolishing a doorstep sandwich and she was pinching the odd bite. The kitchen was like something off a TV commercial. High gloss white units. Surfaces with mottled white marble-effect laminate. If the sun shone in here, you'd need your Ray-Bans. The soundtrack, provided by Jazz FM radio, seemed to match the TV commercial vibe.

The ice in her drink came from a fridge which actually had an ice dispenser. She didn't know such things existed in real life. Mrs Fernandes must have some cash. It wasn't just the kitchen that was immaculate. She herself was also perfectly turned out. Like her own mother, her make-up was carefully done, although more subtle and less tarty if she was being honest. And those perfect teeth, and high cheekbones. A designer face. Did she have discreet gentlemen callers like her mum? Is that where the money came from?

God's sake! Listen to yourself. Not everyone is like your own mum.

'Are you sure you don't want your own sandwich, love? It's no bother. No bother at all.'

'No thanks, Mrs Fernandes.'

'You'll have a biscuit at least?' No one could say Mrs Fernandes didn't play the part of a mumsy mother, which considering everything was so tidy and spic and span, Catilin found weirdly odd. Also odd was the fact that she'd never said to call her by her first name.

A plate of biscuits appeared on the shiny breakfast bar. She thanked the woman and took one, but hesitated to bite into it. It was the sort of kitchen where a single crumb would stand out like a bad pimple on a pretty face, but Mrs Fernandes appeared with a plate for her.

Caitlin smiled; this must be what it's like to have a real mother.

'She's a bit of a control freak,' Bert whispered when she moved away to put some washing in the machine.

The jazz stopped and the news came on. To her dismay, she found herself having to listen to some random MP going on about Riley's Law. He was going to introduce an Early Day Motion in Parliament, whatever that was.

She'd seen the clip of the interview with Darren Burgess. She remembered him from the trial all too well. He never took his eyes off her. She avoided looking his way as much as possible, but whenever she glanced over, there he was, staring at her. Eyes smouldering with hate. If they ever came face to face, he'd kill her. She knew that.

She'd got a bit obsessed with that clip. There was something fascinating about it. At first, she'd enjoyed how he looked so nervous and out of his depth on the TV, served him right for trying to get to her with his bloody Riley's Law. Amanda Cheshire had been great, the way she'd taken her side and not his, and she couldn't help but laugh when he stomped off the set like a bad actor in a soap opera. But each time she watched it, she laughed less and began to see something unsettling about the man, huffing and puffing in front of millions. Impotent. Inconsolable. She could see the pain he was in. And she, Caitlin, was responsible.

She mustn't go down that road. She wasn't Caitlin – child killer. She was Anna now. Amazing Anna. But if Riley's Law ever became a reality, then there'd be no leaving Caitlin behind would there? If that happened, she might as well jump off the end of the pier.

'Earth to Anna!' Bert was saying.

'Sorry what? Distracted by the news.'

'Why?'

She shrugged. 'Just a thing about Riley's Law.'

'Oh, right.' He turned to his mum. 'Anna's applying to take law at uni.'

'Well, good for you.' Mrs Fernandes nodded approvingly. 'Perhaps you'll end up at the same university.' Then added with emphasis, 'If Bert takes up his place in mathematics.'

'Yeah, maybe we will.' She winked at Bert.

'There's more in the paper about Riley's Law, if you're interested.'

'It's okay. Just in case it comes up at my interview.' She tried to sound like she couldn't care less, but felt a sharp twist of anxiety in her gut.

'Interview?' Bert said, frowning. 'Kept that to yourself.'

'So what will you say to them, if it does come up?' his mum asked.

'Mum, she's not here for the third degree.'

'It's practice for the interview,' the woman said, put out.

She was getting herself in a tangle. She shouldn't have mentioned Riley's Law. Or a non-existent interview. Mrs Fernandes was looking at her, waiting for an answer.

'Well, I'd say…' How should she answer? If she said what she felt, it might reveal too much. But she couldn't bear to say Riley's Law was a good idea. Her heart was starting to race. 'If someone has served their time,' she said, struggling to keep her voice steady, 'don't they deserve to be left to live in peace?'

'Well, I'd want to know if a child killer was living next door. Wouldn't you?'

'I…' She couldn't speak. She coughed. Tried to take some Fanta, but her hand was shaking. Mrs Fernandes's stare was freaking her out. She gave up and put the glass down. How could there be such a treacherous bear-trap in a suburban kitchen?

Mrs Fernandes carried on, 'You know they've got over a million signatures now. That's how strongly people think.'

She was going to give herself away. The woman would be

able to tell that she was part of it. 'I suppose,' was all she managed.

'You agree then, with Riley's Law?'

'Mum, give it a rest will you.'

She sat rigid. Feeling faint.

'Are you all right, love? You're looking a bit pale.'

'I think maybe the acrobatics… Given me a funny tummy. Excuse me.' She jumped down from the breakfast bar and rushed into the garden. Took slow deep breaths and tried to calm herself.

Bert followed her out. 'What's up?' He looked concerned, but she found it hard to meet his eyes.

'I'll be fine in a minute,' she said with false brightness. 'Just give me a sec. Let me chill.'

'It's my mum, isn't it? She should be a lawyer herself, the way she cross examines everyone.'

She managed a weak smile at that. 'She's all right. But I think I'll head off, if you don't mind.'

'Oh. I thought we were going to hang at Battery Point later.' He looked deflated, like she'd just cancelled Christmas.

'Soz. I'm just not feeling it.' She did feel sorry. It wasn't his fault she freaked out.

'Buy you a drink then?'

She didn't have the heart to refuse, so they went to The Tudor.

After a pint of cider, she began to relax. She'd over-reacted to Mrs Fernandes's questioning. The woman could not see inside her soul. She needed to toughen up. Face people down, not act weird and guilty. Think Amazing Anna.

She looked around the pub, suddenly worried that the gorgeous, braided haired girl might show up. Just the thought of her caused a stab of jealousy. The way this jealousy thing ambushed her was disturbing.

'You expecting someone?' he asked.

'No. Why? Are you?' she said, searching those pale grey eyes.

'No.'

'Sure you're not waiting for anyone?'

'Like who?' His look was open and sincere. And she was not going to come across as a jealous bitch by asking about that girl.

'Well then, shall we go back to mine?' She said it without thinking. It was probably a bad idea. Would she go rigid and close down like she'd done that day in the pillbox? Or would she drop her guard and say too much?

TWENTY-SEVEN

Boggart Hill, Pennywell

H e zipped his navy fleece against the damp chill. But the dismal atmosphere seemed more than just weather, as if some bad energy was lurking on Boggart Hill. He felt uneasy as he made his way through long wet grass towards Riley's tree. He was carrying a bunch of red roses bought from a kiosk at the railway station.

'Who's the lucky lady?' the woman had said as he paid. He didn't know how to answer. 'Or man,' she added hastily.

The flowers he'd left at the base of the lonely tree last time were still tied to its base, petals discoloured and on their way to slime. Stooping down he replaced them with the fresh flowers. The card he'd written was still there too, but he was taken aback by what he saw. Something was scrawled across it in thick red letters.

Sorry

Looked like it had been written in wax crayon.

The card was softened with rain and damp. The blue ink from his own dedication had leached into the cardboard, fading and blurring the message.

To my Riley. Love Daddy.

The new message was written right across his, in large badly formed letters. Who was the author? Who wanted to come up here to say sorry after all these years?

Grady?

Was that her writing scrawled across his card? It must be. Who else? His anger began to well up, a torment in his belly. He clenched his jaw trying to push it back. How dare she come up here, to this spot? To this sacred spot and scrawl her half-hearted apology. He wanted to spit.

She must have sneaked up here under cover of her new identity. He looked around, half expecting to see her. But he was alone. A dog barked in the distance. A hollow sound that echoed around the inside of his skull.

He folded the card carefully, placed it in his jacket pocket and wandered over to the edge of the railway cutting. Below him, a freight train was rumbling down the track. Its wagons, piled high with stones, stretched way into the distance.

Down there somewhere were the mangled parts of dolls that Tracey and Grady had left. Squashed and mutilated limbs by the side of the tracks. Confirmation of Grady's malicious nature. He felt compelled to see evidence of her handiwork with his own eyes and found himself slithering and sliding down the steep embankment. At the bottom of the slope, he pushed through the remains of a rusty fence. In front of him, the endless freight train was still thundering past. The heavy wagons made the ground shudder and the tracks move as axels passed over.

Then it was gone. A strange, unnerving silence descended on the tracks, the air moist and still. He searched amongst the stones, old wooden sleepers and scrub at the side of the railway, but all he found was the odd crisp packet, a couple of shredded plastic bags and a rotting fag packet. That was about it. No broken dolls or children's toys. Pity. He could have sent photos to the papers.

Inside the sick mind of Caitlin Grady.

A train came fast, out of nowhere. Blasted its horn as it screamed past. He hadn't heard it coming and it gave him a shock. If you didn't watch out, you'd end up splattered over the front of a train. What kind of kids came down here to play chicken? It beggared belief. He grimaced at the thought, just as another train came past. Why did no one stop them?

He didn't much fancy the climb back up the side of the cutting. It was steep and he'd have to scramble on his hands and knees to get to the top. Instead he walked along the railway, hoping to find a place to get to the road. A couple of minutes' walk and he was on the embankment overlooking Pennywell City Farm. He stopped to peer through a fence at the gardens and allotments.

The day it happened started like any other day. There'd been no hint of anything bad in the air. No bird flew into the window that morning as he was spooning Cheerios into Riley's reluctant mouth. No black cat crossed their path on the way to the city farm. The day was so ordinary, it hurt to think about it. How could things have gone so wrong, so quickly? If there'd been a clear omen, it might be easier to accept. It would have meant a dark force beyond his or anyone else's control was at work. The very ordinariness of the day made it worse somehow.

He set off down the tracks again, but came to an abrupt halt when he saw a couple of men emerge onto the railway a few hundred metres away. Railway workers sporting orange high visibility jackets. Or were they transport police looking for metal thieves?

He turned back and finding a weak point in the fence, managed to get through and scramble down the embankment, push through some undergrowth into the allotments and safety of the city farm. The foliage here was still thick from summer growth. He couldn't be seen from the railway; he was safe among the familiar paths and borders.

But the fact that Grady had been to Pennywell was disturbing. He couldn't shake off the feeling that she might still be in the area. Maybe she was right here, at the city farm, skulking amongst the shrubs and bushes.

There was no one much around, apart from a middle-aged woman in muddy jeans digging at an allotment. But the more he thought about it, the more he became convinced that Grady really was here, and began to look for her, driven by a kind of belligerent excitement. Like a thug looking for trouble on a night out. He double-checked all the allotments, the Vegetable Corner and Healing Herb Circle. Then headed over to the goat field, and the pig pen, that Riley had hated the smell of.

Stinky pig!

Finally, he went to the farmyard, where they'd let the chickens out to cluck and roam. There was no sign of anyone that could conceivably be Grady. All the same, that didn't mean she wasn't here. She could be hiding from him. Watching him. The way she must have watched Riley that day. He spun around suddenly as if to try and catch her out. Course she wasn't there, but it felt to him that she was never far away. Everywhere and yet nowhere, something illusive and spectral.

Why had she come to the city farm that day? Was it with the intention of abducting a child as the prosecution claimed? She must have been watching Riley and then waited for her opportunity. Otherwise how had it happened so fast? But why did she pick out Riley? Of all the kids there that day, what had Riley done to be picked on and murdered? Was there something that attracted her? Or had Riley done something to offend Grady, pulled a face at her, or something like that.

The reason Grady chose Riley never came out at the trial. But now he wanted to know. Needed answers.

'Why? For God's sake, why?' he appealed to the indifferent grey sky.

He was in the farm's café, sipping tepid tea, wondering what to do with the teabag which had been left in the plastic beaker. A kid in a nearby highchair was staring at him, the way kids do sometimes, without any inhibition. The kid was trying to avoid his mother spooning something gooey into his mouth. Darren pulled a silly face making the kid laugh, allowing the mum to pop some food into the child's mouth, which he automatically swallowed. Darren gave the kid an exaggerated wink. The child distorted his face trying to wink back without success. His mum managed to deposit another spoonful.

Darren grinned to himself. Felt a glimmer of dad-like pride. He was still a man who could relate to kids, something he learned when he became a father himself. The young mother glanced over, looked like she was in her mid-twenties. Her hair was untidy, but her eyes were bright. He smiled at her. She allowed a shy smile and tilt of the head. He suddenly felt emotional. Moved that he'd managed to connect to this mother-and-child world. A world he'd been running away from for ten years.

He'd been in two minds about coming in here. But Jedd was on his way, and he couldn't think of anywhere else to wait. He had to steel himself to get over the threshold though. The entrance to the café was where the nightmare began.

Riley was by the duck pond that day. He had one eye on her, but was arguing with Kerry. She wanted to go to McDonald's. He wanted to wait in the queue.

'You don't even like McDonald's,' he reminded Kerry.

'Riley's desperate to get a diplodocus.' They were giving

little plastic dinosaurs away with kids' happy meals and Riley was collecting them.

'You're always going on about junk food and additives.'

'Then she'll have the whole set.'

'Preservatives, salt, fat, sugar, E-numbers,' he said, quoting her own list of bad things in junk food back at her with sarcastic emphasis.

'Where's Riley?'

It was such a pointless stupid argument.

Jedd looked out of place in his security uniform as he paced slowly and purposefully into the café. People looked over and stared as he approached Darren's table, as though they expected him to make an arrest. Or throw Darren out, like a nightclub bouncer.

He sat down and surveyed the scene like he was looking for felons. The mother and kid in the highchair were just leaving, she gave Darren an acknowledging wave as she went.

'You dirty bastard,' Jedd said with a wink.

'What!'

'You know,' he said. Then got up and, avoiding a piece of discarded sandwich on the tiled floor, went to the counter to order a coffee and a home-made cake.

'Lipstick,' Jedd announced, when he showed him the card with the message scrawled across it.

It was somehow even worse that she'd written in lipstick. Sort of thing a mistress might do, writing an intimate message to her illicit lover.

'This is not half bad,' Jedd said, washing his cake down with coffee. 'Want a bite?'

He did not. The thought that the message on his card was written by something that had touched Grady's lips made him feel sick.

'She's taking the piss, isn't she? Big time,' Jedd said, examining the card again.

A kid ran past, bumping into their table and spilling some juice on Jedd's shoe. He bristled and muttered under his breath, then seemed to realise he was supposed to tolerate kids in a place like this and smiled. 'Kids, huh.' But the smile was thin and false; he was uncomfortable in this world.

'We can go somewhere else,' Darren said, feeling a bit smug. Here in this café, he felt a certain superiority over his friend. He had been an actual father, whereas he could tell that kids were an alien species to Jedd.

'No it's fine,' he said, rubbing his scar.

'Grady's barred from Bristol. Shouldn't ever go up to Boggart Hill. We should tell the police.'

But Jedd seemed to have already thought things through. 'They'll just sit on it. Nothing will happen. Won't change anything. Maximum, just give her a slap on the wrist.'

He sighed, the guy was probably right about that.

'They might even have allowed her back to the scene anyway. Part of her rehabilitation or whatever, cus they are all such a bunch of bleeding-heart liberals, aren't they?'

'Too right.' Darren looked at the scrawled red lettering. Dug his fingernails into the back of his neck.

'It's not just taking the piss. It's personal. Making a fool out of you. That's what she's doing.'

'You think?'

'What makes it personal, is writing over your card. If she was genuinely sorry, she'd have bought her own damn card.'

Grady was trying to get at him, wasn't she? Make some sick minded point. Well he'd make her eat her words. Literally. Shove that card down her throat so she choked on it.

A nearby toddler let out an ear-piercing high-pitched scream. When Riley tried that trick, screaming like that, he took her outside to calm her down, instead of inflicting the screams on everyone else. He tutted loudly, attracting nasty looks from a couple of women on the next table. Well fuck them. These people who don't control their kids. Don't care what they get up to. These were the sort of people who'd simply shrugged their shoulders when they'd seen Riley being dragged off by Caitlin Grady.

Jedd raised his eyebrows and smirked. 'Welcome to the monkey house.'

Suddenly he didn't want to be sitting in this café sipping tea, putting up with kids shouting and mewling and spilling things. The bits of food dropped all over the floor were disgusting. He got to his feet.

'Hey, mate. You okay?' Jedd asked.

'Need some air.' He stomped outside to the car park where Jedd caught up with him.

'I need to get to the train station. Get back to Swindon.'

'Oh.' Jedd looked disappointed.

'Sorry. Shouldn't have dragged you out here.'

'No worries. It's good to see you. But it must be tough being back here after what happened.'

He nodded. Grateful that Jedd understood.

Jedd added, 'I'll just carry on here for a bit.' There was something in his eyes, not exactly a twinkle but something.

'Carry on?'

'Yeah you know. What we're here for. Finding Grady.'

'I checked the place already. There's no sign.'

'Yeah, but you know, I'll feel better if I check before I leave. If another child were to disappear…'

He hadn't thought of that. That Grady might have returned here to repeat her crime. He couldn't let Jedd search alone.

'I guess four eyes would be better than two.'

Jedd grinned. 'They would.'

They were standing in silence looking at the plastic dinosaurs swinging around in the breeze. Their colours seemed more faded than ever in the light. They were losing their essence. The only bright spot was the bunch of red roses he'd left earlier.

They'd come up here after spending more than an hour searching the city farm for Grady.

'Perpetrators often make repeated visits to the scene of a violent crime,' Jedd said. He sounded grim. 'I even saw that toe-rag, the one who killed my sister, hanging round the intersection where he mowed her down.'

'Really?'

'Not long after the crime, out on bail he was, went back there.'

'What a bastard.'

'Can't leave it alone can they? Have to come back. Relive it. Their moment of glory.' He gave a hollow ironic laugh, but his face was full of disgust. 'Taking a life, you know it can make you feel like God. Powerful. Invincible. The moment in their life when they really lived. When they were someone. Their moment of actuality. Going back to the scene is a way of squeezing every last drop of pleasure from what they did.'

'That's just so sick.'

'Oh yeah.' He nodded. 'It's a sickness of the soul all right.' He sounded thoughtful. More thoughtful than Darren had ever seen him. Looked genuinely sad. Probably thinking about his sister.

Jedd got a box of matches out of his pocket and lit one. It flared up like a small firework as the phosphorous burned, but then it faded and flickered. The flame managed to hang on a moment, before a gust of wind snuffed it out.

'For Riley,' he said, tossing the match over to the base of the tree. A thin strand of smoke from the smouldering match snaked up into the air, before disappearing on the wind.

He'd been secretly put out that Jedd insisted coming up here. To his private place, where he imagined he was alone with Riley. But something had passed between them. An understanding you couldn't put into words. So now he was glad he'd shown Jedd Riley's tree.

Jedd turned to him. 'Grady made a big mistake writing that card. A tactical error,' he said with a considered smile. 'Showed her hand, hasn't she? The sort of person she really is. People will be outraged about her coming up here to gloat.'

'You think I should tell Harvey Pringle?'

'Give him the card. Get him to create a stink.' He paused a moment and looked out over the city stretching away, in the distance you could make out the hills south of Bristol. 'Someone out there knows something. Maybe after they read about her being here, they won't be able to hold their tongue.'

Jedd wanted to drive him back to Swindon. Darren explained he had a train ticket, but Jedd was insistent, told him he had something cool to show him.

The something was Jedd's new van. 'Bought with you-know-who in mind,' he said, grinning like a kid with a new toy as he showed off its very particular features.

It was a white transit with a couple of dark tinted windows on the side. 'Got it at an auction of ex-police vehicles. Cheap as chips,' Jedd explained. You could still make out traces of the faded police logo on the bodywork. But the highlight was the way the rear doors of the van opened into a cage, where suspects were once detained and transported to the cop shop.

'Grady's new mobile home.'

Darren was gobsmacked.

'We're going to have to keep her somewhere, right? So what do you think?'

He wasn't sure what to think about it. But it was, he had to admit, impressive.

'Is there a key?' Darren said, examining the cage door.

'Yes. Course.'

He was amazed that they hadn't disabled the lock or something. Amazed it was actually legal to sell a prison on wheels in the first place.

'Want to give it a try? Get a feel of what we've got in store for her?' Jedd gave him a playful shove.

'You first!'

Jedd winked and climbed in the back and sat on a hard metal seat. 'There's room for two.'

Darren got in as well. Sat opposite Jedd, who shut the cage door with a resounding metallic clang. They sat staring at each other.

'Cosy, isn't it?'

He wondered how many prisoners had been transported in here. Would he himself ever be locked in a vehicle like this? If they snatched Grady. He might well be.

Between the cage and the driver's cab there were seats and a table, where officers could sit and do paperwork, and presumably eat doughnuts if they got peckish on a job. You could see outside through the smoked glass window, but people couldn't easily see in.

On the drive to Swindon, he began to imagine that Grady was in the back. That they were taking her somewhere. The van made the whole project seem more real. They were actually going to find her and lock her in the back. He would be in control. She would be fretting and worrying, while he took his sweet time deciding what to do with her. Maybe it would go some way to making her feel sorry for what she did. Revenge is a dish best served cold, they said didn't they? Well his heart was cold now. But was it cold enough to kill?

TWENTY-EIGHT

Belsize Gardens, Westcliffe

Her phone vibrated, waking her up. A text. She sent an exploratory arm out from under the duvet to grab it. The warmth of Bert's body caressed her as he slumbered next to her, oblivious to the phone. She paused for a moment to breathe in his musty after-sex smell. It was intoxicating. She wished she could bottle that smell. She peered at the phone, eyes sticky with sleep.

> We need to meet. Urgent.

Her heart jumped, banishing the delicious drowsiness. Something must have happened for George to send a text this early. Sounding so dramatic wasn't his style, either.

She sat up and surveyed the room. They had hardly set foot outside the flat all weekend and the detritus of days spent in bed was all around. Clothes strewn about the floor. An empty bottle of cheap wine. A Domino's Pizza box. A candle burned down, its solidified wax pooled onto the table. Empty pink foil condom packets. Ironic that such a perfect long weekend created such a messy fallout. Every action has an equal and opposite reaction. Law of the universe.

She looked at the naked body next to her and felt a surge of desire. The sex with Bert had been tentative at first. Despite his obvious arousal, he was a little shy, and admitted he was a virgin. She was surprised, but it was reassuringly honest of him to say so. They were in the same boat, although strictly speaking she wasn't sure that she was as pure as Bert.

As they became more confident, she found herself taking the lead, which he seemed to like. So did she, she enjoyed the feeling of being in control. Stark contrast to the rest of her life, in which she appeared to be at the mercy of forces beyond her reach. Forces, that she suspected from George's urgent message, were on the move again.

She slipped a T-shirt on and jumped out of bed. Didn't have time to linger. Texted George suggesting they meet on the pier, then filled the kettle, which caused Bert to stir.

'It's wham bam thankyou man,' she said, flicking the switch to boil the water.

'Eh,' he said, squinting at her, rubbing his eyes.

'Gonna have to throw you out, I'm afraid.'

He sat up. 'Why, what did I do?'

'Corrupted the innocent.' She grinned. 'Coffee?'

'You're so fucking gorgeous! Come back here.' He patted the bed. 'Please?'

She shook her head. 'No way, I gotta go out.' But then softened, went to him, bent over and kissed his forehead. 'Sorry, baby.'

She gave him a coffee and went to freshen up in the shower. Catching herself in the bathroom mirror, felt amazed he could love her despite the mess she looked first thing in the morning.

The sea was grey and the air had a chilling bite to it. Summer was over. Her thin jacket wasn't up to its task, and as she stepped onto the pier, the full force of the blustery wind caused her to shiver.

George was waiting at the end of the pier. He was wearing a long black coat and a scarf around his neck. His face as bleak and disturbed as the heavy sky. He nodded but didn't speak, his cold lips forming a severe smile.

'You should be wearing a hat. You'll get a chill on your brain in this,' she said.

His hard smile remained fixed. The wind made her eyes moist.

'I wanted to tell you in person.' He took a deep breath. 'I've been suspended.'

'What? What does that mean?'

'There's going to be a story in tomorrow's *Daily Herald*. It's about us.'

'Us? You and me!?'

He nodded. 'Alleging we are having an inappropriate relationship, although I doubt that's the language they will use.'

'But we're not,' she said, indignant at the idea. They'd been through this. All right so there'd been some affection. Just friendly affection, that was all. Wasn't that allowed anymore? People just jumped to conclusions and judged. It made her blood boil.

'The newspaper gave the Ministry of Justice the opportunity of responding before publication. Which is why we know about it.'

'So we're not allowed even to be friends?'

'And the response of the department is to suspend me.' He shook his head. 'Pending a full investigation.' He spoke as if the cold wind had got inside him and dried out his heart. 'I have to go up to the head office in London for a debrief. That is, a telling off.'

'Where's all this shit come from?'

'Apparently they have evidence, although what evidence remains to be seen, because they wouldn't tell me anything.'

'My bloody mother!'

He tilted his head. 'Well possibly, but what evidence could she possibly have?' He cleared something from his eye and turned away to look out to sea.

'I'm sorry.' She put a hand on his shoulder. He covered her hand with his, gave a squeeze, but after a moment, he let go and turned back to face her.

'Caitlin, I can't be your probation officer anymore.'

'Okay,' she said, wondering if that might be a good thing. Maybe without pressure, they could be normal friends.

He cleared his throat. 'I won't be allowed to see you, or make contact with you in any way.'

'No! That can't be right.'

'I shouldn't even be here now.'

'That's not fair.'

'Also, if my name comes out, and it might well, I'll be a security risk. People will follow me to get to you.' He looked pained, like he was suffering from some internal wound.

'But they'd have to find you first, right?' She laughed nervously. The situation was slipping away from her.

'It's my fault. I should never have—'

'What? What? We did nothing wrong.'

'I did wrong. I let myself become…' He sighed, unable to finish the sentence. 'Tammy will take over from me full-time.'

'But after this investigation or whatever… then…'

He shook his head. 'I'll probably be transferred to another region.'

'So are you saying… Are you actually saying, this is it? Goodbye?' She swallowed, forcing back threatening tears.

'It has to be. I fucked up. Sorry.' He adjusted his scarf and clasped his hands behind his neck.

'But we can still meet, can't we, whether you're my probation officer or not?'

'I'm not allowed to see you.'

'They can't stop us meeting!' Her voice sounded shrill and desperate.

He closed his eyes and hung his head, but didn't seem able to say anything.

'George. Look at me. Look at me!'

He took a deep breath before he could face her. She could see how tense his jaw was. Holding something inside. She wished he'd let it out, whatever it was.

'I'll be fired,' was all he managed to say to her unspoken question.

'So! So what?'

'I can't. I'm sorry. I can't trash what's left of my credibility.'

Her world seemed to be spinning off its axis. 'I need you,' she blurted out.

'Tammy will take care of you. She's a fine probation officer.'

'I'm sure she'll be very professional,' she spat.

'You've got Bert. And you've university to look forward to.'

'Bert doesn't know me!' She shook her head. 'What do they say? Lovers come and lovers go, but friends, true friends they stay with you. They stick.' She bit her lip.

He just looked blank.

'But you're not a friend, are you?'

'It's more complicated than whether I'm your friend or not.'

'No, George, it isn't. It's not complicated at all.' She swallowed again, desperate to hold back the tears. But it was no good, her eyes filled.

'Hey!' He went to try and comfort her. But she shoved him away.

'It's nothing. Just the wind.' She turned to go.

'Caitlin, wait!'

She stopped for a moment. Feeling his eyes on her. But she couldn't bear to turn and face him.

'Don't let's end it like this. Please?'

Why not? Why shouldn't she end it like this? When it came down to it, he just didn't care enough. Which was about as much good as not caring at all. So fuck him then, for trying to be all civilised about it. She set off again, walking at a measured deliberate pace away from him, towards the promenade.

She thought for a moment that he might come after her. Catch up. Apologise and beg forgiveness like they would in some dumb romantic movie. But it wasn't one of those kind of movies. They weren't those kind of people, so why was she thinking like that? Nevertheless it took will power not to stop, turn and go back.

As she walked past the amusement stands, she noticed the Ten Penny Falls was closed for winter. Irrationally she thought of Tracey. They'd only been kids, but she'd never managed to have another friend as close as Tracey. Probably never would.

TWENTY-NINE

Woodside Garden Centre, Swindon

W ater cascaded down a small rocky waterfall. He was at the garden centre in search of roses, making good on his word to create a proper back garden. But he'd got distracted by the water features. Fountains which spurted high into the air when you approached, or more modest bubbly affairs with water spilling over smooth silver orbs.

Then, he saw the mermaid and was smitten as a sailor. The green copper-effect creature was sitting on the edge of a pond, her tail in the water, while more water cascaded from a shell she was holding. Her face passive, but thoughtful.

Kerry loved mermaids. And he loved Kerry. Still. He let out a tired groan.

Give it time, Darren. Give it time and she'll be back.

He watched as other men, some with kids in tow, were buying bags of compost and mulch, or rakes to clear up the autumn leaves that would soon be falling. He imagined them returning to their warm bright houses and the family life they had built. Well then, he'd do some building of his own.

He was mulling over the idea of buying a preformed blue plastic pond when he noticed someone looking at him. A big bloke. Overweight. Legs too short for his bulky torso. The man looked away pretending not to have seen Darren. But he was sure he knew him from somewhere.

He got it when he was looking at rolls of heavy black waterproof membrane. It was mole-wrench Jim, Kerry's workmate, who'd helped her with the dripping tap. They'd met a few times at Kerry's work Christmas dos and such. Had Jim heard from Kerry? Presumably not, if she really was on her mum's boat. But he couldn't help feel a pang of suspicion, especially because of the way Jim had pretended not to notice him and seemed over-keen on inspecting a garden shed. But Kerry couldn't possibly fancy him, could she? Since when had he become so suspicious?

He was distracted by a text from Jedd.

Riley's Law war chest now at £5000.

Jedd had been spending the last few days setting up a site dedicated to the Riley's Law appeal. For a security guard, he seemed to know a lot about how to build websites, handle online payments and so on. Darren was convinced that no one would send any money, and they'd be lucky to get more than a few quid. How wrong can you be? All the publicity surrounding Riley's Law was building up momentum. Money was flowing in. It was a vote of confidence that he was doing the right thing. People were on his side. Jedd's idea was to use the money to lobby members of parliament. He wasn't sure quite how that worked, but whatever, Jedd was on the case.

'We'll need some tame lawyers on side and they'll want their pound of flesh.'

He was constantly surprised how resourceful and knowledgeable Jedd was. There was clearly a lot more to him than being a simple security guard. He wondered about Jedd's past. He didn't really know much about him. Well whatever

Jedd had done in a past life, he Darren was getting the benefit. It seemed at that moment like it was a match made in heaven. Jedd had come along, just when he needed him most.

The mermaid was perched at the front of Darren's trolley, like a ship's figurehead as he sailed into the car park. She was kept in place by the wherewithal for making a garden pond. He saw Jim again, leaning against an ugly oversized four-by-four. The fat car suited the fat man. There was no avoiding the guy; his car was parked in the same row as Darren's.

'Jim.' He gave an acknowledging nod as he wheeled the trolley past.

'Darren. How's the missus, all right?' There was a sneer to his voice. He knew that Kerry had walked out.

'All right thanks,' he said with an aggressive stare, daring him to say something else.

Jim nodded, opened the door and shifted his bulk into his car. Darren loaded the mermaid and pond equipment into the back of his van. As he returned his trolley, he saw Jim was still sitting there. The man glanced up from his phone as Darren walked past giving an embarrassed smile.

Back home, he carried the mermaid to the front door, like a bridegroom taking his new wife across the threshold. But as soon as he opened the door, he sensed something was different. There was a faint smell of perfume in the air. Kerry's. He shouted her name in a rush of enthusiasm. He wanted to show her the mermaid and tell her about his planned water feature. But there was no reply. Then he noticed that Kerry's winter coat and thick jacket were no longer hanging in the hallway.

'Kerry?' he shouted again, running upstairs to their bedroom still holding the damn mermaid. The wardrobe doors were flung wide open. Kerry's clothes were gone.

For a confused second, he thought the place had been burgled. But that didn't make sense. The small bedroom TV was still there and so was all his stuff. He threw the mermaid on the bed. Sat next to it, his head reeling.

She'd sneaked in while he wasn't there. That was low. And he knew who'd put her up to that. Bloody fat Jim whatisface. He'd been spying on him. Watched the house, waiting till he went out, then texted Kerry the coast was clear. Followed him to the garden centre to keep an eye on him, while she cleared out her things. The bastard! He shook his head, trying to clear his brain.

He phoned Kerry, but she didn't answer. So he sent a series of angry texts. How could she do this to him? How sly she'd been. How they should at least try and talk. Sneaky, underhand, bitch-move.

She didn't like that word: *bitch*. But she was. In a way, he really had been burgled. Robbed of the chance to make it up to her. He'd been banking on trying to win her over when she came back for more of her things. Well she wouldn't be back anymore, she'd taken everything. For a second he felt like crying. This betrayal was hitting him harder than when she'd first left. That had seemed little more than a difference of opinion about Grady. But now, taking her stuff made it really hit home. Like someone had nutted him.

He needed a drink, but couldn't face going out. Found a bottle of lurid green liquor someone had given them one Christmas. Took it upstairs to the bedroom and sat next to the mermaid to drink it. Got through the whole bottle. It made him feel sick and gave him a headache.

Thoughts chased each other around his brain. She was stupid for throwing away the marriage like that. Not giving it more of a chance. But she'd realise eventually. She'd see what a fat bastard Jim was. She'd miss him and be back. Once he'd dealt with Grady. It was Grady's fault. Grady had wrecked his marriage. Round and round, over and over the same thoughts. His brain a hamster on a treadmill.

His mobile rang; the number wasn't in his contacts. Had Kerry changed her number?

'Darren?' A woman's voice, not Kerry. But sounded familiar.

'Yeah,' he slurred.

'It's Tracey.' She waited as though expecting a reaction. 'From Pennywell?' she prompted.

'Yeah, whadyouwant?'

'Are you all right?'

'Never felt better.'

'If it's not a good time…'

'Great timing. I'm having the best bloody time in my fucking life. How about you?' He took a swig from the bottle, but then remembered it was empty.

'It's about Caitlin.'

'Having a party here. Why don't you come over?'

'Are you drunk?'

'Maybe I am.' But he was still thirsty. He'd go to the Spar shop later and get a few beers in.

'It can wait.'

'No, no spit it out.'

'I met her mum in Asda.'

'Lucky you.' He wondered why she'd bothered phoning if that's all she had to say.

'Well… if you're not interested…'

'Like I give a fuck about that bitch.'

'Suit yourself.' The line went dead. He sighed, and overwhelmed by sudden tiredness, flopped down by the mermaid.

THIRTY

Garland Avenue, Westcliffe

'D'you want to hold Charlie?' She was staring at a baby, a tiny pinched-faced thing. It was only a few weeks old apparently, but already had a thick mop of blonde hair. Bert's mum was looking at her, eyebrows arched, waiting for an answer.

The only other baby she'd been this close to was when they arranged for some unsuspecting new mum to come to Lowood Secure Children's Home and exhibit her bundle of joy. They all had to have a turn at holding the baby, even though she was terrified of dropping the thing. That one had been older, more robust looking. This tiny creature looked so vulnerable she thought she might ruin it somehow, just by looking at it.

'Um, no thanks. I don't know how,' she stammered.

The baby's mother, Chloe, Bert's aunt, looked uncomfortable, like she knew Caitlin couldn't be trusted with a baby. Looking at Chloe you'd never have guessed she'd given birth a few weeks ago. She was slim, with perfect skin. Neat and petite with her blonde bob. She reminded Caitlin of a china doll. Not a toy to play with, but the sort they have in museums. She was a younger, more flawless version of Mrs Fernandes.

'Just form a cradle with your arms,' Mrs Fernandes said.

Bert was looking on, smirking. 'Maybe you'd like a go?' she said to him pointedly.

He squirmed. But Charlie's father, Steve, looked up from his phone and intervened. 'This is the twenty-first century and men hold babies too, Berty.' Steve had the look of a bespectacled snake about him.

'Yes, *Berty!*' she said stifling a giggle.

'Steve's been hands-on since day one,' Chloe added, looking adoringly at her husband, who appeared considerably older than she did. Steve took the baby from his wife and then passed Charlie to Bert giving him no choice but to hold the child.

She watched Bert with the baby. As he got used to holding Charlie, his awkwardness melted and he smiled at the little scrap. She couldn't help but wonder if he'd make a good father. Probably. Bert was one of the good guys.

He caught her eye. 'Don't get any ideas!'

She laughed. 'No fear!' But she went over to take a closer look. Little Charlie was cute and she held her pinky finger out for him to grasp. She watched with a certain awe as he wrapped his own tiny fingers tight around hers.

But then she was ambushed by the memory of Boggart Hill and little Riley crying and wailing for her mummy. She winced and moved away. Went over to the window and stared hard at the front garden, concentrating on a blackbird poking the lawn for worms.

She could never have a baby of her own. Not that she wanted one. But even if she did, got herself up the duff, they'd probably remove it for its own safety.

'Getting broody?' Mrs Fernandes said, coming up beside her.

She shook her head. 'Don't think I'm the maternal type.'

'Neither was I until I had Bert,' she said, with a meaningful look. 'And it's taken a few years for Chloe to get there, but look at her now.'

When Bert had phoned her and invited her to Sunday lunch with his aunt, uncle and new baby cousin, she complained that it wasn't her scene. He said it wasn't his scene either, and it would be purgatory without a kindred spirit.

'And don't worry about my mum. I made her promise not to do her cross-examination act, on pain of death.'

She hadn't seen much of Bert since *The Herald* ran the story alleging an affair with George. She'd been keeping a low profile. As it happened the story came across as more of a gossip piece than anything else and George's name hadn't come out.

An unnamed case worker has been suspended pending an investigation.

Not so bad, but it left a sour taste in her mouth. And she was still smarting from the way George had cut himself off from all contact. She didn't want Bert to know how upset she was, so took extra shifts and tried to avoid him generally.

'I'll love you forever, if you say yes,' Bert had said over the phone. 'And mum cooks a lush roast dinner.'

Bert was right about one thing: Joanna Fernandes did make a delicious roast dinner. With all the trimmings, as they say. It felt like Christmas. They always had a Christmas dinner at the secure children's home, and even at Thornhill, they tried to produce something vaguely resembling a Christmas dinner on the day. It tasted shite. Watery gravy and spuds you could use to break a window.

They ate at the dining table in an actual dining room. It had a sideboard full of posh plates and sparkly glassware. The table was covered with a crisp white embroidered cloth, which she had already stained with gravy. But no one seemed to mind. The conversation was baby talk: how his smiles were real, even though the books said it was just wind at his age. Would his eyes remain blue or turn brown? The colour of his poo.

Gross.

The star of the show, however, was absent, having been put down to sleep in the sitting room.

Later the conversation moved to who Charlie took after. And as if that wasn't enough, they were already planning the kid's whole life. Bert, who was sitting opposite, kept theatrically rolling his eyes at her when no one was looking and also played footsie under the table, which made them both giggle as they knocked back the wine. So what if the conversation was boring and not something she could join in with; with free wine, who cared? She might even come to Sunday lunch again.

Steve was droning on about how they were going to move. Their 'bijou' flat in London wasn't suitable to bring up a child, and they were looking for a house in a 'good area' to accommodate their growing family and so on. Blah blah blah.

'The problem is finding a safe place to bring up the sprogs,' Steve said, helping himself to more wine, finishing the bottle. Steve had an app on his phone that rated different areas for safety. 'Burglaries and muggings,' he explained.

'Also tells you about convicted criminals living in the area,' Chloe said.

'Can they do that?' Caitlin said casually, but an alarm was already chiming in the back of her mind.

'Murderers and rapists, that kind of person,' Steve said. 'I don't know about you but I wouldn't want to live next door to someone on the sex offenders list.'

Caitlin groaned silently. *Don't say anything. Focus on the food.*

'Let's see what the app says for Garland Avenue, shall we?' Steve said.

'I don't think I want to know,' Bert mumbled, finishing off

his potatoes. They exchanged looks. Thank God he didn't like the way the conversation was going either.

'Well maybe you don't now, but when you're a father, Berty, you'll think differently believe me.'

'You can't tell me what to think,' Bert muttered.

'When you are a father, you have to take your responsibilities seriously,' Steve said, typing into his phone.

'What are you going to do if you find some undesirable living next door. Go round an lynch them? Hang 'em from the nearest tree?'

'I do think some of them should be hanged actually,' Chloe said. 'Paedophiles and child murderers.'

Caitlin felt for a moment like she was falling. Plunging down a rabbit hole, like Alice in Wonderland. She'd landed at a table with a woman who wanted to see her swinging in a noose. How nice. She looked at Bert, willing him to make an excuse to get them away from the table, both having finished their plates.

'Some of these perverts can't help themselves. It's a genetic defect,' Steve added.

'Cleanse society of the degenerates, that's what I say,' Bert chimed in. 'Cheers, Adolf.' He raised his glass.

'Bert! Don't be so rude,' Mrs Fernandes snapped. Turning to Steven she added, 'I'm sorry, he's had a glass too many, I think.'

Bert did sound a bit pissed. But she loved him anyway.

'Trying to impress someone?' Steve said with an unpleasant curling of his lip.

Caitlin felt herself flushing up, and so offered to clear away the plates as a way of escaping to the kitchen.

Once there, she was in no hurry to go back, so fixed herself a glass of ice-cold water from the swanky fridge. Savouring the freshness on her tongue, she wondered how long she could hang about in the kitchen before she was missed. There were raised voices in the dining room. Happy families. After a moment she was joined by Chloe carrying another couple of plates.

'Boys will be boys!' she said, plonking the dirty dishes on the draining board. 'They do like a bit of a punch-up don't they?' The porcelain doll face broke into a nervous laugh. Caitlin didn't feel like laughing, she felt like punching something. That stupid face. This was what they were like – the people who wanted her strung up. And she was having lunch with them. She hated it. Hated having to pretend and be nice.

Then Mrs Fernandes appeared. Her face was strained, but she put on a smile and said it was time for dessert. Trifle apparently, so Caitlin helped carry the wherewithal for dessert through to the dining room. Things had calmed down when they went back in, even if Bert looked like he was working out who to kill.

No one spoke. The only sound was the scraping of serving spoon on china as Mrs Fernandes doled out the trifle.

Eventually Steve broke the awkward silence. 'Joanna tells me you are going to be a lawyer?'

'Was thinking about it. But not so sure now.' The law was a minefield in this house. 'I might be a vicar instead,' she added as a joke. Which made Bert nearly choke on his trifle.

It also had the effect of shutting Steve up, who seemed to think she was serious. Mrs Fernandes gave her a quizzical look, but didn't say anything.

After a while Chloe said thoughtfully, 'Vicar's better than a priest I suppose.' As though her flippant comment deserved a considered response.

Mrs Fernandes frowned. 'What's wrong with being a priest? You're not thinking of leaving the faith, are you, Chloe?'

'Because of the confessional. You know if someone confessed something, you have to keep it to yourself instead of doing anything about it.'

'They're all paedos anyway,' Steve said. 'Priests.'

'Really, Steven, just because one or two–'

'Anna was joking about being a vicar,' Bert interrupted, saving his mum from digging herself into a hole. But then added with a worried note, 'Weren't you?'

'I could never be a lawyer either,' Chloe piped up. 'Having to defend the bad guys. I couldn't do that.'

'Everyone deserves a fair trial,' Bert said, looking at her. Which she found slightly disturbing.

'I do love trifle.' Caitlin flashed a warm smile at Bert's mum. 'Is there any more?'

'Of course.' The woman looked genuinely pleased and served another portion.

'So *are* you going into the law?' Steve said.

She shrugged and took a mouthful of dessert. Food was a useful prop if you wanted to avoid conversation.

'Could you defend paedophiles and child murderers?' Steve looked at Caitlin meaningfully.

'Or priests?' Bert said, grinning.

'I'll probably do corporate law,' she said. 'Or divorces.' She fixed his own stare with hers, which she held as long as she could bear.

That seemed to be the end of the matter and they managed to get to finish the meal without igniting any more flashpoints.

Mrs Fernandes ushered them into the sitting room, moving *The Sunday Herald* off the sofa, folding it neatly and placing it on a side coffee table. The presence of that paper was disturbing. But at least there'd been nothing in the press about her recently.

The coffee was served from a silver coffeepot into delicate china cups. Milk from a jug. That was silver too.

Baby Charlie was in a travel cot and began to make weird gurgling and snuffling noises, so Chloe picked him up and then looked hopefully at Joanna who took the hint and the baby. She paced around whispering inanities and rocking him gently in her arms.

Caitlin drank her slightly too bitter coffee wondering if the coffeepot was solid silver, or was the silver just a shiny veneer on some dull base metal?

'Garland Avenue gets four and a half stars overall,' Steve announced.

Bert groaned.

Chloe said, 'That must be a relief, Joanna. What with all those seasonal workers you get round here.'

'What have they got to do with it?' Bert said.

'Just saying.'

'Cus a lot of them are immigrants. Is that it?' Bert was getting upset again.

'Bert! Stop being so argumentative,' his mum said. 'I don't know what's got into you today.'

Caitlin gave Bert a look, swivelling her eyes towards the door, hoping he'd drink up his coffee. She needed to escape this purgatory.

Chloe snorted and picked up the paper as if to shield herself from Bert. Then tutted loudly. 'Typical!'

'What is it?' Steve said looking up from his phone.

'It's disgusting, that's what,' she said and read out the newspaper article, '*Dad's Heartfelt Message Defaced by Killer Caitlin. It seems Caitlin Grady has broken her parole by visiting the scene of the crime, where she defaced a card left there by grieving dad, Darren Burgess.*'

What the fuck! The bloody *Herald* was printing out and out lies now. It took a real effort not to snatch that paper off Doll Face and rip it up into tiny pieces.

'There's a picture too!' Chloe announced.

'Bloody rag, print such crap,' Caitlin said through clenched teeth, unable to stop the words from spilling out.

Chloe responded by showing the room the picture of a

card, with a close-up insert of red letters scrawled across Darren's message. What fucking game was that paper playing?

'At least she wrote sorry,' Bert said.

'Fake news!' Caitlin spluttered. 'They're just out to get her!' She felt her cheeks flushing and wiped her hand across her face as cover.

Steve sneered. 'Know better than the papers, do you?'

'Yeah. Maybe I do,' she said. 'Maybe I know someone on *The Herald* and know what a lot of shite they print.'

'I only get it for the women's section,' Mrs Fernandes said, suddenly defensive. 'More coffee?' She gave the baby to Chloe and picking up the silver coffeepot left the room.

Caitlin felt like leaving the room too. Not just the room. The building. But didn't want draw any more attention to herself so stayed put. Shaking with rage. Fortunately Charlie started to whimper again and distracted Chloe and Steve.

'He needs feeding,' Chloe said to Steve, who mumbled something about heating up expressed milk. He went off to the kitchen leaving Chloe to it. She gave all her attention to the baby and ignored Bert and Caitlin.

Bert cocked his head towards the door, stood up and led the way out of the room. She was more than happy to follow him upstairs to take refuge in his bedroom.

'I'm sorry,' she said. 'I've upset your mum.'

'Don't worry about it. I'm always telling her what a load of fascist shite that paper is. She likes you. Really.'

She wasn't so sure about that. His mum had looked very offended by her outburst. She thanked him for putting up with her and kissed him. But he seemed distracted.

'Do you really know someone who works at *The Herald*?'

'No, course not. I just said that to shut your uncle up.'

He nodded. 'Right. Course, that's what I thought.' But he didn't look convinced somehow.

'I mean how would I know a journalist at *The Herald*?'

He shrugged. 'It's just, you did seem very sure of yourself.'

'Did I?'

'Yeah… just a bit.'

'Well. You like that don't you?' She gave him a flirtatious smile and then kissed him hard. He succumbed and they collapsed on the bed. But when she put her hand on his crotch, he stopped her. 'Better not. Mum's on the prowl,' he said. But that was an excuse and she felt a pang of rejection. Something was bothering him.

'You mad at me for something?'

'No. Not at all.'

'What is it then?'

'Nothing.'

'It must be quite something for you to suddenly worry about your mum *being on the prowl.*'

'It's just the way you were SO angry about that newspaper report.'

'You said yourself it's a fascist rag.'

'Seething with indignation at that photo of what they said Grady had done.'

'Was I?' Fuck. She should have kept her mouth shut. Fuck fuck fuck.

'Why? Really, why did it bother you quite so much?'

She shook her head and went to his bedroom window which looked out on the street of well cared-for houses and gardens. A place where she had no business being. He came up behind her. Put his arms around her and kissed the back of her neck. 'I don't mind you attacking the paper. But I think there's more to it than you're letting on.'

She gave a long heartfelt sigh. 'I know Caitlin didn't write on Riley's father's card.' Her heart was in her mouth. Should she tell him? Should she come clean? She turned to face him. 'I know that, because it isn't her writing.' Bit her lip. Held her breath.

THIRTY-ONE

Ropeway Café, Pennywell Industrial Estate. Bristol

He was in the greasy spoon opposite The Embassy massage parlour, a steaming mug of tea in front of him and a bacon sandwich in his belly. He watched as a youngish bloke in jeans and a sweatshirt slipped into the massage parlour. A regular guy, nothing special or seedy about him at all. Could be any one of a number of guys he'd worked with over the years.

Now that Kerry had left him, maybe he'd go in there himself one day. Why not? He sipped his tea mulling the idea over. No, he wasn't that desperate. Or low. Not yet.

Tracey emerged from the parlour. Looked around, lit a cigarette, took a couple of drags, then threw it down on the pavement. She had her signature pink neon trainers on, but smart jeans had replaced the short skirt. She was wearing an expensive-looking suede jacket too. He'd phoned her the morning after his drunken dismissal of her offer of information. She told him that Grady's mum had been to a secret meeting with Grady in Weston and so he arranged to meet her.

'Slow day today. So I'm glad you decided to pitch up,'

233

Tracey said as she plonked herself down opposite him. 'Get me a coffee, will ya?'

She looked in better shape than last time. Better complexion and didn't seem so on edge. But still painfully thin.

Waiting at the counter for the coffee, he couldn't help wondering what counted as a slow day. How many men had she 'massaged' this morning? Poor kid. And how could he even have contemplated going into a place like that for one second? He turned to her, holding up a packet of salt and vinegar crisps. She nodded and smiled.

'How long have you been working at The Embassy?' he asked when he got back to the table.

'Couple of weeks. It's all right in there.' She took a slurp of coffee. 'If you're thinking of going, you get a free can of lager on Tuesdays.'

He laughed at that.

'What's funny?'

He shrugged. 'Variation on "a pie and a pint" I guess.'

'Shag and a shandy!' She held out the packet of crisps. 'Want one?' He wasn't hungry after his bacon sarnie, but took one just to be polite and asked about Grady's mother.

'Came across her in Asda, full of herself cus she wants to show off how good Caitlin's doing these days. Let a few things slip.' She nodded her head meaningfully, but wouldn't say more until he paid her what they'd agreed. He reached inside his pocket for his roll of twenties, but she stopped him.

'Not here!' she hissed. He could see her point. Handing over a large amount of cash around here might attract more than knowing looks.

As she was finishing her coffee, she told him she was pretty sure Grady hadn't been back to Bristol.

'But my card? You know she wrote on it?'

'Caitlin didn't do that!' Tracey said, sounding a bit put out.

'How can you be so sure?'

She looked uneasy and stared out the window a moment at a middle-aged man in a business suit who was hesitating outside the door of The Embassy. 'I wrote it. Okay?'

'You? Why would you do that? Write over my message?'

'I didn't mean to *deface it*, like they made out. I wasn't thinking properly.'

'Didn't think at all.'

'Well if you're gonna get all arsey about it!' she said with a mean, defensive look. She stared past him like a girl at a party, trying to find someone more interesting to talk to.

'Sorry… it's just you wrote all over my message.'

'Because the sorry was for you. That's why I wrote on *your* message. Like I say I wasn't thinking properly. Had a couple of ciders, I suppose.'

He nodded, thought a moment and then asked, 'Why did you want to say sorry to me?'

She shrugged. Put her hands around her coffee cup. 'Sorry for what happened. Your loss, kind of thing.' He was sure there was more to this, but didn't press it. Instead he suggested they adjourn to his van to conclude their business.

They walked along in awkward silence. He was pissed off. Not just with her for writing on the card. But because he had wrongly believed Grady had done it. Strangely disappointed too that she hadn't broken her parole after all. He'd keep that detail to himself.

Once in the van, he handed over the agreed amount of cash. The aroma of new suede hung heavy in the air. 'Nice jacket,' he said to try and thaw the atmosphere as she slipped the money into the inside pocket.

'Got it from Harvey Nic's. Was wearing it when I met Caitlin's mum. She was a bit taken aback, cus she knows how much Lorenzo stuff can cost, right. Hah! No Primark for me!'

'Lucky you!' He tried not to sound sarcastic.

'She was boasting about Caitlin going to uni next year.'

Pringle had been right about that, then. It still made him bristle. 'She'd have never got to uni if she'd stayed in Pennywell. I mean look at me.' She gave a humourless laugh. 'Anyway, it put me and my designer jacket in my place, didn't it?'

'Which university?'

'Didn't say. But she's not at uni yet. She's living it up at the seaside. "A nice little resort," is what she said. Got her own nice little flat there too.'

'A seaside town?' It galled him that they'd put her up in a place where people go on holiday. 'Where is it?' he snapped.

'Hey! Don't shoot me, I'm only the messenger!'

'Sorry. I got a short fuse at the moment.' He sighed. 'Because, well my wife walked out on me the other day, so apologies for being a bit narky.' Why did he tell her that? He shouldn't have told her that. She wasn't his friend.

She looked at him for a moment. 'Sometimes I don't think men and women are meant to live together.' There was something heartbreaking about such cynicism in a woman so young. 'Anyway. You're forgiven for being a bit narky.' She gave him a genuine smile, which softened the mood.

'Thanks.'

'She's got a job in a coffee shop. But I don't know the name.'

He grunted. That wasn't much help.

'I got something else: her mum reckons this probation officer, the one she's meant to be shagging, George, that's his name apparently. It didn't come out in the papers cus it might help identify her. Anyway he's West Country. Maybe Devon or Cornwall. Got a definite accent.'

'She told you this?'

Tracey nodded. 'Was adamant that Caitlin is living by the sea, somewhere in the south west. Said that Caitlin had lost the

Bristol from her voice and gone more soft and Devon-like, talked about grockles, whatever they are.'

'Okay.' He smiled. That *was* something.

'When me and Caitlin were like ten, her mum took us on holiday, to a seaside resort. Thing is, Caitlin told her mum the resort she's living in reminds her of that holiday.'

'Could it be the same place?' he said with sudden urgency.

'What I remember was the pier and the amusement arcades.'

'But where did you go?'

'Search me? I was only a kid. I can't remember. I asked my mum, but she can't remember either, because she didn't go. Anyway the seafront had loads of amusement arcades. And there was a pier. We stayed in a caravan.'

Amusement arcades and a pier. A caravan site. West Country. Probation officer called George.

'One last thing, she let slip that Caitlin's hair is dyed blonde. Shoulder length.'

That was about it as far as Tracey's information was concerned. He wondered why she wanted to tell him what she knew. Was it just the money, or was there another reason she was betraying her childhood friend?

She asked for a lift home. 'I'm back living with my mum. It's not far.'

That was why she looked healthier. Home cooking and a mother's TLC.

She directed him to a narrow road of dull grey pebble-dashed Victorian terraced houses. Doors that opened straight onto the pavement. Not a blade of grass anywhere.

'That's where Caitlin lived,' Tracey said, as they drove down the street, pointing out a rundown house. He couldn't help but stop the van outside. He'd never been told where she lived.

'It's not as if you'll find Caitlin in there. Her mum hasn't lived around here since Caitlin got arrested. Got herself re-housed. Don't ask me where, cus I don't know. It was empty for a while, then they put refugee families in it.'

There was nothing about the dull house that made it stand out. No mark to show a killer had been born and bred there. He drove on to Tracey's mum's. This house looked cared for. Neat net curtains and a vase of yellow flowers in the window. Freshly painted window frames and front door.

'Thanks,' she said, but instead of getting out, she simply sat and stared straight ahead. He waited, wondering what was on her mind. Something else Grady's mum told her?

She took a deep breath as though she was going to dive into an unseen ocean. 'That day. I was on my way to school. Caitlin caught me up and went on about how we should bunk off and go to Pennywell City Farm.' Her voice was flat, devoid of feeling.

'That day. You're talking about…' He couldn't finish his sentence. The animal-hide aroma of her jacket was suddenly suffocating.

She gave a barely perceptible nod. 'We pretended to be wicked witches. Caitlin always said she was a witch, so she was chief witch and I was her apprentice witch.' She swallowed, looked like she was finding it hard to go on. 'I'm sorry, I…' She moved to get out of the van.

'You've got to tell me!' He grabbed her arm. 'I need to know.'

She looked down at her arm, still firmly gripped by his hand. Didn't say anything.

He let go. 'Sorry,' he said, feeling suddenly embarrassed for behaving like some aggressive punter. Since when had he been like this?

'You gonna behave?'

He nodded. She looked at him for a moment, deciding if she could trust him. 'It's just been on my mind, since I saw you up Boggart Hill.' She smoothed down her jeans. 'But don't get all arsey with me. I don't have to tell you anything, all right?'

'All right.'

'It was a game. Find a tasty child to put in the pot for dinner. We spied on the little kids running around and we were like, "Shall we have this one or that one? No that one's too skinny; that one too small; this one looks like it would taste bad." It was just an innocent game. We weren't going to actually do anything.'

He stopped breathing, wondering what was coming next.

'We got bored of looking for kids and went over to the goat field, but then, saw a little girl, not much more than a toddler. She was on her own, looking through the railings at the goats. "There's a nice juicy one," Caitlin said.'

Riley had gone to see the goats, not the allotments. That was his mistake. The fucking goat field.

'So we went over, and Caitlin picked a handful of grass and stuffed it through the railings to attract the goat. The girl, Riley as I know now, she took some of the grass and did the same. Then she held Caitlin's hand. "Let's cook you up in our pot," Caitlin said and Riley laughed. And I laughed too.'

The tension in his body was making him shake.

'You all right?'

'Not really.' He wanted her to stop. Not to say any more.

'Didn't mean to upset you.'

But he needed to hear it whether he wanted to or not. 'Go on. Tell me your worst.' He braced himself for more, clenching his jaw so hard it hurt.

'So, Riley was holding Caitlin's hand. "Come on then, me babba," she goes and led Riley away from the goats.'

His mind was racing and jumping around. He just couldn't believe that Riley had allowed herself to be led off. She must have struggled. Grady must have dragged her off.

'Caitlin said we were going to our witch's coven or

something. I didn't think we should take Riley anywhere because we'd get into trouble. Told her we should stay by the goats. But Cait wasn't listening. She was in her own world. Making Riley giggle by pulling silly witchy faces.'

This wasn't what he imagined. Riley should be upset and crying and wanting her mummy and daddy. He didn't want to believe this version. Shook his head.

'She took Riley towards the back entrance, on the far side of the goat field. They closed it off since.'

'Couldn't you see what was happening?'

'I was following behind. Kept saying to Cait, we should take Riley back to the goats. Cait told me not to be such a wuss. I got cross. Didn't want to end up getting into trouble for what she was doing. So I ran off. That's it.'

'That's it! You didn't think to tell anyone?'

'Like who? Was meant to be in school anyway. I thought I'd get in trouble. That's all I was thinking.'

He was sitting in his van with someone who could have stopped it. Or at least raised the alarm. But this kid hadn't raised a finger. Like all the other fuckers who looked the other way. Thought it was nothing to do with them.

'So that's why I wrote *sorry*. All right?'

'But when they said Riley was missing? You didn't tell anyone?'

'I didn't hear about that. Didn't know anything till they said… found Riley's body. Didn't think Caitlin could have done it anyway. And I wasn't gonna say nothing. Didn't want to get arrested for something I never did. I never did nothing!'

'That's the point, isn't it? You never did nothing.'

'I am sorry.'

Was she expecting him to forgive her? He couldn't do that. She was part of it. 'I think you better get out, don't you?'

But she didn't. She sat looking ahead. Chewing at the inside of her mouth. 'Do you want to punish me?'

'What?'

'Because you can if you want.'

Oh my God. What the hell was she suggesting? Did she think he was some kind of pervert?

She turned to him. 'It brought it home to me when I met you. Saw how upset you was. I feel bad about it. So. If you want… Pain's a kind of release for me, you see.'

'Just get out.'

She nodded and got out of the car. He sat, his mind reeling. Had she told him about that day because she wanted him to hurt her? Did she really feel that guilty about what she'd done as a kid. Or was she just so damaged she wanted to be hurt? Would it give him some kind of sadistic pleasure to inflict pain on her?

She could have stopped it. She was on the list of people who were culpable. And it was true he might get some awful pleasure from punishing her. But that was a dark road, leading to an even darker place. And if anyone needed punishing it was him. He hadn't looked for Riley properly. Been convinced she was in the allotments. He hadn't gone to the goat field. If only he'd done that, he would have found her.

But the most disturbing thing about the story was that Riley had not been snatched. She'd gone with Grady willingly. Was it really a childhood game gone wrong? Or was the truth of it, that Grady was even more callous and scheming than he ever realised. Tricked Riley into taking her hand. Trusting her and going willingly to her fate.

THIRTY-TWO

Regal Cinema, Westcliffe

The Regal was all red carpets and art deco light fittings with an ornate moulded ceiling. Some retired banker who was a massive film buff had bought the place and thrown a shed-load of money at it.

There was a row of double seats at the rear of the auditorium for couples to get close-up and cosy. It was, Caitlin had to admit, a romantic place with its period atmosphere and soft lighting.

'I love the movies,' Bert said.

The last time she set foot in a cinema was with Tracey and her mum. They'd gone to watch *Toy Story* at a multiplex which smelt of sweet popcorn.

Bert had chosen the film, even though it was a 'bit of a chick flick', as he put it. But went on to confess that romantic movies were his secret shame. 'Just don't tell anyone.'

'Why not?'

'It's sad. And my mates will take the piss.'

'Well, I think it's sweet.'

'That's what I mean!'

She whispered in his ear, 'Your secret's safe with me.' Then tickled him in the ribs.

She hadn't told him her own secret though. She'd wanted to, but nerves failed her. She told him the reason she knew what Caitlin's handwriting looked like was because she'd known Caitlin in the children's home, and her handwriting was very distinctive. Even that much spooked him and he looked shocked, before he managed to pretend it wasn't that big a deal.

'I didn't realise that it was the kind of place they'd put someone like Caitlin Grady.'

'Well it was. You see it was a secure children's home. You weren't allowed out.'

'I didn't realise. Why did they put you in there?'

'I used to run away. They thought I was "vulnerable", all right? But if you're going to judge me for it…'

'Hey! I'm not my Uncle Steve.'

'You're not to tell anyone that I used to know her. Not a soul.' Even though she hadn't told the truth. It still felt good to hint at who she really was. Eased the stress of lying to someone you cared about. Living a complete lie was a hard thing to bear.

'What was she like?'

'She was all right. Normal. As normal as anyone else in there.'

'You must have been pretty close if you know her handwriting,' he said later.

'I guess you could say we were, mates. Yeah.' She smiled as if remembering a friend. But actually, she decided she liked the Caitlin she used to be. Preferred her to Anna if the truth was known. Anna Moreton was frightened of her own shadow. Caitlin Grady didn't give a shit.

'So you were besties with a murderer,' he said, nodding slowly as the wheels in his brain clicked into a new position.

'Well we don't always know everything about a person

before we become their friends, do we? It's not like they give you their CV. And maybe if you like them, you should give them the benefit of the doubt.'

The film was a story about a boy who loved one of the cool girls in school, but she wanted to hang out with all the macho jocks, and so he stood no chance. But he could sing classical opera, which of course everyone thought was deeply uncool. He got bullied and teased for it. Then one day she heard him singing in an audition for music college and was so moved, she fell in love.

Even though it was cheesy and predictable, she found herself with a tear in her eye at the end. She was embarrassed that such a soppy film made her weep. Blinked a lot to try and make the tears go back inside her eyes. Avoided looking at Bert as the titles went up, taking an inexplicable interest in who had done obscure jobs on the film, like 'best boy', whatever that was. She felt a teardrop escape her eye and run down her cheek. Bert spotted it and kissed the tear away. Which was almost as soppy as the film. But it made her love him nonetheless.

Afterwards they joined his friends for a drink in The Tudor. (Bert never went anywhere else.) She tried to enjoy getting to know them all better, and to be fair, they were a friendly bunch. Even the girl with the braided hair, Chino, made an effort to talk to her. Although she was snobby about the film, declaring it a reactionary throwback. 'The so-called heroine was merely a passive observer to a male psychodrama and offered up as a trophy to the hero at the end of the story.'

Caitlin conceded she had a point, but insisted she enjoyed it anyway. Perhaps she liked male psychodramas.

As the evening went on, she became increasingly aware of just how well they all knew each other and started to resent their private jokes. She was like the shy new girl at school. They'd all grown up together, gone to school together, knew everything about each other, and you could tell how tight they were. She was the outsider.

She'd lost touch with everyone she'd ever been close to. Had no friends from Lowood Secure or HMP Thornhill. Okay, so that was out of necessity, to keep her identity safe, but still made her feel like a social leper. She'd even managed to fall out with her mother. And as for George: she wasn't going to waste time thinking about him.

Later, when they left the pub and were alone walking along the seafront, Bert asked her what was wrong. Out in the black distance there was a lonely light bobbing around. 'D'you think it's a fishing boat?' she said, pointing out to sea. She couldn't see the actual sea though, the promenade lights being too weak to penetrate far enough into the black.

'Don't change the subject. Tell me what's bothering you.'

'It's just when I see you with all your friends…' She took a moment listening to unseen waves breaking on the shingle. 'I haven't got anything like that in my life. Friends. Family.'

'You've got me.' His face looked pale in the light, but his eyes caught it somehow and sparkled.

She smiled. 'I hope so.'

'I love you,' he said.

'Don't say that.' Her voice was strained. 'You don't really know me.' He frowned, not understanding. She was tempted in the anonymity of the semi-darkness to blurt it all out, tell him everything. 'No one really knows me,' she continued. 'Only Uncle George and he fucked off somewhere or other.' She couldn't keep the bitterness from her voice.

'What do you mean? Fucked off?'

'Got transferred. His job. So he had to move away.'

'What does he do?'

She couldn't think of anything quickly enough, so just told the truth. 'Probation officer.'

'Oh? Right.' Even in the dim light she saw something flash

across Bert's face. Something she couldn't read. Whatever it was disappeared as quickly as it came, like a brief chill from a cloud passing in front of a summer sun.

'Sorry. I'm being moody. Maybe it's my hormones or something.' She gave a false little laugh, wondering why she'd made a sexist joke at her own expense. She'd never have done that a few weeks ago. What was happening to her?

He reached for her hand and held it as they walked on. 'Is it because no one knows what it was like in care. Is that what you mean?'

'Yeah. I suppose that's it. And you know if people find out about my past, they'll get all judgey.'

'Well then, we won't tell them.'

She stopped and turned to him. 'You promise to keep all my secrets?'

'I do,' he said before kissing her.

Later, as they were near the flat, he brought up the subject of university. How they'd both be starting again. Both be in the same boat when it came to how many people they knew. 'We'll be making new friends together.'

'Together?'

'If we're at the same uni?'

'I thought you were gonna go to circus school,' she said, frowning, he was assuming too much.

'But if you get into Manchester, I could take up my place on the maths course.'

'Haven't even had my interview yet.'

'I can postpone for a year. Go the same time as you.' He was getting ahead of himself.

'What about circus school?'

'That can wait. Maths is the sensible option, isn't it?'

'Bert. No. That's not right.' She didn't want to be responsible for his life choices. 'You should go to circus school. Follow your heart.'

'I am following my heart. Cus you know, "my heart is set on you".'

'That sounds like a line from a corny film.'

'Yeah, it is.' He grinned. '*Grease*. We did it for the school play two years ago.'

She laughed. 'What are you like!' She gave him a poke and ran off down the road and up the steps to her front door. She turned and waited for him to catch up. He stopped at the bottom of the steps.

'Will you come to visit? If I go to the circus academy?'

'Course! Keep me away.'

He climbed up the steps and they kissed against the front door. She wondered how long their own little play had to run.

The online chatter was getting worrying; it had got out that she was living in a seaside town, somewhere in the West Country. They even mentioned a pier. The newspapers hadn't printed that detail, restrained by court orders, but it was on the HuntAKilla website. How did they know?

There was moral outrage on Riley's Facebook page and an outpouring of poison on *The Daily Herald* comments page. Somehow living in a seaside resort was cheating the system, taking the piss. But would they really be any happier if she was in some grim industrial wasteland, housed in a squalid cockroach-ridden hovel?

She needed George and so tried his number, but was redirected to some reception woman. He'd never even given her his personal number. Felt like another shard of glass in her heart. She'd heard nothing from him. No text, no nothing. She even searched for him online, but failed to find a single mention. The man might have never existed.

'I'm scared,' she told Tammy at their next meeting in the probation office.

The woman did her best to be reassuring. 'Try not to overthink things. It's all guesswork and speculation.'

'The West Country? The pier? Someone's tipped them off.'

'How many piers are there in England? How many holiday resorts in the west? And even if a newspaper reporter were here in Westcliffe, how would they recognise you? Without your new name, without a photo? One of them could go into the coffee shop and be none the wiser.'

Her buttocks clenched at the thought. She wondered again if the suited man might be a reporter. But they hadn't seen much of that guy recently. Brig said he'd defected to Starbucks.

'No one knows what you look like.'

'Apart from my mum.'

Tammy gave her a look which implied she thought her mum was the grass. But she'd been careful not to tell her mum any specific details. Hadn't mentioned the West Country, or the damn pier. Someone else had betrayed her. Someone in the probation office, maybe George even. Or how about Brig? Had she guessed who she really was?

'In any case, we are monitoring the situation closely. So don't worry. Really. You are safe.' She smiled in that genuine way that Tammy had. It was a gift that she gave to the world, making people believe she genuinely cared about them. For a moment Caitlin almost believed in the woman.

'And if it comes to it, we won't hesitate to move you to a new location,' she added.

Caitlin wasn't sure she liked that idea and pulled a face.

'What is it?' Tammy said. 'You surely wouldn't prefer us to leave you *in situ*?'

'It's just, I'm getting to know people at last. I'd have to start all over again.'

She nodded. 'It's tough.'

What about Bert? What would she say to him? What lie would she feed him. Or would she simply disappear out of his life? No. If it came to it, she would tell him the truth. She owed him that much. And maybe, just maybe he'd stick by her.

'I'll discuss our options with my service manager, but in the meantime, I'm only a phone call away. If you feel threatened, you can ring me night or day. But I doubt it will come to that,' Tammy said, winding up the meeting.

'Have you heard anything from George?' She wasn't going to mention him, but it just came out.

The woman shifted uneasily. 'No... I'm afraid not.'

'And just so you know. We weren't shagging. That was just bollocks.'

'Well... I er...'

'In case you were jealous or anything.' She suddenly felt pissed off with Tammy, as though it was her fault that George had been suspended.

'I don't blame you for feeling angry.'

She snorted and went to the window. Someone had tried to clean the seagull shit off the outside, but only managed to smear it around. 'I just want to know how George is doing that's all.'

'I haven't seen George. None of us have. He's still suspended.'

'So, he's at home?'

'I imagine so.'

'On his own?'

Tammy shrugged, and managed a sad smile.

'Does he live local?'

'I don't know where he lives and you know perfectly well that if I did, I wouldn't be permitted to tell you.'

She nodded. 'I get it.' But she wondered if there was some way of putting pressure on Tammy to get her to bend the rules and give out George's address.

THIRTY-THREE

Lyme Regis, Devon

They started their search in Lyme Regis. A genteel town with narrow winding lanes and tasteful little shops selling things like locally produced honey, and galleries displaying pottery and paintings of brightly coloured boats in the harbour. Darren didn't like the place, it was too pretty. No way was this the right place to be looking. No pier, no amusement arcades, nothing to keep the kids happy.

'Don't know why we bothered coming here,' Darren grumbled as they were strolling along the blustery sea front.

'We have to be methodical, mate,' Jedd said. 'Besides, the chase is all part of it.' Jedd was recording their search and posting video clips on @BitchHunt.

He insisted it was helping increase donations to the Riley's Law fund.

All the same, they could have started in somewhere like Brighton; it had plenty of amusement places and a well-known pier. Could have dropped in on his sister. But Jedd insisted they should go with Grady's mother's idea about the West Country.

'The meeting with Grady's mother took place in Weston.

West of Bristol. It could be relevant. It's all a question of statistics,' he added enigmatically. 'Probabilities are key to modern detective work.' That sounded like something Jedd had read in a book.

They went into one of the many fussy little tea shops in the town for a snack. Darren felt immediately uncomfortable. The fine china and cramped space meant things were waiting to be spilt and broken, followed no doubt by withering looks from the surly waitress, who looked like she'd stepped off the set of *Downton Abbey*. The tea shop was designed for little old ladies and it made him feel awkward and clumsy. Jedd seemed to be enjoying himself though, and tucked into a cream tea.

'What's the matter, buddy?' Jedd asked.

'Nothing.'

'Have a home-made scone. They are delicious.'

He didn't want a scone. He wanted to get on with the search. They should be looking in places with candyfloss, amusement arcades, crazy golf and donkey rides. Somewhere with caravan parks. Traditional family resorts. This part of the West Country was far too sleepy and twee. Perhaps he'd be better off without Jedd. He wished now they'd come in separate vehicles. But he'd agreed to go with Jedd in his ex-police van. Why did he always just go along with things?

Feeling claustrophobic in the airless teashop he supped up his tea and escaped, to stretch his legs he said, leaving Jedd to his cream and scones.

Wandering down a winding back lane he stopped at a fossil shop. In the window a range of polished shells of giant snail-like creatures was on display. Creatures that had inhabited the sea round here millions of years ago. Life turned into stone.

In that film, *Jurassic Park*, they took a fossil and turned it back into a living breathing creature. Would such a thing ever be really possible?

The next few towns on the south coast, were in the same vain. More like retirement places than seaside resorts. But Jedd maintained it was important to visit each one, and record their progress. Build up the anticipation on @BitchHunt.

THIRTY-FOUR

CoffeeTime, Westcliffe

Government Betrays Riley!

She was standing over the newspaper rack trying to understand what the headline meant. It looked like the government were not going to support a private member's bill to introduce Riley's Law, which from reading, meant that it stood no chance of ever becoming law. A big ear-to-ear grin began to take hold of her face.

She looked up to see Brig staring at her with a questioning expression. She placed *The Daily Herald* on the rack and got on with her job of dealing with the rest of the morning papers. But she made sure that *The Herald* with its sour grapes headline was on show.

'You're grinning like a Cheshire cat,' Brig said. 'Good news?'

She shrugged in a display of nonchalance. 'Not really.' She tried to look cool, but just couldn't stop herself from smiling.

Brig picked up *The Daily Herald,* so she made herself scarce by arranging the sandwich packs in the refrigerated display. She'd never mentioned Riley's Law to Brig. But a sudden bout of insecurity made her wonder if Brig might be in the 'hanging's-too-good-for-em' camp.

'There is a God after all.' Brig gave one of her lopsided smiles. Caitlin silently agreed that perhaps there was. 'I'm no fan of laws made by the bloodthirsty mob,' Brig went on, looking at her with searching eyes. Did Brig know more than she was letting on?

Whatever, she was relieved that her boss seemed to be on her side. 'Where does that kind of thing end?' she said.

'Burning witches. That's where.'

Caitlin grunted.

'And as we're a couple of witches,' Brig added, 'we'd better watch out!'

They both laughed and before she knew it, she found herself giving Brig a hug. Brig wasn't normally the touchy-feely hugging type, but now held her tight until it was on the verge of becoming uncomfortable. Then the woman pulled away, avoided her eyes and almost fled behind the counter. There, busied herself putting more change into the till.

It was a strange encounter and she couldn't work out what it was about. Brig had let her guard down in some way and then thought better of it. Crossed some line or other to do with bosses and employees. Nevertheless, it felt like progress. Maybe they could be real friends eventually.

After her shift she went to meet Bert for a celebratory drink, although she didn't tell him that. But he seemed to pick up on something.

'You're on good form this evening,' he said when she made some joke or other.

'Am I?'

'Buzzin'.'

'Well cheers.' She glugged a mouthful of cider. They were in The Tudor of course, and that night a well-known DJ was booked for a gig. Some of Bert's mates were already arriving.

Chino was by the bar and gave a wave. She was with Harry, another old mate of Bert's.

'They are always off and on, those two,' Bert told her. 'No one lasts more than a couple of weeks with Chino, but she keeps going back to him.'

'Must be love.'

'Be crunch time for them soon; Harry's off to uni next week.'

She wondered when their own crunch time would come. Whether Bert would go to circus school and meet some lithe trapeze artist or something. Well she wasn't going to think about that. She was going to get drunk and have a good time. Give her brain a fucking rest. It deserved it.

Tables and chairs had been moved to create a dance floor, which was soon heaving with bodies. The whole of Westcliffe seemed to have pitched up. It was the first time she'd ever been to something like this, but easily got into the groove. Got high on the atmosphere. The sweaty closeness of the gyrating crowd. The pulsing music and rhythmic dancing was making her feel connected to something she couldn't name. Her mind seemed to be both inside of herself and swirling around the dance floor, like she was dissolving into the crowd. She loved it. Felt the tension that had been building up over the weeks flow away from her. Everything was going to be all right.

Afterwards they walked drunkenly back to her place. He was going on about what a good time they'd both have when they went to uni.

'Circus school for you, isn't it?' she reminded him.

'Yeah but maybe uni would be more fun. Socially.'

'Actually, I'm having second thoughts about studying law. I don't think it's for me.' She pulled a face. 'People like me don't get to be lawyers.'

'Because you were brought up in care?'

'Something like that. Anyway, it was George's stupid idea to do law, but since he upped sticks and just fucked off...'

'Got a new job, you said.'

'Fucked off! Haven't heard a bloody thing from him since. And he was all, "Don't worry, Anna, I'll drive you to the open days and interviews".'

'Where did he *fuck off* to?'

'Search me? No fucking idea.' They reached her building, she fumbled for the keys as they staggered up the steps to her front door. She had to try the key a few times to get it in the lock.

'Jesus, Anna, how drunk are you?'

'Just a bit. I guess I'll need someone to put me to bed, *Berty!*'

He slapped her arse and they tumbled through into the hallway.

'Shush!' she hissed as they made their way up the stairs to her flat trying not to giggle. Once inside the flat she went to the fridge and reached for a can of cider.

'Is that a good idea?'

'I want to get hammered. And you are sounding like Uncle George. He was such a lightweight.'

'I thought he was a bit of a boozer actually, cus you two used to go out for drinks a lot, didn't you?' Bert had a curious look on his face. Like something was niggling him.

'Not a lot. He took me to the pub a couple of times. You know as part of my education.'

'Education? Weird.'

'He knew I'd spent my life in care, so took it upon himself to teach me the ways of the world.' She pulled off the ring-pull with a percussive hiss and took a swig. Bert was watching her. That niggle was growing into a suspicion.

'You must know where he is, though. He's your uncle. He wouldn't just disappear. Especially if he was *educating* you.' There was something in his tone she didn't like. Was he trying to imply something? Or was she just a bit drunk? She passed him the can hoping to shut him up.

'Well anyway, he's off the scene. No idea where he is. Hasn't been in touch. Nothing.' There, that was it. Subject closed. But thoughts of George's betrayal were still spinning in her mind and she let out an involuntary sigh. She grabbed the can back off Bert, took another slug and wiped her lips with her arm.

'What's the matter, Anna?'

'Nothing. It's fine. It's just he was supposed to take me to the uni open days and stuff.'

'And you needed him to hold your hand, did you?' There was an unpleasant hard look in his eye.

She shrugged. 'It would have been nice to have some support–'

'I don't get it.'

'What's there to get? He's just a bit of a cunt.' She took another deep swig from the can.

'Doesn't seem like something an uncle would do. Ghost you like that.'

'What are you saying?'

'More what a boyfriend would do.'

'Jesus you must be drunk yourself. He's old enough to be my father,' she snapped at him. But was squirming inside.

'Maybe you met him on SugarDaddie.com.'

'What the fuck?'

'Chino's friend did that – Shona. The guy helped pay her uni fees.'

'He's not my fucking sugar daddy! Jesus Christ what do you think I am?' Her mum might be a bit of a gold-digging tart. But she was not.

'Well who the fuck is he then?'

'Honestly you've really got the wrong end of the stick.' She got up and went to the sink to get a glass of water. This conversation was getting out of control. She needed to sober up fast. Took big mouthfuls to try and dilute the alcohol. Refilled the glass and passed it to Bert. He took it with a flat smile. Took one sip and then put the glass down. Sat staring at her. Waiting for an answer.

'I told you George is a probation officer, right?' She took a breath. 'Well, truth is, he's *my* probation officer. Or was. Only since he got himself *transferred*,' she added, 'I haven't heard a pip squeak out of him.'

'Probation officer?'

'And the woman who's taken over. She's well meaning, but a bit useless.' Was that a bit unfair to Tammy? Probably.

'Why have you got a probation officer?'

The alcohol must have really made him slow. 'Oh God, Bert. Why do you think?' She watched his face change as he slowly worked it out.

'You've been to prison?' She could see him trying to get his suburban schoolboy head around what that meant. It gave her a feeling of ironic drunken superiority.

'HMP Thornhill.'

'Right.' He had a wary look, like a tourist who'd taken a wrong turning in a dangerous country. The sheltered little world of Westcliffe was somewhere far, far away.

'Am I allowed to ask what you did?'

I killed someone. I killed a kid. I choked a kid to death.

She winced at the thought. He caught the look on her face. 'Must have been bad whatever it was.'

'Does it make any difference? You're going to run a mile anyway, aren't you?'

'Just tell me the truth. Let me decide whether I'm gonna *run a mile*.'

'I'm trouble, Bert. That's the truth.'

'Yeah. I kinda worked that one out already.'

'I'm not nice sweet little Anna Moreton who works in a nice li'l coffee shop...'

He laughed. 'You were never sweet little Anna. You're different. I knew that, the moment I saw you.'

This was her opportunity. Tell him everything. She wanted to tell him. He deserved to be told. And maybe he'd understand. What a difference that would make to her life, if someone knew her worst secret and still wanted her. That's why she'd valued George's friendship. But in the end he was just doing a job. With Bert it would be different. If he accepted who she was and stood by her. Well that would be love. Real love. In fact, how can you really love and be loved if you tell each other lies.

'Well?' he said, still waiting for an answer 'What did you do?' His body was tense, hands clutching his knees, like he was bracing himself for a crash.

If she could trust him not to tell anyone. Then she would. But she just couldn't take the risk. She knew in her bones he wouldn't be able to handle it. Not yet. Maybe one day. But not today. So she told him a lie. How she'd attacked someone in the children's home. One of the supervisors. And then broken things and smashed windows. Charged with assault and criminal damage.

'I was going through a difficult time, but that was no excuse. Anyway I paid for it by being sent to Thornhill Open Prison for a couple of years.'

He nodded. Accepting.

'Don't tell your mum, will you?'

'You joking? I won't tell anyone. Not a soul.'

She smiled. 'Thanks.'

'And by the way, I don't think I can run a mile.'

'You probably should.'

'We've all done some dumb things. You know they used to call me Bad News Bert, cus of getting into drunken fights.'

'Ah but juggling straightened you out.'

'Kind of. Being sent to circus school summer camp, yeah that gave me something. Plus, there were people there, you know. People who'd done worse than me in the past.'

Sounded like her kind of place. 'Perhaps I should go there.'

'Perhaps you should.'

'I can't juggle.'

'You're learning.'

'Yes. I am.'

THIRTY-FIVE

'The English Riviera', Devon

This town had a pier. A big improvement on the sleepy places where they'd spent the last couple of days. There were even fruit machines in the entrance lobby, which Darren took as a good sign.

He made his way down to the pierhead, attracted by the promise of something he couldn't quite name. Although when he got there, he wondered why he'd bothered. There was nothing to see but a grumbling ocean and an indifferent grey sky. A dark shadow of falling rain was out to sea. A boat, sporting an array of long fishing rods pointing skywards, returned to harbour ahead of the bad weather.

He'd spent most of the day sounding off about the government. How not supporting Riley's Law felt like a knife in his back.

Jedd had tried to sound more positive. 'You won't be the only one angry about this. If you ask me, it makes it more likely than ever that someone will give her away.'

Darren grunted, unconvinced.

'Every cloud has a silver lining, know what I'm saying?'

Looking up at the leaden sky, there was no sign of a silver lining anywhere. Just approaching rain.

The Grand Hotel was set back from the seafront and looked over a small lake with a fountain in its centre. It resembled a palace, complete with ornate turrets. Jedd had texted to say he was in the lobby.

Darren walked up the wide marble steps toward a liveried doorman guarding the entrance. He half expected to be challenged, but the man silently opened the door for him.

The lobby was vast, with a double-height ceiling, pink marble columns and chandeliers. He found Jedd sprawled across a leather sofa.

'What do you think?' He grinned and looked around like he owned the place. Jedd had caught the sun in the last few days, all that sea air and coastal light. But the scar above his eye stayed pale and white.

'What are we doing here?'

'We need a bit of a pick me up, after what happened with Riley's Law and everything,' Jedd said, handing him a key card. Room 1056.

'What! We can't stay here!' Jedd was supposed to book them into a modest B&B.

'Oh, come on, Mr Grumpy,' Jedd said and adopted an exaggerated look of disappointment on his baby face.

'Seriously, Jedd, it's going to cost an arm and a leg.'

'I thought you'd like it here.' The exaggerated face gave way to one of genuine displeasure.

Darren felt a pang of guilt and sat down opposite, sinking into the leather. 'I do like it. It's just the money.'

'No worries on that score. I got it covered.'

'I can't let you pay for me, Jedd.' He was already beholden to Jedd. He didn't want to increase his obligation to the guy.

'Relax. I paid it out of Riley's fund,' Jedd said with a smile.

'The fund? Riley's Law fund? We can't spend that on a

hotel!' Darren gasped, shocked that Jedd would even think of spending Riley's money on something so frivolous.

'What are we going to use it for then?'

'People gave that money to pay for lawyers and the campaign.'

'Yeah, but we don't have any lawyers to pay now, do we? And the people, the people who gave that money, they'd want it to go to a good cause. You see what I'm saying?'

'This hotel is not a good cause.'

'But finding Caitlin is.'

'It's… it's… extravagant.'

'It's just for one night,' Jedd said. 'We deserve a break. You deserve a break.'

Darren didn't think so. He bore some responsibility for Riley's death. He didn't deserve to stay in a luxury hotel.

'No, Jedd, we should be staying in a bed and breakfast place.'

'Look. I had to pay for the room upfront, so it's a done deal. But if you insist, I can pay it out of my own money.'

'You should have talked to me first.'

'It was meant to be a surprise. You know, a consolation present for the Riley's Law thing.'

'I don't know, Jedd,' he mumbled, shaking his head.

'It will hardly make a dent in the Riley's Law money.'

He could feel his resolve weakening and so agreed that just this once they could use the fund to pay for the hotel. He didn't like it. But then again, what would they do with that money now? Keep it in case the government had a change of heart? Donate it to charity? He had to admit, he didn't know. Maybe they should try to give it back.

Before dinner he went for a walk around the town, telling himself that if Jedd had raided Riley's fund for the money, well that was his doing. Jedd had set the fund up and any irregularities were not Darren's fault. It was nothing to do with him.

He discovered two amusement arcades together with shops selling rock candy and buckets and spades to dig up the red sand on the resort's long wide beach. There was crazy golf and a children's play area on the esplanade. It was a good resort for families with kids. It made him feel better. This really could be the place that Tracey had told him about. And if they found Grady here, maybe he'd deserve a swanky hotel after all.

Jedd insisted they eat in the Grand Hotel's equally grand restaurant: sparkling chandeliers, huge windows looking out over the illuminated fountains, and large potted ferns everywhere that made him feel like a wilting greenhouse plant himself. They were pretty much the only diners and he felt self-conscious and exposed.

Jedd ordered the lobster, which was so expensive there was no price on the menu. 'Depends on the size and weight,' Jedd informed him, while sipping chilled white wine. The beads of moisture on the glass made it seem more exclusive somehow. Like an advert.

Darren ordered fish and chips, and a pint of lager, which attracted a barely disguised look of contempt from the waiter. Perhaps he should have ordered wine like Jedd. Or was it his Bristol accent? Jedd's voice wasn't posh exactly, but you couldn't tell where he was from.

The waiter scrutinised him as he buttered his bread roll, as though he was doing it the wrong way and would be asked to leave any second.

Jedd was loving the place. Darren realised the difference between them was Jedd relished attention, whereas he, Darren shied away. If someone was watching him, it reminded him of his father's disapproving looks at the dinner table.

Why couldn't he be more like his brother? Troy never gave a fuck what anyone thought. If he came here, he'd be all matey with the waiters, while still getting their respect for being in the forces.

'Want a taste?' Jedd asked when the lobster arrived. Darren had never actually seen a lobster let alone eaten one.

'No, you're all right.'

'Know what you like. Like what you know. That's you.'

Darren grunted and looked around wondering where he could get vinegar for his fish and chips. He could do with some ketchup as well. He tried to catch a waiter's eye. But failed.

'You should try the lobster, mate,' Jedd said.

'I'm happy with my fish and chips, to be honest.'

'I know you are and fair play to you. But you're missing out.'

He ignored Jedd and popped a chip into his mouth.

'You might like lobster. You might get a taste for it,' Jedd said, teasing.

'I might not.'

'It might become your favourite thing though, and if you don't try, you'll have missed out, won't you?'

'You gonna go on about the bloody lobster all night?'

'I just want to see you enjoy the good things in life, mate.' He cut a piece of lobster and leaning across the table, put it on Darren's plate.

Darren stared at it, resisting the instinct to flick it onto the table cloth.

'It won't bite.'

'Well I won't bite *it* neither. So we'll have a truce then, won't we?' Darren pushed it to the side of his plate.

'How can a big lad like you be scared of a little bit of lobster?'

'Godsake!' He forked the invader and popped it into his mouth. It was a bit chewy, but quite meaty. Kind of okay, but he didn't see why people were prepared to shell out so much for it. 'S'alright.'

'Now your wife's out of the picture, you can start taking advantage of what the world has to offer. See what I'm saying?'

Was his wife out of the picture? And did he want what the 'world had to offer' without Kerry to share it with?

'And at some point, you'll want to sort out that fat cunt, won't you?' Jedd said.

He'd told Jedd about Jim. His suspicions that the man was spying on him at the garden centre. 'She's not with Jim. He was just her lacky. She's with her mother.'

'Are you sure about that?'

'Hundred per cent,' he said. But his voice sounded hollow. Jim was an ugly fat bastard. But could he be absolutely sure she wasn't with him?

'I could find out for you.'

'There's no need.' It was his problem not Jedd's, and it probably wasn't a good idea to encourage the guy to poke his nose into Kerry's life.

'I'm a professional. She won't know I'm checking her out.'

'A professional?' He was a security guard, not a private detective. Anyway, private detectives only existed on films and TV, didn't they?

'I've done surveillance work. In the past.' Jedd was staring at him, eyebrows raised with a half-smile on his smooth face.

'You really done surveillance work?' He had to admit that part of him was desperate to know if Jim and Kerry were really together.

'Police.'

'Police?' He couldn't help but be impressed. If it were true. 'Doing what exactly?'

'Undercover. Organised crime. It was a difficult time, and, well, in the end I had to get out.'

He stared at Jedd long and hard. There was a story there, he could tell. One day he'd get the guy to tell him about it.

'Okay, I suppose you could make some discreet enquiries about Kerry. But hang on until after we've found Grady.'

'Yeah, mate. Of course, Grady comes first.'

He decided he needed another drink, and failing to attract the waiter's attention through looks alone, clicked his fingers which attracted a scowl. But the waiter came over nonetheless.

THIRTY-SIX

Victoria Park, Westcliffe

She was juggling soft blue, yellow and red balls. They were a present from Bert and now, after hour upon hour of practice, she'd perfected a couple of simple tricks. She was bursting to show off her skills to her boyfriend. She smiled at the thought she had an actual boyfriend. The beginnings of a normal life. But the moment's warmth was dispelled by cold doubt. She hadn't seen Bert for over a week.

She told herself not to worry. He was taking extra shifts at Tesco, saving up for circus school, having taken her advice to follow his dream. Good for him. She was tempted to go there too. Fire eaters and trapeze artists, street performers and buskers: they weren't your average run-of-the-mill crowd, were they? Freaks and rebels. People who didn't fit in with mainstream society. People like her. A place where she might feel accepted. A place where normals were the outsiders.

She'd been playing it cool, waiting for him to get in touch. But the insecure worrier in her was starting to get the upper hand so she gave in and texted him, wanting to meet.

No reply. She walked past Tesco, stopping to peer in

through the glass doors, hoping to see him behind the counter. No sign.

Twenty-four hours later, there was still no reply and worry made her send a couple more texts asking him to let her know what was going on. And was he all right?

Maybe he was ill. Had an accident and been taken to A&E, and was languishing in some hospital at death's door. But surely his mother would have got in touch? She tried calling him of course, but it just went to voicemail. All right then, his phone was stolen or broken or had fallen down the toilet.

She went into Tesco, this time asking after him. She was met with shrugs and stonewalling.

Either something bad had happened or more likely he'd had second thoughts about her having been to prison, and had run for cover. The only way to find out the truth was to go round to his house and knock on the front door.

She waited on the doorstep for an answer with lead in her stomach. Through the swirling bevelled glass, she could see the distorted image of his mother coming to answer – her head somehow separated from her body.

Mrs Fernandes opened the door. Gone were the warm smiles, instead unfocused eyes looked past her, flicking up and down the street as though she was afraid the neighbours might see who she was talking to.

'He's out and I don't know when he'll be back,' was all she said, before making an excuse about being busy and practically shutting the door in her face.

He'd told her. Must have done. Told her she was an ex-con. So much for not telling a soul. And not running a fucking mile.

Friday night, she steeled herself and headed off to The Tudor to look for him. Even if he wasn't there, one of his mates would be. Yeah okay, it might count as stalking him, but she needed to know what the fuck was going on. Preferably out of his own mouth.

She found him tucked away in a booth sitting next to Chino. Not just sitting. His arm was draped around her. They looked very fucking cosy. She strode up, blood fizzing in her head.

'If you're gonna dump me, you might be man enough to tell me to my face.' If she'd had a drink she would have thrown it at him.

He looked up at her with clouded eyes, like he didn't recognise her. Then, deciding to speak asked, 'How's George?' His words were thick with booze.

'What?'

'How's *Uncle* George doing?'

'I'll catch you later, babe,' Chino said, unwrapping herself and slipping away. The girl pointedly avoided eye contact. Maybe they'd been shagging all the time she'd been with him.

'I told you all about Uncle George,' she said, wondering what game he was playing.

'D'you call him uncle in bed? Is it like a thing that turns you on?'

'What the fuck?'

'You really took the piss out of me,' Bert said. 'Lying. Pretending that we were something. And meanwhile, you and George.'

She felt a wave of nausea and dizziness. 'There is no *me and George*.' She looked around, seeking a friendly face. The only face was Chino talking to another couple of guys at the bar.

'It's all over the internet, your affair with your probation officer.' He paused and fixed her with a nasty curled-lip stare. 'Caitlin.'

The world keeled onto its side. She couldn't hear anything except ringing in her ears. Like someone had hit her over the head with a mallet. In that moment they were the only two people in the pub. She felt her legs about to give way and grabbed the table for support. Her first instinct was to deny it. Just front it out. But she couldn't speak.

'Nothing to say, Caitlin?' She slumped down on the seat opposite him. 'How could I have been so dumb not to see it? I'm supposed to be good at maths, but I couldn't put two and two together. It's so obvious. But then I thought I knew you.'

'I'm sorry,' she mumbled.

'You're sorry!?' His face twisted in disgust.

'I wanted to tell you. I did. I just didn't know how.'

'Lying bitch. That's what you are. Scheming and—'

'I never had an affair with George. I was telling the truth about that.' She felt tears running down her cheeks.

'I don't believe a word that comes out of your mouth. You lied all the way along: one minute your parents are dead, the next your mum couldn't look after you. Then you were "vulnerable". Lies. All of it.'

'My feelings for you are genuine.'

'You can't help yourself, can you? It's just bullshit, Caitlin. Bull-shite.' He shook his head. 'I really fell for you. Well, not you, I fell for Anna. But I loved a fake. A phantom.'

'What we had was real.'

'Like some saddo who falls for a catfish on the internet. Someone who doesn't exist.'

'I exist, Bert. I am real.'

He shook his head again. 'My girlfriend was called Anna. She doesn't exist.'

'But I am a real person.

'Yeah, Caitlin fucking Grady.'

'That's right. The evil Caitlin Grady. Child killer. That's what I am to the world. That's *all* I am to the world. A headline in a newspaper. But I was more than that to you. And whatever happens, I'll always remember…' She sighed and took a moment to look at him. Those pale grey eyes and that tanned smooth skin. 'I'll always remember, you. You and me. What we had together.' She nodded, as much to herself as to him. 'I will, Bert. I really will.'

He stared at her. She couldn't tell whether it was anger, pain or pity in his eyes. 'You should leave Westcliffe.'

'Probably.'

'While you still can.'

'What's that supposed to mean?'

'They're coming for you. So if I were you, I'd fuck off somewhere, find yourself a dark cave and stay there.' He got to his feet.

'Tell me something? If I had told you who I really was, would it have made any difference?'

He stared at her for a moment, shook his head and left in a drunken meandering walk. He waved casually to his friends at the bar and headed off, out of the pub.

She knew she'd never see him again. He'd walked out that door and taken her one chance of a normal life with him.

She went to the bar, ordered a shot of vodka and downed it to calm her nerves. It wasn't cold in the pub, but she was shivering. She ordered another shot. Wondered how long she had left.

THIRTY-SEVEN

Grand Hotel

D arren was woken by an insistent buzzing from the bedside table. Squinting in the pale early morning light, he reached for his phone. It was Harvey Pringle.

'Big news, mate,' Harvey said in a voice far too excited for the early hour. 'We had a tip-off. Solid information. Source is credible. The lawyers have been on it all night. We even held the front page, would you believe it?'

'A tip-off?' Adrenaline kicked him awake. 'Do we know where she is?'

'We do. But we can't print diddly-squat. Can't even so much as hint. We've all been told of the "very severe consequences" to each and every one of us individually, if we so much as breathe a whisper.' Was this Harvey's way of making him beg for information? Or did he just want to share the frustration around? 'I could be arrested for what I'm about to tell you, so on no account did you hear this from me, okay?'

'Okay.'

'And if I tell you, then I want exclusive access to your story.'

'Yeah, yeah, whatever,' Darren said with growing impatience.

'No, no. Not "whatever". I want you to keep me informed every step of the way. Daily reports: How and where you find her. What passes between you when you confront her. Every last detail.'

'Okay. I get it.'

'Exclusive access. You don't talk to anyone else about what occurs, just me. Deal?' Harvey's voice was hoarse. Like he'd been up all night shouting.

'Deal.'

'You'll say you got an anonymous tip-off.'

'Okay. I understand.' He was fighting to keep the irritation out of his voice. Why did he have to play this game? Spit it out for God's sake.

'Caitlin Grady is living in the seaside town of Westcliffe.'

'Westcliffe!' That was only an hour's drive max.

'Works as a waitress in a coffee shop on the high street apparently, although the source didn't name the establishment.'

'The source? Who is this person?'

'I haven't been told. But they have met Caitlin personally. She is now going under the name of Anna Moreton. She has shoulder-length hair, dyed blonde.'

Hair dyed blonde. Working in a coffee shop. Details that had never been printed, but matched what Tracey told him.

'Big news' didn't cover it. Every cell in his body was filled with a kind of terrible joy at the thought he was finally going to get to Grady. The long search was almost over. The day of reckoning was at hand.

Darren and Jedd were sitting in a coffee shop in Westcliffe. They'd already checked out the other places on the high street and drawn a blank. No sign of anyone who looked like Grady. Prospects didn't look much better here. They'd ordered a couple of coffees from the spikey haired middle-aged woman and took a table where they could keep an eye on the counter.

'Lipstick lesbian,' Jedd said.

Darren scowled into his coffee. He thought people had stopped making snide remarks about the gay community years ago. 'My sister's gay.'

'Just saying.' Jedd shifted in his seat. 'In case you fancied her.'

'You think she runs this place on her own?' he asked to get the guy to focus on the job in hand.

Jedd shrugged. 'Let's just wait and see.'

So they took their time drinking their coffees, which was okay by Darren. He'd had enough coffee and was starting to feel headachy. He left his drink to go cold, but then a slight girl with mousy brown hair appeared from somewhere out the back. Didn't look like Grady. But could he be sure she hadn't dyed her hair again?

'What do you think?' he said.

The security guy shook his head. 'Looks like a school kid to me.' He had to agree, she did look a bit young to be Grady.

When, later, the girl came over to take their cups away, he could see she really was quite young. She was around the same age as Riley would be now, if she'd lived. That disturbed him in ways he couldn't fully understand.

'Shouldn't you be at school?' Jedd said.

The girl was taken aback, as though she'd been told off by a teacher or policeman. The uniform effect.

'It's half term. I'm just helping Brig out,' she stammered.

'No worries,' Darren said, smiling at her.

'How old are you?' Jedd snapped.

'Um… fourteen, I'll be fifteen in January.'

Annoyed at Jedd's attitude, Darren flashed him a warning

look. But Jedd carried on regardless. 'And exactly how many hours a week do you work?'

'My mum said it was okay. D'you want to talk to the manager?' The girl began to back away like a frightened baby animal. Brig was looking at them now.

Darren said, 'No it's fine. He's just checking.'

The girl turned and fled, taking cover behind the counter. Darren could see Brig questioning her, before the girl disappeared. 'I don't know what that achieved,' he mumbled into his coffee.

'Did you spot the CCTV?' Jedd said, changing the subject.

'Yeah, but how's that going to help us?

'If the bitch works here, she'll be on camera.'

Darren nodded. 'But how are we going to get access?'

'Maybe if we ask the lipstick lezzie nicely...'

'Well here she comes,' Darren said as Brig headed over towards them. It didn't look like *nice* was on the agenda.

'Can I see your ID, please?' she said to Jedd.

'Why?'

'My waiter tells me you are questioning her work here. Where's your authority?'

'I'm just a concerned member of the public that's all.'

'Concerned about what?'

'Exploitation of minors.'

'Freya is fourteen, and is therefore permitted to work twenty-five hours a week during the school holidays,' she said with an authority that wouldn't go amiss in the army. She wasn't someone to mess with.

'What about your other employees? They all minors too?' Jedd said, persisting.

'I don't know what your game is, but I'd like you both to leave now, please.'

Jedd stared at the woman for a moment with a half-smile. Like a chess player deciding on his next move.

'Come on,' Darren said, standing up.

Jedd mumbled something unintelligible and dragging his feet, followed him out of the café.

'Don't know why you had to have a go at that girl in there,' Darren said as they walked past Tesco towards the seafront.

'I was just shaking the tree. See what fell out.'

'Taking an interest in her underage workers. The manager probably has us down as a couple of paedos.'

'You know what your problem is? You care too much what people think. Whereas me, I don't give a flying fuck.' Jedd grinned to himself. The dimples on his face made him resemble a hamster.

Jedd insisted it would be possible to hack into CoffeeTime's CCTV cameras. So after they checked into a seafront hotel he went online to consult his new-found friends on HuntAKilla in search of a hacker for hire. Darren doubted that a little place like CoffeeTime would have its cameras linked up to the internet, but there was no arguing with Jedd. He also wondered how much they'd have to pay a hacker to do such a job. But it would at least be a legitimate use of Riley's money.

Darren's room overlooked the promenade. To one side was the pier, with its brash neon-lit entrance, its bright coloured lights making a last stand against the darkening autumn weather. Looking the other way, in the distance at the far end of the beach, was a rocky outcrop. He might take a walk over there this evening, to have a break from Jedd. The guy was a bit much sometimes. He was grateful for his help and all that, but he needed a breather. He didn't like the way he'd picked on that teenager in the shop. Made him feel bad. Like he'd picked on Riley.

———

The next morning, Jedd came down to breakfast beaming and insisted they have Buck's Fizz with their bacon and eggs. Darren had been right about the café's CCTV. So Jedd, ever resourceful, turned his attention to the café's owner. According to an online company database, Brigit Stoneham was the sole proprietor of CoffeeTime.

Overnight, an Israeli hacker broke into her mobile phone and downloaded the pictures stored on it. Darren might ordinarily have been shocked by this, but was too excited by what Jedd showed him.

Two photos in particular were electrifying: the inside page of a passport in the name of a certain Anna Moreton. The mugshot was of a young woman with striking blue eyes and shoulder-length blonde hair. It was her. This time he was sure. And the name matched. Presumably the photo was taken when she had to prove her ID for the job. There was also a pic of 'Anna's' provisional driving licence, which had an address on it.

'Eat up,' Jedd said. 'It might be a long day.'

After breakfast, Jedd went to get the van, while Darren went to scope out CoffeeTime. He hadn't the gall to go in after yesterday, so sauntered past several times, peering in through the windows. There was no sign of so-called 'Anna Moreton'.

Later they were both seated in the back of the van watching a building. In particular, a room on the upper ground floor which had the curtains drawn shut.

The idea was to grab her when she came out, bundle her into the back of the van and boot it out of town. Darren wondered how easy it would be in practice, but Jedd insisted a young woman like Grady would be no match for the two of them.

'Easy-peasy. Snatch and run.' Sounded like they were just pinching some gear from a building site, not abducting a young woman.

Sluggish hours crawled past. The air in the van was stale

and smelt of something damp and rotting. Sweaty policemen's bad breath had got into the bones of the van somehow. Unless it was Jedd's boots.

With nothing happening, questions bubbled up from a part of his brain he was ignoring. He'd been so excited by the prospect of finally getting to Grady, it had been easy not to think. But now questions needed answers. Once they got her in the van, what then? Where would they take her? What would he do to her? Up to now it hadn't been real. Just an idea. A fantasy even. But now here they were, actually sitting outside a flat, planning to abduct a young woman. If they were caught, he'd be sent down. Was he ready for that?

He forced the doubts away with what Grady had done to Riley. Buttressed his determination by torturing himself with memories of the police photographs. The shots of her bruised neck and bloodshot eyes indicating trauma. The pics Kerry had refused to look at. It wasn't how she wanted to remember Riley, she said at the time. Well someone had to remember. So it had to be him.

But he couldn't settle. It was all this waiting. That was the problem. He was a doer, not a sit on his arse and waiter. He sighed and huffed and puffed.

'What's the matter?'

'Nothing.'

'If you're getting restless, then how about you do a pizza run?'

'Good idea.' Maybe his heebie-jeebies were caused by hunger.

'How about you get us a pepperoni to share?' Jedd said.

He pulled a face. 'Bit spicy.'

Jedd let out a disappointed sigh. 'Okay then, margherita!'

He took his time getting the pizza, enjoying the cool air after the claustrophobic van. And he found himself dragging his feet, as if he secretly wanted Grady to make a run for it while he wasn't there. What was wrong with him? He had to do this. Had to. Couldn't be a wimp about it. Troy wouldn't be like this, would he? He remembered the black dog. He had been scared of the beast, but Troy had booted it in the balls.

The pizza cheered him up, but then more hours went by and nothing happened.

'Suppose she's not there.'

'She's there.'

'How do you know?'

'Would you rather she wasn't?'

'Not what I said.'

'You seem a bit stressy though.' Jedd gave Darren a hard look.

'I'm fine.' Jesus, was he that transparent?

'Good. Cus I wouldn't want you to bottle on me, mate.' Sounded like a warning rather than a note of friendly concern.

'I'm not going to bottle.' He thought for a moment and added, 'It's just, where are we going to take her?'

'I know a place.'

'Where?'

Jedd winked. 'All in good time.'

More sloth-like hours. Nothing happened except a woman went into the building, a secretary or businesswoman type. Probably coming home from her office.

Surveillance work didn't suit Darren. Got bored too easily. He looked out of the smoked glass window at the curtained flat. Wondered if Grady knew somehow they were there.

'What if she never comes out?'

'She's got to show her face eventually.'

'We can't wait here forever, can we?'

'Patience. But if we're going to be here for the long haul, we'll have to work out a shift pattern. So take a break. Go and chill at the hotel for a couple of hours. Get some shut-eye in case it's a late night.'

Back at the hotel he went for a badly needed piss. The stream was dark and yellow from too much coffee and no water. Stung his penis as it came out. He watched as the urine formed a sulphurous dark yellow cloud in the white pan's clear water. He gulped down mouthfuls of fresh cold water to purify himself.

He looked at his reflection in the mirror. What were they going to do with Caitlin Grady, really? Once they got her in the van, there'd be no turning back. Justice for Riley, was his mantra. But what did it mean? An eye for an eye? Would he be capable of killing her? Because if it was to be done, then he would be the one to do it. He wouldn't let Jedd do it. She wasn't Jedd's to kill. She was his, Darren's. But could he? Could he take a life in cold blood? Would that be justice? 'An eye for an eye,' he repeated to himself in the mirror. Was he staring at the face of an executioner?

Remembering Grady from the trial. That arrogant couldn't-care-less face. If she was like that, if she wasn't sorry for what she'd done. If there was no remorse, then yes, if he screwed down his courage, he could administer ultimate justice. He'd do it for Riley. And he'd take the consequences.

He flicked on the TV. Some cheerful celebrity DIYer was making over a house for a disabled woman. He had a team of enthusiastic helpers and it was all such fun and in a good cause that Darren found the general atmosphere of doing good rubbed off on him, dissolving the darkness that was gathering in his soul. At least for now.

THIRTY-EIGHT

Studio flat, Belsize Gardens, Westcliffe

She hadn't been able to face going into work, so took a few days off. Told Tammy what happened with Bert and she agreed it was time for her to leave Westcliffe. Promised she was 'putting the wheels in motion'.

She tried not to think about Bert. But couldn't help fantasising about him calling her up to say he realised that despite who she was, he loved her and couldn't bear to be parted from her. What crap. He'd told his mum, that was obvious. And that woman was definitely part of the 'string em up' mob. Even if Bert hadn't told anyone else, his mother was bound to have blabbed to someone. She had to get out of town. No two ways about it.

She wondered if it would always be like this, living the life of a fugitive or refugee. A rolling stone. But then perhaps a nomadic existence wouldn't be all bad. No strings. Be her own person. Nothing to tie her down. Maybe it could be a journey of self-discovery: she could re-invent herself at every port of call, maybe that way she'd eventually know who she really was.

Tinker, tailor, soldier, sailor, rich bitch, poor whore, bag lady. Witch.

She didn't go out except for furtive late-night dashes to the convenience shop two streets away. The curtains remained closed against the outside world and she spent her time on the bed with Teddy Tubby, re-reading the Harry Potter books. Hogwarts had always been her escape. One of Teddy Tubby's eyes had fallen off recently. Poor thing was losing his sight.

At night the fears came. Scenarios where the mob, egged on by journalists, got to her. Tammy shrugging her shoulders and refusing to help.

The first thing she did every morning was peer anxiously out of the curtain crack. A ritual she repeated every few hours. But so far there was nothing. No sign of the feared journalists. No unruly mob. She made herself check the internet regularly. Flinching at the comments on @BitchHunt and HuntAKilla. But so far there was nothing new. Nothing about Westcliffe. No new pictures of her. She was starting to relax a little. She'd be moved any day now.

She looked around the room, which in the shapeless claustrophobic days had started to resemble an animal's cave. But instead of old bones, this cave was strewn with left-over ready meals and drinks cans. It was developing a fetid atmosphere. It was time to tidy up and let some light in, so she bundled the rubbish into a black bin bag. The bins were kept in the basement well at the front of the building, and to get there involved venturing out through the front door.

She checked the curtain crack. Everything was quiet. No newsmen or photographers. The parked cars were the ones she unconsciously recognised as belonging to the street. Nobody was loitering about. The only thing of note was a white van. Probably a delivery guy. Amazon or Ebay.

But there was something about that van. She had the sixth sense of a hunted animal and decided to wait till the van drove off before taking the bin bag out.

An hour later it was still there. She studied it through the crack. Obviously not a delivery guy. Maybe a builder then? But it didn't look like a builder's van. The smoked glass window in the side didn't seem right. The paintwork looked a bit strange too. Patchy. It just felt all wrong. Looked like the kind of van a paedophile would use to snatch a kid.

If only George was around, he'd have come over, checked out the van and put her mind at rest. She wondered again why he hadn't at least got in touch with her. Even once, to say he was okay. It hurt.

She phoned Tammy. Tammy's voice was normally comforting; smooth and rich in a way that made her relax. But today, Tammy sounded stressed and irritable.

'I'm sure it's just a tradesman's van,' she said, before telling her how busy she was which made Caitlin feel unreasonable for bothering her. The woman made it clear she was working her tits off trying to find somewhere to get her moved to.

Hours later and the van was still there. It was getting late. Workmen usually packed up and went home by about five o'clock, didn't they? But no workmen came.

Finally, her anxiety about the damned van made her phone Brig out of sheer desperation to do something. She asked her manager if anyone had been enquiring about her in the café?

'Anyone like who? If you mean Bert, I haven't seen him.'

'Anyone else?'

'Are you all right, Anna? You sound a bit stressed.'

'Yeah, maybe I am, a bit.' She'd already decided that she wouldn't leave Westcliffe without telling Brig who she really was. But she wanted to tell her to her face, so for now, simply said she was afraid some people from her past had come to try and find her.

'No one's been asking about you.'

'No one suspicious in the café?'

'Actually, now you mention it…' She told her about the two

men asking about underage workers. 'I thought they were dodgy. Had them down as a couple of paedophiles, but thinking about it, paedos wouldn't be so obvious.'

'What did they look like?'

'Oh, you know. Average. One had a scar above his eye, I remember that.'

'Did you get them on the CCTV?'

'Probably, I'll be here for a bit, so swing by and take a look.'

'No thanks. It's okay. Never mind,' she mumbled. She made an excuse and hung up. But then wondered why she hadn't just told Brig everything. What difference would it make now anyway? Might as well shout it from the rooftops.

Later, as it was starting to get dark, Brig sent her a still image from CoffeeTime's CCTV. She recognised Darren Burgess immediately. Sat down on the bed, heart pounding. Gasping for air as though there was a lack of oxygen in the room. He was here. And he had a creepy accomplice. They were in that van outside. No question. What were they planning? Wait till nightfall and break in? Murder her in her bed?

With shaking hands, she picked up her phone and called Tammy again. This time at least, her probation officer took the threat seriously.

'I'll have to make some calls to the crisis team. We'll get you out of there tonight. Just stay put.'

But she didn't want to stay put. She paced around her single-room flat wondering what to do. They could come in through the door any second. She packed her backpack with a few essentials in case she had to leave in a hurry. It at least gave her something to do.

She was tempted to simply escape the flat and leg it down the street. But what if they caught her? How about going through the back garden, then? Trouble was she'd have to go through the basement flat, which had its own separate entrance from the street. So in the end all she could do was hope that Tammy would be round before Darren made his move.

THIRTY-NINE

Atlantic Hotel, Westcliffe

H e jolted awake, startled by his phone chiming the arrival of a message. He'd nodded off in front of the TV like an old woman and it was already dark outside. He felt ashamed about how long he must have been dozing.

> Get your arse back here. It's all kickin off!

On his way to Belsize Gardens a siren deafened him as an ambulance screamed past, blue lights blazing. Gave him an uneasy sense that there was trouble ahead. Then as he got nearer, his nose was filled with the acidic smell of something burning. Turning the corner into Belsize Gardens itself, he was brought up short, stupefied by the scene. Two fire tenders, an ambulance and a police car. Firemen in yellow hats were spraying water onto a building. Caitlin's building. No flames as far as he could see, but white smoke, caught in floodlights was billowing from the upper ground-floor window.

Jaw dropped and stomach full of lead, he couldn't move. Prayed to God that Jedd hadn't done this. Surely, he wasn't that crazy? Was he? There was no sign of Jedd or his old police van.

A couple of policemen were cordoning off the area, and trying to get the gathering crowd of onlookers to move back, although it seemed there was no immediate danger and the fire looked under control.

A woman, perhaps in her seventies, was standing near him and as he caught her eye, he could see a tear running down her cheek.

'Are you all right, my love?' he asked, moving closer.

She looked at him surprised. 'Oh yes.' She wiped her face with her hand. 'Just the smoke in my eyes.'

He nodded. 'Would you like a handkerchief?' She looked frail and vulnerable, reminding him of his mother. He felt like giving her a hug. Wanted to comfort her in some way. Or perhaps he needed comforting himself.

'No it's all right. I'm just being a bit silly and emotional.' He didn't think it was at all silly shedding a tear at someone's house on fire and said so.

'It's the shock, I think. Not what you expect around here is it?'

'Was anyone hurt?'

'I don't know. But I heard them say it was started deliberate.'

His jaw tensed up. Worst fears confirmed.

'Who would do that?' the woman was saying. 'If you can't be safe in your home, then where can you be?' She shook her head and wandered off to be alone with her fears.

He should leave too. Just go. Get to the station, catch the first train out of here. Put as many miles between himself, the fire and Jedd as possible.

But what if Caitlin was trapped inside? Suppose they brought her out? Or suppose she'd been overcome by smoke. He imagined her burned and charred body being pulled from the building. That's not what he wanted. He wanted her alive. He wanted to question her and yes, maybe he did want her to suffer for her crimes. But he needed to witness her pain himself. Physical, but also emotional. That would be the sweet spot. He did not want to be simply presented with her dead body because of Jedd's recklessness.

———

Caitlin was in the bathroom when the window smashed. For a moment or two, her brain tried to play down what was happening. It was simply a milk bottle breaking outside, even though no one gets milk delivered anymore. Or maybe a drunk dropping a bottle in the street. Then she thought it was a car windscreen. It couldn't be a window in her building, could it? Not her own window surely?

Brain caught up with reality and she rushed into the living area. Flames were spreading over her curtains. She watched for a few terrifying seconds as fire engulfed the fabric and pieces of charred curtain fell onto the carpet. The flames licked upwards and caressed the ceiling. The room was filling with sooty black smoke.

She grabbed her jacket and backpack and ran out onto the landing screaming, 'Help! Fire!'

But was then paralysed by indecision. Escape through the front door? What if they were waiting? No. Don't play their game. The woman who lived above – she could help. She ran up the stairs, but stopped halfway. A window. Outside she could make out the flat roof of the basement extension. Without thinking, she opened the sash and threw her backpack and jacket onto the extension roof. Then, heart pounding, she squeezed herself through the window, legs first, sliding her body over the sill and then lowered herself, so she was hanging on to the ledge with her hands. It wasn't that much of a drop.

She could do it. She could. Okay, so she might break a leg, but at least she wouldn't be burned alive.

She let go and dropped, landing hard on the roof below, twisting her left ankle. Fucking hell, it hurt. For a moment she thought she'd broken it. The drop was further than it looked. She lay still, allowing the pain to subside a little. Then staggered to her feet. It was painful, but she could walk.

She lowered herself down into next door's back garden via some bins, and then managed to get through the gardens until she reached a house with a side passage leading to the street. She could hear sirens approaching. Emergency services. But she was afraid. The mob might even now be fanning out searching for her. Adrenaline wouldn't let her do anything but run, albeit with a limp. Run as far as she could.

Keeping to the shadows in the back streets, she reached the seafront. At least here there were people around, so she felt relatively safe. Didn't know where to go, so made her way as far from the town centre as she could by walking along the promenade, retracing the route she and Bert had taken on their first date, just a few weeks ago. Eventually she got to the sand dunes. Her ankle was throbbing. She needed to rest it and so sat in the coarse grass, overlooking the dark ocean.

She called Tammy, but there was no reply. She could leave a message. But why bother? If Tammy was any good, she'd have got her out of Belsize Gardens before nightfall. She checked @BitchHunt. They had posted that she was at large in Westcliffe, and put a pic of her up there. Her passport photo. How had they managed to get that? Jesus Christ. Darren Burgess was cleverer than he looked. Could they even hack her phone? Could they track her through the probation service tagging app?

Darren watched as a couple of firemen in breathing apparatus appeared from the building. He wondered if a body was going to come out as well, but one of the men gave a thumbs up to his colleagues. They turned the hose off and it looked as if they were getting prepared to wind down. Looking around at the crowd, he saw Jedd was watching him from the shadows. The security guard sauntered over, with an unsettling smirk.

'So, what do you think?'

'I think you should be locked up,' Darren hissed.

'Aw, come on, you don't mean that.'

'I fucking do.'

'Needs must.'

'You don't deny it then? It was you.'

'Had to try and flush her out, mate. Sometimes you have to do what it takes,' Jedd said, without an ounce of apology in his voice.

'Fucking hell. Someone could have died.'

'Take a chill pill! I called the emergency services myself. There was no danger.'

'No danger!' He shook his head. 'And Grady? Where is she?'

He shrugged. 'The only person who came out of the building was that secretary type. Got rescued by a fireman. Best day of her life!'

He stared at the guy in disbelief. Jedd seemed to think setting a house on fire was a big fucking joke. His scar was more prominent in the floodlights. It had a life of its own.

'I don't want any part of this,' he said to Jedd in a hoarse voice, choking back his outrage. He had to get away from the man before he punched the guy and they both got arrested for fighting in the street. So walked off.

'Don't be like that,' Jedd called after him. Darren took no notice and carried on walking.

He should go to the police. Tell them everything. Get Jedd

taken off the streets. Yes, that's what he'd do. End this now before anyone got hurt. He paced around town in a state of agitation. Where was a policeman when you needed one? Checked Google for the location of a police station, but the nearest one was in the next town. Okay then. He should go back to Belsize Gardens. Talk to the police there. But what would he say to them? That his friend was a dangerous arsonist and had caused the fire? They'd be suspicious of him as well, wouldn't they?

What's your relationship to Jedd, sir? they'd ask. *What's your involvement?* They could easily turn on him. After all he had a bigger motive for the firebombing than Jedd. He might even be arrested and charged for the arson attack.

He found himself on the promenade. Stopped to stare out to sea, his eye caught by a distant light which flashed every few seconds. A lighthouse warning of rocks or treacherous waters. But knowing where the rocks were was one thing. Navigating safe passage around them was another. For that you needed a map or a chart.

There was someone else leaning over the promenade railings, a silhouette caught in the seafront lights, looking out into the blackness. It was Jedd, not more than a hundred metres away. The guy was following him. There was something slumped and heavy about the way he leaned on the railings, as though he needed support. He cut a lonely figure.

Maybe he'd been a bit harsh. He'd encouraged Jedd, after all. Been on at Jedd, asking what they'd do if Caitlin didn't come out. Jedd was trying to help in the only way he knew. He needed reining in for sure. But the two of them were in this together whether he liked it or not and so he went over to speak to his friend.

'You gonna grass me up?' Jedd said as he approached.

'You're going to get us both banged up for arson.'

'So that's what's bothering you.' Jedd sounded relieved.

'Mate, there's no need to stress. You were at the hotel when the fire started. In the clear. And there's nothing to connect me to Grady. I got it covered, mate.'

'You have to promise me, no more firebombs.'

'And don't worry, even if they got me, I wouldn't land my best mate in it, would I?'

Best mates? Is that what they were now? Darren hadn't had a best mate since school. Garry had shagged his girlfriend behind his back. That was the end of best mates.

'You got to swear, no more firebombing.'

'All right then, just cus it's you.'

'Swear on your sister's soul.'

He held up his hand like a witness taking the oath. 'I swear.'

Darren nodded. 'Okay. But pull anything like that again, and I will grass you up.'

'All right. I get it.' He held Darren's gaze for a moment. 'Drink?'

'Might be an idea.'

FORTY

Battery Point, Westcliffe

The only relief from the blackness was the faint outline of the pillbox's slit-like windows. It was surprisingly cosy in here though, sheltered from the icy breeze slicing off the ocean. And her jacket was warm, so she was all right for now. If she peered through the window, she could make out the lights of the promenade in the distance. But her focus had been the causeway; she half expected to see a group of men with torches coming over the sand dunes, like in one of those films where the villagers go in search of the werewolf. But now the tide was in, she could relax.

She opened her backpack, felt for the packet of biscuits in the darkness and took one. She was rationing herself, they had to last till morning. Water was more of a problem; her single bottle was half drunk already. How long can you do without water? A couple of days?

That first time she came here with Bert, she'd freaked out when he touched her up. Ironic that this concrete fort was now her place of safety. Especially as Bert must have been the one who betrayed her.

How else had Burgess found out where she was living? She

should have listened to her body's reaction when he pushed his finger into her crotch. Booted him in the balls and had no more to do with him. Judas. To think that she'd given herself to him enthusiastically after that. And she'd really got into the sex. Made it even worse. Made her want to take a knife to his privates.

But then, suppose it wasn't him? Could be someone in the probation service. Tammy even? Because, why hadn't Tammy rescued her? Checked her into a hotel for the night. Anything, but allowed her to be attacked by a fucking fire bomber. Bitch! She kicked the concrete wall, which jarred her bad ankle.

She needed to chill. Getting angry with Bert and Tammy wasn't going to help. And she needed some sleep. Who knew what kind of shitstorm was going to hit her tomorrow?

She made herself calm down. Retrieved Teddy Tubby from her backpack and hugged him as she settled down for the night on a bed of soft dry sand, using the backpack as her pillow.

'Goodnight,' she said to Teddy Tubby, and blew out an imaginary candle.

Her eyes blinked open. It was still dark, but she was uncomfortable and suddenly anxious. Was she still safe? She stepped outside. Pale moonlight was pushing through intermittent clouds to illuminate the rocks and seashore with its soft light. A shadowy ephemeral world, it seemed unreal, as if she had woken into a dream.

She made her way towards the shore, stumbling over the pebbles and rocks. In the half-light she thought she saw an animal watching her. A wolf? Ridiculous. A dog then? Or a large cat. No. It was nothing, just a rock or shadow.

When she was a little kid, she often saw spectral creatures in the night. They were real to her at that age, but she wasn't afraid because she was a witch and these apparitions were her familiar spirits.

Staring at the black and languid sea, which seemed like thick treacly oil, a wave of despair washed over her. She'd been let down by everyone she trusted. George, Bert and Tammy. And her mum. She could step into the water, load up her pockets with stones and let the sea suck her below the surface into the blackness.

Drowning; gasping and struggling for breath while her lungs filled with water would be a horrible way to die. But now, she wondered if drowning would be better than being beaten to death by an angry mob. She began to get interested in the question. To die alone at night, in private. Or be publicly beaten? One of the mob would film it. It would go viral and add to her notoriety. A public execution. Some people would feel sorry for her, but most would be satisfied. *Serves her right,* they'd say.

'The world needs to punish, so it doesn't have to look at itself.' That's what Sandy, her favourite shrink, reckoned. But then Sandy was a bit soft.

She had so few choices left; choosing how to die was pretty much the only control she had.

Out to sea, silvery patches of moonlight glistened on the water. She imagined that out there, magical creatures, green-haired sea fairies, were waiting in the shimmering light to welcome her beneath the waves. As she stared, she could almost hear them calling.

She began to fill her pockets, stones in her jeans and jacket. Felt their weight pulling down. If she got her backpack, and filled that with stones, it would guarantee she'd be dragged to the bottom.

Then she noticed something. It was almost imperceptible, but the sky had started to lighten a touch. She'd never seen a sunrise over the sea. So she sat down on the rocky shore and waited for the sky to brighten. The first rays of the sun painted the clouds gold and orange. Watching the sunlight sparkle over the sea, and fill the world with its light and colour, aroused something primitive within her. The instinct to survive. To fight. To believe that today would be better than yesterday.

She emptied her pockets of the stones and went back up to the pillbox. Peering out at the causeway she saw that the tide was out sufficiently for her to make her way across. She should make her move, but suddenly felt reluctant to leave this island. This place was her refuge. Her place of safety. What would she face back on the mainland? She'd give it longer, stay put while the tide came in and went out one more time.

But as she kept watch, two figures appeared on the sand dunes. Two men. They were too far off to see their faces, but as they got closer, she could make out enough to recognise Darren Burgess.

She was a sitting duck in the pillbox. It would be the first place they'd look. The concrete chamber would be her coffin. Her throat tightened.

The entrance to the pillbox had an ancient steel door. There were remains of the cream paint that had once covered it, but mostly it had gone to rust. If she could shut it, they wouldn't find her. She heaved and pushed with all her strength but the fucker would not budge a single damn centimetre. She gave up and moved back to the window. Maybe they wouldn't cross the causeway.

Indeed, they seemed to be hesitating. Looked like the tide was coming in now.

Who the hell was the guy with Darren? He wasn't police, so what was the uniform about? Had Darren hired protection? Her fingers were tightly crossed as she prayed that the warning signs about the tides would put them off crossing the causeway.

Darren was gazing at the old fort. Was Caitlin hiding out in there? It didn't seem likely, but then again, if not, where was she? Overnight the hacker for hire had lifted her number from Brig's phone and tracked her to these sand dunes. It was the last place she'd used her phone.

'Maybe she checked into a B&B for the night,' Jedd said.

'Maybe she left Westcliffe.'

'How?'

That was a good question. Before they went for a drink last night, they'd checked out the railway station. There were only a few trains a day and they watched as the last one pulled out. No sign of Caitlin. There were even fewer buses and the fix they had on her phone was well after the last one left town at seven in the evening. There wasn't another train until mid-morning and by then more people would be joining the search. Jedd had put a call out on @BitchHunt and a handful of locals had agreed to check the trains and buses today. There was no way she could get away.

'Police might have moved her.'

'She only made one phone call last night and it went to a voice message service. They'd have had to call or text her. Besides her phone is still off. So she's still in Westcliffe lying low, one hundred per cent.'

He nodded. Made sense. 'How about that old concrete fort up there?' he said, pointing to the pillbox.

Jedd shrugged. 'It's worth a try.'

Darren set off towards the rock causeway. There were signs warning of dangerous tides and currents, but it looked safe enough to cross at the moment, even if some of the rocks were uneven and slippery underfoot.

'Parting of the seas!' Jedd said as they made their way across. Did Jedd think he was a fucking saint?

'It's a lonely spot,' Darren remarked, looking at the low bushes and coarse grass on the island.

'The sort of place anything can happen,' Jedd said with an unsettling smirk.

Darren raced ahead, scrambling up the rocks to the pillbox. It was the obvious place to hide and he wanted to be the one to find her. He was a little breathless when he reached the top of the outcrop. Out of condition from the climb, or was it a panic attack coming on? His heart was certainly racing. He wished it would calm down. He didn't want his encounter with Caitlin to be breathless on his part. He took a few deep breaths and then peered inside the hexagonal concrete chamber.

After the glare of the morning light, he couldn't see a thing in the gloom. For a second, he wondered if she'd use the dark to attack him. But soon realised the place was empty. A strange sensation, a mix of relief and disappointment played on his brain. Understandable to be disappointed. But why did he feel relief? After all he'd been hunting her for weeks now.

There was a discarded water bottle and an empty red cellophane packet on the sandy ground. Jedd came in and stooped to pick up the cellophane.

'Chocolate digestives!'

Darren grunted and stepped outside to survey the island. She was here somewhere.

She was hiding in a grassy hollow, behind a spiky bush. She watched them going up the rocks to the fort. If they both went inside, she could dash to the causeway and make a run for it. They'd spot her, but she'd have a head start.

Burgess was first inside, followed by the security guard. She hesitated. If they spotted her, how far would she get, honestly? Be better to get off this island without being seen. She could wade through the water at the far end of the island away from the pillbox and the causeway. If it wasn't too deep she'd make it across. And really, how deep could it be? There was no water there at all at low tide. She stood and moved out of her hiding place, but at that moment Darren emerged from the pillbox. She dived behind some long grass, just as he turned to face her way.

Shit. Oh Shit. Shit! She was a dead woman. He must have seen her. She pressed her body into the ground and didn't breathe. Waited. Lay still listening for his footsteps. But apart from her thudding heart, all she could hear was the swishing of grass in the wind and waves lapping softly in the distance.

FORTY-ONE

Battery Point

D arren saw a head bob down behind a clump of marram grass.

'Jedd!' he hissed, turning towards the pillbox. There was no reply and Jedd didn't come out. He dithered, unsure of himself. He should sprint over there, take her by surprise and grab her. But didn't. Something was holding him back. He wasn't scared of her. He was sure he could snatch her and bring her back to the pillbox. But still, he didn't act.

Instead, he stepped inside the concrete fort. Jedd was holding the cellophane biscuit packet in one hand and a cigarette lighter in the other. He looked up at Darren.

'Any sign of the bitch?'

'What are you doing?'

He sparked up the lighter, and put the flame to the cellophane, it took light straight away. He held it, seemingly mesmerised by the fire. Like a primitive savage who'd never seen a flame before. Then he dropped the cellophane onto the plastic water bottle. Darren simply watched, speechless as the flames spread to the plastic bottle.

No one came. Tentatively, she raised her head again. There was no sign of Darren Burgess, so she made a dash down to the shore, to a place where she couldn't be seen from the fort. Stuffed her trainers, socks and jacket into her backpack which claimed to be waterproof, rolled up her jeans and set off into the waves. The stones underfoot were sharp and slippery, and she felt unsafe on her dodgy ankle which was starting to play up again. She should have kept her trainers on. Worse, the tidal current was tugging powerfully at her. If she slipped she could be washed out to sea. She wasn't much of a swimmer either. It was too risky. She was forced back to the beach where she sat on the rocks wondering what to do.

Troy went through a phase of setting fires. Started with toys he was fed up with: Transformers, Power Rangers and Hot Wheels cars. Graduated onto bigger things like the waste bins at school and then the skip round the back of the convenience store near Clumber Road. The fire brigade was called that time, and the police came around asking questions, Troy already being on their radar. However, when Troy got interested in girls, he seemed to forget about burning things. But it wasn't lost on Darren, that now Troy was in the army, he was in charge of his own 'fireteam'.

The plastic bottle was burning furiously, sending a thin plume of black smoke upwards and filling the pillbox with the pungent aroma of burning plastic.

'Sometimes I wish I lived in an age when they burned heretics and witches. It would have been quite a sight.'

Was Jedd hinting they should burn Grady as a witch? The thought chilled him. But then, hadn't he himself wished her drowned as a witch after the trial? He moved to the window and looked out, half expecting to see her scampering across the causeway. There was no sign of the bitch, but the tide was coming in fast. The water already licking at the crossing back to Westcliffe.

'We need to get back.'

'Apparently, even after the person is dead, the body contorts and twists itself. They used to think it was the sinner's soul fighting to keep out of hell. But actually, it's the action of the flames on bone and muscle.'

He stared at Jedd for a moment. This obsession with fire was worrying. 'The tide's coming in. We need to go.'

'But someone was here. We should search the island.'

He couldn't bring himself to admit to Jedd he'd seen Grady, and done nothing about it. What the hell was wrong with him? He needed time to think. Right now, he just wanted to get off the island. 'We don't want to get marooned out here do we?'

'We need to be sure she's not here.'

'Come on, I don't want to get cut off by the tide,' he said, heading out of the pillbox. He hurried down to the causeway. The water was surging over the rocks as the tides swirled around the island.

Danger. Do not attempt to cross when water covers causeway. Hazardous Tidal Flow. Risk of Drowning.

The water was still only inches deep. So, despite the sign, he was sure he could make it across if he didn't hang about. It wasn't far, only a hundred metres or so.

'Don't try it, mate. It's too risky,' Jedd said, catching up with him.

Ignoring Jedd, he put a hesitant foot forward but Jedd grabbed his arm.

'Let go of me!' he shouted, suddenly angry. It was Jedd's

fault he hadn't said anything about Caitlin Grady. His fault for fucking around with fire.

'What the hell is wrong, Darren?'

He pulled away from his friend and set off across the dangerous rocks. He was angry with himself as much as Jedd. For not following through and being a wuss about Grady when it came to the crunch. What was he frightened of, for God's sake?

The way across was treacherous and slippery. Water was coming into his boots, cold soaking through his socks. He'd underestimated the depth of the water. The tide seemed to be rushing at him. It was difficult to keep his balance.

'Come back!' Jedd shouted after him. But he wasn't going to be told what to do by Jedd. He'd had enough of the guy. He could do this. He was sure he could make it across and leave Jedd behind.

But the further he went, the stronger the current. Jedd might be right, perhaps he should go back. But something drove him on and he pressed forward against the current. The water surged and pulled. His footing less and less certain. He was losing traction. The only way was to trust in fate and make a dash for the shore.

He felt himself falling into the torrent. Almost watching himself from above as he smacked into the waves.

The cold took his breath away. Shocked his system. He struggled, trying to find his footing again. Managed to touch the bottom, but it didn't help; he had no grip and the waves rushed and pushed him, playing with him like a toy. He was thrashing and struggling and out of his depth.

He tried to swim against the current and get to the shore, but could make no progress and was soon losing strength as his muscles sapped in the cold.

Don't fight it, he told himself. *Go with the current. Just keep afloat, that's all. Slow breaths, calm down, don't panic.*

But he was panicking. He was panicking like shit, because how long could he last in this water? He undid his jacket and slid out of it. Maybe that would help his buoyancy. The jacket floated away from him like a dead man. He struggled out of his boots too and watched as one, then the other slowly sank into the deep green waters. His jacket would be washed ashore one day, but his boots would never be found.

In between the swell, he could see Jedd on the island, looking towards him. Following his progress. He raised his hand to wave but his head went beneath the waves, so abandoned that idea.

Call someone. Don't just stand there! Get the lifeboat.

Maybe he'd called already. Or maybe he was just gonna watch him drown. No. Jedd was his friend. He may be a bit psycho, but they were still partners. And let's face it, Jedd had tried to stop him crossing the causeway. Told him to come back. He should have bloody listened.

He was taken further out to sea. Kept losing sight of land as the waves tossed him around like a piece of driftwood. Helpless and hopeless. But at least the cold wasn't so bad now. He was getting used to it. After all it wasn't winter, was it? Wasn't freezing. Some people still went swimming this time of year, didn't they?

Salt was up his nose and in his mouth. His eyes stung. The ocean was invading his body. His vision was blurring.

There was the land again. Not so far away. But no sign of Jedd. Where was Jedd? He'd left him to die alone. Which by all accounts wasn't as bad as he thought. In a way the sea was like a big soft bed. He should try to float on his back and relax. He closed his eyes for a moment.

He coughed up a mouthful of water. Had he drifted off? Was he drowning? Is this how life paid him back for letting Caitlin Grady go? Concentrate and stay awake. The tide would turn soon. It would deliver him back to the shore. Swallowed more water. Water in his throat. Coughing.

He'd die without ever seeing Kerry again. But he thought of her now. Imagined her voice. Tried to focus on her face. Remembered her smile that day when they met at the Jolly Sailor.

If he died, maybe he'd see Riley again. That would be nice…

FORTY-TWO

Battery Point

S he was witnessing a miracle: someone was walking on the
water. Not just one person either: shimmering in the
morning light, there were half a dozen of them.
Paddleboarders. They were going to paddle right past her,
heading for the tidal passage between Battery Point and the
mainland.

As they got closer, she recognised their leader as Speedo
Boy, the guy she'd seen paddleboarding near the pier that day.
He wasn't wearing his tight Speedos today though, and was in
a sensible wetsuit. She waved her arms, and despite the danger
of Burgess and his sidekick hearing, screamed a panic fuelled,
'Help!'

Speedo spotted her immediately and paddled over.

'Any chance of a lift?' she called out with mock casualness.

'Cut off by the tide?'

'Yeah.'

'Hop on.'

She waded into the water and gripped his hand as he
helped her climb up and straddle the board. She sat in front of
him, hugging her backpack.

A couple of minutes later and she was back on the mainland. Relief made her feel like kissing and hugging Speedo, but instead simply gave a gushing thanks. He returned a patronising smile, like she was a silly kid and he was a superhero. But she'd forgive him for that. He'd saved her life.

She watched the flotilla of paddleboards pick up speed as they approached the now drowned causeway. According to Speedo Boy, the strong tidal currents were cool to navigate in a paddleboardy kind of way. She was sorry she'd been so snooty about paddleboarding before. She might even take up the free lesson Speedo had offered her one day. But for now, she trudged across the sand dunes towards Westcliffe promenade.

Taking a last look at Battery Point she saw the sidekick on the shore.

'Come get me, sucker!' she shouted, giving him the finger. But he was too far away to hear, and anyway wasn't looking her way, but out to sea. There was someone in the water.

Whoever it was, didn't look like they'd meant to go for a swim; they were in normal clothes, not swimmers or a wetsuit. They were in trouble. Could it be Darren Burgess? She was too far away to be sure, but there was no sign of him on Battery Point. The longer she stared, the more she became convinced it was him. She couldn't help the broad grin that formed on her face. He was the one behind Riley's Law. He was the one tracking her down. He was the one who had set fire to her flat. If he drowned, she'd be free. With that happy thought she set off again, kicking sand playfully as she went.

She got a dozen steps before stopping and turning to look at Burgess once more. She needed to see what happened to him. It was bad of her, wasn't it? Staying to see him drown. As she watched, the badness settled in her stomach. Like she'd eaten some rotten fruit. And the more she watched the worse she felt. Well, that was just the price she'd have to pay for being sure he was out of the picture.

But she couldn't do it, just sit there. She hated him, yet couldn't stomach watching his watery end. She rummaged in the backpack for her phone.

After she'd played good Samaritan, she checked @BitchHunt, which made her switch off her phone in a panic. They'd hacked her phone and were tracking her. A lynch mob was gathering in Westcliffe and they had people watching the trains too.

She felt in her pocket for her keys. On her keyring was the key to CoffeeTime. The café didn't open till ten on a Sunday, so she went there to take refuge, freshen up and polish off some of yesterday's left-over pastries.

She used the café's laptop to plan her escape. Even though they were watching Westcliffe station, the train was still the best way to escape. First station stop out of Westcliffe was a little village, Sandford, about two miles up the tracks; she'd go there to get the train. She had no intention of switching her phone on, so drew a map to guide her.

Before leaving, she took the float from the till. Two hundred quid. That would keep her going for a bit. She left a note to Brig apologising and promising to pay her back. She signed it Anna aka Caitlin Grady. Then added another note and wrote *THANK YOU* in large capital letters. It wasn't just about the money, Brig had given her a job, trusted her and been a friend. It was bad to steal from her, but she hoped Brig would understand.

Sandford station was nothing much: a short platform and a little wooden shelter reminiscent of a garden shed cut in half. There was no one else here. No sound apart from birdsong. She stared down the single-track line towards Westcliffe for signs of the promised train. Had no idea what time it was now, because she hadn't switched her phone back on. But the longer she was here on this lonely platform, the more her imagination fucked with her. If they didn't find her in Westcliffe, would they extend their search? Could they track her phone, even if it was switched off? She removed the SIM card as an extra precaution.

Her stomach curdled with a cocktail of anxiety and boredom. Her ankle was playing up again, but she was too restless to sit and give it a chance to recover. Instead she paced up and then down the platform with slow steady strides to calm her nerves. Reaching the Westcliffe end, she stared at the quiet tracks willing a train to come. Grass and weeds were growing between the sleepers, so it looked like trains were a rare event. Maybe she'd read the timetable wrong and they simply didn't run on a Sunday?

A tabby cat padded its way across the line. Planting careful footsteps on the concrete sleepers to avoid the vegetation. Fussy cat. Going down the slope at the end of the platform she went to pet it. It rubbed against her jeans and followed her back onto the platform. She sat on a bench and the cat jumped onto her thighs and lay there while she stroked it. It rewarded her with contented purring.

Finally, the train appeared – rocking and rumbling towards the station like a tired beast. Her muscles tensed as it drew nearer. Its two coaches lumbered up and she stood on tiptoes trying to look through the windows for anyone suspicious. Looked pretty empty. It came to a halt with a rasping squeal. She climbed aboard and checked the carriages out. The first one had a woman with a couple of kids in it. That was all. No danger here. She poked her nose into the other one, but the only passengers were a harmless looking ageing couple and another younger couple, wearing bright orange anoraks and hiking boots. They had those stupid sticks that hikers use to help them walk as well. A bit sad in her opinion, but thankfully not vigilante material.

She bought a ticket from the guard and relaxed into the worn seat. A wave of relief swept through her like a drug. She'd escaped from Westcliffe and was on her way. As the train rattled and swayed along, she felt her eyes becoming heavy, the motion lulling her into a pleasant torpor.

FORTY-THREE

Westcliff District Hospital

There are six stages of drowning. Darren was stage five when he was found floating face down in the sea. Clinical death. The final stage is biological death: irreversible brain damage from lack of oxygen. Resuscitation impossible. Luckily, Speedo Boy was practised in CPR and managed to revive him before that unhappy event took place.

But it was a close thing.

A doctor, who smelled of cigarettes, was shining a torch into his eyes. The doctor moved his nicotine-stained finger from left to right. Satisfied, he went on to ask Darren what day it was.

'Not sure, lost track of things since I came here,' he answered a little breathlessly. His breathing was still not right.

He did better on questions about the capital of France and the President of the USA.

'There's no sign of cognitive impairment,' the doctor announced. 'You are a very lucky man. It's probably the hypothermia that saved you. Slowed your metabolism. Congratulations – you got away with it.'

Got away with it, sounded like he'd deliberately tempted

death. Won a bet. He was going to say something, but coughed instead.

'We need to keep an eye on those lungs, though. You aspirated more water than I would like.' The doctor scribbled something on the bedside notes, and said they'd keep him in for observation for a day or two, nodded to the nurse who drew back the blue curtain surrounding his bed. The doctor swept off like he was royalty, with the nurse scampering after him.

He was in an alcove with three other beds, the nearest of which was thankfully unoccupied. His breathing made conversation an effort, and anyway he was feeling unsociable. Embarrassed at his stupidity. Still, he was glad to be here. The doctor was right, he had been very lucky. Lucky those paddleboarders came along. All the same it chilled his heart that he'd actually been dead when they fished him out of the sea.

He stared at the pale blue wall opposite wondering if there was a reason he'd been saved. It meant something. It had to. Things were going to be different from now on. But how? In what way should his life be different? He hadn't worked that bit out yet.

One of the nurses was keen he should inform family where he was, so he phoned Kerry. She was still his wife after all – his next of kin. But no joy, either she was ignoring his calls or was off-grid. He could phone his parents, but didn't want to worry his mum and anyway he'd be out of here any day.

So it was a surprise when the nurse came to see him all smiles, saying his brother had phoned and was on his way. Had they managed to get word to Troy? He was meant to be in Africa.

'Mate!' Jedd strode up carrying a box of expensive chocolates.

Unable to hide his disappointment that it wasn't Troy,

Darren slumped back into the bed. Okay, so he wasn't his brother's biggest fan, but at least Troy was family.

'You all right?' Jedd said, handing him the chocolates.

'Was expecting my brother.' He looked at the box of chocolates. Probably paid for with Riley's money.

'We are brothers! Brothers in arms.'

Darren answered with a wheezing cough and put the chocolates on the bedside table. Being Jedd's *brother in arms* might be one of the things that needed to change.

'What are you like? Eh?' his new brother said with a condescending grin. As if there was something vaguely amusing about drowning. 'Really, Darren, what were you thinking?'

'I don't know.' Had the guy come to gloat that his attempt to escape the island had ended in disaster?

'Still, something to dine out on. "The day I defeated death".'

'It's not a joke,' he said, a tremor going through him as he recalled the cold dread of knowing he was going to die. 'If those paddleboarders hadn't happened along...'

'I didn't mean it as a joke.' Jedd sat down on a grey plastic chair and pulled it up to the bed. 'Defeating death is quite something.' There was a strange tone in Jedd's voice, as though he'd only come here to see for himself that Darren wasn't dead. 'So what was it like?' he added.

'What? Drowning?'

'Dying. Being dead.'

Despite the fact that it might be something to *dine out on*, he wasn't keen on talking about it. But Jedd was staring at him with bright-eyed anticipation. Like he was expecting some mystical revelation.

'I didn't see any shining light if that's what you mean.'

'Out of body experience? Anything like that?'

'Nothing like that, no.'

314

'What about Riley? Did you see her?'

He shook his head and looked over at the window. It would have been a big comfort if she'd been there with him at what seemed to be his end. That she hadn't appeared, underlined that he'd never see Riley again. Even in death.

'That's a shame,' Jedd said, disappointed. 'Still, I'd have liked to experience it: dying and coming back again like you did. Glimpsing the after-life.'

'I didn't glimpse anything. It was just cold and lonely if you want to know.' He took a painful breath. 'The loneliest I ever felt.'

The two men looked at each other. The atmosphere was suddenly heavy, as if Death heard he was being talked about and had also drawn up a chair.

After a minute, Jedd reached for the chocolates. He unwrapped the cellophane and read the card describing the different flavours. 'I recommend the raspberry smoothie.' He picked a chocolate out and offered it to Darren. 'Open wide.'

'I'm not eating something you've had your grubby fingers on.'

'Don't be so squeamish.'

Darren took the menu card. 'I can choose my own chocolate, thanks.'

'Ungrateful.' His friend pulled a face and ate the raspberry smoothie.

He picked a mousse au chocolate. It wasn't at all bad. The taste lightened his mood.

Jedd's eyes followed a nurse. 'She'd do, I reckon,' he said with a mouthful of raspberry smoothie.

Darren wasn't in the mood for juvenile banter about sexy nurses. And let's face it, NHS trouser suits were not exactly a turn on.

'Any of the nurses given you some bedtime benefits?' Jedd added, winking at him.

'Godsake, Jedd, grow up.'

'Just trying to cheer you up,' Jedd said, scowling and examining the chocolates. There was an awkward pause. Then Jedd dropped a casual bombshell. 'Do you think Riley's angry with you?'

What a thing to say! Why would he say a thing like that? He stared at the guy not knowing how to answer. Jedd didn't look up, just made a show of considering which chocolate to choose next.

'Billionaire's shortbread. Wonder what that's like.'

'What did you mean?'

'Mmm?' his friend mumbled.

'About Riley?'

'Well…' He chewed the chocolate thoughtfully, making Darren wait until he'd finished. 'Maybe that's why she didn't come to you, when you died.'

A wave of regret swept through him. 'Maybe she is angry with me, I was the one who let Grady snatch her.' Not only that, he'd let Grady go when he had a chance to make her pay for what she'd done.

'There's been no sign of the bitch by the way. We lost her.' There was something in the way Jedd looked at him that was unnerving. Did Jedd somehow know he'd let Caitlin go?

'Well, we'll have to find her again then, won't we?'

'Broken her parole apparently. Police are looking for her now as well,' Jedd said with a humourless smile. 'If they find her, she'll be sent back to prison.'

If that happened, he'd never get to confront her. To avenge Riley's death. 'We need to find her before they do then.' He meant what he said.

'Too right! But you are banged up in here, after playing silly buggers.'

There was no need for Jedd to rub it in. He felt like an

idiot. Is that what Jedd wanted him to say? How fucking stupid he'd been?

'So while you're laid up in here,' Jedd added, 'I'll organise a new search. We're getting more people coming forward on @BitchHunt. Good lads, they'll be only too happy to help.'

He got a sinking feeling. It was nice to have support, but it felt like he was being gently elbowed out of the way. 'Look, Jedd, Grady's my problem. You know. She killed my child. I should be the one to deal with her.'

'Absolutely, mate. But if we don't find her before the police do, you won't be able to deal with her. That's why we need the lads.'

He had no choice but to agree with Jedd, albeit reluctantly. 'But no more firebombs. Nothing crazy like that. Okay?'

'Don't worry. I won't let anyone lay a finger on her. It has to be you that casts the first stone.' He gave a meaningful stare before adding, 'Metaphorically speaking.' Jedd nodded, almost to himself and then stood to leave.

Cast the first stone. It sounded like Jedd wanted to turn dealing with Grady into a barbaric ritual killing.

FORTY-FOUR

Boggart Hill, Bristol

The grass was long, wet and yellowing. Darren's boots slipped and slid as he made his way up to Riley's tree. Winter was already in the air, and a melancholic haze was hanging over Boggart Hill.

He wanted to find Grady for himself, confront her one to one, without Jedd and the @BitchHunt crew setting the agenda. He figured that if she was on the run from the police, then she might well come back to Bristol. It was the only place she really knew.

He wondered if Tracey might have some idea about where she was. Might even have met up with her childhood friend. He'd already been round to her mother's house, but no one answered the door when he knocked. So maybe he'd find Tracey up here, the place he first ran into her.

At the top of the hill, the tree formed a silhouette against the grey sky, its branches stark and bare. Riley's toys hung motionless in the heavy atmosphere. But on getting closer, he saw something else in that tree. Something new.

He stopped and stared. What the fuck! How dare someone put that thing up there? A dirty old teddy bear. Threadbare

318

and sodden from recent rain. Deformed too: one of its arms was missing and it only had one eye. It was a grotesque creature, like a small malevolent goblin.

He made a grab for the disfigured thing. Wanted to chuck it down the embankment onto the railway line, where it would be pummelled by passing trains. But he couldn't reach it. It mocked him, perched on a branch just beyond his grasp.

He sensed someone watching him. Tracey? He swung around. But it wasn't her, it was a lad, a teenager, hands thrust inside his hoody pockets. He was watching him, head cocked slightly to one side, like he was about to make some sarcastic comment.

He wondered if the lad had followed him up here. It was a lonely spot and he suddenly worried the lad might be here to sell drugs, or worse, might be a knife-wielding mugger. On the other hand the boy didn't seem much of a threat. He was quite short and seemed pretty young.

'Know anything about that teddy? See who put it there?' he asked. Bit of a stupid question, so he wasn't surprised when the lad didn't reply. Why would a random youth know anything about the abomination in the tree? The boy's hair was shaved into a short buzz cut, but he seemed to have no facial hair at all. He wasn't just young, he actually looked quite feminine, like he wasn't a boy at all.

A dreadful realisation gripped him. She looked different to the passport photo with such short hair, but it was her all right.

'You! What the fuck do you think you're playing at?'

She shrugged and gave him a nonchalant stare. Like at the trial.

The brazen cheek of the girl made blood rush to his head. 'How dare you show your face at this place. At Riley's tree.'

'I've a right to be here, just as much as you.'

'No, you fucking haven't! You are barred from Bristol.' He took a step toward her. 'That's the law.'

'The law! Joke, right? Since when did you respect the law?'

Cheeky little shit. He could wring her neck. He took another step towards her. Wasn't going to let her go again. If she made a dash for it, he'd take her down. But as he approached, she pulled a knife from her hoody pocket.

'Keep away from me!'

Taken aback, he stopped and stared at the blade. In the movies, the knife always glints in the light, but this one had a short dull blade with a curved black handle. He wondered if he could get the knife off her. If Jedd was here, he'd be able to disarm her in five seconds. As it was, he kept his distance.

'Firebombed my flat. That's how much you respect the law.'

He felt his cheeks getting hot. 'That wasn't me. I didn't do that,' he stammered. She'd managed to embarrass him.

'Liar!'

'Wasn't meant to happen. It was Jedd, he…' What was he thinking, apologising to Caitlin Grady? What kind of upside-down world was he in?

'One of your vigilante mates did your dirty work, eh?'

'I've got a lot of people on my side. A lot of people.'

She nodded. 'How nice for you, well I got no one.'

Was he supposed to feel sorry for her? Well fuck that. 'That thing yours?' he said, pointing to the teddy.

'Might be.'

'You take it down, all right?'

'I…' She looked up at the teddy. 'It's for Riley. I put it up there for her. Okay?'

'No. It is not okay. It's not right. Especially a disgusting mutilated… Did you pull it's arm off deliberately?'

'Oh yeah. Deliberate that was. And the eye! Because I'm evil, aren't I, Darren? A sick freak?'

'You said it.'

'No, you did!' She gave an unpleasant sarcastic sneer. 'Told everyone on TV.'

'You're a bit of a smart arse, aren't you?'

'Oh yeah, got my smarts, Darren. Cus you know while I was inside I got GCSEs and A-levels and I'm going to university.' Was she trying to wind him up deliberately? 'All in all, being locked up was the best thing that happened to me. And you know how they say, prison these days is like a holiday camp? Well it's true! We got to play video games and everything. I'm the boss at *Call of Duty*.'

'Good thing you've got that knife, otherwise...'

'What? What would you do to me? Hmm. Let's hear it then? Burning, hanging, shooting, what's it to be, Mr *Respect for the law*?'

He glared at her, hackles raised, and reached for his phone. Called Jedd who picked up immediately, like he was waiting for the call.

'Mate! How's it hanging?' They hadn't spoken since the hospital visit and Jedd sounded genuinely pleased to hear from him.

'Guess who I'm with?' he said still, staring at her.

'Grady returned to the scene, has she?'

'How did you guess?'

'Call it second sight.' The guy laughed. 'Anyway, as it happens me and the lads are in Bristol, so we'll be up there in no time. Don't let her get away.' He hung up and thrust the phone into his pocket. A smile crossed his face. Jedd being in Bristol meant that fate was on his side for once.

'What's the matter, Darren? Afraid to face me alone?'

He made a grab for her wrist but failed. Tried again and got it. He squeezed hoping she would drop the knife. But she didn't. They locked eyes.

'Why did you come here, eh? To relive your crime? Your big moment?'

'Like I want to relive that fucking moment!'

'Made you feel good did it, killing a child?'

Something hovered on her face. Regret? But if so, it was fleeting and went as quickly as it came. 'Oh yeah. Felt real good! Here for the sick kicks, that's me.'

'Don't you feel anything. Nothing at all?'

'No, absolutely fucking nothing!' she shouted and flicked the knife to one side. They both stared at it lying in the grass for a moment. Darren took his opportunity and grabbed her by the shoulders.

'Want to know what it feels like to have the life squeezed out of you? Do you? Well do you?'

'Go on then,' she said, like she was resigned to her fate. 'If you're going to do it. Go on.'

He placed his hands around her neck. She didn't struggle. Maybe she knew there was no point. She was a slight girl and he was much bigger and stronger than her. He pushed her backwards against the tree. It would be so easy to kill her now, before Jedd got here. It wouldn't take long. He knew from the expert witness at the trial, it isn't choking that causes death in strangulation, it's pressure to the vein, restricting oxygen to the brain, causing unconsciousness in seconds. Death follows in no time.

He tightened his grip, feeling her veins pulsing beneath his fingers. Veins filled with the blood of his daughter's killer.

She opened her mouth, but no words came out, she was trying to say something. Tears filled her eyes. He released the pressure a little, wanting to hear her last words.

'Sorry. Truly. I am sorry for what happened,' she croaked. Tears now streaming down her face.

Her tears knifed into him. Made him soften. Then, his own eyes began to blur. He let go and turned away. Couldn't look at her. Felt relieved and wretched at the same time. He could hear her gasping for breath. If she had any sense, she'd fuck off somewhere far away. But she didn't.

'He's called Teddy Tubby,' she said.

He twisted round to see her sitting on the ground, her back against the tree, hunched and hugging her legs. It's where they'd found Riley.

'When I was arrested, they let me keep him with me in the cells. At the trial and everything. It's the one thing left from my childhood. You know, from the time before. I just thought.' She shook her head. 'I'll take it down.'

He stared at the teddy. It no longer looked like an evil thing, but rather a sad broken offering. 'No, it's all right.' He took a breath. 'But you got to tell me something. You got to say… Why did you take Riley?'

'It was the worst day of my life. I'd do anything to put the clock back. Wipe that day from history. But I can't.'

He gave a bitter laugh. 'You and me both.' It was an awful irony that they should have anything in common.

'I don't really know why I took Riley.'

'But you must know!' His voice strained and desperate.

'They said at the trial: *Grady went to the city farm with the intention of abducting a child.*'

'No. You were with Tracey. Playing a game. Pretending to be witches.'

'What? I never said that!' She got to her feet. 'I never told anyone about that. You been talking to Tracey?' He nodded. 'How's she doing? Is she okay?' She gave him a hopeful look.

He hadn't the heart to say what a mess Tracey had made of her life. 'Well, I doubt she's ever going to get into uni.'

'But she's okay?'

'Yeah, I guess you could say she's managing.'

'The way you say it, does make me wonder.'

'Look, I don't want to talk about your best friend. And I

may be some sort of masochist, but you have to tell me. Tell me how it got from a game... to... to what happened.'

'There's stuff I think I remember, then there's stuff they told me I did...' She looked genuinely perplexed. 'For a long time I didn't believe Riley was really dead.' She stared out over the railway and shook her head. 'Maybe they are right. People. The prosecution. You. Maybe you are all right. Something inside me is evil. But it didn't start out that way. It started out as a game. A laugh.'

'She was giggling about being cooked up for dinner and eaten. She liked me. Held my hand. Trusted me.' She took a deep breath. 'And how did I return that trust? I killed her.'

Grady looked in despair. Well, she deserved it. He couldn't help but feel pleasure at seeing her full of pain and self-loathing. Self-loathing was something he himself was all too familiar with. So why shouldn't she have some of it.

They stood in silence. He watched a line of birds flying across the city, migrating south to a sunnier country for the winter.

'I suppose it was all because of the sweets. I always had a sweet tooth. Well what kid doesn't?'

'It's boarded up now. That sweet shop.'

'Fat Fred's. My second home.' She gave a rueful laugh. 'Fat Fred always hated me. Knew I used to steal his pick and mix. Anyway, the joke about cooking her up for the pot was getting boring. That's why I took her to Fat Fred's. Something to do. I didn't take her in, because she might give us away while I was pocketing sweets. Told her to wait outside. She stood by the doorway. I thought she'd wander off, to be fair, so I could keep the sweets for myself.'

He swallowed hard and almost gagged on his own saliva. Struggled to control nausea as she told him about how Riley had waited obediently outside the shop while she went in and filled her pockets with sweets. Fat Fred, the shopkeeper had apparently been too busy with the lottery machine to notice Caitlin. But the CCTV from the shop had led to her getting caught.

'I snuck out and was about to make a run for it when Riley grabbed my hand. So I pulled her away from the shop as quick as possible, before Fred came after us. I can still feel that tight little grip. She had strong fingers for such a little girl.'

That detail caused another churn in his stomach.

'Always came up here to Boggart Hill when we nicked stuff. So that's why I brought Riley up here. We sat on the embankment stuffing our faces with squidgy sweets.'

'Kerry had bad teeth from when she was a kid,' Darren mumbled. 'She was determined Riley's teeth wouldn't go the same way, so we never allowed her sweets if we could help it.'

'She loved the sugar-coated elephants. Couldn't get enough of them. Bit the trunk off first, then the legs.' She gave a hopeless smile.

'And then what?'

'Then there weren't any left. No more sweets.'

'And?'

Caitlin shrugged. 'We watched the trains.' She seemed distracted. Her eyes focusing not on him, but through him somehow. His phone pinged.

> Arrived in Pennywell. Heading toward your position.

There was something about his use of words. Your position. As if Jedd knew his precise location. As if he was tracking him.

'Do you think Riley's still here?' Caitlin said.

'What?' he said, looking up from his phone.

'Do you think she's still here, on Boggart Hill?'

He looked hard at Caitlin's mournful face. Nodded. 'Sort of.'

'In therapy, my psychiatrist made me say sorry to a cushion, as though it was Riley. But really, they should have brought me here to apologise.'

'Bit fucking late to apologise.'

'I know that.'

His bitter words seemed to hang between them in the still damp air. He looked up at the tree, at the dinosaurs and at Caitlin's damaged teddy, hanging motionless from the branches. A mutilated thing that seemed to sum up Caitlin herself.

He felt an overwhelming sense of sorrow. Not just about Riley, but strangely sorry about Caitlin too. What had gone so wrong with the kid? He didn't understand. Moved towards the slope down to the path. No sign of Jedd yet. Looked back at Caitlin. She was standing by the tree looking up at the branches, lost in thought.

He didn't want Jedd to spoil this, whatever it was. And Jedd had the @BitchHunt crew with him. They'd be here any second. He didn't know what they'd do, but he wouldn't be able to stop it. What had Jedd said? 'Cast the first stone.'

He switched off his phone, just in case Jedd was tracking him. Went back to the tree and grabbed Caitlin by the arm. 'Come on.'

'Hey!'

'Come with me!'

But she didn't want to move and resisted. 'Why would I do that?'

'Suit yourself then, but Jedd's on his way. I won't be able to...' He paused, looked around, not wanting to say the words. But made himself. 'I won't be able to protect you, all right?'

'Why would you protect me?'

'Because...'

She looked at him waiting for an answer. He didn't know what the *because* was, so simply repeated himself. 'Just because.'

'Okay then.'

It would be no good heading back down the slope to the path. Chances are they'd run straight into Jedd and his posse. The only option was down the railway embankment. She went first. Skidding down the steep slope like there was no tomorrow. He followed cautiously behind, worried about losing his footing. His experience on the causeway had taken some of his confidence. Watching her zooming ahead, he realised how fearless she was in comparison.

When he got to the bottom of the embankment she was already walking along the tracks. Balancing along one of the actual rails, playing a game with herself, like a tightrope walker. Had she forgotten how fast the trains came? Against his wishes he felt a tightening in his chest at the thought she was going to get herself killed by a train.

'Get off the tracks!' he shouted.

She took precisely no notice. He sprinted over and pulled her to the side of the railway. 'It's dangerous!'

She pulled a face.

They could still be seen by anybody looking down from the embankment top. 'We need to keep going.'

'Quit telling me off then.' She ran off down the tracks. He went after her. She could run fast, he'd say that for her. He kept looking over his shoulder for signs of Jedd, which slowed him down. She was soon way ahead – probably trying to run away from him. But once they were round the corner and clear of Boggart Hill, she stopped and waited for him to catch up.

FORTY-FIVE

Service station, A4174, Bristol

D arren's van was a pit. Crisp packets and old cellophane sandwich packs stuffed into the overflowing door pockets. It smelt lived in. A takeaway coffee cup was rolling around under her feet as they pulled off the dual carriageway into a grimy petrol station.

He could have picked a nicer place to fill up. The pumps were faded and stained dirty yellow with fuel and there was a patch of sand on the concrete forecourt, covering an oil spillage. Caitlin gathered up the detritus from the van as best she could and got out to look for a bin.

When he saw what she was doing, he gave her a small but appreciative nod. She binned the rubbish and breathed in the air which was heavy with petrol fumes. It was probably bad for your lungs, but it was the smell of the road, of going somewhere, which despite the unpromising petrol stop, gave her hope.

Watching the traffic zooming past on the dual carriageway, she wondered where Darren was taking her. He hadn't said. She wasn't sure he actually knew himself. They were simply driving away from trouble.

When they'd set off, he told her he was going to hand her over to the police for her own safety. She wasn't over the moon about that and told him so. They'd send her back to prison for breaking her parole and coming to Bristol. Then he said they'd start by just getting out of town and decide later where to go. So for now, it was destination unknown.

'Want anything from the shop?' he asked, heading towards the kiosk.

'Coffee. Skinny latte.'

'In your dreams. The coffee is tepid and tasteless, from a machine.'

'Make it a Coke then.'

He nodded. 'Safer bet.'

When he got back, he handed her a packet of chocolate digestives along with the Coke. 'Thought you might like these.'

It was thoughtful of him to buy biscuits for the journey. But why would he? She didn't understand what was going on here. Why was she even riding with him? Especially after he nearly strangled her. Was she one of these women who can't leave their abuser? And strangulation would count as abuse in any court of law, wouldn't it? But it was more complicated than that. And at least she knew now he was no killer. He didn't have it in him. Unlike her.

They sat in silence for a moment, he slurped tea from a takeaway cup and she crunched her way through the biscuits.

'You should get a refillable cup.'

'What?'

'Save on waste. You can't recycle them cups – you know that?'

'Who are you? Greta what's-her-face?'

'Just saying.'

'Well don't.' He put the tea in a holder and they set off. 'And you better not be dropping crumbs everywhere,' he said as they joined the traffic on the dual carriageway.

'Not that it would make any difference in this pit.'

'You can travel in the back with the tools if you'd rather.'

'Can we have the radio on?'

'No.'

So, they travelled in silence. She ought to make some sort of conversation, but what could she say to Darren Burgess? Soon they were driving up the slip road and joining the M4 motorway. After a bit they passed a sign.

London 125 Miles

'Are we going to London?' she asked, to break the silence.

'What? To see the King?'

'I've never been to London. There was a school trip, but me and Tracey didn't go.'

He cleared his throat. 'She's still living in Bristol by the way. Staying at her mum's. They still live in the same street.'

She looked at him, but he didn't face her. Kept his eyes on the road.

'I must drop in and say hello sometime.' Felt a pang of yearning, because somehow she knew she would never see Tracey again.

'Seems like a nice kid. So it's a pity really.'

'What is?'

He shrugged. 'Works in a massage place. But was working on the street before that though, so it's an improvement, I guess. Think she's got a bit of a drug habit.'

'Oh. Poor Tracey.'

'No GCSEs for her,' he said, bitterness entering his voice.

'I'd give up my GCSEs and swap places with Tracey any day.'

'Yeah right!' he said.

Why was he mocking her? 'I would. Because if I was her, I wouldn't have done what I did.'

He snorted.

'What? Don't you believe me?'

'Not really,' he mumbled, manoeuvring the van into the middle lane and accelerating to overtake a lorry.

She felt her temper rising at his casual dismissal. 'Well if you aren't going to believe a word I say, what's the fucking point?'

He ignored her and completed the overtaking manoeuvre.

'You calling me a liar?' She undid her seat belt, causing an alarm to start chiming.

'Will you put your belt back on,' he said, irritated.

'Stop the car. I want to get out.'

'No!'

She pulled the door handle and pushed the door open a crack. Wind filled the van, making loose papers fly about. The car veered to the left.

'What the fuck!' He slammed his foot on the brake, she lurched forward into the dashboard. The truck behind let out a deafening honk on its horn. Darren swerved onto the hard shoulder, bringing the car to a juddering stop.

'Jesus Christ what the fuck are you playing at?'

'Don't call me a liar!' she shouted and got out.

'Fucking crazy!'

She walked off as fast as she could, heading along the hard shoulder away from his shitty little van. Cars and heavy lorries rushed past only a couple of metres away, noise and dust thrashing at her as she went. She didn't care. She needed to get away. Why had she even gone with him? Just the instinctive need to escape and some mistaken trust in Darren. Which was insane. He was the last person on the planet to trust.

She resisted the temptation to look over her shoulder and see if he was still parked up. Then as her anger began to dissipate, his van went past and accelerated away. He was giving up on her. Well good riddance. She wondered how far it was to the next turn-off. Maybe someone would stop to give her a lift. Maybe she'd be picked up on CCTV and the police would come. Maybe she shouldn't have been so hasty.

But Darren pulled over a couple of hundred metres ahead. It annoyed her that she found she was relieved. He got out of the van and stood waiting. She paused and stared a moment, considering whether to give him the finger or not. Then carried on walking towards him.

'You're not allowed to walk along the motorway,' he shouted above the traffic as she got near.

She stopped, but said nothing.

'And it's dangerous. People get killed. Stuff falls off lorries. People drive onto the hard shoulder by mistake. All sorts can happen.'

'Trying to make out you give a fuck or something?'

'Look, you made your point, okay?' He walked around to the passenger door and opened it for her like a chauffeur. 'Please?'

She twisted her face, but got in anyway. He took his place next to her in the driver's seat, but didn't start the engine. His eyes flicked around between the rear-view mirror, the side mirror and the road ahead. Looked like he was working up to say something.

'I'm sorry about Jedd, all right? I should never have let him get involved and I'm sorry about the fire. It was wrong.' He scratched the back of his ear. The passing motorway traffic rocked and buffeted the van. He turned to face her. 'This thing is between you and me. You and me alone.'

'Okay,' she said, holding his gaze. That was something they could agree on at least.

'You can put the radio on if you like,' he said as they set off again.

'Sounds of the Seventies?' she said, flicking through the stations.

'Bit before my time.'

'Eighties?'

'Maybe.'

'Nineties?'

'Yeah. Put that on.'

So they drove on listening to REM, singing about losing their religion.

FORTY-SIX

Meadow Farm Housing Estate, Swindon

They were driving through an endless labyrinth of new-build suburban streets. The journey had rocked her into a comforting limbo, which she wished would last for ever. But then Darren swung the van into a short drive and parked with a jolt in front of a neat boxy house.

He killed the engine which silenced the radio. There was a moment's stillness. She stared through the windscreen at the white garage door. She had no idea what was going to happen to her next which twisted her gut. Darren seemed anxious too, craning his neck to peer at the next-door house, and muttering something about the neighbours.

'Why don't you drive into the garage?'

'There's something in there at the moment.'

'What?'

'Garden stuff. And a mermaid.'

She gave him a look.

'Don't ask.'

'You got a thing for mermaids?' He gave a half-smile and shrugged before getting out to check the street for unwanted eyes. Having a mermaid in your garage was a bit weird. She hoped it was weird in a good way.

Satisfied there was no one watching, he urged her through the front door, but she hesitated on the threshold, it felt like crossing a border into forbidden and dangerous territory. She didn't want to be seen by the nosy neighbours though, so made herself step inside.

The only house she'd been in since her release was Bert's. This wasn't as big or as posh, but it was okay. For a moment she imagined living in a boring magnolia painted house like this, herself. A life where no one bothered her and she could be left alone to grow old, becoming an eccentric old lady who kept too many cats.

She followed Darren down the hallway to the kitchen at the back of the house, wondering about his wife, Kerry. She'd been at his side during the trial, so where was she now? Perhaps she was in the garage with the mermaid.

There was a pile of washing up in the sink. Was it sexist to think it was a sign the wife wasn't around? She went over to the window to look into the back garden and was taken aback at what she saw. In the middle of the untidy grass there was a large hole. Big enough for a body.

'Is that for me?' she said in a voice too faltering for the joke.

'It's a water feature,' he replied as though it was obvious. 'Cup of tea?' He flicked the switch on the kettle and went to the fridge, picking up the milk and sniffing it. He pulled a face and put it back. So much for the tea.

The air in the kitchen was stale, like no one lived here. Darren was looking for something in the cupboards, but she was more interested in the 'water feature'. She muttered something about needing air and opened the door to the back garden.

Stepping out she found the air wasn't much fresher out here.

Maybe something to do with the excavation. She looked around the untidy garden with its overgrown bushes surrounding the badly cut lawn. A big fat spider was watching her from an extensive web in one of the shrubs. It was an ugly thing and made her feel uneasy. It better stay in its web. If it came anywhere near her, she'd squash it. But then, the thought of its disgusting fluids splattering everywhere turned her stomach.

She distracted herself by taking a closer look at Darren's earthworks. Next to the hole there was a pile of rubble: broken bricks and lumps of concrete.

'It's for the mermaid,' he said, joining her.

'You going to bury her?'

'It's a pond!'

'Looks like a grave.'

'It needs lining. Waterproof membrane.'

'Like plastic sheeting?' She imagined a body being rolled up in thick grey translucent plastic and then dumped into the hole. She looked around. The garden wasn't overlooked. If you wanted to bury someone here, no one would ever know.

'Not plastic. Rubber. Lasts for ever. Got a roll in the garage,' he said cheerfully.

The sun came out and warmed her cheeks, sending thoughts about dead bodies away to the shadows. She looked at Darren. 'I could give you a hand if you like.'

'What?'

'Build your water feature. I don't mind getting my hands dirty.'

'I don't need your help, thanks,' he grumbled.

'Suit yourself.' Another grumpy dismissal. What was the point of making an effort with someone like Darren Burgess? She picked up a stone from the pile of rubble and chucked it at the spider's web. She missed and the stone disappeared into the foliage.

'Hey! What are you doing?'

'I was aiming for that spider.'

'It's just a garden spider. There's no need to chuck stones at it. For God's sake!'

'All right, Daddy, calm down!'

'Don't call me that! Don't dare call me that. I am not your...' He couldn't finish his sentence or bear to repeat the word. 'I'm not anything to do with you.'

'What am I doing here then?'

'Why d'you throw that stone? Eh? Tell me.'

She wasn't going to admit her spider-phobia to him. 'Dunno. Just cus it was there.'

'That's not a reason.'

'Sometimes there is no reason.'

'Senseless!' he said, shaking his head.

'Yeah, well.' She paused and took a breath. 'Sometimes things don't make sense. They just happen.' Was she just telling herself that, because she had no explanation of what happened with Riley? Why she'd done it.

'Things don't *just happen*. There's a cause.'

If that were really true, then what had really caused her to do what she did to baby Riley? If there was a trigger. What was it? All she could think was there must be something wrong with her.

He looked at her with a stone set face. 'Senseless or not. I want to know what happened to Riley. What you did. Step by step. Every detail.'

She squirmed as the image of Riley's lifeless eyes, pale skin and blue lips came into her mind. The moment when she knew something was wrong. She didn't want to think how it got to that. But she must.

'We ate the sweets. We watched the trains going past and I was saying to look out for the Hogwarts Express, cus that would take us somewhere magical.'

Her brain squirmed and writhed like a trapped wild

animal, refusing to focus and think what happened next. 'And I guess she wanted more sweets.'

'So you choked her.'

'No!' He stared at her, eyes burning with accusation. 'Well, yes, but—'

'Lashed out, the same way you threw that stone at an innocent spider.'

She shut her eyes. Saw herself and Riley sitting on that embankment. Riley getting annoying about the sweets. Ungrateful little baby. She could feel her own irritation at that. Then Riley kicking off. He wouldn't believe her, would he? The perfect child of his memory had a temper tantrum.

'She was whingeing about the sweets. Told her she couldn't have any more. Started crying. So I lifted her up, swung her around, made funny faces. Worked for a bit, the crying died down, but as soon as I put her down, it would start again.' The memory gave her a tightness in her chest. 'I hadn't hurt her, so why was she crying? It wasn't fair. I was never allowed to cry so why should she? And it got worse and worse. Louder and louder, till she was screaming.'

'She had a pair of lungs on her. I'll give you that,' he said in bitter acknowledgement.

It was a festering wound for both of them. What happened had to be remembered and it had to be said. It wouldn't heal anything. But it might clean the wound, stop the poison from spreading.

'Lifting her up didn't work anymore. There was nothing I could do. The screaming seemed to take over her little body. Like it had come from somewhere else.'

'A crying fit,' Darren said, his face pained. 'She had those.'

'She couldn't catch her breath with it.'

'It's hard to watch,' he mumbled as much to himself as to her, clearly thinking about something he'd rather not.

'I didn't know what I was supposed to do.'

He took a shaking nervous breath. 'Sometimes I didn't know what to do either.' He bit his lip and looked away.

'If I'd have had more sweets, I'd have given her more sweets… anything to stop her crying.'

'You should have left her to cry it out,' he said, staring at the earthworks.

'Is that what you did, when she got like that?'

He shook his head. Started to talk. Still not facing her and mumbling, almost talking to himself. 'One time. Riley was about two years old. She was crying, wailing, working up to one of her paddies and I was tired and getting irritated.' He turned to face her. But looked reluctant to say what was on his tongue, holding something that he'd kept inside for years.

'We were in the bedroom, I was lying on the bed, trying to watch the footy on the little TV. But she was kicking up such a fuss I couldn't follow the match: Bristol versus Nottingham Forest. Shouted at her to shut up and of course that made it ten times worse.' He shook his head thinking. 'So, I know what it's like – that's what I'm saying. Does your head in.'

'But how did you stop her crying?'

'Never mind. It doesn't matter.' He looked uncomfortable. His body tense and twisted. His lips moving as if they wanted to say more, but he himself did not.

'Whatever you did–' she began.

'I put her in the car! Okay?' he snapped.

'You put her in the car?'

'Yes. That's what I did.' He looked on the edge of tears. What was going on with him? What wasn't he saying? What was so bad he couldn't speak it?

'Well,' she said, 'I didn't have a car, but I could have run off. Left her there to cry it out like you said. But then I thought she might fall down the railway embankment, cus she was so distressed, she didn't know what she was doing. She could have fallen onto the tracks and got squashed by a train and I'd get the blame. I wasn't thinking straight. The screaming was making me panic.'

He looked past her into the mid-distance. 'People say things like: I just saw red. People say that, don't they? It's like a red mist. A kind of madness. Something comes from somewhere in you, that you didn't know was there.'

Caitlin recognised that. It was what she'd felt. A madness.

Darren's face was full of anguish, but he wasn't done talking. 'I pick her up and I shout, "Shut the fuck up. Just shut the fuck up, you little bitch, or I'm going to throw you through the bedroom window." And I mean it. I really mean it. In that moment I could have.'

She stared at him, mouth open in shock. Then said, 'But you didn't throw her through the window, did you?'

'It terrified me that I could feel that way about the thing I loved most in life. Terrifies me even now.'

'You stopped yourself.'

'Yes. Made myself be calm. Detached. Took her outside, put her in the car. Oh, she was struggling and bawling so loud the whole street could hear. I drove round and round the streets with the radio on. Concentrated on the radio, until she calmed down and nodded off.'

'That's the difference between what you are and what I am. You know how to stop.'

There was a silence. A stillness apart from distant faraway birdsong. The birds seemed in another world. As though this garden was a nether region, too grim for songbirds.

'Tell me how it happened,' he said in a croaking whisper.

'Only thing in my mind: make it stop. Someone might hear. She might have a seizure. Whatever, it had to stop.' She didn't want to say what happened next. But he was waiting.

Just say the words, Caitlin. Just say them out loud.

'What my mum did to me, when I was little. "Stop that crying," she'd say. "Stop that or I'll throttle you, so help me

God." Then she'd put her hands around my throat and shake me.' She paused to take a breath. 'So that's what I did. Put my hands round Riley's neck. Squeezed until she shut up and stopped crying. Kept squeezing and squeezing just to make sure. I couldn't stop myself somehow. Then she went all limp and strange. I put her down. Set her against the tree. Told myself she was asleep. She couldn't be dead. I couldn't have killed her. You couldn't kill someone unless you had a gun or something. She'd wake up and then everything would be okay. But it wasn't. Not for her, not for me, not for you.'

She turned away to hide tears that were streaming down her face. Stared into the hole. 'I'll never forgive myself.' She pushed her hands into the pile of soil and dirt. Pulled them out, stared at the filth and buried her face in them. Breathed in the underground smell of stones and earth.

He was horrified. Couldn't speak. Couldn't think. But at least now he knew the truth. He retreated to the kitchen, leaving Grady there. The dishes needed doing. He shouldn't have let them pile up.

As he was trying to remove the dried-on food from the plates, his mind went back again to the day when for just a moment he'd completely lost his temper with Riley. It was true, he stopped himself from harming her, but what if he'd been eleven years old? He might not have stopped. Or sixteen. Or twenty-one. He could have shaken her in rage. Or anything. He'd never told Kerry or anyone else about that day. The memory filled him with shame. Sometimes he wondered whether that's why she'd been taken. Because he wasn't good enough to keep her.

He wiped his hands on the tea towel and looked through the window at Caitlin. She was sitting on the pile of rubble, sobbing. Inexplicably he wanted to offer her some comfort. Why? This girl had described how she'd killed Riley. He should hate her. Loathe her. But he didn't. All the same, he couldn't understand why he should care. She was nothing to him.

He took a fresh tea towel and went outside to speak to her. 'Are you going to stay out here all night?'

She turned towards him, face smeared with dirt. She looked like something that had come up out of the hole. Or been dug up. An underground creature.

'Or are you going to come inside?'

'Leave me alone.'

He shook his head. 'No.'

'How can you look at me?'

'Spent weeks looking at your face in the courtroom. Looking for something. But I didn't see. I didn't see who you were properly. Now I do. That's it.'

'The face of evil?' She gave a humourless smile.

He shook his head. 'You were just a kid.' He passed her the tea towel. 'Here, wipe your face.'

She hesitated, but took it and cleaned herself up. 'What are you going to do with me now? Call the police?'

'Not tonight. Unless that's what you want.'

'Rather you than the police.' She gave a tentative smile.

'So then, do you fancy something to eat?'

'Not hungry.'

'Pity, I fancy a pizza, and it's too much for one person.' He waited for a reply, and when none came asked, 'When did you last eat?'

She shrugged.

'Do you think you could manage one slice?'

'Well… maybe just one slice. Can we get pepperoni?'

FORTY-SEVEN

Appletree Avenue

S he was woken by a muffled toilet flush followed by water wheezing through pipes somewhere in the building. At first, she thought it was the woman upstairs, the one with the clicking heels. Then remembered she wasn't in Belsize Gardens, but the treeless Appletree Avenue.

Her eyes flicked open and she squinted at a shaft of sunlight streaming through a crack in the curtains. What the fuck was she doing in Darren Burgess's house? What would people think? More to the point, what would the Ministry of Justice do if they found out? She was specifically forbidden to make contact with any member of Riley's immediate family.

But then, Darren would be an idiot to tell anyone she was here. What would that say about him? *The Daily Herald* would crucify him. And the mob: they'd be after his blood as well as hers. She wondered if he knew what a risk he was taking by giving her refuge. Is that what this place was? A refuge? A place of safety? She hoped so.

Last night they sat together, eating the takeaway pepperoni pizza, watching TV. A programme about a couple building their own house. Being in the trade, Darren was full of derision about what they were doing wrong. It almost felt like a normal night in front of the telly with a normal family. Except there was nothing normal about her being there.

She'd forgotten to grab her backpack when they fled Boggart Hill, so only had the clothes she'd been wearing when they arrived here. She was naked under the duvet and felt vulnerable. Her knickers were in the airing cupboard drying after she rinsed them out last night. She threw on the dressing gown he told her to use, but it smelt of another woman. Kerry, his wife, no doubt. Wearing it made her feel weird. She wondered why he hadn't washed it, which made her feel even more strange. But needs must. She crept out of her bedroom feeling like an imposter. Darren was downstairs by the sound of it, filling a kettle in the kitchen, so she slipped into the bathroom, relieved she didn't have to face him yet. A quick splash of water on her face, then she cleaned her teeth with a spare toothbrush which had the logo of some posh hotel on it. She retrieved her dry knickers from the airing cupboard and dived back into the bedroom.

The room had a chest of drawers and a fitted wardrobe. She wondered whether there might be some spare clothes she could borrow in the wardrobe, so opened it to have a look-see. She was greeted with a vaguely damp, old-clothes aroma. No one had been in here for a while.

There were a couple of men's jackets, trousers and shirts on a rail. Nothing suitable for her needs, but she noticed a shabby old cardboard box at the bottom of the wardrobe. She pulled it out and put it on the floor by the bed. Inside it had a lidless shoe box containing Duplo – brightly coloured plastic bricks that click together. A version of Lego for younger kids. She lifted out the box of Duplo and rummaged through it. It had animal shaped pieces as well as bricks: horses, cows and an elephant. She set them on the carpet and then built a little enclosure out of yellow and red bricks to keep them from wandering off.

At the bottom of the cardboard box was a stack of children's books: *Mog the Forgetful Cat, The Very Hungry Caterpillar, The Selfish Crocodile.*

Her mum never read to her as a child. Her gran read a bit, though not very well. But once she herself learned to read, she devoured books. It was before smartphones and as she didn't have a Nintendo or anything, books were her escape.

———

He could hear her moving around upstairs. Wasn't sure whether to leave her to it and wait till she came down, or take up a cup of black coffee. There wasn't much in the way of breakfast though: a slice of toast or the dregs of the cereal packet, was about it. It was embarrassing how little he had to offer his unexpected guest. Maybe he should slip out to the convenience shop and get some eggs. Or perhaps even do a supermarket run and stock up. But that would depend on how long she was going to be around, which was the question he'd been asking himself all night. Now he'd brought her here, what the hell was he going to do with her? In the end he went upstairs and tapped lightly on the bedroom door.

'It's all right, I'm dressed, you can come in,' she called out.

She was sitting on the bed with Riley's brightly coloured picture books fanned out around her. 'Hi,' she said, smiling at him.

'Make yourself at home why don't you?' he grumbled. Getting that box out was taking liberties. No one had touched it since they moved in here.

'You don't mind, do you?' she said, worry clouding her smile.

Did he mind? He should. But somehow didn't have the

heart. What had happened to his anger? His constant companion for the last ten years had gone into hiding. And he had to admit it was sort of nice to see someone enjoying those books again.

'Bit old for kid's books, aren't you?'

'Suppose. But the shrinks reckon I suffer from Immature Personality Disorder. So I'm allowed.'

That made him grin. After a moment's hesitation he went over to her, pulled up a chair and began looking through the once familiar books himself. He wondered if he had a touch of immature whatsit as well.

'What was her favourite?'

'*Mog the Forgetful Cat*. Made me read it to her over and over again. It tickled her the way Mog always forgot about her cat flap and meowed to get in and out of the house.'

He still missed moments like that; Riley sitting on his knee while they read a book together. He couldn't deny the bitterness that came attached to such memories. But he would never wish them away.

'I wanted a cat, when I was a kid. But Mum wouldn't let me have any animals. In any case, a cat would have lasted about five minutes in our place. Would have run off if it had any sense.'

'Riley wanted a cat too. But Kerry's allergic to animal hairs. So...' He trailed off and flicked through the story of Mog and the burglar.

'Do you dream about her?' she asked in a strange, distant voice. As if she was lost in a dream herself.

'Yes. A lot.'

'Me too.'

It never occurred to him that Caitlin might have dreams about Riley. But thinking about it, it wasn't such an odd idea.

'I thought they'd stop after the court case,' she added, 'or maybe when the psychiatrists had finished with me. Or failing that, when I grew up. But she still visits me sometimes at night.'

They exchanged dreams. Dreams in which Riley was alive. Where Caitlin found her wandering along the railway and rescued her from an oncoming train. Where Darren went to the morgue to identify the body, and she sat up wondering why everyone thought she was dead.

He found a curious comfort knowing that someone else was keeping Riley alive in their dreams. Even if it was Caitlin. He knew Kerry used to dream about Riley too, but they hadn't talked about that for such a long time that he wondered now if she still did.

His gaze was drawn to the Duplo farm she'd made. He imagined Riley sitting there on the floor playing with the bricks and talking to the animals in her own little world. For a moment, it felt like there were three of them in the room.

The moment was broken by the shrill warbling of his phone. Not his mobile, that was still switched off. He didn't want Jedd tracking him, nor did he relish a conversation with him about what had happened to Caitlin. It was the landline extension in Kerry and his bedroom.

'Don't answer it,' Caitlin whispered, as though the caller could hear.

'Probably some spammer.' All the same he found himself on edge, hardly breathing. What was he afraid of? It stopped ringing and after a few minutes silence, Caitlin suggested they go to the shops.

'I need some spare clothes.'

'I'm not sure going out is a great idea.'

'Scared I'll show you up?' she said with a cheeky smile that made him uncomfortable.

'It's not that.'

She looked at him, expecting clarification.

'Want to keep you safe, that's all.' The question of how

long she'd be staying floated in the air between them. He still didn't have an answer.

She nodded. 'But I still need some clothes and toiletries.'

'We can get some stuff online. If you can hang on.'

'I can, if you can.'

He rubbed his hand across his mouth. 'Okay. You may as well stay here for a couple of days anyway.'

She thought for a moment. 'We could build the water feature.'

'We could.'

Then the phone rang again. She gave him an anxious look, a look which reflected how he felt. Someone was trying to get in touch. He tried to tell himself that it might be Kerry, which would be a good thing.

'I'd better get it. Might be important.'

'Suppose it's the police?'

'Why would they phone here?' But then he remembered the kerb-crawling letter and felt another twist of anxiety. Ridiculous. He wasn't going to be afraid of a bloody telephone.

He went into the marital bedroom to take the call, but when he picked it up, there was silence. Typical spam call. He slammed the receiver down. Looked up to see Caitlin standing by the bedroom door.

'Who was it?'

'No one. Spammer or wrong number.'

She had the look of a nervy animal about her. A roe deer. One that had picked up the scent of wolf on the air. Glanced past him towards the window.

'I think we should check the street.'

'Why?'

'Instinct.'

He pulled a face, but nevertheless moved towards the net-curtained window.

'Careful!' Caitlin hissed. 'Don't let them see you at the window.'

She was being a bit paranoid, but he snuck up to the edge of the window and peered round the frame into the street.

'Oh fuck.' His stomach lurched and plummeted.

'What is it?' She joined him and looked out too.

Jedd's van was parked in the street. He should have realised the guy would come here looking for him. He'd called the landline to make sure someone was in. And of course his own van was in the driveway. Shit!

He looked up and down the street as best he could from his viewpoint, but there was no sign of the man himself. Then the doorbell let out its cheerful little chime. Just once, like a polite neighbour popping round to borrow some milk. He went to the landing and stood at the top of the stairs wondering what to do.

'Don't let him in!' Caitlin said, pleading and coming up to him. He resisted a powerful instinct to hug her – as if by so doing they could protect each other. The doorbell chimed again.

'You better hide in the garage,' he said. She nodded and slipped down the stairs as silent as a cat. He followed with slow, gentle footsteps. Luckily the front door was solid, with no window for nosy neighbours to peer in. They went through the kitchen to the utility area which had a door to the garage. Unlocking it he ushered her in.

'Don't lock me in the garage!' she said on the threshold.

He gave her the key. 'Lock it from the inside.'

The chime went again. And again. And after a short pause, another two chimes rang out. Jedd was getting impatient.

'If you don't answer he might just go away.' She looked desperate.

'He won't.' Jedd was more likely to firebomb the place than go away but he didn't say that to her. 'Don't worry, I can

349

handle Jedd. I'll get rid of him.' He hoped he sounded more confident than he felt.

She stepped into the dimly lit garage, shut and locked the door.

The doorbell was repeating its chimes again. The sing-song tune now sounding threatening and sinister. He tried to gather himself together. Took deep breaths. Adopted a bleary-eyed, just-got-out-of-bed expression and went to the door. He opened it a crack, keeping the security chain in place. 'Oh, it's you,' he said, feigning surprise.

'You okay, mate? I've been so worried.'

'Fine, yeah.'

'Been trying to reach you.'

'Sorry. My phone. It died. Dropped it and… it's fucked.'

'Oh right.' He paused, looked around. 'You got someone in there with you?' He gave a false smile.

'What?' he said, knocked off balance. 'No. Course not.' It felt like Jedd could see right through him.

Keep it together, Darren. Front it out.

'Well then, can I come in?'

He couldn't think of a half-decent excuse, so there was no choice but to let the guy in. Unchaining the door he led the way through to the kitchen.

'You could have let me know you were okay,' Jedd said, leaning on the back of a chair.

'Like I said, my phone.'

'Got a laptop, haven't you? Could have messaged me.'

'Kerry… it's hers and she took it back. Coffee?' Darren spluttered, turning to the kettle. He began to fill it as a way of avoiding Jedd's penetrating stare.

'No. I won't be staying long.'

Thank God for that. He put the kettle down and turned back to Jedd. Tried not to show the relief on his face.

Jedd looked pained. Like he'd eaten something bad.

Darren resisted the urge to apologise and smooth things over. But that's what this little act was about, wasn't it? It reminded him of the way his father behaved sometimes. Pretending to be hurt, which would then excuse an angry outburst.

'I was worried about you, mate. What with the radio silence, I thought something bad had happened.'

'No, nothing happened.' The awkwardness between them prowled the room, like a snarling dog.

'Look, Jedd, about Caitlin, she got away. That's the truth. She got away and I didn't want to tell you because I knew you'd be disappointed.'

'Got away? Well, that explains things. *Mea culpa*, though, mate. Should have got to Boggart Hill sooner.' He gave a brief, formal smile. Seemed to be taking it quite well. Darren allowed himself a smile too.

Jedd went over to the counter, picked up the empty pizza box, still there from last night. He should have put it in the bin. He should learn to tidy up after himself. Jedd opened the box and looked inside.

'There's none left,' Darren said.

'What was it?' He sniffed the box. 'Pepperoni?'

He didn't say anything.

'Bit spicy for you, isn't it?'

'I don't mind a pepperoni.'

'You told me you preferred margherita.'

'Did I?' He gave an exaggerated frown, as if it was the last thing in the world for him to want a margherita.

'And you are a creature of habit. Fish and chips. Cheeseburgers. If forced into an Indian, it's chicken korma. And Italian means margherita pizza.' He fixed Darren with a meaningful look. 'I know you.'

'I was in the mood for a pepperoni, all right?' He turned away from Jedd and looked through the window at the hole in the lawn. How had the guy managed to get him on the back foot? Again.

'Perhaps someone else chose it. A girlfriend maybe?'

'Godsake!' Was he ever going to shut up about the pizza?

'Got a woman upstairs, have you? Some slapper taken pity on you?'

He laughed at that. 'No! Really, Jedd, how did you get that idea?'

Jedd wasn't laughing though. 'Because that pizza is too big for you. You haven't got any kind of appetite to eat a pizza like that. Especially as you don't even fucking like pepperoni.'

'I was hungry. And I had some more this morning for my breakfast. Okay. Okay? It's just a fucking pizza! What is wrong with you?' He held his gaze. Challenging him to call him a liar. Jedd's scar seemed inflamed, like he'd been scratching it. Maybe it was going to start bleeding.

'How exactly did Caitlin get away, again? How did a kid like that get away from a big lad like you?' This was the nub. What he really wanted to know.

'Pulled a knife.'

'Pulled a knife?'

Was there a hint of sarcasm in that tone? Whatever, he was going to carry on anyway. 'So I couldn't get to her. Then she ran off down the embankment onto the railway line. I chased after her, but she's fast. And there were trains. It was dangerous down on the tracks. In the end, she got away.' It sounded credible, didn't it? And it wasn't that far off the truth.

'Okay.' He smiled. 'I get it. She pulled a knife. I could kick myself for not being there. Because we are a team, aren't we?'

Darren gave a reluctant nod. Felt like he was back at school, trying to placate the playground bully. Pissed off with himself for being a wimp.

'Anyway, not to worry, we found out where she was staying,' he announced, suddenly cheerful. 'Youth hostel in the centre of

Bristol. Cut her hair short so she looks like a boy. But you'd know that, right?'

'Yeah.' His heart was heavy and leaden. He was sure the colour was draining from his face.

'Hasn't been back there, though. We think she's sleeping rough. Unless someone's hiding her.'

Darren closed his eyes. Jedd couldn't possibly know. He couldn't.

'How say you, we go back to Bristol right now and stake out the hostel? She's bound to go back there to get her stuff, because she's still checked in.'

He took a breath. He had to put a stop to this. 'I let her go. She didn't escape. I let Caitlin go.'

Jedd looked at him flatly. Without surprise, like he knew this already.

'I'm sorry, Jedd. I don't want to do this anymore. Go after Caitlin. I think things changed for me after I nearly drowned. It's over. Okay?'

'Okay? You think that's okay do you?'

'I'm sorry, but I'm done with it.'

He rolled his big head around and rubbed the back of his thick neck. 'Is it because she told you she called the paddleboarders. Is that it?'

'What? I don't know what you're on about.'

'Because she must have said something for you to choose her over me.'

'What do you mean about the paddleboarders?'

Jedd shook his head and moved over to the sink. Selected a glass from the draining board and filled it with water. Took a sip and placed it on the table between them. Both men stood facing each other either side of the table. Darren had the irrational idea that he was supposed to take a sip too, as if they were acting out some arcane ritual.

'We could have done things. We were a good team. We

could have gone on to do great things.' He was breathing heavily, as though trying to release pressure from his body.

Darren could feel his own arm tensing, muscle memory forming his hand into a fist.

'But you. You don't care about our friendship. Our bond. When I do something for you. You throw it back in my face.'

'I am still your friend. But I'm my own man. Understand?'

'I love you like a brother. I do. But you!' He shook his head, slammed his fist on the table making the glass jump and water spill. 'You kick sand into my face.'

'Take it easy, Jedd,' he said, still trying to kid himself that the guy would leave without any real trouble.

'Like when I booked you a lovely room in the Grand Hotel. All you could do was whinge on about the money.' He put on a mimicking, sarcastic voice. *'It's too expensive, it's extravagant, too this, it's too that.* And I try to educate you. Introduce you to the finer things in life. Make you a better fucking human being. But all you want is your fish and chips and pints of pissy lager. And then, worse still, when I flush the bitch out with a molly to her flat, risking everything for you, you get all high and mighty and moralistic on me. Finally, you show your true colours: betraying everything we did together – letting the fucking tart go free!'

'I think you better leave.'

'You know what you are? You are a disgrace to the human race. That's what.'

'Come on, Jedd.'

'I tell you who's going to leave. You are. With me. In the back of my van.'

'What?' He wasn't sure what Jedd had in mind. But there was no way he was going to get into that van with him.

'I'll have to incapacitate you first,' Jedd said, matter-of-factly.

He had to get away. Back garden? But he'd be trapped there.

Jedd picked up the glass and threw the water in his face, which caught him off guard. Then smashed a piece out of the rim of the glass using the edge of the table. Waved the jagged edge at him, threatening to slash his face.

Darren glanced away from Jedd towards the hallway.

'You'll never reach the front door, mate,' Jedd said with an unsettling sneer on his big baby face.

FORTY-EIGHT

Darren's garage

The mermaid was lying on her side, as though trying to get comfortable on the cold concrete floor. Caitlin knelt down next to her and stroked her curved tail. The smooth metallic scales were cold to the touch. But her copper green patinated features had an iridescence that lifted the atmosphere in the dim and otherwise colourless garage. The mermaid seemed to be staring at her with an enigmatic smile, so perhaps, like some religious aesthete in a cell, she enjoyed the hardships of the concrete floor. And perhaps too, the smile was due to otherworldly knowledge way beyond that of mortal souls.

Next to her was a roll of black sheeting – the waterproof membrane for the pond. There wasn't much else to see apart from a large grey metal shelf unit attached to the wall. It was stacked with switches, sockets and plugs. Cardboard boxes of stuff electricians use. Adjacent to this, hanging on hooks and pegs were tools: drills, screwdrivers and wire cutters.

There was nowhere to hide. If only she could sneak out and get away from the house. She could escape through the up-and-over garage door, but she had no idea how to open it.

There was no sign of a lever or switch and she didn't want to make a noise by trying to use brute force to open the thing. So if Jedd managed to get into the garage she was fucked.

Being locked in here was worse than prison, even if she did have the key. At least in a cell, once the door was locked you were safe from harm. She tried not to think what Jedd would do if he found her, so took a closer look at the tools to distract herself from going through all the bad outcomes.

She unhooked an electric drill. Felt its weight. She might enjoy a practical job like electrician and wondered about training for something like that. Maybe she could be Darren's apprentice. She gave a silent hollow laugh at the absurdity of the idea.

There were voices beyond the door, but she couldn't tell what they were talking about. She prayed that they would soon come to a conclusion. That she'd hear goodbyes and the sound of the front door shutting.

But then the voices were raised. That didn't sound good. She examined the tools looking for something to defend herself with. There was a decent sized hammer hanging on the hooks. Its head had a flat end for hammering nails, and a curved forked end for pulling them out. She got it and gave it a swing. It was pretty fucking heavy. That metal claw could do some real damage if she put some muscle into it.

She turned to the mermaid, caught that knowing smile, nodded to herself and headed to the door, heart racing at what she might be going to do. But she didn't go out. She stood to one side, her back pressed against the bare brick wall waiting for the door to open. Did she have the bottle to do it? The determination? She'd have to use all her strength, because there would be no second chances. It would have to be a killer blow. She glanced at the mermaid again, gripped the handle with both hands and raised it above her head.

But the door didn't open. Instead there was the sound of a

struggle. Furniture being kicked and moved. What to do now? Wait for it to be over? Or try and get away in the confusion?

Darren pushed the kitchen table towards Jedd, surprising him and causing him to lose his balance for a second. The guy staggered backwards, dropping the glass which shattered on the kitchen floor. Darren pressed his advantage by slamming the table into his opponent even harder, pinning him against the kitchen counter. It gave him the space to make a dash for the hallway.

'You are so dead, you fucker!' Jedd screamed after him as Darren hurled down the hallway.

He heard Jedd coming for him, but managed to reach the front door and turn the handle. The door opened inwards, so there was a moment's hiatus while he pulled the door open to let himself through. A moment in which Jedd got to him and slipped a thick muscled arm around his neck, somehow managing to slam the door shut at the same time. Jedd was pulling him backwards down the hall. Trying to get him to the floor.

Darren's body knew what to do from teenage school fights. He bent his legs and leaned forward, trying to take Jedd's weight on his back like a heavy sack. If he could lift Jedd off the ground he'd lose traction and be forced to let go.

But the arm around his neck was choking and Jedd was heavy. He was too strong. He was losing his own strength and felt himself succumbing, being pulled down. If Jedd got him on the floor, he'd have no chance.

Then an ear-splitting shriek: some terrible demon escaping hell.

A splintering crunch, like a coconut cracked open.

Jedd's arm fell away.

He turned around to see Jedd making a mess on the floor. Oozing blood and brains onto the carpet. Caitlin was standing gripping a bloody hammer. She looked terrified. Dropped the hammer. Stared at what she'd done wide-eyed.

His first thought was how to get the blood out of the carpet.

Neither of them spoke. Caitlin was shaking. There was blood splattered over her clothes.

His second thought was that she needed to get those clothes into the wash.

'Will we call an ambulance?' she said.

He shook his head. He remembered the time Jedd mimed forming a gun. '*Bullet to the brain*,' he'd said then. A primal shiver went through his soul.

FORTY-NINE

Darren's bathroom

Her toes were poking out of the foamy water. She'd painted them red a couple of weeks ago, but the nail varnish was flaking off now. It looked like patches of blood. She tried to scrape them clean, but it was impossible without proper remover.

Downstairs she could hear the washing machine whirring into a spin. Darren had put her clothes in, to try and get the blood out. She wasn't sure if it would work. Even if it did, washing away a murder wasn't easy. Every time she shut her eyes, she saw the back of Jedd's skull, broken and splintered. Perhaps over time it would replace the recurring image of Riley's dead eyes.

She was shocked at what she'd done. What she was capable of. There was something brutal inside her. She could have just run past those men, got out into the street and called for help. But she hadn't done that. Her fury made her kill. And in that moment, lost in the act, she'd felt a frightening wild pleasure.

She wanted to call the police. Get it over with and face justice. But Darren wouldn't hear of it.

'They'll string you up. You were never here. Okay?'

He insisted he wouldn't call the police until she was well away from Appletree Avenue. She tried to point out that he'd probably end up going down for murder. It could hardly be self-defence with half the back of Jedd's head missing.

'If that happens. Then so be it.'

'But–'

'He'd have killed me. He'd have come after you too. We'd both be dead.'

That was the end of the discussion. But she didn't like it. Darren would almost certainly end up charged with a murder he didn't do. She sank down into the bath, closed her eyes and allowed the water to cover her head. Floated away in her imagination and swam with mermaids. Sat up suddenly. It was obvious what to do. If she could persuade Darren.

The body was heavy, so shifting it wasn't easy. He'd rolled Jedd up in the bloodstained hallway carpet, but needed Caitlin to help him slide it through the kitchen and into the back garden. Even though most of the blood had dried up, it still left tell-tale smears showing its path. More cleaning for him to do.

He'd been quite prepared to take responsibility for Jedd's death. Didn't really care about what happened to himself. In fact, he almost relished a spell in gaol now. There were many reasons why he deserved it. Whereas Caitlin deserved at least chance at a life. But if they found out she'd landed the killer blow, he was sure she'd never ever be released.

In the end though, she'd simply refused to let him take the rap. Said they should cover up the killing. Said if he didn't agree, she'd give herself up. She'd saved his life, so he couldn't allow that.

Together they dragged the body to the unfinished pond and

rolled it into the hole. He would stock the pond with ornamental fish when it was completed.

'It's a new take on sleeping with the fishes,' she said. He allowed himself a grim smile, realising just how much he loathed Jedd.

'You got to promise me to make something of your life,' he said to Caitlin later as she helped him lay the waterproof membrane over the soil-covered body.

They were placing heavy stones around the perimeter of the pond to hold the membrane in place. She stood, dusted off her hands and looked at him, squinting against the sun. 'Why would you care what I do with my life?'

He wasn't sure exactly, but he knew it was what he wanted. 'Neither of us can put the clock back, can we? No matter how much we want to. What's done is done. But the future – your future – is up for grabs. Make something good of it.'

She bit her lip. Nodded. 'Okay. I'll do my best.'

FIFTY

Bearland, Gloucester

They were in Darren's van, parked up opposite Gloucester police station, a swanky new building that looked like a finance company HQ. They sat not speaking for a minute until the silence became too much for her. 'I guess this is goodbye.'

He nodded. 'We never met. But I'm glad we did.'

'You don't always make sense, do you?' she said, opening her door.

He grunted, and then before she got out asked, 'One thing. When you were on that island, did you see me struggling in the water?'

She stopped. Didn't look at him. 'Did you see me on the island?'

'Might have.'

'Well then, I might have seen you in the water.'

'And the paddleboarders?'

'What paddleboarders?' She didn't want to admit helping him, saving him. Didn't want him to think he owed her anything more. They were done. She got out and headed towards the police station without looking back. But when she got to the top of the entrance steps she turned around. He was still there, so she gave him a wave before going inside. She knew she'd never see him again and felt an unexpected prick of loss. Then dismissing such nonsense, she went to the enquiries counter to hand herself in.

They put her in an interview room while the slow wheels of the Ministry of Justice ground into motion.

Hours later, they said she'd have to spend the night in a bail hostel, and so moved her to an anonymous downmarket former hotel. It had that familiar institutional smell. Polish and stale soup. Home from home. But at least it was a room for the night and a hot meal.

'Pack your things, Caitlin. Your transport awaits.'

She didn't have anything to pack and followed her minder down to the reception area. There, sitting waiting for her was George. She stopped and stared. What the fuck?

'I'm not sure about that haircut,' he said, standing up.

'Bastard.' She was still pissed off with him and didn't see why she should be nice. They stared at each other for a moment. He looked a bit put out. Good.

'Bastard or not I'm here to collect you.'

'What happened to your friend, Tammy?' she said, adding scornfully, 'Such a *fine probation officer*.'

'I suppose I deserved that.'

She allowed herself a sarcastic smile. 'So, where is she?'

'Suspended. Negligence. Shit hit the fan after the fire. Heads have rolled. Although not mine. I have been rehabilitated,' he said with a smile.

'Don't tell me you're my probation officer again.' She sounded as downbeat as possible about the idea.

'Luckily for you, I'm just the courier.'

'What's that mean?'

'You're going to be moved to a new location and given a new identity. I'm to brief you, take you there and then do the handover to the new team.'

'Oh. I see.' She couldn't hide her disappointment. Yeah, she was pissed off with George. But not so pissed off that she didn't want him back as her probation officer.

'In any case, I've been offered early retirement. So I'm leaving the service in three months' time.'

'Well I suppose you are getting a bit over the hill.'

'Exactly. Too old for this.' He gave her a meaningful look. 'Shall we go?'

'Aren't you going to say where you're taking me?'

'I'll tell you on the way.'

She nodded and followed him out of the building and into the car park. He stopped suddenly and turned to her. 'I am sorry, Caitlin. About what happened. The arson attack. The vigilantes.'

She punched him on the arm.

'What was that for?'

'I guess it's kind of good to see you.'

'Likewise.'

She followed him to the car and they set off for her new life.

Darren kept a close eye on the news. There was nothing about Jedd's disappearance. But then on *Crimewatch* one night, there was a report about a husband who'd disappeared recently. The wife, Jenny, told of how he'd left for work one morning and hadn't been seen or heard of since.

He didn't think anything of it until the pic of the missing hubby flashed on screen. It was Jedd. Except his name was Julian Draper. Julian's job was private detective, although it wasn't clear what case he was working on at the time of his death, but it involved spending a lot of time away from home. Apparently, Julian was a collector of incendiary devices used in warfare. They included an original Molotov cocktail produced by the Finnish alcohol monopoly Alko in 1939.

There was no mention of his involvement in the search for Caitlin Grady nor the ex-police van. Just as well, because the van was still in Darren's garage. He hadn't yet decided how to dispose of it.

He had visits from his sister, brother and mum. They all admired the new water feature. Even Paramjit's husband thought he'd done a professional job and asked if he'd do one for them. The mermaid's knowing smile was commented on and they all said the gurgling water added life to the garden. The ornamental fish were a nice touch. In the spring, the new perennial border would look lovely. Everyone agreed that Darren's life had turned a corner.

Finally, there was a call from Kerry. She'd read the feature in *The Daily Herald* in which he'd declared that he'd forgiven Caitlin and had abandoned any idea about Riley's Law. They agreed to meet to 'discuss things'. He hoped she'd be pleased when he showed her the mermaid. Kerry always had an affinity with water.

THE END

About the Author

Peter Kesterton was born and brought up in Manchester. He went to university in Bristol where he now lives with his wife Adriane. Before turning to novels, he wrote scripts and plays for theatre TV and radio. Girl's Don't Cry is his debut novel. The book was a finalist in the 2022 Page Turner Awards.

To learn more and access free bonus material go to: www.peterkesterton.com

A note from the publisher

Thank you for reading this book. If you enjoyed it please do consider leaving a review on Amazon to help others find it too.

We hate typos. All of our books have been rigorously edited and proofread, but sometimes mistakes do slip through. If you have spotted a typo, please do let us know and we can get it amended within hours.

info@bloodhoundbooks.com